A DUST NOVEL

UNSPOKEN

A NOVEL BY

JANN ALEXANDER

Black Rose Writing | Texas

ISBN: 978-1-68513-622-2
LIBRARY OF CONGRESS CONTROL NUMBER: 2025934576
PUBLISHED BY BLACK ROSE WRITING
www.blackrosewriting.com

Printed in the United States of America
Suggested Retail Price (SRP) $24.95

Cover art and design by Jann Alexander
Unspoken is printed in Garamond Premier Pro

For Lorene

PRAISE FOR UNSPOKEN

"Jann Alexander's blazingly alive novel asks how do we keep a family intact? Here, in a story told by both a mother and her daughter, two people struggle to both understand their world and each other."
–Caroline Leavitt, *New York Times* bestselling author of *Pictures of You* and *Days of Wonder*

"The novel reminds me, in tone, of Texas classics like *The Time it Never Rained* and *Giant*. I loved it. Alexander is a great new talent in the genre of Texana."
–W.F. Strong, author, *Stories From Texas*, and radio commentator for NPR Texas

"Fans of Kristin Hannah's *Four Winds* will devour *Unspoken,* Jann Alexander's tale of Ruby Lee's gritty Texas Dust Bowl journey"
–Cam Torrens, award-winning author of the *Tyler Zahn suspense series*

"*Unspoken* is an evocative story best suited for readers who appreciate historical fiction steeped in grit and emotional intensity. Fans of novels like *The Grapes of Wrath* or *The Nightingale* will likely feel at home here. I recommend it for anyone ready to weather an emotional storm in exchange for a beautifully written tale of survival and hope."
– Thomas Anderson, Editor In Chief, *Literary Titan*

"A literary gem. Her story and character will be talked about and debated in book clubs everywhere."
–Paul Jantzen, author of *Sour Apples*

"Alexander wastes no time snaring you with a double whammy of death in the first paragraph – a visceral description of all-too-common calamity during the Dust Bowl's insipid encroachment that swallowed an entire region in the heart of the US. A sweeping story of many truths during a time little told. Don't miss it."
–Kay Smith-Blum, author of *Tangles*

"*Unspoken* explores themes of perseverance, love, and the resilience of women who redefine what home and family mean during times of great hardship."
–K.C. Finn, Amazon and *USA Today* best-selling writer

"*Unspoken* shines in vibrant details–riding the rails, war brides waiting for their husbands, internal battles inside Ruby Lee and her mother. From the opening blackness of a blinding dust storm to the satisfaction of watching Ruby Lee reclaim her family farm, readers will experience the trials and triumphs of women."
–**Joan Donaldson, winner of the 2010 Friends of American Writers Award for** *On Viney's Mountain*

"*Unspoken* by Jann Alexander has a wonderful voice, is captivating, and is well-written. It's a heart-wrenching story of a family destroyed by the 1935 "black blizzard" dust storms in the Texas Panhandle."
–**Connie Morgan, author of** *More Than Luck Required*

"Jann Alexander brings us Ruby Lee, a feisty, determined gal, who you'll root for, page after page, in this gritty, heart-wrenching story steeped in history."
–**Linda Rosen, author of the award-winning** *The Emerald Necklace*

"One of the better written narratives I've read of late, ranking up with some of the greats, like Steinbeck. He'd have his hats off to the talented Alexander. Highly recommend."
–**Paulette Mahurin, author of** *Two Necklaces*

"A strong tale worthy of acclaim. I highly recommend it."
–**P.L. Jonas, award-winning author of** *Hall of Deception* **and** *Sea of Doubt*

"For an unusual Texas tale told with impressive detail and fine writing, I highly recommend *Unspoken.*"
–**Nancy Stancill, Author of** *Saving Texas,* *Winning Texas,* *Tall,* **and** *Deadly Secrets*

"It all comes down to dust. It all comes down to desperation. It all comes down to survival. This novel is a must-read. Deeply researched, deftly detailed, Jann Alexander's *Unspoken* immerses the reader fully in Ruby Lee's journey as she learns to speak her values, to claim her choices and, ultimately, to breathe."
–**Shirley Miller Kamada, author of** *No Quiet Water*

"Courage is more exhilarating than fear."
–Eleanor Roosevelt

UNSPOKEN

1935

CHAPTER ONE

RUBY LEE

I had never seen anyone dead before.

Momma had hold of my hand, hers larger and warmer and locked tight around mine, while her chest was heaving and she was stifling her gasps in the plain little prairie church so new I could smell its fresh-cut pine boards.

Footfalls echoed as people walked in with tentative steps, as though not to disturb the dead, of which there were two. They were laid out in simple caskets built only yesterday after my grandma, and then my baby sister, died with the brown dirt—*dust pneumonia* they called it—clogging their lungs.

They made my Granny Alma look like she was at peace, with her hands crossed atop her chest. Except she hadn't been, because she was coughing in fits right before her eyes flew open wide and then rolled backwards and she gurgled her way out of this dry, dusty world. My momma had grabbed her hands and begged her not to leave us, sobbing and moaning so loud I was the only one to hear baby Nell's raspy breaths.

I picked her up from the little cradle Pa had carved for my brothers before me and held her close to shush her; she was wheezing so bad. I put her on my shoulder the way Momma had showed me to help clear her lungs. I ran my hand over her silky hair, *shush, shush, take a breath now*, hearing her chest rattle, wiping the brown spittle from her mouth, until of a sudden I heard her silence louder than Momma's wails. I shrieked, handing Nell to Momma; I'd felt the life go out of her. That's when I knew what dying was.

I was ten and prone to coughing up the dust, too.

Momma cradled Nell in her arms, and her screams terrified me so I hear them still.

They closed the wood lid on her real tight; they wouldn't let anyone see baby Nell laid out in her tiny casket, it was too heartbreaking. But I had already seen her, and she didn't look peaceful. She looked startled, the way she had when we fed her cow's milk from a bottle after Momma's stopped coming.

That Sunday in April 1935 in the Panhandle was an uncommon bright day which didn't reflect our family's desperation. What little breeze there was blew gentle, unlike the stinging winds we were accustomed to. The spring air was so clean you could almost inhale it deep without coughing up dirt. The sun was golden and hopeful. Our families who'd been farming this desert during the five long years of the drouth were well acquainted with hope, though it was a currency our town's shuttered bank no longer accepted.

The new windows in the church were propped open to the balmy air that afternoon of the double funerals, and I couldn't see the dunes of dirt covering every square inch of town once I sat down—only the tufty white clouds skating along a blue sky, framed by the church windows.

I scowled at the waste of a fine day, one where there would be no playing outdoors despite the tempting weather.

Behind us I heard much quiet coughing and clearing of throats, and I knew without looking the church had filled up. The minister laid hands upon each casket, the small one beneath his right hand as he began to pray, and then came the shuffling of dozens of parishioners standing up behind us, lifting their voices in unison to drown out Momma's sobs. Pa propped her up, his eyes raised heavenward, his lips moving rapidly.

Outside the church window, birds were flying towards us from the west. I hadn't seen birds in a long time. The years of dusters left nowheres for them to nest, and nothing to eat, like our near-starving family. I was trying to make out what kind of birds they were, some as big as geese, when the breeze gusted and kicked up loose dry earth, which swirled and blew into the church. A fine coat of grit settled on the two caskets, and the folks behind me whispered about it. I turned round and glared at them to quieten them out of respect for the dead, and that's when a panicked bird flew in through a window.

The sky was thick with birds, flying fast and hard. The few which landed inside by accident were squawking and slamming the walls to find their way back out, and the ladies they flew into screeched as loud as the birds did. The disruption was turning to panic as the daylight became the darkening so familiar and fearful—a rolling wall of dark dirt tumbling and climbing and tumbling and rising, wave after wave, chasing the birds, aiming right at us. With the wind howling, my two older brothers shifted back and forth, uneasy on their feet. My momma had not taken her eyes from baby Nell and Granny in their boxes.

The sky grew ominous, very purple, then dark brown descending into near black. When the temperature plunged, the crowd in the church stampeded outside, crying, "Cover your mouths. Who's got the little one? Get in the car! Is it a twister? It's too big for a duster!"

"Where's the sun?" And she was right, my momma, since the once-bright day was pitch black, darker than sin.

The minister was praying hard, standing his ground at the altar. Pa yelled, "Boys, grab Ruby Lee! Willa Mae, we got to get out." Momma screamed, "I can't leave them," and my brothers Will and Earl each grabbed one of my arms, lifting me to run up the aisle with my feet flailing. I cried out for Momma and I guess she couldn't decide who to pick, since she'd collapsed on the floor, clinging to the stands bearing the caskets. Her eyes were riveted to mine. My pa was trying to haul her out, and the screech of the wind competed with my brothers' shouts, "Ma, Pa, come on!"

While the purple sky turned inky black and the wind wailed, we huddled in the church vestibule, each of us praying, I suppose, until a long time passed and we felt Momma and Pa surround us. My brothers scrambled to help Pa shut the church doors, but the silt shot in anyway, finding every crack between planks and loose shingles on the roof, like it snuck in day and night in our sod house.

"I can't see my hand before my face," Pa said.

It was hard to breathe. A coughing spasm overtook me, and Momma ripped some strips from her petticoat, dunking them in the holy water holder for us to cover our faces.

It was the biggest, blackest blizzard of dirt we'd seen, and we'd seen plenty of blinding dust storms. Sometime during the fearsome darkness it had turned to night. As the wind died down, we fell asleep there, knotted close against the chill.

The next morning was calm. We stepped outside. Folks with drained faces, dirt-smeared and silent, shoveled the drifts wedged against their cars. The church's fresh coat of white paint had been peeled sheer off; it hung in shreds off the planks.

"They been in there all night, all alone without me," my momma said when my pa shuffled her gently away.

•   •   •

My momma had done her best to keep the brown plague from our little house for almost four years, but after that blackest of Sundays in the Texas Panhandle, she finally gave it up. Her eyes focused on nothing in particular and she rubbed her hands over and over like she could wash them off as my pa led her to our car. Some kindly soul had dug it out for us, and by then the street was passable for everyone trying to get back home. When we got to our place, sod-roofed, its wood frame leaning but standing, she kept rubbing her hands. I let out a breath I had been holding, testing the air. I couldn't see any sign of relief on Momma's face.

The black blizzard thwarted all our attempts to keep out the swirling murk. The wet sheets we hung across the windows were so heavy with the fine dust they'd fallen down. It had bored inside and left a flour-like coating on what little we had. I dug out my rag doll, but water was too scarce to clean her with. Sand caked her golden yarn hair; her fair skin was the color of bran. I pushed baby Nell's cradle into a corner and laid out my doll in it, and piled the quilts from my grandma's bed on it, but Momma didn't take note.

Will and Pa shoveled and struggled their way through knee-high drifts toward the barn to check on our cow, the hens, and the vegetable garden

Momma had started a few weeks back—if sparks from the storms hadn't burned it down. Earl set to shoveling out the cabin till the only dirt left was our own dirt floor.

"Done, Pa," Earl shouted, always eager to join the men.

"Dig out the fruit cellar, Earl," Pa yelled back, "and haul in the water."

When he shot out the door, I did my best to think what Momma would do, since she sat so still in the rocker, not moving a twitch except what few muscles she exerted rubbing her hands. I cleaned off our skillet and tin plates and cups as best I could, shook out the rugs, and wiped down the fancy Starck spinet piano Granny Alma had ordered all the way from Chicago. Red soil blown in from Oklahoma was wedged between its ivories, which had turned pale brown, and putting a finger on middle C played the nearest keys simultaneously, so stuck together were they. Stabbing at keys that gave up toneless, harsh chords, I watched Momma, but her eyes never left the far-off space she stared into.

I cleaned off the Bible, which was flopped face down in the dirt beneath our table, and lifted Momma's hands to set it in her lap, opened to her favorite psalm. She let it slide off.

The temperature was rising, and any remnants of yesterday's spring weather had vanished. Already blazing hot. How long till last summer's 112-degree days came back? Outside, I shielded my eyes from the glare and followed Pa's footsteps toward the barn. Next to it, our wagon was almost invisible; only the tops of the wheels and its seat rose above the mounds settled onto our homestead. The windmill stood, whipped by the ceaseless wind, but three blades were missing. Dry earth blown into peculiar patterns had banked up against the barbed wire fences that once contained our cattle.

A few days earlier there had been a tank awaiting our next rain; now gritty gray swirls had drifted over it, the last of the water dried up. When I collected the eggs one morning a while back, a brood of wild ducks lay choked to death by dust in the tank-turned-graveyard. Pa said it must have been a watering stop on their spring migrations. Not no more it wasn't. We couldn't even eat them, as hungry as we were, since their bellies were filled with half the dirt in New Mexico.

In the barn, which was part dugout with a sod roof to cover the animals, Pa was worried for our last cow. Patches of hair were missing all over her body, her skin bared by the blowing grit. You could see the outline of her ribs. She didn't have any milk, and she was laboring hard to breathe. I was, too, but I didn't tell Pa. He had enough on his mind already. Earl said we lost the hens for good, but how did he know? Will, going on thirteen and more prone to thinking through a situation, stroked his chin, scanned the desert surrounding us, and said they'd be back.

"Prob'ly took off afraid, but might find their way home."

I looked at Pa for confirmation, but he avoided my eyes.

If they'd laid any eggs before they lit out, they'd been blown away with their roosts.

My brothers kept at their fretting about the condition of the tractor in the barn, though it seemed a long ways off till Pa would use it to plant the next batch of wheat, bound to die from thirst and dust, like every harvest I remembered in my ten years. Pa said we should clean up for supper, not that we could get any cleaner without wasting precious water. I followed the boys back to the house. Will was telling Earl he figured Pa would sell off the tractor next.

"Can't plant with it, and can't sell the car, Earl," he reasoned, "and who'd buy a dying cow." Both sets of shoulders hunched forward as they trudged through the sandbanks.

Momma didn't make any supper. Pa found some canned beans and ladled them unheated onto our plates till we all got equal shares. He guided Momma to the table, but she didn't touch hers, and the boys wasted no time gulping them down. I cleaned up and stole glances at Will, who was writing in his diary. He was scribbling fast and purposeful; for a quiet boy, he had a lot to say. He'd been one of the school's best students till he had to quit going. None of us farm children could get there reliably, with roads drifted over by all the blowing dirt. Mounds of sand piled up around our unused red-brick school.

I settled at the piano and let my fingers slide across the keys like I was playing a song Granny Alma used to entertain us with, singing to myself about gold dust—I waited out a cough spell—on a sunny street. Pa sat at our table, his Bible open, eyes poring over its pages, a long tendon tensing in his neck. Earl traced his forefinger around the grit on the table, writing nonsense, probably. He wasn't the book-learning type like Will.

I missed Granny Alma, who sang the prettiest of us all in her bright, clear voice. Momma would play for her after supper, with Earl and me chiming in to reach for the high notes as she sang "The Very Thought of You," grabbing my waist to cinch me near to her.

Before Pa turned off the lantern, Momma's hands were raw.

I woke with Pa and we went out early the next morning, right as the sun came up. Rubbing sleep from my eyes and wheezing some, I half-expected our rooster's *cock-a-doodle-doo*; then I remembered, he flew the coop. The sun was red, rising huge and slow in the direction of town, and Pa said, "A red sun augurs a bad day."

"Dust-storm weather," he told me with a firm clap on my shoulder. "Wake your brothers, Ruby Lee. We got two loved ones yet to bury."

CHAPTER TWO

There wasn't nuthin to eat for breakfast. Pa said we'd take care of our church business, then have supper at the De Soto's dining room in town. I saw the doubt on Will's face. "More 'n likely at Doc's soup kitchen," he said under his breath. We knew Pa barely had enough money to buy gasoline for his beat-up Ford. When Will had asked Pa why he sold our mule team before the winter came, he had that same look. Like Pa's answer dissatisfied him.

"No need to feed mules all winter if we can't plant a crop, boys," Pa said. "We'll buy new ones come spring."

Last winter, Momma sewed me two dresses from flour sacks, saying, "No need for fancy fabric if we can use what we got." Except I still remembered the fine linen dresses with pearl buttons she'd worn until they turned to rags.

My brothers knew the sole Hartless bank had closed its doors for good with our money inside—I'd overheard them whispering about it. But most folks in town didn't whisper. They were still dang angry three years after the bank holiday. I'd heard my fill of stories straight from the wives of farmers whose wheat crop was gold dust under their plows and gold bars in the bank, till the years of the drouth and the dusters made everybody hungry and broke. Will told Earl all our money was gone; Earl slugged him hard on the chin. Then they were both hollering and throwing punches that mostly missed.

"Is not gone!"

"Is so!"

"Liar!"

Pa broke it up when they were rolling around in the dirt. "You boys know better than that. Now, what's this all about?"

They hung their heads. Both said, "sorry, Pa," in one voice, and I saw that losing all your money was a thing to be ashamed of. One of the unspoken things.

My belly was grumbling. When the bulldozers came to dig a big ditch last year, and they rounded up the cattle which were just skin and bones, everyone gathered to witness the dozen or more men aiming rifles at their stock. Pa stood with the next-year folks, glad of the cash the government men handed him afterwards. "Couldn't keep 'em fed anyways," his voice broke. "But next year, when it rains . . ."

The farmers were shaking their heads. "What a thing," they said as they counted their twenties. "Sixteen bucks a head. A damn shame."

Even the growed men had tears in their eyes.

Helping Momma get dressed for the burials was near to impossible. She was froze in that spot.

I coughed. Then came coughing fits. I settled next to her, hoping she'd rub my back, feeling nothing but the hacking that hurt clear inside my chest.

Will brought the Vaseline and said to dunk my finger in, rub it in my nose, and handed me a moist cloth to breathe through. He was real gentle with Momma, leaning her back onto the bed as he whispered, "Lay back down next to Ruby Lee and keep her warm."

I was shivering. He layered some quilts on me, saying, "I'll fetch Pa."

Before they returned, I'd quieted my coughing and was remembering when the little airplane took off at a neighbor's farm to make it rain—by inciting the atmosphere, the rainmaker promised. We craned our necks backwards to watch the plane soar up, up, up into the few gray clouds. We exclaimed when rockets and fireworks exploded over and over, showering down white sparkling trails swallowed up by the blue horizon. It took a few moments after each skyrocket burst for the sound to find us, like a cannon firing at the circus.

The airplane put on a good show. We all oohed, we all aahed. Once when the plane rolled and spiraled down, we gasped. But it righted itself and climbed so high we couldn't see it anymore.

The plane never landed. We got no rain.

I hacked up the gritty mucus caught in my throat and Pa peered at me, his hand rough on my forehead, a peculiar, confused expression on his face. I saw how hollowed his cheeks were, how the lines became crevices for dirt, how deep were the sockets under his eyes.

Pa leaned over and gripped Momma's hands so tight the veins in his arms bulged.

"Willa Mae, come with us? Time to go to church. Willie? Come on now. We got to fetch the doctor for Ruby, too."

I bolted up; a coughing spasm got me real bad.

That was one of those times Pa didn't know quite what to do. Momma always nursed us on the rare days we were sick. If we needed doctoring, she'd send Pa for him. It was always up to her. Except this brown plague was different. Nobody knew how you could fix air that wasn't fit to breathe.

The drive into Hartless was bumpy—slow, too, in fits and starts, since Will and Earl had to jump out to shovel drifts so we could pass. In front next to Pa, Will leaned forward, his bony elbows on the glove box, eyes darting around, keen on what lurked ahead in the haze hanging from on high. Folks had plenty of near-misses and some crashes out here during the dusters, where the road got so lost in the murkiness a car'd run off into a ditch, with no way to haul it back out. Pa's A-Model dragged a chain, like the few automobiles we passed, to ground the static the dusters kicked up. Our headlights caught the electricity sparking off the barbed wire fences with a fuzzy glimpse of what we approached. Always more mounds of brown grit, what itched under our seats and fixed itself in our teeth. Our sponge masks and goggles lay in a tangle on the floor. None of us felt like strapping them on.

Momma sat beside me in back, while I tried not to gag up dirt from my chest. Sweating, I slid nearer to Earl, whose rail-thin body had less heat. Dead jackrabbits and field mice, hundreds of their carcasses, were half-buried in the drifts. We passed a fencerow with dead snakes hung belly-up on it.

"Pa," I tugged on his shirtsleeve, "look."

"Some folks think it'll bring rain, Ruby. Some folks'll try anything."

"Are we going to church?" I asked anyone who'd answer. Momma's gaze was as distant as before. My brothers waited for Pa.

"Yep. We'll see the doc about your cough, too." I took one of Momma's hands in mine. It was so cold. Or was I so hot? I took small breaths to keep from wheezing.

CHAPTER THREE

The doc's dark Stetson was as familiar to me as the smell of the strong black coffee he served in the Haven, in the back of his old clinic building. Most days after we got our free helpings of beans and boiled potatoes there, Earl and I wandered past the kitchen to peek into the room with glass jars holding pickled babies, goiters, and in one what he said was a human heart, lining dusty shelves stacked high with old medical books. But I was burning hot, my ribs sore from coughing, and too weary.

A fearful look crossed Pa's face. "Let's see what Doc Lawler has to say, Ruby," he patted my hair. "Boys, you stay here with your momma awhile."

He settled me on a hardwood bench, where I watched the farmers, cowboys, and Mexicans line up for a helping from steaming pots of beans. More drifters straggled in. They looked as down on their luck as us, and disappointed in what they found upon jumping off the Rock Island line at our depot. Some were kids as young as Earl.

Everything burned—my eyes, nose, throat—and I had hold of the table to keep the room from spinning.

At the makeshift counter the doc eyed Pa, then me, while he ladled beans onto tin plates. He aimed a stream of tobacco juice into his spittoon, removed his apron, and headed for us. The colors in the room grew bright, then dim. "Doc," nodded Pa.

"Beck," he said to Pa, his eyes on me as my wheezies started up.

"What have we got here?" Doc kneeled beside me. "Stick out your tongue, Ruby Lee," and I did. "Let me put a hand on your forehead," and he did. "I'll listen to you breathe now," and I waited.

He brought the stethoscope he always wore out from under his shirt with a shaky hand, placing the cold disk on my back. Before he told me to, I breathed in, out, deep slow breaths that came out raspy, and I gagged up dirt. And with it, some pink froth. The doc rubbed at his beard and his knees cracked when he stood.

Right above my head, Doc Lawler and Pa were having a whispered discussion I strained to hear.

"No need to run the X-ray," the doc was saying. "She's got the dust pneumonia, same as . . . She needs to breathe easier." That's what he'd said about my grandma and baby sister.

Pa looked at me. "We're fixin to visit the Trinity hospital, Ruby," which was odd since the sick ones were already dead and lying in their wood boxes.

"Don't we got to bury baby Nell and Granny Alma," I reminded Pa.

His eyes were so grim I wished I could take it back, and I clung to him tight to feel the life in him.

•　　•　　•

I remember the sponge baths, so cool and calming at first.

Water was so precious, I never got many baths at home. But in the hospital, the Sisters always bathed me in my bed with those little sponges. "Bless 'em and bathe 'em," the oldest one said. The Sisters whispered their prayers over me as they dipped their sponges into the water basin, the cool water pressed by gentle hands to my forehead, my chest and tummy, my arms and legs. Their fingernails were cut straight across, so clean, their hands so soft and white.

I longed for Momma's hands, hers much browner, the skin much coarser. When I slept peaceful, I dreamed of her hands on me; if I woke up gasping and hacking, her name was on my lips.

My nose itched from the smell of the kerosene and lard mixture they put on my chest and throat when my breath came in short bursts and I coughed up dirt and blood through the gauze mask I wore. *Oww*, I cried. My chest hurt so bad. My eyes burned. The bedsheets were scalding.

"Why are you putting hot water on me," I asked the Sister with the sponge. She laid a finger to my lips while I thrashed off my covers, my arms and legs going wild so's I could get back home, but they surrounded me, making a wall of black habits that blurred into another duster. Their white hands held me down. Their loud prayers turned into wind, all those Sisters round my bed, their fingers working their rosary beads, till I drifted away toward the light above them. It glowed white and grew so bright I closed my eyes. Granny Alma sang to me, she quieted me, while she rocked sweet baby Nell.

When I was well enough to sit up and take my supper on a tray, the Sisters smiled and called me a blessed miracle.

"What day is it," I asked. "How long have I been here? Am I going home?"

I set my bare feet on the cold tile floor. My legs buckled and the Sisters hauled me back into bed. They kept on smiling. They clucked their tongues, said, "Be patient a few more weeks while you get your strength back."

Half the summer passed by since the black blizzard at the church.

Pa came. The doc with him. I threw my arms around Pa and wouldn't let go. During the entire visit I was lookin at the doorway for Momma. "There, there, Ruby Lee, you gave us a scare," Pa hugged me back till I could feel his bones, he was so skinny.

"Is Momma comin, Pa," I asked, "Are you takin me home? Where's Will? And Earl?" But Pa just wiped at his eyes.

"Let the doc have a listen, Ruby." Pa stepped away while I showed Doc Lawler how deep were my breaths. He smelled like chew, holding a lump in his cheek. He laid his stethoscope to my chest, pressed around on my neck with his thumbs, looked into each ear, thumped me in a few places on my back, my belly, my chest, watched to see if I hurt. I didn't grunt one bit. I looked at his clenched fist, which he turned and opened like a magician. A piece of hard candy! When I popped it into my mouth, he grinned at Pa.

"She's fine, Beck. Long as she doesn't go back to breathing the brown dust."

I laid back on my pillow, looking up at the two men. They shifted uneasily on their feet. The doc spun his black hat around and round in his hands, eyes intent on Pa.

Pa stroked his chin. The furrows in his forehead made deep ravines. Craggy lines traveled from his eyes to his mouth. His eyebrows sagged around the outsides of his eyes to the dark sockets under them. The whites of his eyes were red, like they get from the sting of the wind and the dust. There were tears there.

"Ruby," he said, so soft I barely heard him. "My sweet Ruby Lee."

•　　•　　•

The Catholic Sisters had found me a hand-me-down dress that looked near new, and shoes a little big so's I could grow into them. They put on a cardigan sweater that was too tight, then a wool coat, and buttoned it up to its velvet collar. Then wrapped an itchy mohair scarf around my neck twice. "Keep yourself warm now."

Inside the coat pockets I found a pair of gloves some other girl had worn, and a hanky she'd blown her nose on. I threw them on the bed. The Sisters hugged me, reminded me to say my prayers. I didn't say nuthin.

Pa and Will fetched me from the hospital.

Pa didn't drive to the farm. His eyes were straight ahead, his hands high on the steering wheel, holding it so tight his knuckles popped out white. Ever' now and then, Will looked over his shoulder at me, and I looked out the window. I didn't see nuthin. If the dirt drifts were still piled up high along the street, I took no notice. As we passed the church, I turned my head to the other window. The train whistle blasted, and I knew we were going to the depot.

The train rumbled in, wheels grinding, cars groaning, and squealed to a stop. Pa lifted a cardboard suitcase from the boot and handed Will his rucksack. Then he came for me, offered me his hand. At the window, he asked for two tickets to Waco, a place I never heard of, and gave them to Will. From his pocket, he pulled out a wad of bills. "You be careful with this, son. You'll need it for food and your ticket back."

That's when I teared up. Maybe that's why I didn't see Momma while we walked to the train, my eyes were so full I blinked away the tears.

Pa took some paper from his shirt pocket, unfolded it, and squatted down opposite me. He fumbled in his other pocket, pulled out a few safety pins. I couldn't read much yet, but I could make out my name, Ruby, with six other letters, B-E-C-K-E-R. Will squeezed my hand. The train whistle blew, sad as me.

Pa's hands were shaking, pinning that paper on my coat. He opened the cardboard suitcase and took out Momma's soft hat, the one with a ribbon and a cloth button on the side. Inside were my old clothes, folded neat, next to Momma's tortoiseshell brush and comb set, her fine kid leather gloves, and my rag doll, which was so clean she looked brand new. Her skin was pink, with small red dots where her cheeks were, and her hair looked like the color I always wanted, golden yellow. Her eyes were painted back on, bright and blue like mine.

When he pulled the cloche hat that was Momma's on my head, it came down past my ears. Pa's dark eyes were level with mine while he crouched in front of me, his face mixed up in confusion and determination.

"Your momma ain't well, Ruby," he told me. "She packed some of her things you like and put a letter for you in your suitcase."

He wiped at his eyes and kept on, "You're going east to stay with Granny Alma's cousin, Bess, till the rains come. Can't be long now, when these dusters quit . . . You got to go stay with Cousin Bess, so's you don't get real sick like you was."

I couldn't look in his eyes anymore.

"It's for your own good"—his voice cracked—"Won't be long till you're home again. Will's going with you. Bess'll meet you at the station. She'll take real good care of you. Now don't fret girl—"

Tears trickled down my cheeks and I struggled to free his hands from my arms, shaking my head, *no!*

No! No!

My whole body was shaking. I stamped my feet on the wood platform, crying and hollering, causing a ruckus so's people looked our way. Pa lifted me up the two steps inside the railroad car. I was smack up against a man in uniform and Will bounded up behind me as the whistle blew again—longer, lonelier this time.

Pa handed the man a dollar bill, said, "I'd be mighty grateful if you'd look after these two till the Waco station."

"Yessir, thank you, sir." The man tipped his round steward cap and caught me as I fell limp. The last words I heard from Pa were, "How much more, Lord."

As the train got up a head of steam, my eyes roved the station stop in a panic. Momma wasn't there. All I could think was, *what had I done to make Momma send me away?*

CHAPTER FOUR

WILLA MAE

Bored eyes. "And you are?"

"Willa Mae Eckhart. Willie."

"Your last name?" Not looking at me.

"Ek-erd," I say, enunciating carefully.

"Spell it."

"E-c-k-h-a-r-t. Ek-erd, as I said." I watch her write a loopy E, upside down, then the rest, making sure she spells it correctly, since she must have a hearing problem.

My hearing is acute since arriving here.

The whistle blast of a departing train pierces the quiet. From the Wichita Falls depot, the train Beck takes home.

It's for your own good, Willie. I'm sorry. Beck's last words, his voice gravelly.

The reluctant scuffling of my shoes as he led me inside. My memories jumble—Ruby Lee's cries, my protests when Beck took her from us.

Hushed whispers. From somewhere upstairs, a moan lingers.

She doesn't react to my heart-rent wail, so loud it might deafen me. *How long can I last without Ruby?*

A bell blares. Soft footsteps shuffle past.

Typewriter keys clack next door.

Blunt footsteps in the hall, the squeak of door hinges.

An orderly, rigid, in white. "Ready?" A command.

I tense. He taps his shoe, impatient.

She pulls a draw from a cigarette. Still she avoids my eyes. "The orders say Mrs. Becker."

I shake my head. *No longer.*

"Do you realize where you are?" Her question floats by me, airy.

The starchy crunch of my gown when I nod.

My own voice, scarcely a croak.

"The state . . . asylum." The word catches in my throat—*Lunatic*—silent.

The softest of drips. My tear falls to her desk.

A pen scratches on paper, more scribbling on forms.

She yawns, almost inaudible.

Her inking pad lid snaps open.

"Do you know why you are here?"

I nod. *Driven mad by dust.* My memory is clear—the judge's rich baritone, declaring his ruling. Beck nodding, complicit.

My protests stifled by the gavel strikes.

The echo present now, thunder in my ears, hammering the bench.

Another slam—I jump. Her weighty rubber stamp.

There it is, the court order. On the papers bearing my name, in inky red capitals.

COMMITTED.

CHAPTER FIVE

RUBY LEE

As the train picked up speed, leaving our tiny corner of the Texas Panhandle, we passed deserted farmhouses where I noted no living thing, not animals nor crops, only wavy sand patterns making mounds of the flat plains. Front doors left wide open, drifts blowing into living rooms.

We passed shacks where dirty children with dull eyes wore rags, turning their heads with effort to watch our train rumble by. But what little life I saw outside was more than was inside my heart.

I felt chilled, then feverish, then weak. Leaning against Will's shoulder, I drifted in and out to the rhythmic rocking of the train.

"Let's get some sleep, Ruby," he said, and soon he was snoring gently with his newsboy cap pulled over his eyes. But try as I might to keep them shut, my eyelids kept flying wide open, waiting for the dust to give way to dawn, looking for the daylight that would shine on what my future held.

·   ·   ·

The hissing, clanging steam locomotive roared awake, and us with it. Looked close to daybreak.

"You hungry?" Will reached into his pack for two apples. We bit into them in crunchy unison. I looked at the travelers and saw none of our family. My mind was foggy from sleep. I worked at assembling the events of the last weeks into some kind of order but only one thing screamed at me, shattering beneath my skin, paining my soul raw.

What had I done to make Momma so mad? Did she blame me for baby Nell?

I didn't realize I'd let go of my apple till I heard its dull thud on the floor. As it rolled down the aisle and passengers' heads swiveled to look, I shivered—like a blanket of snow had been thrown over me. Views from the windows swirled past, flashing dizzying turns of dead crops and cracked brown fields and scrawny cattle. I sucked in quick shallow breaths but weakness made me slump toward the wall.

Will grasped my hands and rubbed them in his own. Everything blurred. I saw how Momma's eyes were hard on mine when Nell's spittle came up brown as dirt, and she choked her last breath on earth.

"Ruby, Ruby," Will was saying, his hand on my forehead. "You're so clammy."

The concern creasing his brow turned into Momma's frown. She knew. It was my fault Nell passed.

•   •   •

Will's warm hands were under my arms, lifting me upright. I must have fainted. He patted my cheeks, gentle, and my eyelids fluttered into the present, the place where I didn't want to be. I batted his hands away. I muttered, "Leave me alone." *Like Momma did.*

It made no never mind what happened to me next. I refused to ask, I wouldn't speak. In my ten-year-old mind, that was the only control I had.

At the Waco depot, riders made ready to disembark. Will, holding my suitcase, reached for my hand. My toes tingled first, then my legs went numb on me, and my heart pounded. Little pins jabbed me all over. Will tugged on my hand. He didn't know how terrified I was.

I was lightheaded, everything was spinning, and my legs were powerless. I broke out in a sweat. A breeze blew in and transformed into fingers tightening around my throat. A lady passing by stopped, told Will, "She doesn't look too good."

"Yes, ma'am." Will, ever steady, sounded uneasy.

"I'm a nurse. Let me help you with this child."

She sat beside me and smoothed my hair. She took my wrist and gently placed her fingertips on my pulse. Her face was so near mine, her eyes looked crossed. I moved my head away from her stale breath.

"Let's count together now, one-two. One, two, breathe in. One, two, breathe out. One . . . two. One . . . Two. In, and out. That's it. In, out," and after a time, my breathing moderated. "Calmly in, sigh it out," her voice was melodic. I inhaled deeply, exhaled more slowly. Air filled my chest—clean, pure air—I could gulp it in and not cough brown spittle back out.

She regarded Will. "You're her brother?"

"Yes, ma'am, I'm Will Becker. This here's Ruby Lee."

"I can see that." She touched the paper Pa had pinned on me. "Just a little nervous distress."

She kept at me with the counting. "One, two, Ru-by. One, two, Ruby Lee." I focused on her. Her face came into sharper view. Faint pink lipstick coated her lips. Her skin was smooth, powdery white. Her eyes glowed, the palest of blues. She laid two delicate fingers on my wrist again and watched me awhile.

"There, little sister, your pulse is normal. You're doing swell."

The other travelers had cleared out. The steward hovered nearby. "Lost her vertical hold, did she? Well, she looks fine now," he pronounced, the first words he'd uttered to us since taking Pa's dollar. "Off you go."

"We'll set a while longer." The nurse was firm, not taking her gaze from me. "When you're ready, Ruby Lee."

I relaxed. I stretched out my legs, lifted my feet, and rolled them round at my ankles, first one way, then t'other. Seemed like they'd work. I was breathing normal again. I stood up.

Will let out a sigh, saying thank you. We took it slow walking till I froze at the steps. Will stood below with outstretched arms to lift me down to the platform. Behind me, the nurse gripped my shoulders, whispered, "You can do it."

You can live without Momma.

1936

CHAPTER SIX

RUBY LEE

"It's bound to rain soon, Ruby," Will said, the doubt apparent in his eyes before they skated sideways. "That's what Pa says, you know, next year—"

I sent him the stink eye. I'd never seen any rain in my lifetime, and he knew it, being three years older than me. I'd grown outta diapers listening to Will question Pa's stubborn belief that next year, the land would make good again.

"Lookit here, Ruby," Will pleaded, crouching to tuck his finger under my chin. I gave him no quarter, wouldn't look him in the eyes while he kept at his lies. "Pa will send for you, soon as the dusters are gone for good and the air's clear. So's you can breathe again."

He had me there, didn't he. How could I ever go home when the very air I breathed came at my lungs like an enemy invader?

As it was, though, I hadn't a penny to my name except for the twenty dollars Will had left me, all in one-dollar bills, which he'd told me to save for a rainy day.

If I'd been speakin then, I'd have asked him, "Will, when do you ever expect to see a rainy day?" When Will stuffed those dollar bills in my pocket, I didn't let him know how he tore my heart; I didn't say thank you or nuthin.

I was righteous mad at him for leaving me with Cousin Bess, smiling as he backed away like his eyes had no tears coming. I had no words for him, neither.

But no sooner than he'd left Waco, it did rain, steady and all day long, and it was the first summer rain I'd ever seen in practically eleven years on earth. I ran outside to feel it all over me, I whirled and twirled around in it, I let rain run down my skin and chill me, I let it drench my clothes and hair and fill my shoes. Bess shouted from her covered porch to come in. I ignored her.

"You'll catch your death, come in, Ruby," she insisted. She splashed through the waterlogged grass with a big black umbrella and dragged me inside. Weary flowers in the beds lining the yard had raised up their heads, their petals thirsty for rain, opening into subdued versions of the brilliant colors they would become. She didn't notice them for scolding me. Holding my arm, she fussed. "Why, you're shivering!"

Inside, she dried me with a soft towel and left my clothing in a puddle of water near the deep-pile foyer rug. "Let's get you upstairs into some dry things."

All I could think when she led me to my bedroom was how the rain would change everything. The farm would be saved. The '36 winter wheat would make a crop. Pa would get his mules and cattle back. Momma could raise her vegetables again. I could go home.

•　　•　　•

I became a fastidious student of the *Old Farmer's Almanac*, and a regular consumer of the farm report and weather conditions published in the *Waco Tribune-Herald*. That was before I even learned to read, but I stared at those pages long enough every day, the numbers started making some sort of sense to me. Nonsense was more like it; reading them nowadays, I realize I made them say what I wanted them to say: Nine inches of rain fell in July, a record for Dallam and Hartley Counties. August saw ten more. Twelve inches is predicted the first weeks of fall. The dust storms of 1929-1936 are a thing of the past as the moist soil holds and crops take root.

On the day I read that forecast, I promised myself I'd take the next train back. I kept my cardboard suitcase packed and ready.

•   •   •

The thing that near startled me into speaking again was the colors. I took in all the colors everywhere, and I hardly had the names for 'em, accustomed as I was to the brown life I'd led back home. I wanted to exclaim at all of them, ask Bess how many kinds of blues were there, what were the reds of her rosebushes called? How many words for green did they have—for the ones more yellowish, and the greens with more blue in them? The aquamarines, the deep purples, violets, crimsons—all names I learned later on—what were they called? I couldn't sleep past sunrise, I was so excited to look out my upstairs window at the colors each morning.

But I was so mad, I refused to speak. I didn't appreciate my four-poster bed with satiny pink bedding and soft downy pillows. I didn't want the fancy clothes Bess dressed me in, or the special outfits with hats for Sundays, nor the manners she tried to teach me. My heart hurt too bad. I made myself believe being mute was justification for what was done to me. I didn't utter a word.

If I confounded Bess by staying silent, she'd get so exasperated she'd send me home.

I learned the colors instead by studying the smooth color plates in her flower books. She had a collection of them in her library, lined up on a set of golden oak shelves built into the wall opposite her black lacquer piano. Each volume I opened yielded a heady odor of ink and paper in one whiff. She didn't mind me using her books, and sometimes she'd sit with me and read from them, trying to teach me, asking me to repeat the words back to her. But I refused to talk. I made her think I was too pained to speak. Which in a way, I was.

Bess got impatient with me sometimes, but more than that, she must have felt just plain inadequate. Cousin Bess was a widow who'd never had a child; she'd wanted one some kinda awful, you could tell. She was proud of her husband who kept his bank afloat after the crash, but the bank holiday took the wind out of him, she'd say. He musta left her more money than she could say grace over. But I wouldn't let her spoil me.

I contrived to make her hate me, so she'd send me home.

And I didn't understand what the consequences would be for what I was doing, by not doing what every child can do: talk.

CHAPTER SEVEN

Cousin Bess invited the ladies in her contract bridge group to celebrate my birthday. Colorful streamers hung from the chandelier, fussy decorations bordered her gold-rimmed bone china and Cambridge Glass cut crystal. Fresh flowers, my favorites from her garden, overflowed their cloisonné vases, and the cloying scent of rubrum lilies mingled with the ladies' perfumes. It about choked me.

The ladies brought wrapped gifts from Goldstein's department store downtown. After settling on the next meeting for the Ladies' Service League they'd formed to help needy children—noting in whispers that thanks to Bess's generosity, I was no longer one—they turned to my birthday.

"Why, she's as shy as a crocus, Bess," Mrs. Clifford greeted me.

I couldn't take my eyes off the jeweled brooch Mrs. Clifford had pinned to her velvety green lapel. It was pearly and encrusted with sparkling stones, shaped to resemble a peacock. That bird's blue eye, a color I learned was called sapphire, winked at me when she knelt down.

"You're Ruby? What a perfect name, as red as your cherry cheeks are." Mrs. Barton smelled more fragrant than the blooming magnolia trees.

More ladies arrived, wearing sparkly bracelets over their long gloves. Their day dresses had poofy pushed-up sleeves and their cloche hats were wound with velvet ribbons. A small red fox draped one lady's wide shoulders so its beady little eyes stared at me.

Each of them admired every little thing the others wore, and this took at least an hour. The pile of birthday presents grew with each arrival.

Bess had already indulged me in the only gift I desired. She'd treated me to a day at the Texas Centennial Exposition—the ballyhooed months-long celebration of Texas's one hundredth birthday in Dallas. Amelia Earhart would be visiting. It was the closest I could get to flying, which I dreamed would be my ticket home. The famous aviatrix was made a sky constable at the Jersey Lily saloon (off-limits to a child my age). Amelia took a solo Scooter Ride on the Midway. I was keen to try it. But Bess regarded the Midway as too rough for a girl. Amelia flew westward in her two-motored Lockheed Electra before I ever caught sight of her.

The present from Bess was no surprise and nothing I wanted. She paid five whole dollars—a sum I'd have liked in cash—for a Texas Rangerette doll: Shirley Temple, decked out in suede chaps with a leather holster for her six-shooter. Her ten-gallon hat was cocked back on her famous pin curls.

When she'd stopped at the barker hawking Shirley Temple Centennial dolls, I glimpsed a boy who coulda been Will. I lunged for him, my hopes raised, but Bess clamped my hand tight. He disappeared into the crowd surging toward the lagoon promenade.

I trudged behind her, stalling at Midget City. One hundred costumed little people "lived" in a tiny town, as trapped in their scaled-down village as I felt in Waco. My childish hopes were dashed, that boy long gone.

Another of Bess's guests tucked her polished finger beneath my chin. "You are as pretty as a pie supper, aren't you?" Her voice was rich and throaty, like Momma's.

Tiny needles prickled in my feet and worked their way up to my chest, where my heart began pounding. On the walnut chest in the front hall, the vase of flowers I'd picked from the garden began to blur, its riot of pinks, yellows, and violets running together like unconfined watercolors. Cold beads of sweat dampened my sleeves.

I wouldn't let myself shiver, though. I wouldn't let myself wheeze or cough.

I trusted myself with two small steps backwards, and stayed upright, taking more steps till I was out of view. But at that instant, with grand ceremony, Cook brought out the birthday cake she'd baked in the Florence gas range.

"Ruby, your cake looks delicious. Is vanilla icing your favorite?"

Returning, I scowled at Mrs. Barton, who uttered, "brat," behind her hands. Having never tasted icing till Cook let me lick it from the Mixmaster beater, I didn't know there were choices.

"Already eleven!" Mrs. Clifford said, counting candles. I grimaced—one more year away from home.

Bess struck a match and lit all twelve. Candlelight licked her face, reminding me of the witch who lured Gretel to her oven. "An extra candle for good luck. Go ahead, Ruby, make a wish."

I pictured Momma's pound cake smeared with her dark-red tuna jelly. All I wanted for my birthday was my momma, who didn't want me.

I took in a gulp of air and blew hard, spit flying everywhere, making my wish.

I wished Cousin Bess would die so I could go home.

•   •   •

Once everyone left, I slipped into the kitchen. With Cook nowhere in sight, I licked the batter from her cornbread bowl and heard a sharp rap on the screen door and jumped higher than a kickin mule.

Two boys waited outside the screen door. They took off their newsie caps, and the taller one smiled widely. He was missing a front tooth, and another near it was turning brown. The breeze blew their odor inside, and I pinched my nose.

"Sure hate to disturb, ma'am." The tall boy shifted from one wore-out boot to the other. His eyes were steady, though, and deep brown. Like Will's. "Wonder if you could spare us some leftovers, or anything." You could practically see his ribs under his shirt.

"We can mow the lawn," he finished, and got an elbow in his rib from the short boy.

Both boys had rough hands, dirt under their fingernails, and dark stains smeared across their rolled-up trousers. The short boy fidgeted with his cap, twirling it round and round till he dropped it. He bent over for it and fell backwards off the steps, caught himself, and loosed a sheepish grin, his freckles spreading across his whole face.

They watched me looking them over, hands shoved in their pockets. Their shoulders drooped, and the younger boy, who reminded me of Earl, turned to go.

I pushed open the screen door. "Come in. You got to wash up first." The first words I'd spoken in months and my voice cracked funny.

They stood there scrubbing their hands, on up their arms, and even washed their faces. The grime left our white porcelain sink black, swirling down the drain.

I pulled out two chairs from the kitchen table, and one gave a low whistle. "A set-down! Thank ya kindly, ma'am."

I laughed when they called me *ma'am*, but not too loud. I didn't want to draw any attention. Before I rummaged in the icebox for leftovers from last night's pot roast, I tossed some Snickers their way. The short one caught two bars midair. Their eyes lit up.

"I've developed a taste for these myself," I said to the older boy. "I'm Ruby Lee. Who are you?"

He stood quick, like he had manners. "Hello, Ruby. I'm Carl. This here's Walter. Pleased to make your acquaintance."

The swinging door burst inwards with a shove from Cook, who sized up the boys and moved me aside.

"Sit with these young men, Ruby Lee," she told me, "and practice talking while I heat up their supper."

She had me trapped. I busted out of the kitchen like a duster was coming for me, running so hard I ran right out of breath a block away. Gasping for air, I sat under a shady live oak till I quit huffing.

That night I had a craving for my two brothers that beat any desire I ever had for Snickers.

CHAPTER EIGHT

WILLA MAE

A crack of lightning, followed by the thrum of a downpour—sounds I haven't heard in years—startle me, lost in my memories of Ruby. My letter finished, I'm sketching her face as I remember it on her first birthday, and on her last birthday. "I need another drawing pad," I say to the orderly as he hoists me to my feet, "more pencils and charcoal sticks, a set of pastels."

He stills my hands, which never fail to commence rubbing one another when robbed of pen or pencil.

"Writing your letters again? The nurse will attend to that, and she'll collect all this." He gestures to the stacks of portraits layered on the table and the dozens of letters no one has troubled to mail for me. "But now it's time for your hydrotherapy treatment."

It is a daily ritual after lunch I dread. I will be taken to the psychopathic wing, where I'll be made to strip and lie on a rubber sheet in a frigid bath. Nurses apply sheets drenched in steaming hot water and set a cold ice cap on my head. My entombed skin prickles till it burns in the icy water. They'll strap me down with more sheets to still my muscles, and cover me with more heavy blankets to contain whatever heat I summon. An itching that can't be scratched overtakes me, and in my helplessness I become drowsy. Within the hour, I am falling asleep.

Some days the treatment consists of continuous baths. Strapped into a bath full of scalding hot water that gradually warms, trapped for hours, even overnight, powerless. Then they stand me in the shower for needle-like sprays of cold water that pierce my reddened skin and shock me into consciousness. When my legs cramp and I crumple, they massage them until I can stand again.

I get no hint of which treatment I'll endure today, and it is as pointless to ask as it is to expect stamps for my letters to Ruby.

Thrashing and resisting, as I did at first, causes the staff to recommend sterner treatments. I know from other patients I will be subjected to the loathed cold packs if the doctors don't see improvement from these hydro treatments. I might be laid naked on a canvas hammock in a bath with the rubber blanket placed over me and shrouded in cold, wet sheets. If I struggle, as everyone does, I'll be held down and bound by two attendants, aided by other patients, as they add more wet sheets, a wool blanket, and a hot bag beneath my bare feet. Last comes the ice pack on my forehead. The effect is the same as hydrotherapy—sleepiness—but the methods much crueler.

In the worst cases, patients receive hypo injections—increasing amounts of insulin each day—until they go into convulsive shock. Women speak of awakening with the taste of blood in their mouths. Their gags must have slipped, they are told. Their tongues are raw, they complain. Nauseous and foggy, they struggle with splitting headaches.

"You're causing trouble for your husband and your family in this condition," doctors tell the women who protest, as they increase the duration of the shock treatments. Sobbing, the women rail against the shock hypos. Emerging from shock makes them cloudy, unaware. Confused and drained. Their memories are lost to them, they cry. They jumble words, speak gibberish, until they are reduced to begging. It's to help you recover, they are told.

Always, the staff claims, these methods will help us recover.

Flashes of lightning blind me while I walk along the corridor docile as a lamb, rubbing my hands for comfort, focusing on the rain pelting the windows, and sending my mind elsewhere to set my memories in place, determined to endure the next hours.

CHAPTER NINE

RUBY LEE

After a summer so dry and scorching the folks at church pronounced it hotter than the hinges of hell, we had so much rain in September Cousin Bess fretted about her house floating away.

But the storms was exciting to me. I pictured her house drifting off so's I could rejoin my family. I got a vision of Pa outside our farm shack in his dust-caked brown field, his eyes raised heavenward like they often was, praying for rain and getting his prayers answered. Momma, she'd be pulling fresh peppers and potatoes from her garden, her head tilted back, her mouth grinning open to catch buckets full'a rain. They'd be sending Will for me any day now.

A messenger boy bicycled up with an envelope. "Telegram for Mrs. Elizabeth Eckhart." He handed it to me. "See that she gets it, little missy." He shot me a stern glare from under his Western Union cap, but he was just a kid, younger than Earl. I stared him down till his eyes veered sideways then slammed the door.

I turned that envelope over and around to make out where it came from. But I'd just started school—not where I belonged, not even third grade as Bess promised, but a whole three grades behind. They'd put me in kindergarten with the little panty-wetters, where we were learning the alphabet. The telegram came from Hartless, though. I didn't deliberate long. Bess was at one of her Ladies' Service League meetings, probably doling out re-soled shoes to the needy families they talked about in hushed tones when I was around.

I opened her telegram carefully. All I could read was our last name, Becker, same as the name on the paper Pa pinned to my coat. It had to be from Pa.

Those two boys at the kitchen door who'd loved Snickers—one of 'em was bound to be reading-age. I grabbed two candy bars and tucked the telegram inside my raincoat on my way out the back door.

•　　•　　•

I was on the lookout for Will where the drifters waited for dark to catch out on the freight trains.

It was rotten of me, how I'd spurned him with no words, no goodbyes. He musta felt so low, proud and smart as he was, being a hobo. Will didn't hesitate when he handed me the money he needed for a ticket home. He must've known it was his future he was giving up—his dream, to be educated and go to college—and he let it go in one guilty gesture, to feel better about leaving me. In spite of my regrets, there were no tears on my cheeks, only rain, as I rubbed my coveralls pocket out of habit. I always kept that twenty dollars close.

I tied my rain hat tighter under my chin, kicking through the puddles, walking faster, then racing, conjuring Will at the freight tracks so we could go home.

It was coming down cats and dogs. All the earthly colors and shapes had merged with the clouds—like being in a dust storm, only gray, not brown, wet, not gritty. The creek got on a rise; usually a near-dry culvert a few blocks behind the house, it was creeping into our backyard. I raced ahead of it, knowing the creek took a turn ahead of me. I'd have to beat it.

Getting to the river on foot took longer than I'd figured. Riding in Bess's custom DeSoto with mohair seats along Waco's tree-lined streets, I'd gape at stylish mansions with attached garages and deep front porches and ogle at the Cottonland Castle's sandstone turret before the next marvel appeared, like the iron-crowned cupola atop the blue-and-white Cameron House—

the trip went too fast. On foot, I dodged puddles spreading into lakes and jumped ditches fast becoming creeks while daylight dimmed into gloom and an hour passed.

I guessed I was at Market Square when oranges and apples bobbed past, their wooden crates trailing them in the muddy water coming up fast ahead.

A chicken on a chair floated by.

Near the Suspension Bridge, I'd need to head right to reach the tracks. But now I cut east quick. I passed around a shallow lake that had been Eighth Street when an unfamiliar roar caught me, powerful and deafening. I was horror-struck but spellbound at the Brazos, raging up the riverbanks, nothing to contain its thunder and power.

Like the Sunday a black wall as high as the heavens had rolled over our new church. And had taken me from home.

•   •   •

I ran for the freight yard in the direction of the tracks, I thought, blinded by rain and frightened by the river churning close. When I pressed my hands over my ears, all I heard was Momma's wailing on that black Sunday.

I stumbled under an awning, catching my breath, trying to make the world go silent. Beyond the square, the muddy brown Brazos River was surging up to meet the Suspension Bridge. Nearby, the Cotton Belt line had abandoned its freight cars on the railroad bridge where the rising river readied to meet it.

As if to prove Bess right, a rooftop bobbled up and down and out of sight as the crazed river carried an entire house away. Then came more houses. My mind was racing and a sudden desperation for Will overtook me.

I tore out from the false safety of my overhang and ran pell-mell into it, looking for signs of the trains. It was hard to see, even harder to breathe, and I slowed my steps. The rain came fast in gray slants, so hard it stung. Next to me, someone was walking, keeping pace. I looked over. It was Will.

I rubbed my eyes; it was raining so hard I couldn't trust my vision. I stopped.

So did he.

He wore a poncho; he threw it over both of us and yelled over the pummeling rain and river. "We got to get to higher ground, this way! River's coming over the banks."

Inside his poncho, it was dark, drier too, and warm with our bodies close. Comforting. I followed what I could see, which was his stompers, grateful to have him guiding. "I've still got your twenty dollars, Will," I huffed as we ran.

"What—" he yelled, but the force of water crashing into buildings and trees made it too loud to hear.

He drew us to a stop. I peeked outside the poncho. We were stuck where we stood by a white cow with wild eyes, carried by the current. He grabbed my hand and we whirled to beat feet around the water, running so fast in the dark I quit trying to figure where to.

At last he put his hands around my waist and boosted me up— "Scramble up, now"—and I smelled its smoky stink before I could see. I was inside a boxcar. He came right up after me. The only light was from the ember falling off a cigarette a kid in the corner had rolled.

"Ruby, right?" asked the boy who was Will, his voice not at all like my brother's, but still familiar. "Remember me? Carl . . . Walter's friend. Got any of those candy bars?"

It was darker than coffin air in there. Somebody lit a match, and a dozen pairs of eyes, at uneven heights, were on me for the flash of a Brownie Hawkeye. The stink of wet wool and unwashed men and pine tar inhabited the place. The open door was where the air was clearest, but when the rain slashed inside, I scooted away from the storm's power.

"Hard to say if she's gonna quit. River's still comin up," Carl said, causing everyone in the boxcar to thud to the side door, their dull footfalls rumbling and shaking the car. Sound was contained inside here, as I was with these strangers, and it felt cozy—more at home, among my kind, where my choices were few. Everything at Bess's was complicated.

Murmuring and disagreement rumbled among them as to the nature and duration of the storm, but all agreed on two things: they were lucky the bulls had been scared off by a little rain, and as hungry as they'd got from doing nothing, there'd be Mulligan for supper. "Hobo stew," one said, his laugh forced. "Hope we got more than onions tonight."

"Why doncha drop a line, junior?" asked a deep voice. "Catch us some trout." That got a chuckle.

A boy with a squeaky voice spoke up. "Got a stale loaf. A few moldy potatoes."

None of that sounded good to me.

I shoved the telegram at Carl with a Snickers bar, waiting on him to down it. "Can you read this to me?" My eyes were adjusting to the dim light. The young men and boys who watched us were older than me. Teenagers, mostly.

"Where's Walter?"

Carl stopped chewing. "He got homesick."

"He went home?"

A quiet pall took over the place. "You tell it, Whitey." Carl's voice had a hitch.

From the other side of the boxcar came the strike of a match. The boy next to Whitey reached across him to hold the flame under his chin, and Whitey's face glowed up to the dark sockets circling his eyes. "Walter was catching out, running alongside the train, matching speed, and he got his first handhold. He kept running, then he got his other hand up—you know, he's a short guy, it was hard for him with that guitar case across his shoulder—but it looked like he had a grip. Then he had to lift his foot—and he, well, he musta chickened out. The train gave a jerk, you know, he didn't anticipate it. He wasn't too experienced, that kid. Too young." He shook his head mournfully as the match sputtered out.

"What?" I whispered. "Then what?" A memory of the grinning boy, his erratic freckles like Earl's, came at me.

Carl spoke. "Walter—he fell. Under the train. She dragged him under." He choked up. "From now on, I'm a loner. No more partners for this 'bo."

The fright of Walter's death, ground under the train wheels, made me itch to scram. But I needed his help. "Read that to me, will ya?" I waggled the telegram Carl still held.

Carl thrust it back at me. "It's too dark in here to see. What's your hurry?"

He glowered, turning away, and slid closer to his kind.

Outside, the river crept closer, thundering and muddy, carrying felled trees and stolen roofs as it surged through downtown. I leapt out of the boxcar into the storm, running fast as greased lightning for home—what passed for home—panting and grateful for its welcoming warmth when I got there, chilled to the bone and sopping wet.

Thinking back on it, I think Carl's tears for his buddy embarrassed him. And maybe he couldn't read, neither.

CHAPTER TEN

The house was gloomy without Bess and Cook. When the grandfather clock struck seven, I pondered whether they'd gone off hunting for me in a raging storm, shoving down a twinge of guilt. Outside, across the backyard and the alley, lightning flashes lit up downed tree limbs and leaves, strewn like unshuffled playing cards. The garage doors stood wide open, coach lights blazing, and the DeSoto wasn't inside. There'd be a reckoning later, I could be sure. Or maybe they hoped I'd float away like a house, as sullen and contrary as I was. I half-hoped they never came back, always meddling with me, improving me, and thwarting my plans to get home.

A crack of lightning struck so near I jumped, and Bess's heirloom flower vase wobbled. I lunged, but it escaped me, crashing to the tile, scattering shards and petals right as the lights blinked off. I sank down, furious.

I wanted Momma. *I wanted out.*

I felt my way along the dining room furniture into the kitchen and to the drawer where the candles were. A second lightning strike lit up the Hoosier cabinet long enough for me to spot the matches under a dusting of flour on its enamel countertop.

I crept upstairs by candlelight to the bathroom where Bess had insisted on fixin my hair this morning. The tip of my ear still stung where her hot curling tongs got too close. She'd pinched my cheeks, admiring my single dimple.

"All you need is pin curls, Ruby. You'll look as adorable as Little Miss Marker."

Her lips widened in pleasure, leaving a smear of mauve lipstick on her top teeth. I could smell the baby powder under her arms as she leaned over me and fussed with my board-straight hair. "It doesn't take too readily to curls, does it," she sighed.

Of course I would never resemble Bright Eyes, mine being a pale blue and my hair much darker than hers, set in her fifty-six perfect ringlets. I was lean as a bean to little Shirley's chubby sturdiness. Bess needed new specs, or less wishful thinking.

She styled my straight hair with her heated curling iron and dressed me as she would her doll. "We'll go to the Orpheum! Everyone will think you're a famous movie star!" Her voice was light and breathless.

Peering at my dim reflection in the mirror, I hated what I saw. Every little change Bess made to me took me further from home.

Now those curls, nearly straight after the soaking I'd endured, were what I hated most. They were for rich girls raised on concrete. Using the scissors she'd trimmed my bangs with, I started below my right earlobe, cutting around to the back as even as I could. Then I hacked those limp curls from my left ear. Pretty soon they were in a tangle of dark swirls covering my shoes, which I moved the candle closer to, savoring my loss. Savoring Bess's reaction, when she discovered them.

Where was she, anyway?

I was consternated, alone during a dangerous storm. In the pitch black.

I held the candle near my face so the flame flickered light across me. My hair was as jagged as a broken bowl.

Just then, the lights turned on—startling me—and I let go of the candleholder. It spilled hot wax on me on its way to the black and white tile, and I yowled. The rag rug underfoot sizzled like it might flame up. I stomped on it, but the fire flared up and took off around the oval like a racehorse running the track.

I pushed the sink stopper down and opened both spigots full out, using my cupped hands to splash water over the porcelain onto the rug. When the bowl filled up, I stepped back to admire how it gushed over the edge, like a waterfall. It sounded pleasant, similar to the Spanish fountain across the street, water spilling from basin to basin. I never tired of watching the fountain attract birds who splashed their wings in the copper bath with its green patina, a prism of colors glinting in the sunshine.

But I tired of watching the water overflow the shiny white sink, ringed by minty tile.

I hop-skipped downstairs to the library. Bess had a gleaming mahogany stand where her prized volume, *Birds of America*, lay open, displaying a color plate. I was fond of that oversize book. Its cover was smooth leather, embossed with bright gold letters, so heavy it needed its own stand to support it. Every page you turned showed another painting of a curious bird. They were exotic, some bigger than life. The numerous small birds, striking in their varying yellow and black patterns, were my favorites. I flipped through the book and came upon a vivid pink bird with a long curved neck, standing on one tall, spindly leg, I'd never noticed.

With my scissors, I carefully cut it out, picturing it above Nell's crib. When teardrops moistened the page I fell to the floor, sobbing. For my loss, the little sister I could have had, the family I missed.

Later, I wiped my face and carefully positioned the pink bird back inside the book, closing the cover. I imagined water pooling on the bathroom floor above, ready to spill down. If I lifted my face to it, I might be cleansed.

Instead, headlights played through the glass panes of the French doors that led to the garden. The low hum of the DeSoto followed. I ran to my room. The auto pulled into the garage and I pulled my comforter over my head. Before the kitchen door swung open, I heard the splash of water flowing carelessly from the bathroom sink.

Cousin Bess said, "I pray she's here, safe and sound. You look upstairs, I'll check here." She called out my name, then Cook joined in, "Ruby! Ruby?"

In the front hall, their shoes crunched bits of broken china as they expressed concern. From the library, their cries turned anxious. On the staircase, hurried footsteps ascended between heavy breaths. In the bathroom, curses and the sharp twist of spigots.

From the hall came Cook's voice, thick like a growl. "Meaner than a mama wasp."

I turned on my stomach and pulled the covers higher before tears came.

CHAPTER ELEVEN

I woke early the next day to rain, still pounding. Padding downstairs as silent as a ghost, I found nothing amiss. Every little sign of the havoc I'd wreaked had vanished, all tidied up and *Ladies' Home Journal*-perfect.

Another one of those shameful things you don't speak of.

Cook wasn't yet there, so I sliced her sourdough loaf and made toast, slathered with the last of the blueberry jam she put up.

The telegram was in my raincoat pocket. If this storm ever let up, I'd stop by Kress Five-and-Dime and ask a clerk to read it to me.

I'd heard no sound yet from Bess, always up with the roosters. I dressed in my coveralls—the ones Bess sneaked away each week on laundry day, which I always retrieved from her donation pile—and studied my short hair in the mirror. I looked more like a boy than a girl, plumper and taller than the girl who'd been sent away from Hartless on the train.

The silence in the house unnerved me. The hands on the kitchen clock said half-past seven, late for Bess. Soon Cook would arrive to make me breakfast. I walked back upstairs, where the door was shut to Bess's lavish bedroom.

I knocked gently, then harder. I fidgeted with the crystal doorknob, waiting. I knocked so hard my knuckles stung. About to call her name, I stopped myself.

Though I didn't yet know it, I'd be getting over my habit of being mute real soon.

The door creaked open, wide enough to stick my head inside. The heavy satin draperies were drawn. Bess was still tucked in, asleep in her four-poster bed. I listened a moment, and if she'd a dropped a pin, I'd have heard it; but she didn't move a muscle, not even her satin coverlet rose up nor down. I tiptoed in.

Looking down at her head sunk into her lace-edged feather pillow, her silver hair wrapped around rag rollers, her lips more blue than rose, Bess looked a lot like her cousin, my Granny Alma. Dead.

Before I left her there in peace, I stuck my pinkie under her nose but felt no air come out. I lifted her hands and crossed them on her chest to pray, like they'd done with my grandmother, though it was too late now for her to do anything but beg at the gates of heaven, or hell. I was pretty sure Bess would get into heaven, considering how kindly she'd looked after me despite the righteous amount of grief I'd given her.

That's why I rummaged around in the little dish of loose coins she kept on her bureau for two nickels. Her eyelids already shut, she'd gone in her sleep, and I took care as I laid a nickel on each one.

I didn't take another dime, though I'd a'been rich if I took all her coins. I backed out of her bedroom and closed her door in respect for the dead. That made three for me.

· · ·

While I packed all my important things in my cardboard suitcase, which was everything I brought with me from home and none of the things Bess got me, plus the unopened letter from Momma, I pondered my power over the living to make them dead. I ratcheted into panic, first dizzy, next shivering and freezing, then wheezing, and when tiny pinpricks crept up my legs, I yelled at the top of my dirt-congested lungs.

"Stop!"

My scream echoed around the empty house and by the time it stopped rebounding, I was calm again.

That power of mine came to be like the unspoken things—*one of the things we don't even think of.*

I made sure my twenty dollars was still in my pocket and retrieved the telegram in my raincoat before I sat on the bottom step to wait for Cook.

• • •

The terrible pourdown must've delayed her, I decided, my stomach growling for lunch. I didn't know then it was the flooding on Elm Street, all fifteen feet of water, that kept Cook from crossing the swollen Brazos to get to her job. "Never missed a day in my life," she proudly declared each morning she opened the back door.

I stepped out onto the verandah to watch for Cook and spoke a forbidden cuss word.

Austin Avenue had become a raging stream. I'd never seen skies let loose like this. Rain gushed in sheets from gutters on rooftops. Water poured down porch steps like waterfalls onto the street. A few abandoned cars tipped, swayed, then held in the murky river rising to their floorboards.

Then a Chevrolet touring car let loose and floated away.

I counted the steps up to the porch—only four—and watched the water swell towards the lowest one. The sky was so dark it was unlikely to fair up for hours. If anybody ventured out, they'd need a boat. More 'n likely, the neighbors were hiding out in their attics, praying for deliverance like Noah in his flood.

Those boys in the boxcar yesterday, what happened to them? If a cow and a car got swept away, and a rooftop and a house, what about a train?

I sized up Bess's house. There'd been a fierce flood in '13, she'd explained at the start of these unlikely September rains. Back then, it rained so hard the animals paired up. Her house took in nary a drop of water, since her beloved Everett had invested in a home of quality.

The striped window awnings bulged with the rainfall's weight. The river that took over the street was spreading. We had two stories and an attic, too, if the water got on a rise.

I reckoned Cook wouldn't be coming.

Maybe this rain would find its way to our farm, and I could go home.

CHAPTER TWELVE

WILLA MAE

There are times my memories are so clear.

The odor of burning paper that accompanies a blue norther in March, with its low, blue-gray clouds stretching across the horizon

I can smell the acrid reek behind the glove factory where the smiths tanned the hides they hung and stripped. The smooth feel of the leather on the table where my sewing machine sat, as I fed it into the stitcher, the smell of it I came to love once it was tanned and dyed. The plum leather was my favorite of the ones I fanned out on my table, their edges revealing the warm sienna, the reddish rust, the rich chocolate brown, the deep black, the lovely pale cream color, all in a blend I would rearrange daily in a daydream until the foreman yelled at me.

The rumble of thunderheads massing north and northwest of Hartless that signals a dry norther

I hear the freight trains thundering past our little shack near the Rock Island tracks, where Beck found work after we married in 1921. The earthy smell of the cattle and their dissatisfaction sounding in low moans as the FW&DC train rocked past to Denver. How slippery the soapy water was when we paid a nickel to wash in the bathhouse tub.

The sky makes us feel as though we have no limits. It's as endless as our promise

The sound of rain hammering the roof, soaking the tracts we'd buy from the land agent. The rainfall nearing thirty inches in 1923 alone.

All around us, wheat growing tall and strong, finally golden and ripe for the cutting. Combines crawling the vast fields. Bins overflowing with unending yields, prices steady, demand rising. Good harvests for the big wheat producers, better for the small farmers we'd become.

The look of pride on my husband's face when he made his down payment and signed the deed at the bank for our section carved from the old XIT Ranch. How secure his hand felt, tucking mine inside his, as we walked out of the bank together, standing on the brick-paved street a moment, allowing our adjustment to our new status as landowners.

The way the Panhandle wind shifted our bountiful wheat crop lazily, gold and green waves shimmering in endless Texas sunshine, ours blending with everyone's as far as the eye could see. Plentiful rains, as the land company promised, making for fertile fields

Beck coming home after a September morning of setting the winter wheat to eat his noonday supper, sitting down to my rabbit stew and the buttermilk biscuits I'd pulled hot from the oven. Ladling thick honey onto one, his eyes lighting up at the mingling of the sweet and warm. The way our humble dugout smelled from my home cooking and his sweaty earthiness. The feel of his rough finger, dunked straight into the honey pot and rubbed across my lips, our happy laughter, his insistence on kissing the honey from my lips.

The way we made our first baby

I knew then William would be a boy to name for the rambling father I had craved in my childhood, so willing to send me off with my new husband yet certain he'd never see me again. Daniel Wilhelm Eckhart, my father the geologist, ever exploring, mapping new terrain in search of oil, and leaving little to recall of our times together. Yet asking that one thing from me. *Keep my name alive.*

Those things are as vivid to me as the sharp chill of the ice baths they force me into each day, before the shock injections.

For my memory, they tell me.

CHAPTER THIRTEEN

RUBY LEE

I spent the rest of the day of what was later called Waco's worst flood in history watchful of muddy water creeping through the garden as yard furniture floated down the street. The prized DeSoto that had belonged to the late Mr. Everett was sure to get drowned out. My stomach was in such a tumble I forgot to be hungry. If the flood came up the lawn to the top porch step, I'd best get upstairs to the attic.

I couldn't admit I was afraid to pass by Bess, dead in her bed, abandoned in a storm like her cousin Alma and my baby sister Nell.

I felt ashamed, being ugly to Granny Alma's favorite cousin. I heard Alma whispering in my ear, *you'd steal the nickels off a dead man's eyes.*

Except I'd put nickels on her cousin's eyes, didn't that count for something, I argued back. *I did respect her!* All the while uneasy about acting so low I'd have to look up to see hell.

Well, hell—isn't that what I already been through? Black blizzards, dust pneumonia, a biblical flood. How could it get any worse?

Turns out, you never know what you don't know. If I'd a been a diviner, I wouldn't be stuck in this fix. But at age eleven, I could no more see the future than find water in a drouth or safe harbor in a flood.

•   •   •

At dawn I lit out with my cardboard suitcase in my raincoat and galoshes. The pourdown had let up; the blacktop was layered in muck instead of currents of muddy water. A Model T rolled by, the milk delivery boy dashing from its running board to the front porches lining the street, switching out bottles of fresh milk for the empties. I took ours from him and asked for a ride to town.

"Sure, if the boss says so."

I climbed in. "Thanks for the ride, mister."

"Your momma lets you ride downtown?" he replied in a mix of incredulity and indifference. "Where to?"

"She's already gone to tend my sick aunt, and I got to get myself to school. I'll go as far as you go."

From his perch on the running board, the milk boy gave me a suspicious look, but before he jumped off again, his lips shifted to a sly grin. I gave him the A-Ok sign and slurped down the cold milk.

The driver turned on Franklin Avenue after he finished the delivery route. It was coming to life on a Monday morning, street vendors knocking on doors with pots and pans to sell, a man sharpening knives, Cooper grocery trucks delivering sacks smelling of spices and coffee. An ice truck pulled into an empty lot, where two men hauled enormous blocks of ice onto beds of pickups lined up. From the bottling company lot, a green Chevrolet truck rumbled over the tracks, its racks lined with Dr Pepper, 5¢, painted with a slogan Cook declared often, *Good for Life!*

Newsboys not much older than me walked towards the pickups, hawking the latest issue of their papers.

"Get your *Tribune-Herald*! Read about the flood . . . Flood invades East Waco!" they shouted. "Two thousand homeless!" Like it was something to get excited over. "River rises up forty-one feet, covers the Suspension Bridge!"

Folks forgot about their ice blocks and dug in their pockets for a nickel.

"Thanks, mister, this'll do her," I told the milk truck driver, jumping out for news of the flood. I sidled up near a few men who were exclaiming over the stories they shared: If it weren't for the lake dam, there wouldn't be anything left of East Waco. All the rail traffic across the bridges is stopped. The WPA levee's swamped, it's about gone. All the telephone lines are down in East Waco; in fact, Elm Street's under fifteen foot of water. Fifteen feet, can you imagine? The Brazos put three feet of water over the concrete of the Loop Bridge. Folks in East Waco and Little Mexico are being rescued by trucks and boats and the National Guard, on and on they rattled off the news.

"From a rowboat you could touch the traffic light at Elm and Turner Streets at 6 p.m.," one man read and looked around the small crowd, awed. People walked towards the river and I followed them, my plan to catch out with the road boys now sidetracked. If the bridges were washed out, there'd be no train to Amarillo. Might as well sightsee the Brazos, where the freight cars were (if they hadn't floated off), and maybe I'd run into Carl, or—what was the other boy's name, Whitey? Whose soot-smudged face was anything but white. They'd have the scoop, when we could hop the next train.

"Heavy rains in the Panhandle! Snow in Texline!" shouted a newsie, adjusting a cap that coulda swallowed his head while striding down the block, his paper held high. I chased after him.

CHAPTER FOURTEEN

I wished I'd taken a nickel from Bess for myself cause the newsie wanted one for his paper. I pulled my only Snickers bar from my pocket, peeled back the wrapper, took a bite. Relished it, real slow.

"Say. That looks good. Tasty?"

I bit off a sizeable chunk, chewed it awhile. "Sure is."

"I'll let ya see the story for a bite."

"No, you can read it to me."

"Two bites, then."

"All right, get to it." I gave him the candy. He savored it then began haltingly, "Says it's from Amarillo, yesterday. Winter came to the Texas Panhandle . . . Temp—temp-er-ra-tures thirty-eight to forty . . . first snow at Texline."

"You're leaving parts out."

"Just the boring parts."

"The big words. You can't pronounce 'em, can you."

He stuck his tongue out but kept on. "Heavy rains fell over the entire Panhandle—downpours to the east and north, in Child . . . Child-ress," he struggled, "Stratford, Clar—Clar-en-don . . ."

He regarded me, sheepish. "I quit school. Pop said I was old enough to earn my keep."

"Okay." I waited. "That all?"

"About an inch of rain fell. End of story." He shouldered his newspaper bag, but it dragged him down. "What's it to you?"

"I'm from there. Ain't ya heard? The drouth? They need rain."

We both grinned at the irony of it.

"Here. Take the paper. Line your boots with it if it gets cold." He touched the brim of his cap. "Appreciate the candy."

•　　•　　•

A small crowd surged along the few blocks toward the Brazos, every one of 'em having jumbled, frantic conversations about the flood. I followed the tracks, hoping to find the boxcar where I'd seen Carl during the storm. What the telegram said didn't much matter anymore with Bess gone. Surely Pa would send for me, there wasn't nobody else here who'd take me in. What mattered was getting home.

The crowd got thick and grew more excited as we approached the Brazos. Everyone gathered at the riverbanks, exclaiming at the swift swirling waters lapping over the Interurban and licking at the floorboards of the Suspension Bridge. Past the Washington Avenue Bridge, where the river swamped Elm Street into East Waco, trolley lines menaced the boatmen attempting rescues and maneuvering against the current. The signal lights dangled, skimming the floodwaters, blinking red, then green, and jangling faintly on cue. The floodwaters had reached for whatever they could take, leaving mud as a marker when they receded—mud on rooftops, mud on abandoned cars, mud on the lower half of any wash left on the line.

A man at the riverfront shouted for volunteers to shovel mud for coffee. Downriver, the Cotton Belt Bridge looked like it might sink into the murky river under the weight of the boxcars lined across it, that's how high the water got.

Catching out for home seemed like a childish delusion.

A hand on my shoulder, and I turned. It was one of the youths from the boxcar, the one who held the match under Whitey's face. "Is Carl with you?" He shook his head.

I swear a tear did not come to my cheeks, but he made to sweep one away all the same. "You sweet on him?" He smiled. "You look a bit different."

I touched at my hair self-consciously. "I just need to find Carl, that's all, to get home. To find a freight west."

"That so. Your timing's not so good." He jerked a thumb at the railroad bridges. "As you can see."

I raised up my chin.

"Kinda young for the tramp life, aren't you, little sister? Even though you could pass for a boy. A little lamb like you, the wolves'll be after you." We were walking along the river where I'd been last night, but things were mixed up. The boxcars were stuck on the bridge, the river was in the streets, and the rain we needed at the farm came here instead.

"There's a soup kitchen this away, at the Mexican Mission." He pointed at a cross scratched on a telephone pole beneath an arrow. "Let's get us some angel food."

His language was mysterious and he navigated by symbols. "How ya figure?"

He laughed. "That cross? Hobo symbols. Talk religion, get food." We walked along, peering inside the closed tortilla factory and barber shop and snow cone place till we rounded a corner. "Looks like there ain't no chow today." At the banks of the river where it crept up to the doors of the Baptist Mission, we watched a family row by, their father at the oars, their hens atop their belongings.

He hooked his thumb round to the alley. "Let's spear some biscuits."

Examining the contents of the garbage cans, he palmed himself something gray and half-eaten, handed it my way.

"Ick," I declined.

"Suit yourself. Tasty if your last lump was Saturday." He sized me up. "Can't see you stemming. How ya gonna eat?"

"All I need's a ride." I pulled out my hard-won newspaper, the candy bar still sweet in my mouth. "There a train schedule in here?"

He laughed. "Too young to read?" Then, more incredulously, "How old are you anyway?"

"None a'your business, mister."

"That so." He scanned the news, page by page, till I cleared my throat.

"Okay, you seen for yourself how all the bridges are flooded. Says here the Katy's the only train running, over the Santa Fe lines through Fort Worth."

"Fort Worth? How far's that?"

"Too far for you. You ain't the type to flop on a newspaper bed. Or hop a blind. C'mon. They're setting up housing for the homeless at the Cotton Palace coliseum," he said. "I'll walk ya over."

"Homeless?" I was indignant. "Tell Carl I'll see him around. I got somewhere to be."

I walked real purposeful to Austin Avenue, like I knew where I was going.

But as it turned out, I didn't.

●　　　●　　　●

Cook was waiting for me. "Well, missy?"

She gave me her arch stare, which meant, *no bull-sheet.* It generally had the effect of making me feel ashamed of myself, but then I remembered I wasn't talking. I'd got used to talking today, and I kinda missed it.

She poked me in my chest. "I know you got a voice. Speak up. Loud and clear."

Did she know Bess ate a bitter pill? And I'd left her lying upstairs?

Of course she did, Bess couldn't put those nickels on her own eyelids.

"Ruby Lee Becker!" I heard a frightful tone in her voice. "Don't you have any feelings for anyone?"

It was so preposterous I had nuthin to say.

She was shaking her head, *my-my*-ing to herself like she did over bread that didn't rise.

"I am sorely worried for you, girl."

I dared a look at her face, and there wasn't any vinegar in it, more like molasses. Her eyes were glistening. "Miz Everett is dead upstairs in her bed. I reckon you know that."

I busted out crying despite myself and shoved my head into her belly, reaching my arms as far around her as I could to hold tight and quell my sobbing.

"You got no home no more, little miss, don't you realize," Cook said. "Mrs. Bess got no relatives to fetch you. My house been washed away. The cotton fields are flooded, my husband can't pick. Come here to find out, I got no job, neither." She sniffled, then pulled out a handkerchief and blew her nose with a goose honk.

I settled myself, wiping my tears on her apron real easy so's she wouldn't notice.

"Don't you worry, Ruby, you'll manage. Even a blind squirrel can find an acorn." She led me to the kitchen where she had a plate ready. Mashed potatoes, chicken-fried steak, her thick cream gravy. She stood at the sink, her back to me, motionless.

Through the window, sunlight came in, giving a gleam to the porcelain and putting a shine to the chrome fixtures she kept clean. Cook became a dark silhouette, her edges blurred by bright light.

I still think about her, her tolerance of me, which was really a kindness, the way she showed me wrong from right without speaking it, her mothering instincts which came so natural to her. I don't know if she had her own children. In fact, it wasn't till later I realized her real name wasn't Cook. I never even learned it.

•   •   •

The doctor came, with his black bag and stethoscope, though he wouldn't need either. I sat on the stair feeling forlorn as he followed Cook upstairs with the merest glance at me. After her skirts brushed my face, I scooted tighter to the wall, clasping my knees, and hummed the first song Momma'd taught me. *Guten abend, gute nacht, lullaby and goodnight, thy mother's delight . . .*

The next thing I felt was a smooth palm brushing up my bangs from my forehead. Someone whispered, "Ruby, Ruby Lee, wake up, dear." I lifted my head to see Mrs. Barton. She knelt in front of me, full of caring and concern, stroking my arm.

"Come with me, dear," she said in a tender voice that made me trust her. "You've had such a lot of shocks, poor thing." She had my suitcase in one hand, my coat and rainwear in the other. "You're going to a place where you'll meet lots of children. Where you can play, and be happy! Don't worry. Just until your parents come for you."

I shot up. My parents were coming for me?

•   •   •

Mrs. Barton said we'd be stopping to have lunch first. She patted the back seat for me to sit next to her, and told her driver to go to the Hotel Raleigh. "We'll eat at the Purple Cow, Ruby. Won't that be fun?" I nodded, yes ma'am, having decided I had no more need for silence. I would have eaten at a soup kitchen, if she'd wanted, I was so happy on the ride downtown. Mrs. Barton told me to order anything I wanted from the menu. Aside from the drawing of the purple cow in a chef's hat, I didn't understand a thing on it. I said I'd have a coke.

"What kind?" asked the waitress, and I spoke up quick, "Doc Pepper."

"Bring her the pork chops, too, and I'll have the minced ham omelet."

"My pa, when's he coming?"

"Well, dear, that is a bit complicated—"

Mrs. Barton pulled off each of her skintight gloves, finger by finger, placing them on the table. She cleared her throat, speaking brightly. "Why, as soon as we can locate him, I'd expect. Until then—" The waitress put down our plates, and I bowed my head like I was saying grace.

"Let's dive into this divine-looking lunch. No more worries." Mrs. Barton laid her hand atop mine, as though its milky smoothness might provide comfort, instead of my longing for Momma's rougher, sun-browned hand.

"Worry," she said, "often gives a small thing a big shadow."

My stomach flipped; I was no longer hungry. Later events proved me right to worry.

CHAPTER FIFTEEN

During the long drive we'd taken from the Raleigh Hotel, I fell asleep. The sharp crunch of gravel under the whitewall tires needled into my skin, waking me in a prickling panic. I made my eyes focus. We were parked at an imposing three-story hall on a sprawling property with dozens of modest red-brick buildings, trimmed in white and scattered along gravel pathways across fields and among trees. The whole business was fenced all around to keep people out. Or as I would soon learn, to keep people in.

Mrs. Barton was speaking in her discreet manner behind her hands to a stern woman. I made out "no telephone service" and "dirt poor" and "can't find any family," before the stern woman strode to the Packard.

She peered in. "Another ward of the state. Wasting daylight, might as well come out." I dug my fingernails into my palms, my dread like a horsehair blanket. The chauffeur tugged me, commanding, "Out."

Mrs. Barton slid inside. Before the door slammed shut, she directed the driver to take her to Goldstein's to purchase an Atwater Kent console radio for her husband's birthday. She lifted a gloved hand, waved farewell, and her auto glided past me.

Pa would never find me here. Even if he *could* get across the river.

I took off after the Packard at a gallop, which the stern woman must have expected. Next I saw was cut grass coming up at me. I hit hard.

"You tripped me," I screamed, rubbing my jaw dramatically, but she gripped my arm in her vise of a hand and dragged me inside. "My suitcase!" I hollered. I stomped on her foot, twisted away, and gave her a knee in the thigh for good measure, escaping to the portico. Outside on the lawn, my suitcase had popped open and scattered my meager belongings hither and yon.

"You're in for it now," an older girl with a superior air sneered. "Welcome to the Waco State Home for Dependent and Neglected Children, of which it's obvious you are one and both. You oughtn't irk Matron like that." She whisked herself inside. A young girl with an awkward gait rounded the corner of the portico. She stopped, sizing me up.

"You . . . you . . . you . . . do-don't have haaaaave to wor-wor-worry," she said. "They give you-you a un-un-i . . ."

"A uniform," the head matron announced, shoving the jumble of Momma's things with my rag doll back into my suitcase, its cardboard seams about to bust. I snatched it back.

The matron berated the stuttering girl, who tucked her tongue outside her mouth, inert. "Mollie, don't stand there like a retarded idiot. Walk the new girl to the hospital."

The tongue-tied girl couldn't spit out so much as a syllable. She held out her hand to shake. I ignored it.

"I'm Ruby Lee Becker and I will not be here long enough to wear your stupid uniform," I informed them, which upon closer inspection, I realized Mollie wore, crooked stitches, flocking, scalloped trim, and all.

"My pa will be here any time now to take me home," I said with more certainty than confidence.

A slew of older boys in coveralls walked by with hoes, shovels, spades. One hooted. "Ain't that what they all say!" The gang busted out laughing. "If mine showed up, I'd light out for the highway," a gangly boy with wild red hair yucked, rubbing at his behind, the boys' faces sour with knowing smirks. Then more laughter.

"Your old man couldn't be any worse than Coach," someone whispered loud enough to catch the matron's ear, who slapped the switch she carried.

"Put a move on, boys."

The red-haired boy began whistling a tune Granny Alma had played on her spinet for us to sing, one she called "The Gold Digger's Song."

Mollie leaned close. "Come-come-c'mon unless you wan-want to get a li-lickkkk."

"Or a whippin with a hairbrush," the redhead kid said. "Or a bustin'— with the paddle."

"You young men are due at the farm, keep your opinions to yourselves. Unless you want to get campused," the matron glared. They picked up their pace, but not before the red-haired boy winked at me, I swear.

"Tonight," Red mouthed it, "at the barn."

•　　•　　•

Almost two weeks passed before I even saw the barn. They had me under quarantine in their dispensary. They rubbed me down head to toe with scalding water and lye soap on a rough cloth, and deloused my hair. I knew they wouldn't find any, since an upstanding lady like Bess wouldn't allow lice in her house. Which I yearned for the first night on the ward.

I was the only one confined in that sterile place. I chose the bed nearest the door, since it would be easier to slip out. I dreamed of my journey back to my real home.

•　　•　　•

Three sisters showed up the next night before lights out. The youngest of them hopped in unsteadily on crutches, one withered leg flailing and unable to touch the ground, sniffling. The other two lagged behind her, teary and holding hands. A lady in a hurry ushered them in. "I am making a speech tonight to the PTA in Corsicana on the work being done for the crippled children of Texas, and I must leave promptly."

She introduced herself as the local representative from the Texas Society of Crippled Children.

"These are the Rudolph sisters. Viola, Clare, and little Celesta, step forward—" The representative's eyebrows waggled as she tapped her foot in offbeat syncopation between the thud of the girl's crutches and her heavy hop. "She's had infantile polio paralysis. She'll get surgery, and custom-fitted for a new steel brace. Won't you, Celesta?"

Celesta's eyes darted between the representative and her sisters.

"And your leg will be good as new!" the representative finished brightly.

The relief nurse raised a skeptical eyebrow.

"This one's too tight, it rubs on my skin," Celesta said miserably, indicating a wood-and-iron contraption bound by leather straps buckled to her heavy lace-up boot.

The local representative instructed the nurse to sew cushioning strips. "I look like a seamstress?" she sniped, peevish.

Viola fixed her with a sullen look, taking a step towards her, hands clenched. It looked like fisticuffs.

The local representative stopped them and lectured the relief nurse on the importance of being positive, for little sister's sake. She'd visit Celesta to check her progress. Ignoring their crestfallen faces, she left behind a cloud of Cousin Bess's perfume.

The nurse cussed, maneuvering the two older sisters to bed in the same chlorine-smelling gowns I wore. "Undress quick and get to sleep," were her parting bedtime words.

She turned to the crippled girl, who looked tired enough to topple off her crutches. "I want to sleep with my sisters." Tears rolled down Celesta's cheeks, bigger than her voice.

Glowering, the relief nurse led Celesta to the next room. "Get yourself to bed." She locked the door, hanging a sign on it.

"What's it say?" I whispered to the oldest sister. The letters were tall and very bold.

"QUARANTINED," Viola said. "Poliomyelitis. Celesta's got the crippler."

I wasn't sure what that meant, but I yanked the sheets tight over my head to keep out the crippling air.

·   ·   ·

I laid there till the sisters' slow breathing convinced me they were asleep. Scrounged for my socks and shoes, and pulled my nightgown off. I'd gone to bed wearing it over my clothes, and of course the nasty nurse never noticed, so absorbed in her pulp magazine was she.

Quieter than a church mouse, I swung my feet to the floor and listened.

At the other end of the long row of beds, the light in the nurse's station burned, but I heard snoring. I could see the nurse in her chair, head tilted back, mouth lolled open. Sawing logs.

I made my move to the door.

"Take me," a voice hissed behind me.

It was the cripple's oldest sister. The sullen one.

I moved for the door.

"I'll cause a ruckus if you don't take me."

I kept tiptoeing out.

"I mean it. I'll holler." She raised her voice up on "holler" and I lunged for her. Got hold of her ponytail and tackled her onto an empty bed with one hand clapped across her mouth while she kicked and wiggled and we rolled over, thudding onto the floor like cats in a bag.

"Shush!" I pleaded. The nurse shoved her chair from her desk. We dove for our beds. My heart was beating crazy. I counted, slowing my breathing. I counted her deliberate footsteps as she approached, remembering Momma's steadfast voice, counting sheep during those howling dusters that kept sleep away.

CHAPTER SIXTEEN

Our chances for escape from isolation dwindled.

The night nurse had a snoring habit but she slept with one eye open. There'd been no chance to tiptoe past her with that sullen girl shadowing me.

The teenage girls who worked in the dispensary introduced us to the game of Monopoly. The teenagers took note of the big QUARANTINE sign with a chorus of "not here!" and "oh no!" and "not the crippler!" and herded us to the opposite end of the ward. They gossiped about a child confined inside an iron lung for her bulbar paralysis— "so she wouldn't suffocate," one teenager said—and about avoiding any suspected carriers: ice cream cones, summer playgrounds, stray cats. They relived the horror of two little boys from the same family whose bodies became so twisted and shriveled they were put in turnbuckle body casts for months.

The best thing that could happen to me during my spell in the dispensary was not getting paralyzed by polio.

The teenagers set out the board, counted out our play money, told us the rules, and rolled the dice. They claimed they were needed on the first floor, they'd be back later.

The sister named Clare announced, "I'll be the banker. I count real fast." One of her eyes was cloudy and set too close to her nose for her to appear trustworthy.

She moved her token four spots and paid the bank one hundred dollars for a house on the square where she'd landed.

"Now I own Vermont Avenue," she said like a real gold digger. "And my own house."

They weren't playing Monopoly like the teenagers explained. These sisters had their own rules.

Viola took a few turns, putting houses wherever she landed.

Finally, I got a turn. Viola watched while I pretended to read the Chance card I drew.

"You can't read, can you."

I stalled. "You two don't favor each other much. Don't favor your little crippled sister in there, neither."

They exchanged glances. "Celesta's got a different daddy," the banker girl said, her cloudy eye adrift.

"So do we," Viola sniped. "Ma wanted to be a musician. But it was hard to get a break. So she slept with the orchestra." She giggled herself into a fit. "Closest Ma got to music"—she wiped at her eyes, convulsed in laughter— "was naming us for the instruments our daddies played."

"How old are you," I said, as if I cared.

"Viola's about fourteen." The cloudy-eyed sister twirled her thimble, her good eye on Park Place.

"Older 'n you. And I can read. That's why you need me to bust out of here." Viola's smile was smug. "My turn. You save that card. It'll come in handy when you need to get outta jail."

"About fourteen?" I scoffed, counting while she moved her thimble token. "You don't know?"

"St. Charles Place! I'll buy two houses—one for us and one for good measure. Here's two hunnerds, Clare."

"I got real dollar bills. Twenty of 'em," I said. "I don't need you or nobody to get home."

She sneered. "How's a kid like you gonna get home? All the way to the Panhandle, practically Oklahoma, you said. That's more 'n a day away by train."

I didn't answer. I was working out where to put my hat marker.

"You can't land there. It's the railroad. You got to buy it," Viola sneered.

Clare said, "Two hundred for the bank."

"That's just what I'm gonna do," I said, firmly placing my silver top hat onto the black train engine on the board, my lucky Chance card in my other hand. "I'm buying a ticket back home. And I don't need no help from you."

Viola rolled her eyes and spit out a guffaw. "I'm gonna pee myself, you're so dumb. They won't let you buy a ticket. You're just a child."

She had me. I hadn't thought that far ahead.

"They'll put out the alarm the minute they see you're gone, and then look out—Katy bar the door. They'll close the bridges, shut down the highways, stop the trains; nobody will cross state lines, sister," she said. "You'll be on the lam, with all the coppers after ya."

I glared at her. "How do you know?"

"I been to the movies!" she said, as if that settled it.

•　　•　　•

The afternoon wore on around the Monopoly board, till we tired of playing. I packed up the scrip money. Viola leaned in, her long black hair swinging to cross her face. "I got a way."

I had no reason to trust her, but I had no other ideas, neither.

"My cousin. He's got a truck. And you don't need even a ten-spot for a train ticket. It'll only cost you two. Split your twenty smackers with me and I'll get my cousin to take us to the depot. He can buy your ticket for you."

I pondered her proposal, unable to see its flaws, except I knew what that twenty dollars cost Will to give up, so I wasn't likely to part with it easy.

"Show the money to me," she demanded.

"Where's your cousin now?" I asked. "He got poliomyelitis too?"

"Heck no," she scowled, "Celesta had a little bout. Went to Dallas for her treatment. The doctors at the Scottish Rite gave her braces so she could walk."

"Then why's she in quarantine—"

Viola kept talking right on over me. "My cousin does odd jobs for my grandpa, near my uncle's farm in Hillsboro. He's got a quarter section. Raises cotton. The whole family worked at the mill till it closed. The fields might be flooded out now, account'a the river gettin on a rise. Did you see it flood?"

I coulda told her I saw it and more. But I stared at her, dumbfounded. "You got a whole family like that and you're here? Why?"

Viola looked at the game board, embarrassed maybe, and folded it up. "Hey. You mixed the scrip money all up. Stack the dollars in one pile, the fifties in another, the hunnerds—" she paused. "Look. It's easy, if you sort it by the colors."

I worked at that for a while, a little more inclined to consider her offer.

"My folks have too many of us to take care of. It's hard times. My aunt brought us here, just for a while. Till they get back on their feet. Lots of families do it."

That was news to me.

The nurse came in, wearing a mask, to take our temperatures and pulses and listen to our hearts and record everything on her clipboard. She warned us not to go near the crippled girl's room, since infantile poliomyelitis could spread from the air or a sneeze, or flies, swimming pools and movie theaters, or even along telephone lines. The poor young victims showed no signs or symptoms, or sometimes a little fever and headache, she explained, till all of a sudden it would paralyze their arms and legs or even worse, stop their diaphragm muscles from breathing.

"How do they—how—why, they have to breathe!" Clare said, needlessly.

Viola nodded at Clare. "Sharp as a mashed potato, ain't she."

The nurse said, "Those poor children live inside giant iron lungs, which breathe for them."

My forehead felt warm to my touch. My temples perspired, then pounded.

"And you will need haircuts," the nurse continued. Viola's hands flew to the curls at the tips of her long hair and her face heated. Clare gasped, her good eye darting around, and tried to hug her older sister, whose hands held only her hair, clinging as if for dear life.

"For hygiene. As soon as the hairdresser can get over here," the nurse added. "Of course yours is already short as a boy's, Ruby. You're exempt." With one last firm look at us over her mask, she stomped out.

My hair still felt itchy from my barbering. Would Momma recognize me? I pushed back at the prickles climbing my arms and the drumming in my head. *Pa will never find me here.* The same thought, over and over. I started wringing out my hands to settle myself. *Shut up!* I said, not aloud. But Clare and Viola stared at me, open-mouthed. I stilled my hands.

Viola kept an eye toward the door and clamped her hand around my arm and said real low, "Show me your money so's I can get my cousin."

"Why you gonna help me?"

"I don't want any dang haircut, you ninny!"

Viola sat back on her heels, gazing at me frankly. "I'm in it for the dough."

She grabbed the pile of blue fifty-dollar bills and flung them in the air. "I mean the real deal. My family needs money to feed all of us, back home."

"We didn't want to come here," Clare said. She was on the verge of tears. "But Daddy run off with a gal who didn't have no kids. Ma couldn't stand to let us go. Our aunt brought us."

"Cause Ma was sloshed, more 'n likely," Viola muttered, looking at the door where the bright yellow QUARANTINE sign forbade entry. "And our little sister needs her operations." Her voice caught. "Split your twenty bucks with me and let's light out."

"Not till we get to the depot. I'll show you the money after your cousin buys my ticket home. How ya gonna find him?"

Viola figured on her aunt visiting weekends, like she promised. Clare was sure she would. While the nurse was occupied with a phone call, they tiptoed closer to Celesta's room, cracked her door open, and slipped inside. They weren't a bit afraid of catching the poliomyelitis.

I never slept at all, curled into a tight ball under the covers, trying not to breathe what was in the stale air. I pictured myself trapped inside some iron monster but unable to catch a breath. I was terrified the strangers around me would become my family. When the sun rose up at dawn, I shimmied my legs and arms, hoping they still worked.

CHAPTER SEVENTEEN

WILLA MAE

I shove their hands away, wobbling after the shock hypo, dazed, searching for the words I'd repeated to myself before the injection began. I spit the gag from my mouth, surprised to see blood on it. The words are there—right at the edge of my mind—I'd summon them soon, once this throbbing in my head ebbs, to enter in my diary.

In 1920, when we first fall in love, I envision our lives together with the expectancy of a grand adventure, hand in hand, where things will only get better as we hold tight to each other

"A farmer? In no man's land?" asks my astonished mother, who'd imposed her squandered hopes for a college education upon me. My short-lived freshman year at Texas Women's College and my desire for a degree in art are now dashed—for us both

"A man who won't leave me," I correct her. My father sought adventure under the guise of discovery and wealth, and scuttled my mother's dream of true partnership. Beck is a man who will never abandon me for wanderlust. I love him precisely because he is a farmer tied to his land

The next year, we marry. On my wedding day, I'm dressed to please Beck's maternal grandmother, Adelheid, who is seventy-eight and stern and insistent on Old Country traditions. Beck's parents speak German with her, and to him in heavily accented English. I understand little and wonder what I'm getting myself into. I remind myself I am with a man who'll hold fast, to me, to our land

My new husband takes my hand in his, a working man's hand, leathery, capable. Mine an artist's hand, spattered with cerulean, viridian, burnt umber, and creamy smooth inside his

By year's end, I am expecting. Will is born in 1922. My paints and brushes are set aside to make room for his cradle. Beck packs my art books and paintings in a trunk. A hobby I won't have time for, he says

It's much later I realize Beck is a man whose roots are so firmly grounded in his ancestors' quests, any deviation from the paths they followed will be the end of ours

• • •

The familiar commotion comes: the roar of a train. Whenever one passes I run for the window to search the faces of passengers in compartments and hoboes in boxcars alike. For a glimpse of my husband, of my boys . . . wondering . . . are they among the wanderers riding the rails, longing for home . . . and coming for me?

Has an afternoon passed? An entire day, two days, more? I reread the eloquent words I've written and recognize them as gibberish. I am disintegrating. Without my art, I have no memories—it's the painting that summons them. Becoming lost in my art means survival.

I reach for my sketchbook. There's no escape from this pounding headache. I fear there's none from here. I swipe the flat edge of my charcoal along my girl's hair, picturing her alert blue eyes.

CHAPTER EIGHTEEN

RUBY LEE

The hairdresser made it before Viola's aunt did. Viola twirled her curling tresses while we sat cross-legged on the floor in front of the door. To thwart escape attempts, the nurse brandished the yardstick she'd used to measure the cotton batting cushioning Celesta's brace.

Amid the hollering going on during Viola's haircut, they brought in a girl from the tuberculosis preventorium in Amarillo. She was pale, with big puffy eyes and a tiny chin, her wispy hair matted and tangled. She got the same delousing and head-to-toe scrub down we did. The hairdresser began to shave her knotted hair off.

"You're so cute and tiny, Katherine. Your hair will grow back thick and strong," the hairdresser assured the little elf girl, who threw her arms around her. "Call me Kitty! I'm ten! You can be my friend!"

"Friendly, isn't she." Viola was bitter as gall, standing amidst her long curls now spiraled around her shoes.

The relief nurse came on duty for the weekend. Ugly as a scar and rumored to be even nastier. Beneath the hum of hair clippers, she observed, "Feeble-minded nitwit."

Kitty took no offense; she threw her arms around the nurse's legs. The nurse swatted her away. "Tuberculosis germs—you belong in the preventorium, with the rest of the lungers."

The matron, on her daily rounds, observed the commotion. "Now, don't you worry about the TB, girls."

The adults were always telling me not to worry, while I knew better. A pint-size girl with too many cobwebs in the attic arrived with tuberculosis. A crippled girl with contagious polio was next door in the QUARANTINE room.

I didn't say nuthin. Talking got me nowhere.

•　　•　　•

The relief nurse gave the elfish girl a spoonful of Pinex syrup, which must have tasted fearsome, the way the girl bared her tiny teeth to spit it out. When her coughing woke me up, the fuming nurse was forcing another spoonful down her throat. Again, later, the nurse whacked Kitty with the spoon before she administered her Pinex syrup.

I bet Pinex went down smoother than the kerosene and lard Momma gave me when I hacked up dirt.

The relief nurse was done with Kitty by Saturday morning. Viola and I crept over while she dialed her telephone, handset to her ear. She yelled at the candlestick phone, "I don't give a dang if the flood's keeping the gates of heaven closed! I'm off duty whether she shows up or not!" She slammed the whole talking contraption onto the desk, where it clattered off, lifting her coat from the hook and stomping down the stairs without a backward glance.

Viola and I eyed each other, giddy at our luck.

Quick as a lick, she was inside the nurse's office, dialing the phone. Its magic still worked, since she whispered into it a short time, her voice wheedling. Then she grabbed up her belongings.

"Clare, you take care of Celesta. I'll be back for you both," she said.

Clare's eyebrow fell over her lazy eye. She looked more forlorn. "Viola— wait, I'll get my bag."

"Clare. No ma'am." Viola's face turned hard. "We are not abandoning Celesta. You stay here."

I got a funny premonition—she could leave me behind, too. I rushed for my suitcase and heard Viola laughing.

"Think you're ridin in the sidecar, do ya?" She was near the stairs.

"Wait! Viola, wait!"

"Don't need your help, Ruby," she called from the bottom of the steps.

I scrambled downstairs, holding up my twenty dollar bills.

She stopped short and whistled. "Well. You had the dough, after all. C'mon."

•   •   •

We skirted the grounds, hiding between buildings and bushes, Viola leading us through an orchard like she knew exactly where we were going. The campus was silent but for the lowing of cows, whose earthy manure smells followed us. We reached the barbed wire fence without being noted. Viola was undeterred by the sharp prongs and slunk along the fence until she found an opening barely large enough for us to shimmy through on our bellies. I was to follow a few steps behind on the opposite side of the street, since they'd be looking for two of us.

"You called your cousin?" I said. "To come get us?"

"Who d'ya think I called, the mayor? Duck if a car comes along."

That seemed unlikely, since we were surrounded by farmland. Wily as she was, I kept a close eye on her. But we had a deal, and she wanted her ten bucks.

We walked a long ways in silence.

"Viola? Is he coming?"

She looked peeved. "Of course he is. Any time now."

I was oddly heartened by the devastation surrounding us. Corn dead on the stalks from summer heat was afloat in flooded fields. A whole river of rain had come to Waco, and who's to say it didn't flood our farm, too?

In the distance, a truck backfired and grew bigger till it was a busted-up old Ford with a rangy brown-haired boy behind the wheel. Viola waved and waved like he might miss us. The brakes squealed and the truck lurched to a stop as he leaned over to open the passenger door, but Viola ran to his side of the truck, yanked open the door, and pulled him out. They were laughing, his arm wrapped around her hips, her hand found his rump, and she tipped her head back. They were real friendly cousins, I guess. She kissed him, and he kissed her back, longer, until he held her away, inspecting her.

"Your hair?" He had a deep crease in his frown. "Your long hair I loved to run my hands through, Vi, what'd ya do to it?"

Right then he noticed me.

"Clare?" He looked closer. "No, you're not—who's this?"

The more puzzled he got, the deeper the crease in his frown got. He cocked his head in a boyish manner, but he had the scheming eyes that come with a hard-knock life.

Viola took me possessively by my shoulders. "This here's Ruby. We're taking her to the M-K-T."

"The depot in town? Hell, Vi, I ain't got enough gas. Costs too much."

She leaned down, hissed, "Show him the money, Ruby."

No, I shook my head.

She gave me a little shove.

"Don't be a ninny. You want your train ticket, we want our ten bucks."

The crease in his sun-browned forehead faded into an uneven white scar as Viola's cousin understood. "Sure, we're headed that way, Miss Ruby. Hop in, ladies." The seat coils squeaked and gave up some chicken feathers, which floated around inside the cab.

Viola slid closer to him than a tick on a hound. "We'll get us a Dr Pepper, too."

He smiled, patting her leg well above her knee, pulling and pushing levers in a series of maneuvers familiar to me from watching Pa start up our Model A.

"What's your cousin's name, *Vi*?" I asked, mocking the nickname he'd called her.

He glanced at me as he wheeled the truck toward town.

"Your cousin?" He grinned at Viola. "You'd best let your hair grow long again, Cousin Vi."

CHAPTER NINETEEN

The bumpy drive to the depot was protracted but downtown didn't lack for sights.

Waco had sprung back to life less than a week after the flood. The river was tame inside its banks. I could see no indication the Brazos had got on a rise high enough to touch Elm Street's blinking traffic lights, or topped the Suspension Bridge, where folks who'd paddled boats now strolled across. Boys toting bulgy sacks hollered, "Paper shell pecans, twenty-five cents a pound!" in front of the hatchery. Along Bridge Street, the Square was bustling with farmers selling produce from mule-drawn wagons to hungry buyers. The Negro bootblacks were doing a brisk business shining up all the muddy shoes. Geese honked from cages strapped to the running boards of a car idling at a busy produce market, while the driver hopped out to deliver eggs. Customers in soggy clothes and muddy shoes lined up for haircuts and baths. A freight train lumbered across the Cotton Belt Bridge, the Brazos still muddy but settled well below the tracks.

Men were unloading trucks at the cotton oil mill and sacking the meal, and the powerful stink of cottonseed cakes hung in the air. "Cattle feed," Viola's cousin said ruefully. "Smells like money."

Back home when ours were starving, Pa said it smelled like money going out the door.

I inhaled the sweet aroma rising from the Rainbow Bread Company, struck by a craving for the hot buns Bess served. Nearer the depot, men in crisp uniforms lined up their delivery trucks at the Artesian bottling plant. The streetcars came and went at the Texas Electric car barn, guided by their slender attachments to the power lines.

It made for a decent launching place to travel home.

"Hurry up, I got to powder my nose." Viola pointed to a spot where her cousin could park.

She jumped out on a run into the train station, leaving me with her cousin. "Let's get you a ticket on the Flyer," he said, taking my hand, "C'mon inside."

"I'll be going with Viola, I got to pee." I ran after her. I didn't want to wait alone with a fella who kissed a girl who was his cousin, whose name I didn't know. Let alone hold his hand. But inside, the depot was jammed with travelers. Halted by the noisy crowd, I scanned the immense room for the ladies'; I couldn't see Viola.

He caught up with me. "Thought you wanted a ticket. Line's pretty long."

People jostled for the ticket windows. "The ladies' is in that corner. I'll get your ticket while you go."

"My suitcase—I left it in your truck," I stalled.

"I'll fetch it once I buy your ticket," he said from the corner of his mouth, his eyes trained on the ladies' room door. "Now scoot. Tell Vi I'm in line. Hand me your fare."

He turned to me then, giving me his winning smile, so like my brother Earl's. I looked around the vast room and the unreadable signs, pondering Pa's favorite saying about a fool and his money, as a well-dressed family squeezed past us. Close on the heels of the father, the mother followed, with each of her girls in a firm grip. The youngest girl turned to stare at me. Her scornful eyes showed me all the ways I was lacking.

"Here's my money." I handed it over. "You didn't ask where to."

"You're right." The cousin pocketed my stash. "My mistake. What's your next stop, Miss Ruby?"

"Amarillo," I called to his back. He'd already moved into the line. "Amarillo!" I shouted, and he spun around with a wink, giving me the A-Ok. I pushed through the crowd to the ladies.'

•   •   •

"Viola, let's go," I said as I entered. Viola didn't answer.

I called her name again, bending to look beneath each stall door.

The ladies' was empty.

I ran back out to find her cousin.

The ticket line was moving fast. He wasn't at the end of it anymore. I wondered when my train would leave. I slipped between the waiting travelers to the ticket window.

He wasn't there, either. He musta gone back to his pickup for my suitcase. I shoved my way past the lollygagging passengers to the street where he'd parked.

The truck was gone.

In its empty spot stood Viola so flustered that—to my surprise—she was sobbing.

•   •   •

I took off along Jackson to South Eighth, aimlessly making a circuit around the Katy depot, looking for the low-down crook's pickup. Rounding the corner, Austin Avenue beckoned, busy with late Saturday afternoon shoppers. The afternoon grew dusky, the neon lights flashed, defining the storefronts in an inviting way. Each flicker of the brightening signs, those colorful blades that fought the coming nightfall, made me lonelier.

Inside Pipkin's Drug I sat at the counter. The waitress handed me a menu, useless to me, her look quizzical. "You're not alone after dark? Waitin on your momma?"

"Yep," I swallowed, "you might could say that."

"Well, we don't serve minors in here alone." She bent down, elbows on the counter, and spoke in a hush. "But the manager's not here. Want a hamburger, sweetie, while you wait?" She lit a cigarette, blowing the smoke above my head. I nodded and whirled around on my stool to gulp fresher air. Who should walk in but Viola, tears all gone, heels clicking in haste on the tile floor like Santa Anna on a mission.

"How *dare* you leave me like that. We had a deal."

My mouth fell open so big a fly flew in. I clapped a hand over it and spit as the waitress brought out my hamburger next to creamy yellow potato salad. It smelled thick with grease. When my stomach grumbled in appreciation Viola lunged for my plate, sliding it her way.

"Your momma?" The waitress had one hand on her hip, a beady eye to Viola. "Breeding young, are ya."

I snatched my plate back and downed half the burger in a single bite. Viola glared at me, unrepentant.

"You ain't got no conscience," I told her. "You're gonna pay for this."

"It was *you* scared him off!" She slumped on her stool, allowing tears to form at the corners of her crafty eyes. "Anyway, now I'm out ten smackers."

As brazen as she was remorseless.

My hand lifted of its own mind, aiming at her cheek, longing to smack the forlorn look off her face. With effort I forced my hand to slide under my thigh. I needed a reading instructor.

We made the deal right then. I shoved the menu at her, ready for my first reading lesson. While Viola gulped the crumbs I left her, I made a plan. I needed a place to stay, a telephone, some cash, a car, plus those fine clothes I gave up a week ago.

Viola followed me sullenly to Cousin Bess's house. She didn't have nowheres else to go, neither, except back to the Home. We were both glad to sleep in the caretaker's room over the garage. Mostly, I was glad the DeSoto was still parked below us.

In the morning I checked the kitchen door, which was locked, like I expected. In the garage I grabbed a shovel and used it on a basement window, then dropped into the window well, mindful of broken glass. Inside, the preserves Cook put up still sat on the shelves. The coal furnace was cool to the touch and I climbed the stairs.

The house was so empty it echoed, not a stick of furniture nor a rug on the floor; only the velvet drapes remained, drawn closed across the front windows. The floors glowed with a shiny coat of polish and the place smelled of fresh paint. My footsteps clacked across the parquet foyer to where the telephone once rang, gone with its stand, its thick yellow book, and everything else. Upstairs in my old room, my wardrobe was gone. I ran from one bedroom to the next, but every room was waiting for the next family to live there.

I stuck my head in the kitchen, wishing I'd see the oak Hoosier hutch with its accordion door rolled up, dough rising in a bowl on the shiny white counter. But only the sun came in the window over the sink, the gleam it leant to the chrome the one constant.

•   •   •

Viola met me when I slammed the screen door. "Let me see inside, Miss Fancy Pants. You been livin in tall cotton."

"Suit yourself." I brushed past her.

Like she'd reminded me last night while we walked to Castle Heights, we needed the keys to the DeSoto.

I had an idea where to look, from seeing Bess dither around the garage one time she'd misplaced 'em —I was sneaking a slice of chess pie from the kitchen and heard the pounding of a hammer. Maybe I'd find a nail on the wall she hung the automobile keys.

I hauled open the double doors to let in some light. I ran my hand along the rough wood walls while I paced off the garage, feeling and looking for the nail. All I got for my trouble was a splinter.

I thought back to the last time I'd been for a drive with Bess in the DeSoto, and the memory of my last night in her house flushed over me with the heat of shame. She'd been out looking for me in the storm, and later, she'd rushed in, hoping to find me inside. Only she'd found my hostility instead, and though I did not then, I truly felt some remorse now.

It came to me where to look. The keys were where she'd left them in her haste to help me, of course. On the front seat.

CHAPTER TWENTY

From the front seat of Bess's touring sedan, I got up on my knees to see over the dashboard. Viola scooted forward to reach the pedals, pulled the choke, pumped the gas, turned the key, and the DeSoto thrummed to life with its familiar rumble. I stared at her with newfound respect.

"What," she said. "Think I grew up on a farm and never drove the truck?" She placed her hand on the round knob atop the stick, yanked it down, and promptly popped the clutch. The sedan lurched forward and stalled.

"Sure you did." I sank back in the seat.

"Second time's the charm." She got us out of the garage and halfway down the driveway before she shifted it once more, and it stalled again. She pointed across the front lawn, frowning. "That sign. In the front yard. Your Cousin Bess is selling her house."

If you can sell a house in heaven, I thought.

Bess had never mentioned her dear Everett's accounts were in arrears. But she said his bank failed. Of course. Couldn't make the payments. Like Pa. Except living a lot richer.

"That why she dumped you at the State Home?" Viola turned the key again. The motor got to humming.

"You shut up!" I shouted. "Don't speak ill of the dead."

A pained expression briefly embellished Viola's features before she said, cheerily, "Well! Third time lucky," and we took off.

We got no further than the stone wall around the Cottonland Castle. She braked the sedan with a quick jerk to the curb and rolled down her window. "Well don't that beat all. A real castle."

"Quit your gawking; let's get to your cousin's." I was mighty anxious to find my suitcase.

She took the turn at an alarming speed and narrowly avoided landing us in the bar ditch. Then the crooked farm-to-market road straightened out to a wider berth through the cotton fields. I saw nuthin much to look at till we passed the tractor lot and the John Deere man waved. We came upon a whitewashed motor court devoid of automobiles with a blinking neon sign, then we entered a big roundabout where roads came at us from all directions, bearing signs I couldn't read. I grew suspicious. "This the way to your cousin's?"

Viola nodded, steering us around the rotary a few times like a hamster caught in a circle, finally swinging into the parking lot of a café. A gaggle of uniformed carhops, not much older than me, raced to the DeSoto, the winner hopping up on the running board. "Take your order, ma'am?"

Viola shook her head and shot her elbow out the window into his chest, driving around to the rear where the kitchen was. The lineup of hoboes at the back door turned to ogle our shiny touring sedan. "Till we get our money back, we'll have to get in the soup line like every other tramp," she said.

"Our money?" But she was already striding ahead of me, getting herself in line before a gentlemanly hobo who bent low, tipping his scruffy cap, sweeping his hand in a grand gesture. She paid him no mind, nor me.

"*My* money, Viola." I stomped her foot to make my point.

"Rough as a cob, ain't ya." Viola spoke quiet, her fingertips finding my earlobe, squeezing it tight. "Quit it!" I yelled.

"Little sister here's hungrier than a hibernatin bear," she said apologetically, so's they all could hear. "She'll sweeten up."

"Poor little rich girls," one of the unkempt bums said, and the entire line tittered.

A hauling truck drove into the back lot while we were saying our thank you's to the short-order cook who'd doled out burnt bacon and stale rolls.

An unshaved man in a baggy suit jumped out of the truck and strolled around the DeSoto, inspecting its chrome grille and curving humped wheel covers, poking his head in the window, examining every detail on the dashboard. From his inside coat pocket he extracted a wrinkled paper and smoothed it out on the big hood.

"Prosperity Savings and Loan," he announced. Everyone watched him. "Who's the owner of this fine sedan?"

I stepped forward and the bedraggled gang started laughing. "Got your registration on you, miss?" The man winked at them and joined in the laughter.

"This automobile belongs to my Cousin Bess." I jumped on the running board protectively.

"Not no more, it don't. I'm the repossession agent for the bank to which she stopped making payments last spring." So, Bess was behind on the DeSoto payments, too.

Viola looked surprised. "A repo man?"

"She will need to attend to her loan if she wants to drive this automobile again, miss." The man pulled me off the running board, more like jerked me, and got inside our automobile like he owned it.

"That'll be kinda hard," Viola said. "She passed last week. Left little Ruby Lee here in a rough spot."

The hoboes had ringed the DeSoto to stare down the man. "In an orphanage," Viola continued. "A little orphan, with only an automobile to her name."

One of the boes spit and called the repo man a shyster.

"Stealing from an orphan," they muttered to each other. "Making your living off folks' hard times." They were real riled up over their own troubles. "Just like they come for my tractor."

Then I heard one jeer, disdainfully as you'd call out a false prophet, "What kinda man makes his living stealing from poor little orphan girls," before they yanked the door open and had the repo man on the ground, swatting and kicking at him.

Viola grabbed me and, quick as a hiccup, she had us back out on the Circle, veering at the next right, throttling up to speed and taking wild turns till she figured she'd evaded him.

"That was a close call." She pulled up to the glazed service bay of a Sinclair station and called out to the mechanic for directions. Uneasy, I kept watch till off we sped to get my twenty bucks back.

•   •   •

We were driving north along the lake road when she turned onto a street I recognized. From there the road led straight to the Waco State Home, where Viola braked the DeSoto at the entrance to the sprawling fenced campus with its acres of brick buildings, hay fields and trees, sheds and barns. A burly security guard came walking our way.

"This is your stop, Ruby. Out."

I pummeled at her arms and kicked her shins but she shoved me out. "Don't worry. I'll be back. With your ten bucks." She smiled with a wicked twist to one corner of her lips before she glided away in Bess's DeSoto.

"Twenty!" I hollered after her. Double-crossed again.

I watched the DeSoto's trail of dust balloon out while she took my freedom with her. I thought of the dusters that had taken our farm, before the guard took my arm and walked me back to the home that wasn't mine.

•   •   •

The head matron lectured me the entire way to the dispensary on the perils I faced by running off and the punishments she'd mete out if I tried it again, but was content enough with my tearful apologies to deposit me at the front door. I tiptoed up the stairs to the ward I'd left two days ago. I peered around the door jamb; the nurse was inside the QUARANTINE room, changing the linens. In the nurse's station I lifted the handset from her telephone. A disembodied female voice came at me, "Number please," and I jerked the thing away from my ear.

"Number please," it squawked again, and I took the handset to my ear. "I'm reporting a robbery. Of a touring sedan. A suitcase. And twenty dollars."

"You'll want the police station," the voice replied smoothly. "One moment please."

CHAPTER TWENTY-ONE

I didn't catch nuthin from the sick girls—no paralysis struck my legs, no tuberculosis invaded my lungs, no dust choked off my breath. Because as bad as I wanted to go home, I was even more fearful of landing back with the nuns at Trinity Hospital. The day Dr. Carbaugh came to examine me, I took a huge gulp of air to stifle my wheezing. He pronounced me healthy enough for release from the dispensary.

The next stop would be the littles' cottage, and I balked at being lumped in with crybabies. I'd be nowheres near Viola, who was madder than a red ant once she returned from her pilfering spree. It wasn't long before the police found her leaving her cousin's in the DeSoto. They had her in custody awhile, on grand theft auto charges, until they figured out she was a fourteen-year-old runaway, more hapless than crafty. By then she'd spent more 'n a few nights in juvie, getting herself an eyeful and an official record, and working herself into righteous resentment.

The superintendent himself escorted Viola back, while she was spitting and struggling and protesting her innocence. He instructed the dispensary nurse to put a QUARANTINE sign on Viola's door. "Lock it. Till she cools off."

I laid on the floor with my ear to the crack under the door, listening to her tirade. From the Monopoly box, I took twenty one-dollar bills in play money and shoved them in, one by one. "I'm out here and you're in there," I whispered. "You're quarantined."

Viola quit her ranting. Her footsteps approached the door; she'd lowered herself to the floor.

The door shuddered and vibrated. She musta been lying on her back, pummeling it with both feet.

I waited for her to tire of raging. "I can help you," I offered. "It'll only cost you twenty bucks."

She started up her screeching again. The nurse looked in on us, shook her head, strode to her telephone. Matron appeared.

"You're headed to the littles' cottage, Ruby Lee. Come with me." To Viola's locked door, she said, "The longer you make a commotion, the longer you'll be in quarantine."

Her grip was firm as she walked me around the administration building to the littles' cottage.

It looked more like the T-shaped army barracks it had been, when soldiers at Camp MacArthur trained there for the Great War. The dorm mother assigned me a bed next to the stuttering girl's and showed me where to unpack my belongings, which amounted to none since my cardboard suitcase wasn't found on the DeSoto's rumble seat by the police, which I was sorely put out by.

Worse, I was still minus my twenty bucks.

Viola claimed her cousin stole it. But I blamed her. She still owed me.

"Mind you behave yourself while you're here." The dorm mother spoke ominously to me. "You might be eleven but don't you go acting too big for your britches." Derision was writ plain as the smirk on her face. She'd only met me but she'd read me like a book.

On the first night, I discovered nothing was worse than wetting the bed in the littles' cottage. Even if you were little.

•   •   •

After lights out, Mollie stuttered her prayers on her knees. "Lord, plea-please let me ha-have a fam-fam-fam-i-ly again." I plugged up my ears and put my pillow over my head.

I caught a whiff of ammonia. One of the youngest girls cried she was scared of the dark and she'd wet her bed. She stood at the foot of her bed, muffling her gulping sobs with her pudgy little hand. She might have been four years old. She wanted her momma. She wanted a clean nightie. She wanted dry sheets.

It wasn't long before her crying brought the dorm mother, called Miss Bush by the polite girls and known as Hairbrush behind her back, who threw on all the lights as she tramped in with a hairbrush gripped in one hand. Then the young girl's screams grew louder than her sobs. "I didn't mean to, I didn't mean to," the child kept crying. We all covered our heads with our blankets when Hairbrush pulled down the child's wet panties and beat her bare butt with the brush.

The next morning the bristles had left such angry welts on her behind the young bed-wetter couldn't tolerate pulling on her underpants. Hairbrush threw them aside and yanked a dress over her head, commanding her to line up for the dining hall. "I can't sit down," the child wailed, and Hairbrush told her sharply, "If you don't sit for your morning pablum, you'll stand at the table till supper, Dolores."

The sleepy morning chatter of the girls stopped abruptly. No one dared breathe. Their eyes were on Dolores, to see what would happen next, and if it would happen to them.

Young Dolores wailed. Hairbrush pulled the hairbrush from a pocket on her skirt and the child's chubby little legs wobbled into motion. One by one, Hairbrush fixed her menacing gaze on any girl who was gawking at the raised hairbrush.

Her sturdy pumps resounded through the dorm as she walked the row of beds, throwing back covers to lean in and sniff each girl's sheets, making a chalk mark on the wall from time to time. "If I have marked your bed, get in the bed-wetters' line here," Hairbrush said.

Most of the girls who awoke with wet panties rushed for the door.

I was rattled, but secure in my innocence. Hairbrush made note of the spot where a girl named Emma Sue had hung her doll on the wall. Her suspicious eyes darted around and landed on me.

"The new girl," she said. "You can learn the rules the easy way or the hard way."

Hairbrush directed me to the boys' bathroom, which smelled like the outhouse back home, and handed me a hog-hair toothbrush with a bottle of

Clorox. I scrubbed the bathroom floor all morning, until all the black and white tiles glistened and the grout between them turned snow white.

And still the smell of urine pervaded the baby cottage.

•   •   •

Most of the children in the Home were hoping for their parents to come back for them. Some were hoping to be adopted. If they suspected the worst—they'd be there until they aged out—none of them voiced it. There were many sets of siblings, sometimes whole families of kids. Just until the hard times were over, they said. Hoped. When Daddy gets back on his feet. When the cotton crop comes in. When Mother recovers. When a kind, rich family adopts me. Even the occasional deposit of a foundling left in the night, a baby in a basket who was not wanted, caused the children who knew their names to puff with pride. In their optimism they were certain their families would come back.

My pa hadn't written nor sent my brothers for me, I forlornly noted each day I was trapped there, and I didn't feel any such certainty I was wanted. But I was determined to get out.

Some kids shared their stories. Emma Sue's mother had remarried after her father had divorced her, and her new stepfather didn't want kids. So Emma Sue and her two sisters stood in the courtroom while a judge declared them wards of the state and ordered them to the State Home for Dependent and Neglected Children in Waco.

Mollie was the youngest of eight children, living in a Hooverville, and started stuttering while she was learning to talk—about the time her father hopped a freight to find work and never came back. Her mother told the oldest to find jobs and took her youngest to the Home. But she'd promised to return for Mollie and her sisters, soon as she'd saved some money. By Christmas, she'd said. Her mother gave Mollie a 1936 Dionne Quintuplets wall calendar to X off the days until Christmas Eve. In the calendar's photo, the five famous well-fed, rosy-cheeked babies from Canada sat on a soft gray-

and-pink blanket wearing their pink booties, leaning upon plump pillows and one another, staring at the camera with dark startled eyes.

Nobody asked me where I came from, or where I wanted to go. Nobody cared what I was hoping, so I didn't say.

1937

CHAPTER TWENTY-TWO

WILLA MAE

We are mere numbers to the taciturn doctors, troublemakers to the stringent nurses, less than human to the reproachful attendants. We stand in an assembly line on bathing day to undress, to delouse our hair in carbon oil, to be scrubbed two by two in cold showers and dried with caustic towels till our skin rises red and cracking.

We are reminded we weren't wanted at home, we'd failed our husbands—we are high-strung, nervous, irritable, or depressed, prone to laziness, and require ice baths. Perhaps we are delusional and forgetful, unable to care for our children—we let our families down. We are reclusive, even paranoid, and require electroshock treatments. Some are boisterous and volatile and are restrained.

And always there are the incessant bells.

They control us with bells and orders. So many bells: to awaken from mattresses jammed into hallways, nooks and crannies; to eat cold meals in shifts, silently; to line up for the toilets, for our treatments, for our single-file walk back to our overcrowded wards. We heed bells until bedtime. Locked in for our own safety, we're told, no matter how we pound on doors to escape our private terrors. If sleep comes for me, curled up for warmth in a thin blanket on the floor, I hear bells in my nightmares.

We are tracked, numbered, monitored, and fenced. To keep the godforsaken backwoods out, and us within.

The orders are all-consuming, all day long—I follow them obediently; to ignore them is to be confined alone for a day or a week. I want to recover and go home, but month by month the doctors' assessments are I've made little progress.

You're rambling incoherently, states the doctor at my monthly examination. You're mumbling and constantly counting, why, Willa?

We are just numbers, too many of us for the beds crowding the wards and halls, prodded by the staff to stay silent and stay in line

It's true I count each bell aloud. I repeat each order aloud. The penalty for mistakes—restraint, isolation, or worse—is too severe to allow any errors. And so I keep track.

I have to keep track of my memories. After each hypo injection to induce shock, and finally coma, I keep track. Hazy and nauseous, sopping wet, I count my memories to be sure I don't lose one

If there had been any letters I would have counted them too. But I never receive any letters in response to mine.

And no word from Beck

Nervous agitation is noted on my chart, adding to the assessments of hopelessness, despondency, acute melancholia, and generalized insanity. Metrazol to induce grand mal seizures may be indicated, I read upside down as the doctor writes.

CHAPTER TWENTY-THREE

RUBY LEE

We went by bells and whistles, lining up for every activity under the pergolas connecting the buildings. I counted every clang and trill.

We were schooled proper, and I consumed the reading and writing lessons as a sponge absorbs spilt milk.

We all had jobs. We worked in the kitchens, dining rooms, laundry, cannery, barns. We cleaned windows, floors, rooms, dorms, and helped in the dispensary. We sewed our clothes from the same fabrics and patterns; we trimmed and styled each other's hair. The boys baled hay, mowed lawns, worked on the dairy milk gang, fired boilers for the radiators, butchered hogs and chickens and steers, tended sheep and cows, mixed grain, and fed the livestock. At meals we had all we wanted to eat, and stuffed ourselves with food we'd grown in the fields behind the dorms, vegetables we'd canned from the Bosqueville Farm, milk and ice cream from the dairy barn, meat the boys had slaughtered, eggs we'd gathered. We ate what we prepared in the kitchen—cornbread, macaroni, beans, potatoes, peas, cucumbers, tomatoes, watermelon.

We were a family—that's what they wanted us to believe. I was the black sheep.

• • •

And like one big happy family, we sat for our portrait.

The little boys were dressed in sailor suits. The older boys wore their ties. We were dressed in our Sunday best, donated to us by the Service League of Waco. We'd polished our shoes. We'd combed our hair neatly. We'd scrubbed our faces till they glowed like the floating soap we shared. We sat in arranged rows curved like the letter *C* on the lawn, in front of the administration building, with a fresh chunk of juicy red watermelon placed on the grass before each of us. We were not allowed to eat the watermelon.

We were excited to be outside on a summer eve past our bedtime. Fireflies winked around us.

A short photographer wearing a beret who had arrived on a motorcycle, with his assistant in the sidecar and another following in a Model T, directed us to smile on his command. His assistants had set up flash powder guns high above us and behind us, to flood us with even, bright light. The men sprinkled flash powder onto each tray. One assistant took a glass plate from the wooden case and loaded it into the view camera mounted on a tripod. They arranged the teachers, nurses, matrons, house parents, and staff in an arc on the stone steps. The photographer stepped behind his cherry wood camera, made a frame with his index fingers and thumbs, and peered through it at us. He shifted his tripod to the left. He removed his cap and lifted the camera's black cloak, large enough for him to disappear beneath. The assistants urged us to scoot in more tightly, and move our watermelons along too. The photographer ducked out from beneath the black hood and shouted.

"You must be ready when my camera begins its pivot. You must hold still until it finishes." While he yelled, *smile! keep smiling, smile,* he pulled a trigger to light the flash guns in one dazzling, blinding moment that resounded *whooo-o-o-m!* and scattered powder, smoke, and debris over everyone's Sunday best.

His camera circuit complete, the assistants packed the flash guns, the tripod, the cumbersome glass plates, and the weighty view camera, while the photographer spoke to the superintendent. With elaborate gestures his hands painted pictures. His specialty was making wide panorama photographs of large groups—the Shriners banquet in the Heart O' Texas coliseum, actors onstage at the Cotton Palace, the Masons dining in a gymnasium, the Baylor football team on the field.

"I cannot linger," he announced. "I have another orphanage to photograph, the Methodist Orphans Home."

"We ain't orphans!" But he'd kicked his motorcycle into gear, its noise drowning out my scream.

The kids who weren't orphans pounced on their watermelon chunks and devoured them happily, spitting out seeds with soot, blackened juice dripping onto their Sunday best.

•   •   •

Hairbrush deemed me ready for the girls' dorm, where my new dorm mates were gathered round the Philco. They listened to a pitch for the brand new Little Orphan Annie Shake-Up Mug, free, if they mailed the thin aluminum seal under the lid of an Ovaltine can—plus one dime to cover the cost of mailing and handling. Nobody had any dimes to spare, but the girls were excited and took no notice of me. I recognized Celesta in her leg braces, her bug-eyed sister Clare, and that pale wisp from the Amarillo TB preventorium, Kitty the chatterbox.

The dorm mother interrupted the radio serial to introduce me. No one looked delighted by my arrival except Kitty. She stuck to me like burrs on socks. Mrs. Croucher waved her off with an irritated flick of her hand, and Kitty bounced away in a steady patter of changing conversational topics.

At bedtime, Celesta thumped in on her crutches, and Clare helped Celesta unstrap the thick leather bindings around her knee, foot, and hip that kept her metal leg brace on. Celesta's taut face grew lighter as each loosening relieved her, till she puffed out like a prairie cloud. The reddened rings the straps left on her skin had dug deep. When her eyes met mine, they glistened.

"The cotton batting didn't work out so good," I said.

She yowled, burying her face in her pillow.

"Where's Viola?" I asked, itching to get my money back.

Clare yawned, focusing one eye on me. "You'll see her soon enough." Our dorm went dark.

•   •   •

From Celesta I learned her sister Clare had spent months in the dispensary (after Viola had connived to steal my money), tears splashing on the window where she fruitlessly watched for her mother and aunt. From Clare I learned Celesta would require surgeries, all painful, and further confinements in a Bradford frame (some awful apparatus that kept her immobile in her bed). Afterwards she'd wear Toronto splints and learn to walk again. They pinned their hopes on the famous Dr. William B. Carrell, who cured young cripples like Celesta—not with surgeries and splints but with hydrotherapies— owing to the mineral properties in 106-degree natural spring waters in Gonzales. Clare was selling orange Easter seals for the National Society for Crippled Children to raise money for the doctor's clinic.

"Buy one, Ruby? Put them on your letters. From the president's hospital in Warm Springs. They're sticky, see? You can put on lots."

I stared at Clare, making her uncomfortable, till Celesta thumped and half-hopped over, planting the crutch to steady herself.

"I wrote the president. His picture's on the wall in our ward. He wrote me back!" She brandished an envelope, wobbling precariously on her crutch. "Read it to Ruby," Celesta instructed her sister.

"The president is confident your determination will help you overcome the tragedy of your infantile paralysis. It is grand to know you are keeping up your cheerful spirit. With very best wishes, Grace Tully on behalf of President Franklin D. Roosevelt." Clare looked proud and Celesta's eyes lit up like firecrackers.

"That's fine," I said. "I can't buy any of your seals till you get Viola to gimme my money back."

CHAPTER TWENTY-FOUR

Saturday night movies in the auditorium were the only escape most of us managed, no matter how much we dreamed of it or tried.

One summer night in June, they were fixin to show a newsreel about Amelia Earhart who was making a flight around the world. The boys were restless, some of 'em whistling, *here he comes,* and shooting at each other with their fingers, faking like they caught a bullet and falling down dead. They only cared about *Hopalong Cassidy.* The boys never failed to shout in unison with Bill Cassidy (recuperating from his leg injury), who told the Kid, "I can hop along with the best of 'em."

Some of the mean kids shouted it Celesta's way. That's how she got her nickname.

The boys recited the opening they knew by heart over the stirring music.

"Bill Cassidy from Texas!" someone exclaimed to hoots and hollers.

Among the chattering girls and rowdy boys, all ages, was Red, whistling along with the chorus.

I hadn't seen him since the day I arrived.

Now he was the one clamoring, "Bill Cassidy!" The boys took up the chant. "*Texas! Texas!*"

But the social studies teacher was running the show, and our lessons followed the exploits of Amelia Earhart since her June 1 announcement she'd be circumnavigating the globe in her airplane. The teacher was a fast talker and all wound up about the flight, speaking so quick her words ran together. Every day in class since Amelia Earhart had begun her world tour (*Not-a-stunt-it's-a-scientific-expedition*, she said in a rush, when the criticism was leveled), the teacher chalked a city (*Oakland-Tucson-New-Orleans-Miami-San-Juan*) or a country (*Venezuela-Brazil-Mali-Sudan-Pakistan-Burma-Papua-New-Guinea*) on the blackboard. She'd pull down the roll-up map of the world as rapidly as she'd said call me *Miz-Wills*, making us search for the destination. Our class project was to map the route Amelia would fly.

Miz Wills showed us photographs on the projector of Amelia Earhart: in her one-piece flight suit, standing before the propeller of her rebuilt twin-engine Lockheed Electra, admiring a trophy she'd won. Wearing her short leather bomber jacket, she was freckled and beaming as President Herbert Hoover presented her with a gold medal from the National Geographic Society.

Miss Arnold, the English teacher, assigned us to write the famous pilot's biography. Amelia Earhart wanted to be the first woman to fly across the Atlantic, and she was. She saved up enough money in six months to buy her own airplane, and she named it the Canary. It was bright yellow, and she flew it to set women's altitude records. New York City gave her a ticker-tape parade. Amelia Earhart's wavy hair was thick, unruly, tousled in a short bob like mine, and with a mind of its own like mine. She wore men's trousers with tailored shirts and looked stylish in them. She looked like I wanted to look. I adored her.

The teachers shushed everyone and started the British Movietone newsreel first. Hoppy on his horse, competing with a celebrity pilot in her airplane, would have to wait.

I was spellbound by Amelia Earhart's silver plane, heavy with extra petrol, shimmering, then soaring, over the San Francisco Bay Bridge on the start of her triumphal flight round the world. The newsreel ended too quick. The lights came up, and Red gave me the A-Ok. Then clapped crazily as *Hopalong Cassidy* began.

In contrast to the dramatic takeoff into the heavens around the world, Hopalong plodded over the plains on Topper, through cattle rustling, gunshots, and ambushes. When the boys struck up their soprano with

Johnny and sang about following along through the tumbleweed, too, I moseyed out to see the stars and imagined myself among them.

If only I could fly.

After that, my eyes were always on the sky, scanning for any soaring plane.

•   •   •

At supper, I spotted Red sitting with a slew of boys sharing war stories. I inched nearer to listen to an older boy telling how his pa got his airman training at nearby Rich Field, before the Great War, when the Home was part of old Camp MacArthur. His father was trained to fight the kaiser, the older boy said between bites of fried chicken and succotash, and he survived the Spanish influenza that struck the soldiers at the camp in 1918. A German U-boat torpedoed his division's transport ship, and he survived. He fought in the Red Arrow on the front lines in France, and survived. His division cracked the Hindenburg Line, and survived. The boy glowed with pride.

"He came back a war hero," he said. "They shipped him to West Texas to join the cavalry—"

His audience was captivated, except one, who jerked his head. "If he's such a hero, what're you doin here?"

The older boy's stare was hard. "His memories didn't survive."

Everyone got quiet. A lot of kids knew how bad it got, having a pa who lost his vertical hold. Or a ma crazier than a bedbug.

"He wasn't never right again," the older boy's voice cracked. "Ma called it shell shock. Doctors called it melancholia." He stopped with a buttered biscuit halfway to his lips.

"They put him away." The biscuit slid from his hand. "Like my ma did me and my brother." He jerked his thumb towards Red.

Red's eyes were fixed on his full plate. "We ain't seen him since."

The boys welcomed me into their horse apple fights among the bodarks lining the cyclone fence and in the trenches and ropes left over from the

Camp MacArthur soldiering days. Red introduced me to Farmer Krewell, showing me around the dairy barn where he collected empty cans on the milk gang. Red was a herding boy, and he thought it was a prize, waking the cows for 5 a.m. milking. Next he'd join the experienced boys who milked them.

"When I can work the pasteurizer, I'll join Future Farmers of America." He said it right pert.

"They let girls in?"

"You mean you?" he laughed, and I pretended to.

The boys had a radio in their dorm. "That how you come by those songs you're always whistling?" I asked. He had one for every occasion.

"We listen to *The Lone Ranger* and *The Shadow*," Red said. "If Coach ain't bustin someone."

"You ain't following Amelia Earhart's circumnavigation?" In social studies, Miz Wills had us plot every stop the flying laboratory made on the map. In English class, Miss Arnold had us mark each location where she stopped with her navigator for refueling on a wall calendar. She showed us a picture from the newspapers of Amelia Earhart and her navigator grinning as a viscount greeted them upon landing in Karachi, after they flew from the Red Sea to the Arabian Sea in one hop. In the newsprint photograph, the wind blew her short bangs off her forehead. She looked fresh in a pearl-snapped, dark, western-style shirt with white trim. Her face was electric with her energy. She was luminous.

"Say that nickel word again—circum-what?" Red's eyebrows angled into a lopsided quiz.

His thick dark eyebrows that contradicted his crazy red hair were his best feature.

Impatient to read the exploits of the world's most famous aviatrix, I became a quick study. My reading and grammar got so good I showed it off, explaining the exotic stops Amelia Earhart made and the many seas she'd flown over along the equator route. "She's s'posed to be landing her monoplane on Howland Island soon."

"Where's that?" Red's face opened with curiosity, which was what I liked most about him.

"Ever heard of the Pacific Ocean?"

He considered this for a split second till he saw I was cracking wise.

"Fourth of July's this Sunday," he said. "Fireworks at Cameron Park and the ice cream social here. Mr. Berkman's got the band ready to march. I'm on brass horns. You coming?"

"Who else?"

"The gang," Red said, meaning any or all of the boys. Unlike the girls, they weren't shy about leaving the grounds to play at the Bosque River, shooting squirrels, swimming, catching catfish or trot lining at Lovers Leap, and risking licks for their rock fights. The boys figured they'd get campused by Coach, and they'd still play ball for him—even endure his beatings—no matter what they did. They took what fun they could.

"You skipping church? Those divinity students need some sinners to practice their preachin on." Red gave me his puzzled look again. I busted out laughing.

I admired some of his gang—show-offs and smart alecks, all—brave while enduring their whippings. "You don't dare cry." Red shook his head. "Coach'll give you a worse bustin next time."

Kids skedaddled to their dorms in the dusky summer heat at the last-call bell.

"See ya Sunday." I was poised to fly to my dorm. "Listen to the news broadcast for me. I got to know about the world flight."

•   •   •

Like most nights before we fell asleep, that night we played a round of *If Only*. Lots of girls missed their mothers, who'd been widowed and destitute enough to give them up; or had a case of nerves and couldn't care for them properly; or who'd been deemed neglectful by a family service caseworker, despite being on irregular piecework and starving like their children. If only Ma was right in the head. If only Ma married a man who wanted someone else's kids. If only Ma and Pa would come back for us like they promised. If only Pa could get a job. If only Pa wasn't a bum. If only Pa laid off the sauce. If only Pa hadn't beat Ma. If only Pa hadn't left us.

Some girls had brothers and sisters scattered among the dorms. If only we all lived under one roof again. If only we were a family again.

For me it was, *if only I was home.* I pictured Pa—*if only it would rain.* If only Pa would fetch me. If only I could fly. If only Momma loved me . . .

Friday night, way past lights out, I imagined making my escape like Amelia Earhart, flying high away from these hard times. Comforted by my one hope, I grew sleepy, *if only.*

When I am home, I whispered, conviction besting hope.

CHAPTER TWENTY-FIVE

After the Baylor religion students preached to us to save our souls Sunday morning, we were free for the holiday. The band played "The Yankee Doodle Boy" while they marched down the street, and we lined the route cheering and waving little American flags the matrons handed out. Later Red found me at the ice cream social in the ball field, where we were playing stickball, hide-and-seek, and tag. We got our fill of peach ice cream made from our cows' milk and peaches the dairy boys had plucked from our orchard.

While Red whistled *I'm a Yankee Doodle Dandy,* I tagged along with the boys roughhousing and chasing each other to Cameron Park. The fireflies began to blink. We were heedless of the trouble we'd face if we were caught off-campus, excited to see the fireworks—I had never seen a Fourth of July show. When the first booms and bursts went off, I thought of the airplane back home that dynamited the clouds to make it rain. All that plane yielded was sparkly showers from fizzling firecrackers, no substitute for the long, steady downpour we needed.

Red had been quiet since we got there. Lying on our backs in the grass, our eyes fixed on the illuminations sprinkling the stars with color, the fireworks encircled us like a dome, so close, their smoky embers flickered out as they landed around us. An ember sizzled in Red's wiry hair, and he pantomimed slapping it out like wildfire. We oohed and aahed and said not much else.

The darkness wrapped me in a sense of security I rarely felt. I nudged him. "You got a real name? Like one your momma gave you?"

His voice carried a smile. "Sure. Oris. Oris Burton Hubbard."

I tried to wrap my gums around that and giggled.

"Go on," he poked me. "Call me Red."

"Whad'ya find out on the radio about Amelia Earhart? She make Hawaii yet?"

"Ain't listened to the broadcast today. But yesterday, no."

I sat up, paying no mind to the firecrackers. "What ain't you tellin me?"

"Don't get riled up, Ruby. Her plane has buoyancy, they're saying. And a rubber raft. She hit some headwinds on her way to Howland and the navy's out hunting for them now. She's sending signals to wireless stations. Some shortwave operators are picking them up."

"Her plane's down? Where?" I felt frantic.

"The Coast Guard's working that out. Maybe she passed over Howland, it being such a small island, with the sun glaring in her eyes. They'll find her. Don't fret." He reached for my hand. I yanked it away, stood up.

"When did she get lost? Why didn't you tell me?"

"Ruby—rest easy. They probably found her by now. They lost track of her Friday night. But Saturday they heard her calling SOS. They got aircraft carriers and everybody looking for her. The whole navy practically."

I took off for the dorm.

"Hey—wait, it's the grand finale," Red yelled. He kept pace with me, racing through the park, panicked, lost in the dark like Amelia, then led me to the edge of campus, where we ran through the hayfield. He whispered, "Be real quiet. Follow me."

We crept up the stairs of the deserted boys' dorm to the living room. "This is a AM radio and a shortwave, too." Red sat in front of it. "If Coach isn't around, I come in to listen to the shortwave. I can get signals from everywhere, all over the world."

He turned the tube radio knob, which moved a lighted strip of numbers that looked like a tape measure. He kept tweaking it, forward, back. "Can't find KDKA," he muttered, but the crackling static came to life with a smooth, dramatic voice.

". . . have come to grief in their perilous round-the-world flight several hundred miles from Howland Island in the mid-Pacific. Their great plane fitted out as a flying laboratory is down, stranded on a coral reef, it's believed from fragmentary and weak radio calls for help . . . Coast Guard cutters and navy ships and planes are rushing to their aid, among them the aircraft carrier Lexington under forced draft from San Diego with seventy-two planes aboard. The two intrepid fliers missed the tiny dot that is Howland Island in their twenty-five-mile hop from New Guinea and were forced down by lack of fuel for hours . . . The Coast Guard cutter *Itasca* is now reported near them, certain they are still safe and sound. And now we return to the Big Broadcast."

Red played with the dials some more as the radio dispensed fragments of people talking in distorted bursts, interspersed with static and echoes, occasionally a clear phrase.

"How can you understand any of that?" What I heard was garbled and distant.

"That's the shortwave frequency. I'm used to it." He looked mesmerized, his head cocked to one side near the speaker, like the dog in the Victrola advertisements.

"I'm gonna listen for her signals too. Lots of kids are." Red turned off the radio and led me outside through the dark. "See? The whole world is helping. She'll be found. No call to worry."

"That's what Mrs. Barton said," I murmured.

•   •   •

Needles pin-prickled my face as we walked to my dormitory. Then everything around me was spinning like a top. My feet went numb, and my heart galloped as we passed the administration building, which was blurry, and my breaths came in choppy little bursts. A cough began aggravating my throat. I tried counting, *one-two, one-two*, and Red noticed. "Whad'ya say, Ruby?"

He touched my forehead, appearing startled by my condition. "You're shivering like you seen a ghost. Sweating all over."

Red found us a bench under the pergola. I couldn't get a breath. I was wheezing, then gasping, trying to say, *I can't get a breath*, but I couldn't get the air for the words.

That's how I ended up back in the dispensary, with a hot water bottle on my chest, inhaling Potter's powders through a metal funnel and crying over Amelia Earhart.

●   ●   ●

The night nurse sat me up halfway through the night to listen to my chest and my back. She heard a pronounced wheeze and would call for the doctor in the morning. I might have to go to Rexall pharmacy for a pneumostat.

"What?"

"The electric nebulizer," she said as if it was an explanation. "Try to get some sleep." She propped me up with pillows. "It's better if you don't lie down."

I was restless and wheezy all that night; I couldn't quit thinking about Amelia drifting somewheres in the dark, far from home, sending her call letters K-H-A-Q-Q, S-O-S, K-H-A-Q-Q over the wireless, her only hope of rescue relying on folks who might never come.

CHAPTER TWENTY-SIX

WILLA MAE

In the ward where I spend my days, I am among the elderly and the very young, and all ages in-between, where some hallucinate and tear out clumps of their hair, some hug themselves while rocking back and forth, and some converse lucidly until they cackle in distressed laughter. Occasionally someone flies into a rage, or claims she hears voices, or babbles gibberish. I am also among patients who remain calm, and some who are gregarious and witty. Those with a book or magazine read quietly. Many times, patients are good-natured and helpful, but some are politely reclusive.

In here we cycle endlessly, from resignation at our fate to resistance of our treatments, through despair at our confinement to hope we can be released. Sometimes we show flashes of defiance. If we do, we quickly learn we'll be living in locked wards with nothing to do all day long. None of us think our commitment is warranted. We know the doctors aren't helping us—because we know we don't belong here. But none of us have any expectation of release.

Those who have been here the longest have lost the means of expressing their emotions. They have acquiesced. Surrendered.

And one day is like another, the endless boredom of our meaningless day-to-day subsistence.

I spend hours drawing them and their faces of despair, acceptance, fury, in tones of gray, the only tool I'm given, apt for our world here.

I write this in letters to Beck, even though he never answers. He put me here. It is high time he comes for me; I still have expectations. They can't take those from me with their never-ending hydrotherapies and injections.

Time is the enemy here, I confide in the doctor who examines me. *Please post this letter to my husband.*

CHAPTER TWENTY-SEVEN

RUBY LEE

Dr. Carbaugh produced a glass nebulizer from his black bag the next morning. "Open your mouth. Say *aah*, there, that's it. You'll inhale these tiny droplets from this adrenaline mixture by squeezing the compressor here." He indicated a rubber bulb at the bottom of a glass vial with a curved neck. "Place the nozzle right inside your mouth, not too far in. Now squeeze the bulb and inhale at the same time. Pretty soon it will be second nature."

He handed some papers to the night nurse. "Directions for how to sterilize it. She'll need to visit here each day to use it, under your supervision, of course. If this is ineffective, notify me and we'll arrange a trip to the pneumostat, but I don't think that will be necessary."

He turned to me. "If you have another acute attack of wheezing and you can't breathe, get here to the dispensary right away to use this—anytime you're having trouble. You don't want to bring on paroxysmal manifestations."

The doctor must have seen my face screw up in a question mark. "Nervous distress, my patients call it. You feeling better now?" He listened again to my chest. "How'd a little girl like you get such a rattle, anyway?"

I gave him the stink eye. "I'm not little. I had the dust pneumonia's all. I'm dandy now."

"That so." The doctor closed his black leather bag. He must have been in a hurry, since he didn't pursue it, which was lucky for me. I made quick work of lacing my shoes.

"I'll walk you to school; my shift's about over." The night nurse handed me a cherry lollipop. "All the good patients get lollies." She was nicer than the regular weekend nurse but I had no time for kindness.

"I can't be late to class—" She stopped me.

"Hold your britches—I got something for you."

I said my first class was social studies, which it wasn't. "I *have* to keep my high marks in the geography unit," I was emphatic. What I *had* to do, actually, was learn if they'd located Amelia. But the nurse took her considerable time walking me to class, while I fumed a few steps ahead of her. We rounded the corner to school but she stepped into the copse of trees and called to me, impatient. From her pocketbook she extracted a slim orange and black tin can.

"Flip up the lid. They're Kellogg's asthma cigarettes. See? They won't bite you. Doctors prescribe them for older kids. You're on the young side, is all. If you get to wheezing, you smoke one, it'll clear up your breathing."

She lit one up and took a deep drag, and handed it to me. "I use these when I need some bronchodilation."

I waited for her to explain that word, which she mistook as skepticism. "They aren't tobacco cigarettes, if that's what you're thinking." I inhaled it tentatively, coughing, and she whacked my back a few times.

"Try another drag. Slow, take it down your throat, inhale, relax, breathe it out through your nose. You'll get the hang of it." I choked, but less.

"They're packed with dried crushed herbs. Nothing to hurt you. See? Aren't you breathing easier?"

I was, and I nodded. Inertia struck me as I practiced. The nurse lit up another one for me, then gave me the tin pack with a book of matches which read, "MARIHUANA Thrills at a Price" and showed a burning cigarette. It spelled, "R-E-E-F-E-R."

"For bron—bron-cho-di-la-tion." My tongue felt thick as I practiced the word, really wanting to know, *reefer*?

"That's medical talk for expanding the air passages to your lungs. Look, you can get these at any pharmacy, any brand, Potter's, Schiffman's, Asthmador—buy the cheapest."

As if I could afford any. She must have noted my hesitancy.

"If you need more, come see me. I'm here Sundays, sometimes other days. Now get along to your—what class was it? Ge-og-ra-phy?" She drew the word out syllable by syllable, smugly, and left only the echo of her pumps thunking on the sidewalk.

•   •   •

Miz Wills let an eyebrow rise as I eased into her social studies classroom, sitting quiet in the back so's I didn't interrupt her lecture about when Texas was Mexico.

"Class, turn to page forty-seven in your textbook," she said. "Ruby Lee, come to my desk."

None of the kids turned to page forty-seven. All eyes were on me as I walked to her desk.

"Good morning, Ruby, you are early for your class but late to this one."

"Yes, ma'am."

She stood and clapped three times. "Class. Attention." She wrote a big word on the blackboard, and I sounded it out silently while she told the class to busy themselves reading the section titled "Stephen F. Austin."

"Be ready to define *empresario* and name two of them."

She asked me, "Are you here about Amelia?" and her voice was softer. "You've taken such an interest in her flight. Miss Arnold told me your paper was the best anyone submitted."

I didn't show her how little I cared what the shifty English teacher thought. "Is there any news, ma'am?"

She glanced at the classroom globe, where I'd run my finger around the world every day, tracing the Electra's route. "There is. Come back at lunchtime. Now get to where you belong."

I thought about that, where I belong. Where I belonged was *not* the Waco State Home.

•   •   •

"I have yesterday's *Amarillo Sunday News-Globe*." The big banner headline in block letters read, "Chances for Rescue of Amelia Earhart Diminish."

"What's *diminish*?" I asked my teacher.

"Diminish is to fade, lessen, dwindle," she said, making a circle with her finger and thumb that got smaller and smaller.

"Why?" I counted, *one-two, easy*, slowing my breath, focusing on the picture of Amelia Earhart smiling in her leather jacket, a crisp white shirt, and a man's tie.

Miz Wills read, "'Heavy snow, sleet, and lightning storms turned back a big navy flying boat that set off from Honolulu . . . but the Coast Guard cutter *Itasca* is searching . . . Miss Earhart's technical adviser puts stock in the amateur wireless operators who heard messages she reached an atoll in the Southern Pacific.'

"We mustn't give up hope, Ruby. Look for it on the globe, then get yourself to lunch." She handed me the newspaper. "It's good practice for your reading."

Elsewhere on the front page was a muddled picture of ten combines lined up on the wheat fields of Mr. C. L. Ludwig of Moore County, preparing to harvest seven bushels (and perhaps fifteen) to the acre, after emergency listing had saved his land from a spring blow on his contoured land. The headline over the photograph said, "This WAS The Dust Bowl."

"Moore County?" I asked Miz Wills. "Isn't that in the Panhandle?" She opened her atlas to the page for Texas, and told me to find it. "You're sure learning your geography, Ruby."

There it was, a rectangle on a state map full of rectangles running all the way up the Panhandle, next to Hartley, and Dallam County above it, names I remembered on signs in town. This bit of good news lifted me as I got to thinking how Pa's farm would be saved, too, and I'd be going home.

If only Amelia would be, too.

•　　•　　•

"Listen, Ruby, we aren't giving up on Amelia Earhart," Miz Wills told me the next day while my tears spilled on the newspaper, blurring the ink.

"Here is what her grandmother, Mrs. E. S. Earhart, says: 'If she is in trouble, she will find her way out.' *She will find her way out*." She emphasized the phrase like it was a message meant for me.

I didn't say nuthin. It was all I could do to keep from sobbing.

"A grandmother ought to know, ought'n she not?"

I felt a fleeting memory of Granny Alma's reliable belief in goodness which never materialized for our family. "Yes, ma'am."

"Pour over these and find words of hope." Miz Wills indicated the newspapers she'd bought at the newsstand. "Read what you find while I grade papers."

All the headlines from papers across the country screamed, "Amelia Earhart Feared Lost at Sea," except one, she explained, pulling out the *New York Times*. "Look where it says, 'Word is official: Amateur operators had told of hearing voice of aviatrix.'"

She pulled another from the pile. "This first."

The *Rock Springs Rocket* in Wyoming reported "a sixteen-year-old Rock Springs boy picked up a message from the flier." I gave a whoop.

"A boy heard Amelia Earhart on his shortwave! 'Young Dana Randolph, who is not a licensed operator, had the thrill today of having done his share in the search for Amelia Earhart and her globe encircling companion, Captain Frederick Noonan!'" Miz Wills read intently, pleasure spreading across her face.

"Randolph twirled the dial of his small, inexpensive shortwave radio set Sunday morning about eight o'clock. Suddenly he was startled when he heard what he described as a faint but distinct voice saying, 'Amelia Earhart calling.' Over and over again, he heard the call but could distinguish no call letters such as the missing aviatrix would have for her radio station.

"The lad called his father, who heard the woman's voice come again from the speaker, repeating her name, the call letters of her station, and fading away again as she began to give her location. He rushed to the telephone office where he contacted the wire chief, who in turn notified a department of commerce official from the bureau of aviation.

"They rushed to the Randolph home where the lad told his story.

"The signals, he said, came in for twenty-five minutes before they faded out. He could hear something about a 'ship being on a reef south of the equator,' and added some unintelligible figures also were given which may have been latitude and longitude, but he was unable to copy them down.

"The department of commerce official and amateur radio operators here think it was possible Randolph received a radio call from the missing flier."

She rolled down the big map of the world and I looked for islands south of the equator, tiny golden specks set here and there in all the blue. "A reef won't show up there, Ruby," the teacher said.

"What's a reef?" She found a book about oceans, told me to look it up.

Satisfied, I turned back to the first article, which told of Wyoming and Ohio radio listeners who believed Miss Earhart was trying to give a position near Howland Island. Radio workers in Hawaii and on the mainland reported hearing wireless and voice signals almost hourly. Everyone refused to give up hope, because Amelia wouldn't.

"She's signaling to KGMB in Honolulu! They told her to send out dashes and she did!" I said. "The *Itasca* has four crewmen in the crow's nest on lookout! They broadcast a message to her, 'keep your spirits up. Ships and planes are on the way.'"

"That's right, Ruby. Keep your spirits up. Now get to class."

•   •   •

Before bedtime, I slipped outside while Croucher was occupied by two girls arguing over their pillows, one having accused the other of switching them to steal the plumper pillow, as if we even had such a thing. I lit up my asthma cigarette. In one-half less than no time, Kitty was on me like a flea on a dog, skittering about as if afflicted. "What are you smoking! Can I try it!"

"Shush," I warned her, "this is my medicine."

"Here's mine!" She held out her tin of petroleum jelly.

"That's Vaseline. Shut up. Quit your jumping."

Those were the two things Kitty could not do.

"I love Amelia Earhart, don't you? They might not find her!"

I'd taken the last pull, but started wheezing, desperate for any breath I could get. I stubbed the ember of my cigarette into Kitty's bare arm to shut her up, and took off for the dispensary.

●　　●　　●

After I breathed in the nebulizer and calmed my lungs, they called Dr. Carbaugh back, which is how I ended up stuck there. Wednesday afternoon, Miz Wills tracked me down with her stash of newspapers.

Some good news had come. Experts and the plane's builder all agreed the Electra's radio batteries wouldn't work if it was floating in water.

Some bad news had come. Even with all the mysterious messages picked up by radios all over the US and Canada, the ships couldn't get bearings on the plane's signals.

Then came news the battleship *Colorado* was steaming at top speed toward islands south of Howland, to catapult its three Corsair observation planes spokewise to search for reefs where a pilot might make a forced landing.

But that would take till Saturday or even later.

There was nuthin to grip to.

"You look lower than a crippled cricket's ass," my social studies teacher mumbled under her breath, not without sympathy. She spoke loud and direct, like a voice coming through a radio. "Remember, if she is in trouble, she'll find her way out."

Red found me at supper Sunday, busting at the seams to tell me about DiMaggio's perfect day for the Yanks. "They're calling him the next Ruth! He hit two homers himself, then a triple, a double, and a single. Then he rammed in another seven homers—four of 'em he made himself!" He had to pause for a breath. "And the Iron Man, he hit his fourteenth homer and hammered in four runs. They sure sandpapered the Senators!"

He offered me some of the Cracker Jacks he was crunching and began whistling "Take Me Out to the Ball Game."

I waited for him to run outta air. "You caught all that on your radio, did you?"

"Sure, Coach listens to the ball games 'cause he's a Yankees fan. It was dang exciting! Ooh, and then they started throwin punches—the first basemen started it—they all got into it, the umps, the catcher, even the manager. The crowd was pitching soda pop bottles from the bleachers, we heard 'em break." He chuckled, his eyes keen with enthusiasm.

"What about Amelia?"

All the vitality vanished from his eyes. "Well . . . Nothing good, I reckon."

"Tell me."

"A naval officer, he said only a chance in a million for a rescue."

Red hung his head as if to shoulder the blame.

"That all? No more transmissions?"

"The *Colorado*'s floatplanes quit their aerial searches, to refuel—"

I cut him off. "Anyone picking up her radio transmissions?"

"Ain't heard'a none." He looked low as I felt. "Ruby? You're takin this so hard, why?"

"I know how she feels," I said, soft as butterfly wings beating. *Trapped somewheres we don't want to be, with nobody coming for us.*

"Say again?"

I got right in his face, gritted out my words. "None of your business."

"Okay, sure." He put his hand on my arm, real gentle. I jerked it away. "Anyways," he kept on, "they're sending a giant aircraft carrier, the *Lexington*, to the South Pacific and keep up the search. See? There's still some hope . . ." His voice had a pleading quality I found unbecoming.

"Some hope." I sniffed back tears.

•　　•　　•

It was another week before the navy announced what everyone knew was coming—the aviator and her navigator were given up for dead, all ships ordered back to their bases.

When the navy quit their hunt in July 1937 was when I quit Red. I'd come to expect it from adults—saying not to worry. Adults never lived up to their promises. Red gave me his assurances, and I'd trusted him.

But Red was like all the rest—another betrayal. He had no right to give me hope.

I wrote him off, but he didn't let up easy. He brought me a bunch of wild yarrow with its strong, sweet smell, tied with a pink ribbon. I flung 'em down and stomped on 'em. He kept at it, every day, an extra slice of peach pie from the dining hall, a bottle of citrus-and-vanilla-flavored Sun Tang Red Cream Soda, a handful of orange-tinged Mexican hats. When I flipped the pie into the trash can, poured the pop on his shoes, tossed the wildflowers back to the breeze, his eyes had the hurtful look that really got to me. All the whistle went outta him.

Because my tender spot ached, I sheltered my heart from Red. Even a dead snake can still bite.

1938

CHAPTER TWENTY-EIGHT

RUBY LEE

If only I could escape. That was my obsession. Except I had no place to run to, no home to escape to, nowheres anyone wanted me. I smoked my asthma cigarettes nightly, contemplating how I'd get out for good.

The whip-poor-wills struck up their song. Croucher was doing bed check when I crept back in. Tardy again, she said without looking at me, a satisfied expression crossing her chronically constipated face. They all registered pleasure from my comeuppance, like that's what they expected from someone so worthless her own mother abandoned her to the Waco State Home.

I would have to run away.

I discovered the heap of wrapped packages in the closet under the stairs accidentally and read labels, saw postmarks dated years ago. I hoped for mail from Momma and Pa. Or Will, who'd left me behind in 1936. Rummaging through undelivered mail, inspecting it, I carefully opened each item. Most kids had outgrown the clothing or toys they'd been sent. Some had cards enclosed—messages handwritten. "All I can spare, here's four dollar bills," or "Buy a toy with these coins," and "It ain't much, we'll send more soon."

I never found any cash or coins. Plenty of packages were wrapped in Christmas paper, though we rarely had gifts under the tree.

There wasn't nuthin for me.

•   •   •

One evening the still air was so hot, I waited till late for my asthma cigarette, taking my chances with the chiggers. A sliver of moonlight outlined Viola, sneaking under the cyclone fence.

It wasn't her cousin's truck this time, it was a Cadillac convertible coupe gliding to a stop. The streetlamp illuminated its glossy paint, the silvery goddess hood ornament atop the egg crate grille, its wide whitewall tires. The canvas top was down and Viola snuggled right up to the driver. *Babycakes*, she cooed in his ear.

He didn't look like any baby driving off with her. He looked like the coach's buddy, Shotwell, the former disciplinarian, whose severe whippings were an open secret. His habit with a heavy razor strap injured so many teen boys, even some girls, he'd been fired.

By supper the next day, the story of Viola's night out at the Alamo Plaza Courts spread like a prairie fire with a tailwind. Everybody knew it was her fault, since she was looser than ashes in the wind. She came back smelling like bathtub gin, as stewed as prunes. She had to be locked up before she got knocked up. They'd stashed her in quarantine, for her own good.

•   •   •

Mollie, still stuttering and crossing off each day on her 1936 wall calendar, got old enough to move into my dormitory. When I flipped through it, an X marked on every day, she got flustered.

"You started over?" I asked her. "Your mother didn't come for you like she promised, so you started marking your Xs all over again each year?" Mollie nodded like that wasn't odd.

I guess it wasn't. None of us expected much of anything good.

"It's 1938 now," I pointed out.

Her eyes glistened, and she sniffled. "Nuthin to feel bad about," I said.

Truth be told, the parents mostly never did come back. If one did, it was front page news around the campus. Some fathers, and lots of mothers, came for family visits, bringing their promises but always leaving behind tearful kids. A few times, kids got adopted. One boy was adopted by a well-off lady, real sweet and unmarried. Envious, kids speculated about the toys and clothes and love he was getting. Six months later, the well-off lady returned him—she'd married a man with three rowdy boys. Any more was too many. The boy was devastated, being returned like a mantel clock that ticked too loud.

•   •   •

Celesta took up with Mollie, and soon they were fast friends. Mollie helped her with her heavy leg braces, encouraged her to join the other kids, was patient with her, and defended her against anyone who called her a cripple. Mollie even stood up to a bully who hollered, "Hey, Hoppy, hop on over here."

Mollie was always reminding Celesta to pay the bullies no mind with homespun wisdom that made her laugh. "She's not worth your cryin over, Celesta; she don't even have enough sense to spit downwind." Somehow Mollie could say all that without stuttering or garbling it or stepping on her words.

Mollie lost her stutter whenever she was with Celesta. None of the adults could pinpoint why, though they claimed it was due to their attentive diction and speech training.

CHAPTER TWENTY-NINE

In the dormitory, the air was stifling and so close, the room spun round me. I ran outside for clear air. My sense of dread lessened in the nightfall, when I crept to the hay barn. It was dark inside, but I heard whispering. Sitting on a hay bale, I let my eyes seek the shapes in the shadows. Boys were digging tunnels through the stacked hay bales, their footsteps crunching on dry hay, and smoking cigarettes. When I lit up my Potter's, the match's flame illuminated a tall boy coming my way.

"I'm Red's brother, Clarence. Clay." He'd stunned me with the story of his shellshocked father, the war hero who'd lost his memories. "Want one of my smokes?"

I was taking a drag, inhaling it slow. I shook my head no.

"Huh. That smells different."

"It's not tobacco. Made from nightshade herbs, makes breathing easier. The nurse gets 'em for me." I showed him the Potter's tin.

"For asthma, hay fever, bronchitis," Clay lit a match to read, "and diseases of the respiratory organs." He set it down between us. "Helps you out, I reckon?"

"Yep," I said, not really sure but I did like how it lulled me.

"Hotter 'n Hades in here, isn't it? We're heading to the river later, if you wanna come."

The moon had riz, lending its light inside the open doors, and I made out shadowy boys shifting in the dimness. "Maybe. You in high school?"

"Tenth grade. I'm a few years older 'n Red. He's sweet on you. Wouldn't ever say so. I can tell."

One boy emerged from the hay bales and started climbing up the stacks, where stored sacks of onions and potatoes dangled from the rafters.

"Red here tonight?"

"Don't think so. He wanted to go to Cameron Park. None of us did. Prob'ly took off on his own, he's kind of a loner."

The climber called out from the rafters overhead, "Heads up below," then let loose a few sacks, yelling, "Onion team versus potatoes," and dozens of boys appeared from their hiding places in the hay, their smokes hanging from their lips, chucking the onions and pounding potatoes at each other.

"You in the coach's dorm?" I asked.

"You mean the Mauler," he jeered. "Most of us here are. We'd get campused if he caught us. Or worse."

He took a long pull. "Makes us call him our dorm father. Ain't no kinda father any of us ever had. More like a warden. Last week he beat a kid so bad his butt was bleeding."

My skin prickled. "Was it Red?"

"No, he's been lucky so far." The older boys, Clay went on, were long accustomed to vicious beatings by the coach and called him the Mauler, an unkind allusion to their heavyweight boxing idol. Jack Dempsey, known as the Manassa Mauler, was famous for his slugger-style of fighting, which the boys admired—but only in the boxing ring.

"This kid, Coach made him pull down his pants, gave him a busting, ten licks, bent over the bed"—Clay drifted a minute, then resumed, his voice deeper— "It's a nasty paddle he made, from a baseball bat, with notches. Everybody hates him."

Two potatoes thudded at our feet, then an onion, another. I ducked as a potato shot over my head.

"What about the matrons?" I dodged a golden onion. "Or the superintendent . . . Why don't they do something?"

"Heck, it's no secret. They think it's good discipline."

We were quiet awhile.

"You know," Clay said, "Coach is a big guy, tall, must weigh two-fifty or more. There's something wrong with a man like that, beating up kids."

The air inside felt close, making it hard to get a lungful. "I got to get out. Stuffy in here."

"Yeah, hay dust in the air." Clay stood on the hay bale and sniffed, turning his head. Just then a flame ripped up the middle of the barn and caught the surprise on the faces of the boys who'd frozen with their arms mid-windup.

"Fire! Fire! Get the hoses and buckets!" Clay yelled. More flames erupted, surrounding them, all snaking through the hay bales towards us.

Somebody yelled, "Everybody out!" and I led the way.

We scattered in the dark. From the safety of the dormitory portico, I watched flames spew from the barn, the groaning of frightened cows overpowered by clanging fire engines on approach.

CHAPTER THIRTY

WILLA MAE

A fire broke out yesterday in the third story ward for seniles, I note in my logbook of memories both written and drawn. Five women died, whether from shock or smoke inhalation, no one is sure. But I am sure. They suffocated because they were locked in. Trapped, without a fire escape, unable to breathe, plumes of smoke overtaking them. This building has no fire escapes at all. Tonight I refuse to sleep anywhere but on the ground floor, my memories of being encased in black blizzards too haunting to be shocked away by their hydrotherapies and insulin treatments.

An altercation with the attendant, angry words echo down the halls, a doctor summoned with his syringe.

He grasps my hands together, stilling them, and steers me to the psychopathic wing. My eyes water from lingering smoke and chemicals. We pass a row of inert, likely unconscious, patients. At an empty bed, he tells the nurse he'd sedated me lightly and to prepare an injection of Metrazol to bring on a seizure.

"The therapeutic convulsions cause a strong sense of doom but that's normal," he explains with no apparent emotion, tightening the arm and leg restraints. "Nothing to distress over so relax as you convulse." His lips flatten into a terse line and he turns away, addressing the lone nurse as though he would a university lecture hall packed with medical students.

"It's not unusual for patients to experience paroxysmal manifestations before grand mal seizures, but this therapy is safer than the daily insulin hypos she's been receiving, simpler to administer, without the need to surveil for hypoglycemic aftershocks. The cost savings is significant. The seizures bring the patients to a state of compliance, calmer, with agitation reduced. The resultant amnesia seems to relieve their anxieties"—*Amnesia, I struggle against it in trepidation* — "We should see a resolution of her involutional melancholia within weeks. Occasional mid-thoracic vertebrae and mandible fractures are the major complication, thus the patient must be well-padded here and here," he slides his finger under my back and my legs, "with the rubber ball positioned securely in the mouth." He finishes as the nurse pries open my jaw and jams in the foul black gag.

The dark curtain descends. I hear Beck's voice under the howl of the wind lashing the church doors on that Black Sunday.

"I can't see my hand before my face."

CHAPTER THIRTY-ONE

RUBY LEE

Teaching us was a wasted effort the day after the barn burned, as we gossiped and speculated as to who or what started the fire. Arnold, at her wits' end, didn't even try. She smacked a few hands with her ruler and banished a boy to the closet and threatened another with her paddle, but she was more frazzled than fearsome, and eventually dismissed us early.

Next weekend, we boarded the bus to attend Mary Holliday's Saturday morning show, Jones' Fine Bread Kiddie Matinee, broadcast live each week from the Waco Theatre.

We were excited. The bus rolled along Austin Avenue, where memories of Cousin Bess pained me.

When we unloaded we became objects of curiosity to the onlookers, who paused their shopping to read "State Home for Children" painted in capital letters on our bus. I scowled at one who remarked, "Here come the poor orphans," and veered away from indulgent smiles.

Austin Avenue was busy even on a stifling summer Saturday. Ladies in navy blue sleeveless polka-dot dresses with white hats and gloves strode into Goldstein's, their children in hand. The evolution of children's dress, on exhibit in its big display window, featured young girls in old-time skirts and in today's styles, posed on risers in two levels. They stood stock-still before a painted backdrop, caged in the window for the benefit of onlookers. Clad in dresses we'd sewn for ourselves from cheap bolts of cotton, we ogled them.

Pipkin's Drug and the F. W. Woolworth Company were crawling with customers. We were allowed to shop before the broadcast with what nickels and dimes we'd saved from our chores, which suited me, since I needed more asthma cigarettes.

A few days after the barn fire, I'd felt wheezy and reached into the pocket of my overalls for my Potter's. I came up with lint. Then I remembered, the last time I'd had 'em, I was showing the small green tin to Clay. He'd set the tin on the hay bale we sat on.

Everyone agreed after the commotion died down it was a miracle nobody got hurt. The smoldering ruins left little to save, but the older boys stayed busy hauling off the remnants. Word went round, in the rubble, they'd found a tin, its paint burned off but still recognizable as a container for something illicit, possibly cigarettes. Anyone who'd been in the barn that night was white-knuckling it. Gossip flew about who they'd blame for the fire. Whoever was guilty, she'd be shipped off to the Texas State Training School for Girls in Gainesville, where they always threatened to send the worst delinquents.

Of course, they didn't figure a girl had burned down the barn. The coach vowed to send the boys responsible to the State Juvenile Training School in Gatesville, which everyone knew—despite its euphemistic name—was a youth prison.

I should have been cautious, buying a package of Potter's at the pharmacy. The matrons, impatient to usher us to our matinee seats, hustled us out of Pipkin's. I didn't think nuthin about Hairbrush, tapping her foot, demanding, "What took so long, girls." When Celesta said innocently, "We were waiting on Mrs. Pipkin to ring up Ruby's—" I cupped my hand over her mouth before she spilled the beans.

What I didn't know was the coach had already decided on the culprit, and had already determined guilt.

CHAPTER THIRTY-TWO

The coach, whose shirt contained him like casing on link sausage, held my flame-scarred cigarette tin in one hand, twirling it, and his paddle in the other, tapping it against his leg. It was a hideous thing, rough-hewn of some dark-veined native hardwood, maybe hackberry, and cracked, its edges ragged. Holes near as big as pennies were drilled into it. The paddle looked oft-used, as powerful and big as the man's arm.

"I knew it was Red who started the barn fire." His eyes held nothing but meanness. "Now I know where he got his ammunition." He pointed at me, his finger so close to my chest I shrunk back in my chair.

I'd like to think I stayed mum because I meant to sass him, but truth told, I was too scared to make my lips move. I looked at Arnold, who always told me I had the storytelling gift after she graded my English essays; surely she would defend me. But she stayed silent in her chair before the superintendent's massive desk, her eyes fixed on the coach's hand as he slid my burnt Potter's tin across the polished desktop. The superintendent examined it carefully like he was handling the Hope Diamond. I held my breath, wondering what conclusions he could draw from a smoke-blackened tin that had rusted in the rain weeks after being scorched clean of color and identification by flames. Finally he set it on his desk with a hollow clunk and leaned back, his chair creaking.

"And this tells you what, Coach, someone's cigarettes started the fire?" the superintendent said. His face was impassive. "Whose?"

The coach's investigation found two at fault. "The younger Hubbard boy, Oris, was smoking in the barn with"—he pointed at me again— "Ruby Lee Becker." I jumped up to protest and Arnold slammed her arm across my chest to silence me.

The coach continued, "This tin held the cigarettes given to Ruby Lee by the night nurse. The nurse admitted as much."

Again I leapt up to explain. Arnold narrowed her eyes in warning. "You only speak when spoken to." She helped herself to the ruler on the superintendent's desk and slapped my hand hard enough to sting, and then looked to the superintendent for his approval.

She betrayed me that easy.

He nodded at my English teacher and turned to the coach. "This night nurse, she's been relieved of her duties, I understand."

"She was uppity. Insisted she knew more about medicine than me— what she prescribed to patients was nobody's business." The coach smirked, his stout chest swelled up with his confidence. "Yes. The head matron agreed. Gone. Good riddance."

"Well, I should have liked to speak with her," the superintendent mused. "This young Hubbard boy, Red, his name is Otis? He's behind the fire?"

"Oris Hubbard. The night of the fire, we couldn't find him. When the barn went up, he was in hiding, see, but he ain't gettin away with nothing. I've had eyes on him ever since; he's guilty, alright."

The superintendent raised his eyebrows. "He is? He confessed, then."

"Won't admit to it," the coach said. "Stubborn. Got twenty-seven licks from me when I took the strap to him, and he's still denying he done it. His only alibi is his brother, Clayton."

"The Hornets quarterback?" The superintendent looked queasy, appearing to think hard.

"And some of the team, they're backing up Clayton."

I said politely, "Sir. Please—"

The coach gripped my arm tight, his breath hot in my ear. "You're fixin for a bustin too—"

The superintendent cleared his throat, loud enough for the coach to release me. "Miss Arnold, take the child out."

"Nossir! Excuse me!" I set my mouth firm. "I'm waitin on Miz Wills! She'll vouch for me." I didn't budge.

The superintendent just tipped his head towards the door. Arnold had to drag me out while the coach continued his lies. "These delinquent brothers need to go to the reformatory in Gatesville" were the last words I heard him say before Arnold shut the door. She loosened her grip, that turncoat English teacher. I asked, "Where's Miz Wills?"

"She's tired of inferior children like you! Tired of no-account parents dumping their no-good kids on us!" I inched away. "Miz Wills went home to her own family. Why don't you."

I bolted into the night, flying faster than any airplane ever flew.

•   •   •

What little shut-eye I got was in the supply closet beside the social studies classroom. The click of Miz Wills's high heels preceded her arrival the next morning. She looked fresh, like she always did, her straw Scottie cap fitted over her tidy brown bob, her fingernails glossy with polish. She valued appearances, she told us, and we must also. We were exhorted to make the most of what we had to offer. First impressions, she lectured, mattered as much as what we had to say.

The muggy morning had yet to dampen the crispness of her swagger suit, but left me limp after my airless night in the closet. I ran my fingers through my hair, smoothing it, pressing out wrinkles creased into my smock, newly aware of my raggedy edges. Miz Wills said we had to value ourselves before others would.

I tried to stand taller.

I was afraid she wouldn't believe me, since I barely believed in myself, stuck in a place where endurance counted more than loyalty or love. The family I was part of in the State Home wasn't my own, but we were like brothers and sisters to each other and the big kids looked out for the littles. The adults called us *wards of the state*. They didn't talk to us like parents, and showed us little reason to trust 'em. We fended for ourselves; it was the only way to make it through.

Miz Wills would want me to find my own courage, and I wished I could, like the Lion found in the book we read about the wizard in Oz.

I wished for so much, in those hard times.

Placing her hat and pins on her desk, Miz Wills didn't look surprised to see me. "Good morning, Ruby. You're here so early you forgot to comb your hair. What's so important?"

"Yes, ma'am." My voice cracked. "There's a yellow jacket in the outhouse."

"In plain English, Ruby."

I hesitated. "Well, there's trouble goin on . . ."

"Trouble," she said, as if it was expected.

It was a relief to spit it all out. "Clay and Red, maybe even the team, are gettin sent to Gatesville, the night nurse got fired, Red didn't set the barn fire . . . and me, if the coach finds me, he'll whip me and send me away." I wiped my eyes where tears waited to spill. "To the state training school." I gulped at the prospect of Gainesville, where the worst girls were sent.

"Why, Ruby," she said, her voice gentle, "you can't be in that much trouble. I've heard from Miss Arnold what an imagination you have—"

"No ma'am!" I blurted out, not thinking. "You can't trust what she says!"

She frowned.

"Excuse me, ma'am, for being disrespectful . . ."

"Then what, Ruby." One of her eyebrows was arched like the Washington Avenue Bridge.

"I meant, I mean, it's j-just n-n-no, the coach is ly-ly-lying—" I stuttered like Mollie. "Miss Arnold—she doesn't understand . . . The superintendent, he believes Coach."

Miz Wills reminded me, confronting our fears is the best way to overcome them.

CHAPTER THIRTY-THREE

Getting things smoothed over took awhile. Miz Wills spoke up for me and reminded the superintendent the fire chief and police chief had the necessary expertise to determine the fire's cause and identify suspects. She thought the *Waco Tribune-Herald* would like to report the story of a coach who was a more capable investigator. That troubled the superintendent, should our talented quarterback and team be unjustly accused. Without a solid finding of guilt, he agreed, no more punishments should be doled out.

Afterwards, Miz Wills assured me I need not worry. She was as convinced of her belief as Mrs. Barton. "*Worry often gives a small thing a big shadow,*" I heard her matter-of-fact voice as Miz Wills patted my hand, saying, "Only the guilty have cause to worry."

Two days later, the superintendent delivered my punishment privately in his office, after his secretary left for the day: ten licks with his willow switch, hard enough to make me stifle my cries, just enough to put me in my place.

The coach, always administering licks, had his allies, among them Hairbrush and her bristle brush; Croucher, loyal to whoever buttered her bread; Arnold, slippery as a river rock; and the mean relief nurse, whose lips flapped when she was lying like a tombstone. The coach counted on certain dorm parents and the superintendent, who were thick as fleas on a farm dog.

They had me in their crosshairs so I gave 'em no further cause to catch me contravening the rules. My grades were all A-plus. I helped teachers tidy up after school. I volunteered for extra kitchen duty each night. I spoke to adults only when spoken to, a polite *ma'am* or a *sir*, never asking for nuthin from anyone. I was no trouble to anybody.

Even so, I was lucky the night nurse had a motivation of her conscience after being fired. Eventually she came forward on my behalf. She defended the medically approved benefits of asthma cigarettes for girls with wheezy lungs scarred by the dust pneumonia. And she scoffed at the notion the rusty, burnt tin had ever been mine, much less held my asthma cigarettes. She pulled out her own package of Elliotts in its green package, and a gold box of Potter's. She had a third box with red lettering, Asthmador Cigarettes. She set all three cardboard boxes in the superintendent's ashtray and lit a match.

"Here's what would have happened to Ruby's, if it was anywhere near the barn fire," she said with a fierce gaze at the coach. Before she could ignite the three packages, the coach leaned over and blew out the match.

"So much for your evidence. That all you got on her? Leave the poor kid alone. Ain't it enough she's gettin over the brown plague?"

Croucher stood and harrumphed. "I observed Ruby buying those same cigarettes in Pipkin's, on the field trip to Miss Holliday's matinee show."

My throat constricted and felt ticklish. I took that prompt to start up my coughing and wheezing. I doubled over and rocked myself in my chair, then leapt up and thrust my chest out, gasping, croaking, hacking.

The coach set his savage eyes on the nurse, then on me, and back to her. The nurse didn't flinch. She steered me to the open window where I gulped in fresh air and settled down.

The superintendent looked around the room at each of us, his face wrinkling in perplexity, mirroring a rodeo clown's.

He stood and began to utter a thought that must've escaped his addled mind before it could ever form.

He sat back down, then dismissed us with an impatient wave and immediately returned to his paperwork. Viola's dorm mother said something under her breath. *"Don't that beat all."* The coach crept out like a cornered coyote.

The nurse handed me an asthma cigarette as we turned for the door.

•   •   •

There were no findings from the fire and police investigations that would lead to charges. They considered it an accidental fire, case closed. The coach, though, never forgot. And never forgave.

Fall color came on, somber golds that went brown without the brilliance, and gave way to a bitter winter. I didn't see Red much, except on days when the bare trees were sketched like charcoal, bent against a slate sky. Red traipsed across the campus, hunkered into the wind, alone and looking so defeated he coulda carried a cross. His cheeks were hollow but if he was whistling, he managed without moving his lips. In the dining hall, there were continuous whispers about the Mauler administering fearsome bustings to the renegades in his dorm, Red among them. During that frost-bound season, news came in the *Tribune* of three runaways, two brothers and an older teen from the coach's dormitory which, to us, was confirmation of the rumors. Police had been alerted by State Home officials to be on the lookout for the eleven- and twelve-year-old brothers in brown jackets, and the teen boy in a plaid coat, after they left without notice in broad daylight. The teen had to be Red, one zig and a zag away from freedom each day he'd zigzagged the grounds in his hand-me-down plaid wool coat. I hoped it was a warm one.

That Christmas was another lonely one away from home. Mollie marked off another holiday without her mother on her 1936 wall calendar featuring the baby quintuplets, and started again in the new year. It would be New Year's of 1939 and the Dionne quints would be four, going on five, years old, as confined by that calendar as we were by the campus.

CHAPTER THIRTY-FOUR

WILLA MAE

The Duchess is writing to her lawyer, again, demanding a meeting to secure her release, or perhaps she's writing to friends in Dallas, pleading for their help. She writes regularly to the hospital superintendent and the state attorney general, proposing she be discharged. She never gets any replies, but she never tires of it—a habit I understand.

Because my many portraits of Ruby have been noted, I'm in demand by the patients and nurses, even a few doctors. I finish my portrait of the Duchess while she writes, dating it "*1938, Madeleine in the Asylum.*" Madeleine is an educated and well-traveled patient, perhaps twenty years my senior, who insists in her French accent she's been confined unjustly. Since she claims she descended from the fourth Maison d'Orléans, the nurses mockingly call her the Duchess, though it's a title that suits. There's something about her aloof air, an oft-disdainful manner, and her knowledge of fine art that makes me yearn for the art professor I studied with in 1917.

The Duchess rasps some pinkish phlegm into her lace-edged hankie—her cough having become habitual, and worrisome—and resumes writing her inquiries.

Miss O'Keeffe's doctor took her chronic cough seriously enough to send her away, like Beck later insisted we do with Ruby, but there's no such attention paid here to Madeleine's deteriorating condition. My hand trembles at the memory of losing Miss O'Keeffe as I take pen to diary.

The imperious woman of the classroom—dark hair swept to a topknot, her fists stuffed into the deep pockets of a knee-length tailored suit jacket over a crisp white shirtwaist, her full skirt skimming the tops of high laced boots, her impression severe—was sprawled immodestly across the porch floor of a new Craftsman bungalow clad only in a loosely tied katazome-stencil kimono of silk, barefoot and holding a stub of charcoal, transfixed by a train approaching from afar across the Staked Plains. Watercolor paintings, still wet in pools of rich hues, were laid about as if discarded in favor of a sketchpad over which her hand moved rapidly, her eyes never leaving the oncoming train.

This was the daring suffragette art professor with close ties to the founders of the National Woman's Party, rumored to support the women picketing the White House for the vote, who was the new head of the Art Department at West Texas State Normal College in Canyon. She'd already exhibited her colorful abstracts from Texas in a one-person show in New York City last April, a rare feat in an art world where few believed women were legitimate artists. She was the sole reason for my enrollment here as I turned seventeen.

By some sixth sense she summoned me onto her porch, pointing to a pack of cigarettes as she added shadows in broad sweeps to her landscape with the flat edge of her charcoal stick, her eyes focused solely on her drawing. "Evening, Willa, light us some Fatimas, will you. You must call me Georgia, by the way."

Red Mesa, *Miss O'Keeffe called her finished watercolor, showing me the abstract mesa painted in vivid brick-red with surrounding areas of blues, some splotches of gray-green at its orange base, the magazine-sized cream sheet barely containing its exuberance and tempered only by the sky rendered a hazy blue. She'd captured the shales my father would call the Quartermaster formation along the edge of Palo Duro Canyon, combined with less brilliant maroons, magentas, yellows; and outcrops of Triassic red beds higher in the wall, hinting at the Greer gypsum exposed below. Did my teacher know, I wondered, the names of the formations? I'd been taught them after my father returned to Chicago from his field surveys in Texas with specimens and fossils and maps, bursting to tell my mother of his discoveries. Quartermaster, Tecovas, Trujillo, Ogallala—formations I could have recited to Miss O'Keeffe. Names of exposed rock layers I repeated even as my mother, exasperated after his years of long absences followed by complex science lectures upon his return, had redirected her attention to her recital music. As my mother played Schubert and Debussy, practicing to become a concert pianist, I longed to take my pastels to paper but instead became his unwilling geology student.*

Excited, Miss O'Keeffe selected another of her watercolors to thrust at me, asking, "What do you think of this one, it looks like Hell let loose with a fried egg in the middle of it, doesn't it? I'm crazy about it. See how the evening star is visible even in the daylight?" We both looked up at the star—and I saw how she'd used sweeping curves of vibrant watercolor so simply and evocatively, as carefree as her own personae, a yearning I felt, too.

I accept my confinement here, trapped in the middle of nowhere, fenced in and surrounded by deep woods and a lake, with no bus service, no cash to my name, and wearing asylum clothing. It's odd, how content I am here with my art, in a way I couldn't be with Beck, ensnared in his dream.

I hear Beck's gravelly last words at the asylum entry. "It's for your own good, Willie. I'm sorry."

But he got it wrong—they all did. I wasn't driven mad by dust. I was driven to *my* dreams, and denied.

1939

CHAPTER THIRTY-FIVE

RUBY LEE

Some news out of the Panhandle set things in motion in 1939. The government's soil conservation expert in Amarillo, Mr. H. H. Finnell, said the Dust Bowl had shrunk to one-fifth of its original size in February, and in some places the soil was wet as deep as four feet down. Even more promising, things were in the best shape they'd been since 1932.

I spent that day and the next trying to remember the successes my momma and pa must have celebrated on our farm seven years ago. I'd been nearly seven that February, and was sure there were plenty, though I couldn't put my finger on any one thing.

•   •   •

Minus my twenty dollars, I had only one way home. I pulled on my overalls, jammed on a cap I'd found near the boys' dormitory—my hair newly cut and short enough to stay under it—and lifted my sack.

It was early on Sunday in March, and the campus was still quiet. The only activity beyond the gate was a messenger boy on a bicycle. He pedaled onto the campus to the administration building and hopped off his bike. He was a half-pint, maybe eight or nine, his Western Union cap sunk low enough to cover half his ears. His baggy uniform was belted tight and patched in a few spots.

"Who ya looking for?" I asked. "Main office is closed."

He read the superintendent's name from his Western Union envelope.

"Then you want the auditorium, there, go to the office backstage. He sets up early for church service." I pointed out the route through the trees. "Easier to run over."

"Thanks. I'm in a hurry—first day on the job."

When the double doors of the auditorium swallowed him up, I pedaled his bicycle lickety-split to the highway.

•   •   •

I crossed the river on the Suspension Bridge and pedaled up Elm Avenue, parking the bike beside a spanking-new Ford Deluxe parked at the Alamo Plaza Courts. The massive white complex took up a whole block with apartments for tourists and looked like our history book's pictures of the Spanish mission which hosted a famous Texas battle. I sat awhile on the front verandah's rocking chairs till the motel clerk shooed me away.

Somewheres along the Meridian Highway, a dark-skinned boy with a truckload of sweet potatoes stopped, said he was going to Mexia. I ditched the bike and hopped in. He saw me eyeing his raggedy dungarees and bare feet. "What you looking at, sister," he grunted.

"Nuthin." I smiled, big.

He let the scowl above his eyes ease. "Beg pardon. We're jes like most folks. Poor as rats." His grin showed uneven teeth, like half the kids at the Home.

We'd been poor as rats, too. "Like most folks, alright."

"But I got sweet potatoes to sell, and the CC boys at Camp Mexia got to eat."

We took a quick turn, and a dented trumpet rolled across the floorboard. I picked it up, the dull brass hot to the touch.

"Hey. Take care there. Gonna play Saturday night, the CCC's puttin on a dance."

"Like Count Basie?" The boy had the renowned band leader's wide amiable smile that was all teeth, except for his being broken and discolored.

"Ha. Gonna join the CC boys myself when I'm eighteen, get work in the quarry, three hots a day," he kept on. "There's a big dam goin in, right over the Navasota."

"Na-va-what?"

"The river. To make a lake at Fort Parker." He saw I was flummoxed.

"To the east, where the old fort was? The Injun raids where they scalped the men and carried off that little girl, raised her Injun. Don't they teach Texas history where you're from?"

I shook my head and his mouth formed a big round O at my ignorance.

"You ain't from around here. Where you headin anyway?"

I didn't say nuthin.

•   •   •

He left me off at the Elm Mott junction, where two hoboes strode westward, a tall man in a black hat carrying a strapped suitcase, and a shorter one in a western hat, bundle and bedroll slung over his shoulder. The sinking sun made their shadows sharp and long across the road. Up ahead, a billboard showed a well-dressed man, leaning back comfortably in a plush Southern Pacific seat. *Travel by train next time*, the billboard advised, in tall capital letters, *RELAX.* I got closer and realized the two men were scroungy boys, mostly skin and bones.

We arrived at a package house and sat in the shade. They talked of finding a Sally nearby to flop.

"A Sally?" That was a new one.

"Sure," said Mick, the taller one, removing his black hat to rub his hand over his head. "Sermons and sour stew?"

The other one, Tubbs, took in my boy's cap, overalls, and a jacket tied around my waist I'd pinched from the boys' laundry. He got real close, peering at me.

"You studying for a test?" I shoved him away.

"You a frill?" He looked pleased with himself. "Mick! She's a frill!"

"Neither of you smell so good. You ought to be looking for some Ivory soap."

"Salvation Army," Mick said. "At the Sally, they got soap. Well, sometimes newspaper for towels and cold water. But it beats a jungle. Let's see how you look without that cap."

I stood and lifted my cap. "You too." He obliged. I was seeing a growed-up young man who looked like Walter might have in a few years, if he hadn't given up his guitar for a harp, after he and his brother Carl showed up at Bess's back door. Who coulda been my older brother Earl, his eyes the same carefree and devilish ones, a born troublemaker, but more guarded. I got a craving for Snickers. And my brothers.

"You're cute as a bug's ear. You clean up, you'd do swell on the stem with a sob story, maybe some mush talk," Tubbs said. "If you could stand the gaff."

I shoved my cap back down on my head and tucked up what hair escaped, wondering what language he spoke.

In the package house I heard some shouting, and a tall tramp emerged in a hurry. "Hoof it, scram, hightail it, for cripes' sake!" He grabbed his suitcase and ran off like a rabbit to the hole.

We took off with him and rounded a corner to find ourselves in the small town of West.

"She's not a frill, Tubbs, just a swell kid," Mick huffed, panting, when we'd gone a ways.

"Huh. Where you from," the tall tramp said. "You come from Waco? I got a stepbrother there, in the orphan asylum. Elmer Joe Junior, ya know him?"

Mick had to haul me off that Tubbs tramp, I kicked and stomped and swatted at him, like a frill, Tubbs said, which made me even madder. He dragged me off, the Czechs watching us like the outsiders we were.

"I'm hungry. Let's find some grub." I settled my cap on tight.

They led the way, like they knew where we were going, which was more than I knew. At Nemecek Brothers Meat Market we walked around back and Mick pushed me forward to the door. "Ask for dog meat scraps. Say you got a sick mother and lot of sisters at home, starving. Also a mutt."

It worked like a charm, and away we waltzed with a ring of fresh Czech sausages. The scraps, the butcher said in halting English. We fell upon them, and the puffy sweet jam- and cream-filled kolaches we had rummaged from the garbage bins behind Kapavik's Bakery before we set off for the M-K-T depot. The strains of some lively squeezebox music came from the Czech Corner till a train's whistle drowned it out. Mick said, "There's grub at the mission and a flop at the relief station. C'mon."

Tubbs pointed at the tallest steeple in a town full of 'em. "St. Mary's. The Sisters are serving Lobster Thermidor with steamed asparagus in truffle sauce. Hungry, toots?" They laughed at how big my eyes got.

"Those Sisters gonna eat you up with a spoon, cute l'il June bug like you." That got a guffaw outta Tubbs.

The gang of tramps who'd rolled off the freight train before it jerked to a stop shuffled along behind us, their baggy wore-out trousers dragging over their split-soled shoes, hands shoved in pockets, or whistling, or tugging a hat down over sheepish eyes. The slouch of a tall boy looked familiar, and then the whole gang did. They looked alike the way Carl, Walter, Whitey and the boxcar boys, the 'bo at the Brazos, even Mick and Tubbs, all resembled one another. Aimless. Adrift. Aged beyond their years.

•　　•　　•

Tubbs wanted to hit the stem awhile.

"We'll make our fortune." He squinted, casing the street, up and back. "The cops ain't glimming."

I shook my head. "Not gonna beg."

"Proud, are ya? You'll get over it," Tubbs laughed, short and harsh. Mick was shaking down a proper lady entering West Drug and earned a few dimes. He mouthed, "Baby's getting new shoes!" Tubbs trotted after a fresh-shaved man exiting the barber shop.

The train track ran beside the west side of the street; a locomotive waited at the coaling station, giving off steam heat in bursts, smoke billowing from the wheels; the hissing and screeching of brakes still echoed in my ears. Under the coaling tower its tender took coal from the chute like a hungry behemoth. A barrel-chested man with thick shoulders and big arms stood ready to shovel the coal. Freight cars stretched into the distance, more than I could count and I gave it up. I wandered Main Street while Mick and Tubbs went after their small change. What shop windows weren't soaped up, I peered in, drawn to the round awning at Best Theatre. *Held Over!* read the marquee over *The Wizard of Oz* poster. Far from home, Dorothy looked troubled and the Lion tentative, both unaware their harrowing journey would end happily. They must not have read the book.

Dark was coming on fast, with Mick and Tubbs nowheres to be seen. I skedaddled towards the tall steeple, St. Mary's with its mission. A hobo fell in step beside me with the familiarity of the pack of lost boys fleeing the train. "You're a long ways from home, little sister. Last time I saw you, Waco was flooding."

I turned to him. "Carl?"

"Guilty as charged. Got any Snickers?"

I busted out laughing.

"Ruby Lee, right? You look different."

"You do too. You need a shave."

He rubbed at his cheek self-consciously. "And a haircut . . . and a shoeshine. Got two bits? What're ya doing here?"

"Going home," I said brusquely, to hide my uncertainty. "Ain't that what we're all doing?"

CHAPTER THIRTY-SIX

When I woke up after midnight surrounded by the restless breathing of strangers on pallets around me, the air was still and stifling. I was stuck, tangled in rough blankets, swirling back to the home that wasn't mine, spiraling like the northern wind that delivered red New Mexico dirt to Hartless, dropped yellow Kansas soil on the Panhandle, and blew gray Oklahoma silt into our lungs. Spinning in the black blizzard that took Granny Alma, baby Nell, and me from my momma.

I gasped, my nightmare as real as the coffin air that choked me on Black Sunday.

The St. Mary's Sisters saw through me in between their sermons and stew. Their suspicious questions after supper stoked my worries into nightmares. They'd figured me for the runaway I was, homeless and recently of the State Home for Dependent and Neglected Children in Waco.

Sure enough, by breakfast the next day the superintendent was there in his Graham-Paige Supercharger to retrieve his wayward charge. My heart sank like every stone I'd ever tried to skip.

Carl got a whiff of me being wanted and dogged it outta there, his uneaten bowl of watery porridge still steaming on the table. "After Walter, I made myself a promise. No more partners." He'd abandoned me so easy.

The superintendent's specious smile was for the Sisters at the mission. The switch was reserved for me. I knew what would come next. After a silent drive back, with me stuck in his back seat eyeing the slender willow switch, he'd strong-arm me to his office, close the door, and give me my licks.

And I'd refuse to count them, to allow him that authority.

The shame would linger longer than the sting, boring its way to the surface unexpectedly.

I walked amiably enough with him to his car, and once he opened the door, I landed a solid kick at his fly. I squirmed for a split second when my foot made contact. Then I sprinted for the tracks.

•　　•　　•

Past the depot the Katy was building up steam, making momentum while I ran alongside it, waiting for my courage to boost me aboard. The whistle blew in haunting deep chords as the wheels kicked into a *chuka-chuka* racket to remind me about the fate that befell poor Walter. I dared not look at those deadly black wheels. I kept my eyes on the loaded cars passing by more rapidly now, looking for a safe way up. The superintendent was breathing down my neck, I was sure of it, though I didn't dare make time to look. Over the hissing of the steam that shot out around me, I heard a sudden hoot from someone who stuck a hand out from a boxcar door. I lunged for the offer, felt hands on my arms as my feet left the ground. I kept my eyes shut till I was sure I'd been dragged aboard, feeling the rough planks tearing at my dungarees and the release of the hands gripping me tight. I looked cautiously back at the West depot, now a blur in the distance, imagining the superintendent's pique.

"What're you smiling for," the owner of the strong hands asked, a worldly looking sort of uncertain age who wore the road on his face along with several layers of shirts and coats on what was a gaunt frame, all in need of a scrubbing. "You about took the Westbound back there."

"This train's heading north." I was puzzled. I'd studied the train routes for as many years as I'd read the forecasts in the *Farmer's Almanac*. The M-K-T carried cotton, crude oil, and paying passengers to Fort Worth. From there, I could ride it to practically the Oklahoma border—Sherman, where I'd catch a train west across the Panhandle and on home.

"New at this, aren't ya." He smiled ruefully. "Drag your feet a split second too long, you'll get sucked under the wheels. I seen 'em turned into ground round."

If he meant to spook me, he'd never know it from my poker face.

I scooted away from the open doors as the train shifted in a quick swerve, jolting me sideways.

He nodded. "Now you're catching on. Seen the new ones lose legs at the knees, dangling them out the open boxcar doors."

I pushed myself back further to lean against the wall. The creosote-infused smell, the splintering wood, the stink of unwashed hoboes took me back to the crowded boxcar on the rainy night the Brazos flooded. Where I'd encountered Carl, friendly then, absent Walter.

"Thank you for lending a fella a helping hand."

He let a slow grin play at his mouth. "Never forget you're not a paying customer, young fella"—he emphasized *fel-lah*— "the bulls'll toss you off like any old sack of flour. Or do worse."

Not wanting to let on I was a girl, I kept my thoughts to myself.

We approached Fort Worth. To steer clear of the railroad bulls, he said, we oughta bail out before the depot. I could wait on the next freight north in the side yard. He was catching out for Kilgore, to join the East Texas oil field roughnecks on easy street. He pulled a crumpled dollar bill from one of his many pockets.

"For a rainy day, little brother." I hesitated, then made to shake his hand.

That would make nineteen bucks more I'd need, since Will's rainy day money had been liberated from me by Viola's cousin.

"Go on." He shoved the dollar in my palm. "I'll be rolling in the dough soon enough."

Flustered, I thanked him. He motioned toward the side yard. "Stay in the shadows till you see your chance to catch out. And be careful. Don't trust nobody."

CHAPTER THIRTY-SEVEN

WILLA MAE

Madeleine has been scrutinizing my diary entries and the color pencil drawings I make to keep Georgia's watercolors alive. *Evening Star*—the one she'd painted many times—her various versions of *Blue*, her nude self-portraits. "To keep your memories alive, you say?" Madeleine's palm lays gently on my shoulder. She darts a glance around the empty room, holds back a cough, and whispers to me, "Your memories are intact, my dear, do not worry."

After sharing a ride from campus with one of Miss O'Keeffe's suitors, in his loud yellow car—open, the wind blowing, the way she liked it—she led her art students to the canyon edge. "This wide, wide land is like an ocean, so vast, let's walk it together." The students carried palettes and pads, dressed in tunics over their long cylinder skirts. We'd both worn what I came to think of as her uniform—white shirtwaists with sleeves rolled up and voluminous scarves tied loosely around our necks, our cloche hats pulled down on our heads against the eternal wind, our cuffed jeans swiping at the tops of our laced boots. In Canyon, the provincial townspeople chanced judgmental looks at her, but she was embraced on the college campus. Her colleagues respected her. Her students appreciated her affinity for their struggles, having a hard time going to college and paying the bills. She respected them, and they did her. She was alert, quiet, patient, and well-liked by her students, who followed her advice about dressing to suit our shapes. Though none emulated her every movement, action, and wardrobe selection as I did, signing up for the National Woman's Party and even risking unchaperoned automobile rides with male students. Her very actions gave us permission to free ourselves. I was drawn to her man-like independence and of course to her artistic spirit.

She wanted to cut her hair short but was warned she might lose her job, she'd told the class, complaining, they're trying to make everybody alike. She disapproved of the locals' patriotic fervor to wipe Germany off the map and send their own young men off to do the job. "Like sending the cattle to market," she scorned.

I liked how forthright she was, but other students, all local or from nearby towns between Dalhart and Lubbock, looked thunderstruck. "Scandalous, isn't it, to speak one's mind?" She posed the question for class discussion.

As we walked, I pulled off my hat to show her how I'd cut my hair below my earlobes in solidarity. There were a few gasps but Miss O'Keeffe nodded, approving. "It suits you."

Last week she'd shocked us with a model stripped to his skivvies for the life drawing segment of our instruction. After we'd endured endless classes on costume, interior design, and advertising illustration—the commercial end of the business, she called it, how we'd make a living—we were to concentrate on form and shape. An unfamiliar quiver took hold from my heart to my hips as I concentrated on his muscular shape and chiseled form, and though its heat wasn't unpleasant, I had difficulty selecting from my Conté crayons to begin sketching. Miss O'Keeffe, however, seemed utterly at ease near the unclothed young man, tracing sections of his anatomy with a finger hovered inches above his skin as she lectured on figure drawing methods. He maintained an unflappable countenance but for his eyes, which danced when hers met his.

Later that afternoon, gathering my books to walk to my dorm, a melody familiar to me from my mother's enthusiastic piano practice sessions filled the hallway. I walked toward the music classroom and peered into the rehearsal space. Miss O'Keeffe was seated at the piano, her head at a cant, eyes closed, her fingers flying over the ivories.

When she critiqued my work the next day, she said I had a natural knack for capturing anatomy on paper and I'd likely be tempted to focus on portraiture. But it would be a waste of my talents to pursue the traditional art path so many chose. Instead I must explore the abstract—look for spatial movement and dynamism, try to express the harmony and rhythm of music on paper, show its dissonance. You can translate music into art, she explained, showing me a charcoal drawing she'd made a few years earlier, From Music.

Now at the canyon the wind lifted her hat like a tumbleweed and she barked, "This wind blows like mad!" She ran for it, kicking up dust and laughing, "This wonderful great big sky—there is so much of it! Let's paint this view. Think about how you'll divide the space on your paper; look at the vivid oranges and reds and exaggerate them to convey their shapes." We plunked ourselves down by some scraggly locust bushes. I turned toward her profile and began to sketch her as she took in the long stretches of white and sand-colored and greenish-gray cliffs marking the start of the Palo Duro—the Grand Canyon of Texas, the students called it—which Miss O'Keeffe referred to as a curious slit in the plains.

That would have amused my father, who'd joined the covered wagon geologist Dr. Charles Newton Gould to investigate the geology and underground water resources west of Indian Territory and east of the Rocky Mountains, including the water sources of the Canadian River drainage area in the Texas Panhandle. Their field party traveled by horseback and covered wagon in 1903 and 1904 for the United States Geological Survey, and in 1905 they'd explored and prepared a geological map of Palo Duro Canyon, giving names to the formations.

And now Dr. Gould's men were at it again, as my father led a plane-table survey party along the breaks of the Canadian, searching for oil among the anticlines—the domes they'd noted on their first trip fourteen years ago.

I could have given Miss O'Keeffe a lesson in geology as we sketched the terrain that day in 1917, but instead I invited her to accompany me to Amarillo, where we'd be my mother's guests for her piano recital at the Grand Opera House.

The seat reserved for my father remained unoccupied for my mother's recital, as I'd feared. My mother had said its purchase was a waste, but she'd relented after my pleading. Miss O'Keeffe was polite enough not to comment. She lifted her mother of pearl opera glasses to gaze upon the pianist on stage, whose fortissimo had enthralled Miss O'Keeffe at first sight during an Amarillo recital. While Bach's "Chromatic Fantasia and Fugue" made me tearful, as usual, Miss O'Keeffe's face was intense with concentration. She was enchanted by my mother's romantic renditions of Schumann's "In the Evening" and Debussy's "Toccata." Liszt's Mephisto *waltz, one of my favorites, brought the packed house to its feet. My mother glowed as she took a bow and accepted the well-earned applause, her gaze falling on the empty seat beside me.*

Alma Wentworth, my mother, was born in Chicago in 1877 to a society ingenue and a lawyer who was a partner in several businesses. The only child of a wealthy couple, she was well educated and well traveled and inherited the musical talent of her grandfather, a symphony violinist and music composer. Her talent at the piano was nurtured; she attended the Oberlin Conservatory of Music. When she fell in love, though, her musical career was derailed. She met my father, Daniel Wilhelm Eckhart, in 1897 at the Field Columbian Museum in Chicago where sixty-five tons of fossils from Wyoming's Upper Jurassic beds were on exhibit. The whole country was excited by the discoveries of dinosaur hunter Dr. Barnum Brown, who would unearth the first skeleton of a Tyrannosaurus rex *five years later, and my mother was no exception. But for my father, whose passion was terrestrial vertebrates in the Permian period, securing a spot to study the huge fossils with Brown's mentor would quench his thirst for vertebrate paleontology, and later lead to geological exploration. Daniel always claimed the chance encounter with Alma was love at first sight, but as my mother would realize during childbirth in Chicago while he was somewhere in the Tahlequah quadrangle of the Cherokee Nation, his pursuit of rocks and minerals would always come first. Like he'd been for my birth in 1901, Daniel was overdue again.*

CHAPTER THIRTY-EIGHT

RUBY LEE

A whole flock of dusty road kids and unshaved hoboes flew out from the shadows thick as blackbirds on a line, hopping on the roofs, the decks, the cushions, the flatcars, in the boxcars and the reefers, even crowding in-between cows in the cattle cars. Nobody paid me any mind as I flipped a rattler, busy as the yards were with crews loading crates and switching cars.

I followed a boy in oversized duds up the grab irons to the rooftop of a boxcar, watching him unfasten his long belt, loop it twice around the catwalk rail, and buckle it up again. "You'll want to get yourself a big man's belt, if you're fixin to deck the train," he said.

With a jerk and a waffle the train lurched ahead faster.

"I take your point," I said. "Got any extra there for me?"

He told me to belly over to him and he'd lash me up too. He unbuckled another belt from around his waist, slid it off, and hooked me up, too.

He introduced himself over the clamor the train was making. "They call me Belts!"

I couldn't say nuthin for the racket.

We laid there hip to hip as the train gained speed, plumes of black smoke blasting from the stack back into our faces. I squinted till I had to shut my eyelids tight against the wind.

"Ouch!" I exclaimed, wiping at my forehead and cheeks, bit by cinders blowing back and becoming blinded. I heard his laugh over the racket.

"You'll need a wet bandana if you're gonna make a career outta this." He extended his arm and yanked his flapping jacket over my head, but no sooner he'd offered me cover, the brakes squealed and the train slowed.

"There's a curve ahead; c'mon, follow me down into a boxcar," he said as he quickly unbuckled us. The mighty train groaned and creaked to a crawl as we took the curve. I climbed down the irons after him, dangling there, watching him stretch one arm and a leg for the boxcar door while he coiled to shove off. I shut my eyes and prayed.

When I dared open them again, he was gone.

He musta landed inside the car, cause I didn't see him greasing the tracks.

I stretched my arm till I could reach no further and was more than a foot away from the opening. My leg made it a little further. The train was nearly done rounding the curve, rattling and picking up speed again. Belts stuck his head out and reached for my hand. I sprung myself off the irons, clasping his hand and landing inside on top of a pile of hoboes who'd hauled me in like a sack of potatoes across the splintered wood floor.

By then our boxcar was rattling fearsomely, tearing through cotton and wheat fields, jostling us together and muzzling conversations into fragments that came forth in loud bursts. We were a motley bunch of road kids, boxcar boys, harvest tramps, and older train-hoppers who called themselves knights of the road. Some introduced themselves by their road names, Gondy Galahad, Kansas Clay, Peg-Leg Al, Sammy Spats, Flatcar Floyd, and told how they got their hobo monikers. Belts got a big laugh when he opened his jacket and showed off six strapped round his waist. While they talked of where they were from, I closed my eyes. They talked of the bad luck and the hard times and the big trouble putting them on the bum, riding the rails, tramping from town to town, and I jammed up my ears. Their sob stories weren't any easier to tolerate than the ones I already knew by heart from the State Home. They toted their belongings in embroidered pillowcases, torn army haversacks, unraveled burlap feed bags, rank-smelling rolled-up blankets. I held my potato sack of belongings tight to my chest like a shield—against their tired faces, their dirt-smeared and hollow cheeks, their dead eyes, their plight. Maybe I looked the same to them.

Boredom soon overtook us. The flatness and fallow fields were monotonous. When we saw a gang digging irrigation trenches, we waved wildly at the Works Progress Administration laborers. "Lucky to be leaning on their shovels," a smart-alecky hobo said of the WPA men, to rueful chuckling.

Welcome to Denton, a sign read, 1846.

The train slowed as we approached the town's outskirts, where a tangle of tracks peeled off into warehouses, outbuildings, and a soaring grain mill topped by the Morrison's Peacemaker Flour sign. Then Denton divided itself neatly into a college town of prosperous frame houses where abundant roses bloomed in every yard to our west; and east of the tracks, the colored section where tiny swept yards were overtaken by overalls and aprons hung on the lines.

That much was the same in Waco—the divides. The Brazos River made the divide convenient, given the geography: cross the Suspension Bridge to the flood-prone section of Waco called Bridge Street, where colored students walked to A. J. Moore School on South First Street, while in the Silk Stocking District of Waco where Bess had lived, white students took busses to the Sanger Street School. The public burial grounds, Greenwood Cemetery, had a white section and a colored section, separated by a cyclone fence. The whites had their own fountain at the Montgomery Ward downtown, and across the river, Negroes had the Gem, the exclusive colored theatre on Bridge Street. The Pullman cars had sections for whites and sections for coloreds, and so did the railroad station waiting rooms. The soda fountains and the streetcars divided us by our colors. The county fairs had a free day for the colored children, a free day for the white children.

The fairs had yet another day for the orphans. Everyone assumed we were unwanted, and had no families. But we had homes, and families waiting there for us, eager to have us back when the hard times were over.

Their faces appeared in my mind. Lonesome as I was feeling, I got sentimental for them—Viola, Celesta, Clare, Red and Clay, Mollie, little Dolores, Emma Sue, Kitty, Thelma, the boys in the barn, the football gang— family, all of them. We were family, not by choice, but hitched together nonetheless, and divided, too, from our real homes and real families.

CHAPTER THIRTY-NINE

The lone Negro hobo in the boxcar got talkative, pointing to landmarks he claimed to know well, his bone-thin fingers sketching out the lay of the land.

"Grew up here, can't make a living here," he said, adjusting his crooked specs. "Passing through's all this old boy do." His name was Frederick, still had family here. He pulled off his specs to clean them—or perhaps wipe at his teary eyes. He readjusted his specs back on his nose but the hairline crack in the right eye glass had widened, threatening to pop out of the frame.

We unloaded to wait out the switching and stretch our legs. Frederick squinted through his cracking specs at me, said he was off to see an aunt who made fine biscuits. "I'll bring ya some leftovers."

Two men decided they'd batter the stem, having discerned a lead by interpreting the mysterious hobo symbols marked in chalk around the rail yard.

I yanked a coarse wood splinter from my leg without a yelp, and rubbed at it till it bled.

Frederick returned as the train made ready to leave Denton, where the state college women with well-heeled daddies studied literature, languages, domestic arts, business education, the sciences, and lived in spacious, brick, vine-covered buildings built along modern classical lines, surrounded by a grove of oaks, berry gardens, lily pools, lagoons, flower beds, and orchards. The train signaled the outbound whistle and we flocked back to the cheap seats.

"Ought not fuss at that scrape." Frederick dropped two biscuits in my lap. "Gonna make it worse. Next stop's Whitesboro."

Just a whistle-stop, the seasoned hoboes agreed. Better chance of catching out for home if I kept on to Gainesville, since I was headed west.

That was home to the Texas State Training School for Girls, a dressed-up name for the juvenile delinquency reform school, as every State Home kid knew. The superintendent would have put the word out to the Texas Rangers to look out for a female runaway of my description. They'd deliver me straight to reform school, which they ran like a jail. Where they chained the no-good girls to the beds and served inedible swill, practically starved 'em to death. Where wardens loaned the girls out to local farmers on work crews in their fields. Or worse.

Where they'd lock me up and throw away the key—as Hairbrush had often decreed to any unruly girl. I didn't doubt her for a minute.

Even dressed as a boy, there wasn't a snowball's chance in hell I'd risk going near Gainesville. I preferred a through train, I told the tramping travel guides wearing raggedy secondhand clothes and kicks with cardboard soles.

A handful snickered but Frederick signaled an okay. A hobo with a wolfish grin leered at me and I paid close attention to my biscuits. "You wanna deadhead, you'll have to backtrack, thumb a ride east, or walk; it's not too far to Sherman," he said. "Catch the Katy Flyer straight on to Wichita Falls, nonstop."

●　　●　　●

We neared Whitesboro. The gang of us ditched the train when the M-K-T depot was in sight. They'd speculated it was a hot freight yard and weren't taking chances with the railroad bulls. Been known to use saps, and worse, on freelance passengers like us. I was in no hurry to meet bulls, nor saps, whatever they were, and I leaped off too. I hit the grit palms first, dragging my wounded leg across the cinders, and cussed. The splinter scab opened up and blood soaked through my pants. I rubbed at it to stop the bleeding, dragging myself from the tracks.

Frederick lent me a hand up and his dirty bandana, shoving his cracked specs up higher on his nose. They were permanently crooked.

I held his bandana there till a scab crusted over. The hoboes discussed the limited possibilities of working the stem in a railroad station stop without one.

"City of the Divide," Frederick mumbled to no one in particular. "Rain falls on the south side of Main Street; it drains into the Trinity."

His bandana was red with my blood and he told me to keep it.

"The rain fallin on the north side, off she goes to the Red River."

He pointed toward Oklahoma but nobody paid him any mind.

"We can jungle up behind the coal yards," a lanky hobo pointed past the coaling tower straddling the tracks, its chute filling a hopper amidst plumes of black soot.

That didn't look too appealing.

"A hobo jungle," Frederick explained. "Where we can camp, cook us a Mulligan stew."

Even less appealing. My belly was empty. "Thanks anyways. I'll take my chances at the depot."

"Gonna ride the cushions?" Belts said. "Lucky lady—lad—if you got the do-re-mi."

Everyone looked me over carefully, likely making me for a frill.

Another hobo shared a wink with the leering hobo. I deepened my voice. "No partners for me. That's my policy." Like Carl said.

"Would ya look at that, a real Robinson Crusoe. Got policies to go with the petticoats," the winker smirked.

The leering hobo cleared his throat. "No fraternizing with the coloreds, neither."

The hoboes got real quiet, eyes darting to Frederick. He blinked once behind his cracked spectacles, fists clenched, still as a statue.

After the leering hobo slow-rolled his eyes over them, taking everyone's measure, they landed on Frederick. His big frame vibrated, he was that tense for trouble. He took one step forward. The hoboes groaned, shook their heads.

I sucked my mouth dry, balling up a big wad of saliva, and spit it out impressively at his feet.

Enough laughter ensued to make the wolf-eyed hobo turn red. Frederick regarded me through his cracked spectacles with awe and admiration thrown in. Belts emitted a sound, part cackle, more whistle.

"Moxie," Frederick said low. "You got it."

I made my voice deeper. "Don't let me hold you fellas up."

Belts said so long and joined the hoboes tramping off for their coal jungle. He elbowed the leering hobo who'd merged in. I hooted. Frederick began to laugh, and I did too, then his got bolder, booming, and mine followed his lead, till we both balled over in belly-whoops.

It took a while to laugh out the relief we felt.

"Lookit, Frederick, I got to get along. On my own, no offense."

"None taken. Keep the peace. 'Spect you can take care of yourself."

I mumbled some thanks for the bandana and biscuits.

"Made with Peacemaker Flour." He gave me a two-finger V-sign, and I lit a shuck for the Katy's expansive red-brick depot.

Whitesboro may have prospered in its day with both the M-K-T and the T&P serving the cotton, corn, and wheat farms, but drouth had dried the fields, and except for the train yards' bustle, it was a forlorn tear-down town. Like Hartless might could be.

The harsh sun etched the depot against a cornflower-blue sky. Inside the cool waiting room no one waited. My footsteps echoed as I crossed the tile. The station agent gave me the stink eye but no more heed. I studied the timetable map and set out, figuring on a half-day's walk.

The constant wind made me clamp my hat down. The temperature was brisk but the sun would warm me while I followed the T&P tracks. I could make Sherman by sundown.

Frederick's parting words echoed on the wind.

"You keep pickin at a wound, it ain't never gonna heal."

CHAPTER FORTY

My shadow kept me company till mid-afternoon and I stopped to rest in the shade of the only tree I'd seen for miles. I'd passed drained stock tanks where no cattle gathered, Farmalls rusting and useless in thirsty pastures. Remnants of crops browned in fallow fields, dotted black with crows. If ever a farmhouse loomed, I scanned for signs of life but instead saw weed-grown grave plots, sagging buildings that were paint-stripped and grayed, shutters dangling from busted windows. Torn screen doors struggled to flap in the sluggish breeze. Even the windmills had quit turning.

I savored the biscuits, refusing to allow our farm was in the same sorry state.

As quick as the air stilled around me, crows surged up in a V and winged it dead ahead. Low clouds scuttled in and the temperature plunged. The horizon turned steely blue, darkening with erratic wind gusts swirling around me. The shock of cold air braced me for what I saw when I wheeled around.

A red sun augurs a bad day, Pa's pragmatic voice in my ear. *Dust-storm weather.*

The sun in the west was a red orb. The wind came on fast, whipping up a sky-high wall of dark dirt. The rolling black cloud whistled shrilly, blotting out daylight, tumbling relentlessly and towering higher as it bore down on me.

It was black as sin.

I let out a belly's worth of air, not daring to breathe till I covered my mouth and nose with the bandana. I felt my throat constrict. It was too late to find cover in one of the abandoned farmhouses, too dark to even see my hand in front of my face.

I can't see my hand. It was Pa, addled and woeful during that awful Black Sunday at church. I crawled blindly for the tracks, hoping I'd feel them before they got buried in silt.

The shrill whistling came again—it pierced through the pitching wind, came regularly in blasts. I felt frantically for railroad ties. A dim light glowed intermittently, hazy in the inky blackness—a beacon to crawl towards. I moved gingerly on my knees, extending a hand to wildly grope at earth disappearing in the dark. The surface was hardpan, the feel of it thorny, crunchy, pebbly, and yielding no clues until I shrieked at a wood splinter forcing itself into the fleshy thick of my hand.

Quick as a wink I forgot my pain. I'd found the tracks. I trudged near-blind through the black blizzard, my toes seeking the wood crossties under the drift, trying not to notice my constricting lungs, counting *one-two*, breathing *one-two*, dust swallowing me, strangling me, so blinding I blinked till tears came, and I shouted till my lungs near burst, *one-two! One! Two!* Aiming for what I hoped was a locomotive headlamp, my heart sinking when it dimmed, and swelling when it glowed again.

The storm shrieked over my shouts, scattering my numbers and along with them, my confidence. Sand bit at my ears, my brow, my fingers, prying at my efforts to still my panic. The familiar wheezing breaths began with my heartbeat quickening, then the pin-prickling crept over me and heated my skin. I cupped my hands over my eyes, focused on the glow of the light, steady, then dimming.

The black blizzard grew too dense. I couldn't see the light at all.

I ran but quickly stumbled, fell, pushed myself up, and willed myself to slow down. I extended my left arm out, waiting to feel the locomotive's cold steel, taking one careful footstep after the next in the pitch dark, kicking at the tracks to keep myself aligned with the rail.

It was blacker than midnight under an iron skillet.

Over the wind's drone a piercing whistle blasted, then another, and a third. I jumped out of my skin, raced for the sound, and was stunned backwards by something so impenetrable it could only be the hard steel of a locomotive. My forehead stung where I'd made contact. I crouched, moving slowly around it, touching the cinders edging the steel rail, my hand circling the lead wheels, the big drivers, the trailing wheels and on to the tender, counting its four wheels, feeling my way along the length of the train, imagining each tank car and gondola but sensing no haven. Till I felt the rough board-and-batten that signaled a boxcar. I hammered on the doors with what power I had, shouting to be let inside, hearing no response. I moved on to a second boxcar, then another, so many I lost count and sank to the cinders, exhausted, hacking up phlegmy dirt clods. My chest burned. I couldn't get a deep breath.

I pulled myself up by the grab irons and forced myself forward, certain I'd find someone in the caboose, sure I saw the glow of window lamps. My breathing came in shallow huffs. I was dizzy. Maybe the lights were the mirages thirsty people see, lost in the desert. I was swirling in the blackness again, out of my mind, choking, drowning in dust, and then dragging myself up steps to a shimmering lamp and had hold of a door handle when I tumbled into the light.

CHAPTER FORTY-ONE

WILLA MAE

A blue norther whistles in with a deluge of rain, the wind shaking the asylum windows, and the memories surface—the dark ones I keep at bay by making my portraits of Ruby. I pester the staff for sharper pencils, another notebook, the words coming faster than the writing supplies.

1925. For nearly five years, the rains were steady enough we ignored an occasional sandstorm, paying no mind to that harbinger of black blizzards to come. Back east there'd been a stock market crash, but we didn't feel it till the next year when signs went up on the grain elevators: No Wheat Accepted. The Depression arrived here hand in hand with the dusters and drouth in 1930. The next year, we couldn't make a crop. By 1933, there were days we accepted Doc Lawler's charity, standing in line for beans alongside the jobless vagrants he served at his soup kitchen. "Pride won't keep hunger at bay," I observed to Beck.

The portrait classes I taught in a small meeting room in the library brought in no money—who could afford anything beyond the necessities?—but my half-dozen students were grateful and paid me in sacks of flour, preserved fruit, beans, sometimes fresh eggs. Enough to help feed us without charity. Until Beck discovered me modeling for my students, partly unclothed—and was so angered, he kicked everyone out.

A nurse interrupts, the bell's been ringing for supper and I haven't heard it. The ward has emptied out and the silence suits me. No, I shake my head. She grabs my arm. *No!* I push her away, turning on her and feeling my teeth bared in rage. She backs out, mutters about reporting me.

After the bank failed—our life savings swept away like so much sand blow—I acquainted myself with Mrs. Stewart at the state relief office. She agreed to keep it from Beck when I applied for the dole; she knew plenty of farmers too proud to take President Roosevelt's government handout. Their wives, on the other hand, became very pragmatic when faced with their children's hunger.

Fallow fields were swept into the blizzards of loose topsoil, every duster succeeded by worse. The dust storms turned fatal. Babies' lungs were sand-clogged and elders couldn't get a breath of clean air. Starving cattle dropped dead from dust fever.

The sticky dirt in our children's hair was perpetual; grit coated every rooftop and penetrated every bedroom, kitchen, and table in town; we ate it unintentionally. We breathed the suffocating fine silt; we choked it up; we blew black snot into our handkerchiefs. Then came a month of dusters, one a day, where we barely saw the sun. So many blinding dust blows we lost count—until that swirling high wall of black silt slammed Hartless on April 14, 1935, and we couldn't even bury our dead. Beck's voice of doom, I can't see my hand . . .

My sketches and paintings have become gloomy, brooding re-creations of the years of maddening, inescapable dust I endured . . . and for what? The man I trusted deceived me, abandoning me here. I count my losses: my husband, my beloved children, my absent father and dear mother, my home, my art, my self-worth, my sanity, unable to stop, over and over I count. The doctors eye me suspiciously, readying their Metrazol syringes.

CHAPTER FORTY-TWO

RUBY LEE

I was delirious. I couldn't stop coughing. I counted, panic rising. Cool hands soothed me, propped me up against downy thick pillows, laid a warm moist towel upon my chest—*am I home, oh yes I am home—she stands so tall above me she has aged something awful, oh help me breathe, Momma, this dust is strangling me, let me sleep I'm so tired—I never meant to hurt Nell I didn't want Bess to die I miss Granny Alma—why did you send me away*

My eyes fluttered open to dust motes hanging where daylight streamed in. The view was obscured by smeary windows. I took note of my surprising surroundings: a small wood-paneled parlor, mahogany walls curving into the ceiling, a daybed with an upholstered headboard and footboard. On the floor, a thick-woven rug; at the windows, sateen drapes cinched with velvet togs. Plush velvety lounge chairs, the color of red wine, were bolted to the floors, polished tables between them, and a small davenport built into the wall. I squinted at the hazy window in the door where I had tumbled inside. Then it came rushing back—the black blizzard of dust I was sucking down my windpipe, blinded, groping for a door and finding a Pullman car.

At the other end of the lounge, a very tall woman sat at a desk, picking at a typewriter erratically, surrounded by stacks of letters, newspaper clippings, books, a knitting bag, scattered issues of *Collier's*, *Look*, *Reader's Digest*, pamphlets, and a pile of crumpled yellow handkerchiefs. When she stood, the top of her wavy brown hair grazed the ceiling, forcing her to bend her neck. She handed me a clean hanky, with its fine monogram embroidered in golden thread, the letter *E*.

"My dear, I am glad you're back with us. You've been struggling for breath all night. We'll have a doctor examine you."

Her eyes were as blue as a cloudless sky, warm, caring. She smiled and bared teeth a mule could've been proud of, her chin disappearing into folds of skin that puddled into her neck where three strands of pearls were nearly camouflaged. The pearls, shimmery and smooth, begged to be touched.

"You've had a time of it, haven't you. Well, you're on my private car attached to the T&P line and we've had to wait out what they tell me is the heaviest blanket of dust they've seen in years. It was a terrible dust storm, though they told me they never have bad ones in this part of Texas, but I could smell and taste the earth swirling around us. It settled and lifted, like one of those heavy fogs in the mountains . . . They tell me these storms were getting worse in the Panhandle and Oklahoma this month, but in Sherman—well. No one expected this!"

I said nuthin, feeling secure but bone tired. She was like Bess, with her proper diction, her draped crepe dress, even her perfume.

"You're breathing easier now, aren't you? How did you get yourself lost out there? Why, the engineer stopped the train, he was so blinded . . ." Her voice was shrill, wavering. "They tell me we'll return to Dutch Branch Ranch after they clear the tracks—"

I was too sleepy to ask where that was, or even to give worry a big shadow. I fell into a fitful sleep.

•   •   •

Late morning sunlight streamed through tall windows in a whitewashed bedroom. A chubby-faced girl stared solemnly at me. She was five or six, holding the hand of a brown-eyed boy half her height, dark where she was fair. He babbled and squirmed. "Hush, Tony," she admonished him to no avail.

The room was comfortably furnished and decorated with cowboy paintings and framed photographs. A picture sat on the night table—not a person, but a little dog with long straight black fur. In the corner, something familiar caught my eye—a pair of brown ankle-high brogans, with steel braces and leather straps attached. The shoes were much larger than Celesta's, but the torturous contraption was meant for the same paralyzing condition she had.

"Grandmother brought you to our ranch. You got lost. I'm Ruth. What's your name? Are you hungry? Where did you come from?"

Outside the window was the well-kept terrain of a cattle ranch, occupied by barns, stables, a corral full of cutting horses in training.

"We can ride horses to the fishing hole when Grandmother exercises Dot."

"Or shoot snakes!" Tony said with a slight lisp.

"Let's ask her!" Ruth dragged Tony down the hall. We found her seated outside on the gallery of a rambling white-brick home—the lady from last night, who'd rescued me from drowning in dust. She looked me over with grave concern before settling her brilliant blue eyes on mine.

In the sunshine she was ugly enough to make a freight train take a dirt road, but those eyes radiated a compassion that warmed my heart.

"Good morning, my dears, do you want breakfast?" The boy climbed into her lap but squirmed, enclosed in her arms.

Ruth said, "She doesn't talk much. Perhaps cat's got her tongue."

"Nonsense, there's no such thing, darling. She'll talk when she's ready," their grandmother said, giving Ruth's hair an affectionate tousle.

She set the letters she'd been reading aside. "Let's fix flapjacks."

"Can you make mine without the burned edges, Grandmother," Tony said darkly.

She threw back her head and laughed, an exuberant wide-mouthed guffaw that featured her sizable teeth and pink gums.

She guided her grandchildren, stirring batter, heating the griddle. Her voice was the high-pitched, sometimes-uncontrollable falsetto of the lady whose famous husband had launched the March of Dimes last year with Shirley Temple and Eddie Cantor, the popular radio show host. I'd seen newsreels of the president's Birthday Ball, held every January to raise money for curing the polio; they were Celesta's favorite. We'd watched the newsie where Shirley mailed her dime to the crippled president himself, and Celesta had insisted we donate our dimes like the dimpled movie star did.

"Grandmother Roosevelt," Tony said solemnly, "they're starting to burn."

Eleanor was what she was more familiarly called. That unmistakable face appeared in the newspapers and magazines and newsreels all the time; she was always traveling, visiting the Civilian Conservation Corps work at a new park or inspecting a WPA bridge, giving speeches about peace in Europe or halting the criminality of lynching or solving the world's gravest problems, giving interviews to the press girls to promote the president's New Deal, surveying the National Youth Administration training programs, talking up the Federal Theatre Project, and signing the autobiography she'd published, *This Is My Story*. Miz Wills, Arnold, even Hairbrush, had devoured it. The papers ran pictures of crowds greeting her at every whistle-stop she passed, touring her husband's projects in her private rail car where she waved from the rear observation platform and accepted their flowers—the same platform where I'd found shelter during the black blizzard.

She put a plate heaped with steaming flapjacks before me. I didn't pay no never mind to the crunchy blackened edges. She beamed her warmhearted smile at me.

"Mrs. Roosevelt." I stood. "I'm Ruby Lee Becker. And I thank you for your hospitality."

●   ●   ●

Where's home, she wondered, saying she'd like to hear about me and my family. She was on a tour of Texas, having begun in Beaumont on the private Pullman car the *Alamo*. Her first stop was at the Agricultural and Mechanical College of Texas to tour the animal husbandry projects. She gave a talk in Abilene called "A Day at the White House," then spent the weekend at her son's ranch. The day trip in Sherman which ended in her first-ever dust storm had been for a lecture to the American Pen Women, to bolster their creative work. She would give a luncheon speech in Dallas, and spend an evening at the Fort Worth Fat Stock Show with the governor and his wife. She'd depart Monday for Rich Field to see the NYA boys' construction for the municipal airport, and that night, to make a presentation at Baylor University in Waco, before traveling to Houston.

"Waco?" My throat tightened. "Your train's not going toward Amarillo, Mrs. Roosevelt?"

"I'm afraid not, my dear. I've had enough of those dust storms, haven't you?" Did she have clairvoyant powers to complement her charm? "I'll be addressing a large audience in Waco Hall on Monday evening on the importance of peace. I'd be honored to have you as my guest, Ruby Lee."

"Ma'am, where are we?"

"We're at my son's ranch. Southeast of Fort Worth." Her smile was compassionate. "You came aboard in a dust storm outside of Sherman. Now where were you heading in that dreadful weather? Isn't your family worrying about you?"

I was calculating. From the T&P depot in Fort Worth, there'd be a train to Amarillo. I hoped I had enough for a ticket.

"When you go to the stock show, ma'am, I'd appreciate a ride to the T&P station, Mrs. Roosevelt."

"Let's see what the doctor thinks." She patted my hand, which I quickly withdrew.

"I'm fine."

"You were most definitely not fine last night, Ruby. The doctor must listen to your lungs. I could never forgive myself if I let anything happen to you. Your mother would expect—" She broke off, thoughtful. "Your mother . . . You called out for her, tossing and turning, half-delirious, coughing up dirt. You asked why she sent you away . . ." She waited.

I didn't say nuthin. How could I? It wasn't right to lie to the First Lady, and it sure as heck would be just as wrong to argue.

•   •   •

She spoke gently of her growing up years as an orphan. She was left in a French convent by her parents when her mother was expecting, a lonely six-year-old, English-speaking outsider who didn't fit in with the French girls.

At age eight, she said, her mother took ill with diphtheria and died; she wasn't even ten when she lost her dear father, a troubled, depressed man who died from drink. She was passed around to aunts and uncles, to and from cousins, finally to her stern grandmother. She spent three years in a London academy, where she found her fortitude.

She wanted me to believe she'd felt like me, worthless and abandoned.

"I was lonely, and timid—though timidity seems not to have afflicted you, my dear. You're a very pretty young girl, too. I was an ugly duckling, which I very well knew. I did so crave affection, and approval . . . and it was my longing to be needed and loved that forced me to find my mettle. To stare down my fears."

She wanted me to think she understood me, and I allowed her to, saying nuthin.

"Where's your family, Ruby?" she asked gently. "You mentioned Bess, and Nell, and your grandmother, Alma."

I pinched myself to stop the pinpricks crawling up my arms. A lump in my throat kept me from speaking. I was shaking my head to keep from seeing them dead and gone. I pushed their faces away.

As for the living ones, it was over three years since I'd laid eyes on any of them.

She waited, gathering herself, her eyes moist.

"If you're all alone, as I was once—you will learn not to be afraid. By conquering—Do you understand, Ruby, what it means to face down your fears? You learn you can live through the panic so you can take the next thing that comes your way. That's how I found my strength."

I listened, mindful of what Mrs. E. S. Earhart said of her granddaughter. *If Amelia is in trouble, she will find her way out,* I said to myself, but Mrs. Roosevelt had the hearing of a barn cat.

"Trouble. Well, one must make oneself succeed. It takes courage to get oneself out of sticky situations —"

I protested. "Amelia Earhart didn't. Even though she was very brave." A tear rolled down my cheek of its own accord.

"She was a good friend to me, Amelia, and it was from her I learned danger lies in refusing to face your fears. You mustn't let fear or failure take away your courage."

I swiped at my eyes.

"Where's home?" she asked.

"Far away—" I couldn't make myself say where. I pictured rows of thriving crops and a spacious farmhouse with windows of glass near a bountiful vegetable garden, my brothers in the wheat fields with Pa, Granny Alma on the front porch rocking baby Nell, and Momma brushing my hair. I pictured the farm I wanted, my family intact.

My eyelids closed. I knew where my dream lay. *Hartless. Where the air I breathed was deadly.*

"Ruby. We've got to get you home. Is Hartless the town where we'll find your family?"

I blinked open my eyes.

"Whatever you think you cannot do, you must do it," she said firmly.

I felt moisture in my lashes, full-on tears spilling over, but I could see clear as crystal.

"Waco," I said. "My family's in Waco."

"Well, then, we'll get you there." She looked relieved. "We're flying out early tomorrow. Don't worry, flying is fun."

Flying was everything. It was where freedom lay. It was the way home. I didn't even try to repress the smile curling my lips. It was the first time I was ever tempted to believe an adult who told me not to worry.

"But I can't go there." I'd be shipped off to Gainesville.

"Nonsense," she said. "You'll be on that biplane with me. You must come to grips with your fear. You think you cannot do it, but you must," she repeated firmly, her certainty visible in her crystalline blue eyes.

CHAPTER FORTY-THREE

For a second time a doctor pronounced me recovered from the dust pneumonia, but prone to flare-ups in dusters. In prolonged storms I'd have trouble breathing and need to be hospitalized, because the brown plague was deadly in children and old folks. But in Waco, where dusters were unheard of, he reckoned I'd be fine.

I could've told them all that, but Mrs. Roosevelt wanted to hear it official. So I stayed mum.

Mainly I was preoccupied with staying out of detention in Gainesville. The minute I got back to the State Home, the superintendent would mete out his worst punishment, the one he saved for the incorrigible runaways. They'd shave my head, chain me to the filthy floor, feed me nothing but moldy bread and water. Make us live in squalid little rooms, locked from the outside at night.

During the drive to the airfield, Mrs. Roosevelt described her many adventures in the air. She flew every chance she got; the next best thing to flying was driving her sporty Buick Roadmaster with the convertible top down. Once she went skylarking in a big Condor plane with her dinner guest, Amelia Earhart. They'd flown from her formal White House party to Baltimore, all the while wearing their white evening gloves. It marked an epoch, she told me, when a girl in an evening dress and slippers could pilot a plane at night. "There I was, flying a plane!"

She'd taken flying lessons and joined the Amateur Air Pilots Association, despite the president's cautions against piloting a plane herself. "Being out, where I could see forever—it's like owning the world!"

I wanted to own that world, to hear everything about Amelia Earhart. But all I could think of was Red, how he'd come back from his time in Gatesville bruised and blue—the scars that were visible—believing what they'd called him: unredeemable. How he'd said, "Everybody deserted me."

I knew he meant me. A wave of guilt overtook me, what I could never make up to him.

Even more fearful was what he said next. "They pissed me out there on the loose with wolves."

I knew how that felt. I nodded at the First Lady's words but in my head I was speculating more deviously than a suitcase farmer, wondering when the weather back home would turn in my favor. Was the drouth coming to an end? Were dusters still raking Hartless dry? The newspapers sometimes carried ominous headlines about black gales howling and dusters making deserts of farmland, but by 1939, there'd been so many dust storms, most stories were briefs relegated to back pages.

I worked the conversation around to the plains states, what they were calling the Dust Bowl. I'd read about the Dust Bowl shrinking last month, I told the First Lady, things being in the best shape since 1932. Some places, the soil's wet four feet deep. Could she ask Mr. H. H. Finnell what the soil men predicted?

Mrs. Roosevelt regarded me with respect. I hoped she admired my awareness of conditions.

"Mr. H. H. Finnell, why yes, he's one of my husband's most highly regarded soil conservationists, in charge of Operation Dustbowl for the SCS. The Soil Conservation Service. He's been diligent about putting methods of moisture retention in place. I'll inquire about conditions in Hartless."

"Yes, ma'am, thank you."

She squeezed my hand. "You're a sharp girl, Ruby Lee. I bet you'd like a seat next to the pilot on our flight to Waco."

The very thought thrilled my pounding heart.

"Yes, ma'am!" But could she keep the superintendent from banishing me to the Gainesville Training School for Girls?

Her son's white WACO-ARE biplane swept along the ranch's dirt runway, lifting its wheels at the pasture edge, chills flooding my flesh. That dip in my stomach gave way to awe, being in a landscape of clouds as varied as the view below.

But I could not keep my mind from the thing I most feared. While she spoke of her interest in tackling youth problems with the NYA, her favorite program, I contrived to get Mrs. Franklin D. Roosevelt to protect me from the superintendent.

•   •   •

If she was surprised to enter the grounds of the State Home for Dependent and Neglected Children instead of a run-down rent house in a hard-up part of town, Mrs. Roosevelt had the good manners not to show it.

I counted, *one-two*, awaiting Mrs. Roosevelt's reaction as our driver entered the State Home grounds. Silently, she took in the dormitories, administration buildings, cottages, barns, rambling fields, orchards, and crops, occupied by gangs of children young and old, and she must have understood. There may have been a tear in her eye, I couldn't be sure, for I blindly pointed at the superintendent's house and inhaled sharply, my skin on fire, sure my panic would shut down my windpipe. Her hand grasped mine, warm, her long fingers wrapping tightly.

"You must do—" she began.

"What I think I cannot," I finished.

•   •   •

I'd no sooner alit from the motorcar when the superintendent's front door flew open and he stomped out, red faced, frowning, and slapping his willow switch against his trousers.

"Sir, I've brought a guest to meet you."

Rage spewed out in a rush of crude words which stank like stale cigar smoke. The gist was, "Guest, my ass—where the hell you been, the state's been looking for you—you little sneak—I told you—this is your last warning—you are heading straight to Gainesville—" while he made futile attempts to land his switch on my arms, legs, anywhere, which given my agility and his girth and short stature, was nowhere. By then the driver snarled, loud and firm enough to get the superintendent's attention, as he was assisting the First Lady from the motorcar.

"Superintendent, I'm Eleanor Roosevelt," she said graciously, extending her gloved hand from her far greater height. "Why, Ruby Lee told me what a fine institution you run here, and we've become dear friends in the short time she's been our guest in Benbrook."

He was speechless, staring up at her, so unable to believe his eyes he actually rubbed them with knuckled hands.

Still she stood calmly awaiting his handshake, a graceful tower of a woman who had not vanished when he peered again. He shook her hand, sputtering, and I understood he was afraid.

Her eyes gleamed devilish beneath the brim of her ever-present hat. "I'd love for Ruby Lee to give me a tour, if you'd accompany us, then I'm off to Baylor for my presentation at Waco Hall tonight. I'd like you both to be my guests."

"Yes, ma'am, I'd be honored," his voice cracking. "I'm afraid we have a strict curfew here for our young charges, as Ruby knows, don't you."

He regarded me sternly.

Mrs. Roosevelt placed her hand firm on his arm. Her piercing eyes were lit a brilliant blue in the late sun.

"Sir," I said, "the curfews ain't applied to all the girls, for example, when Mr. Shotwell—you know, the coach's pal—wanted to elope with Viola. The girl I told you about," I turned to the First Lady.

The superintendent cleared his throat.

"Of course we make exceptions, Mrs. Roosevelt, and Ruby can certainly attend your lecture. I understand over two thousand tickets were sold, to benefit the Girls Club?"

"Twenty-five hundred," she corrected him.

"That's marvelous. The papers reported former Governor Neff will introduce you, with the president of Baylor. Why, Mayor Jones even declared today "Our Day" in your honor, ma'am . . ." His blathering continued as we entered the visitor's hall. Mrs. Roosevelt held my hand, and I didn't let go.

CHAPTER FORTY-FOUR

A group gathered to follow the First Lady like the Pied Piper to the hall. Following Emma Sue's eyes to Mrs. Roosevelt's face, I overheard her whisper, "ugly as homemade soap," beside a rail-thin boy, who asked, "How do all those teeth fit in her mouth?" I wedged myself between them, ground my heel on their toes.

"You want the wire brush treatment?" I spit at them.

Inside, I looked again at Mrs. Roosevelt, realizing my mistake. She wasn't ugly; you'd see how lovely she was once you knew her. Her beauty shone not from her face, but her heart.

Before we climbed the stairs, Matron made a fuss. "I'm an admirer, ma'am, like the latest Gallup poll says, you're more popular than the president . . ."

That's when I flung the under-stairs closet door open. Matron lunged for it. "She doesn't want to see a closet, you ninny—"

Mrs. Roosevelt's eyes darkened like a blue norther. I said, "Ma'am, here's where they hold our packages from home." She took in the matron's reddened face.

"Undelivered," I continued. "And our money's missing."

The matron, sputtering, couldn't explain. Mrs. Roosevelt wanted paper and pen for a list, asking to see the infirmary, classrooms, and dormitories.

At the dispensary I took the stairs two a time. The nasty relief nurse greeted me with a glare until the First Lady loomed in the doorway, ducking her head to enter. We stood together at the quarantine room, reading the yellow notice taped to the door.

<u>QUARANTINE</u>
<u>Contagious Disease. Infantile Paralysis!</u>
<u>Posted No Entry—Waco Health Office.</u>

"There's someone I'd like you to meet, ma'am. At the girls' dormitory."

•   •   •

After we'd toured the school, dining hall, the creamery and cannery, vegetable gardens, orchards, and barn, we traipsed to my dorm. Mrs. Roosevelt never once flagged. She made more notes—the bristly hairbrush, Coach's notched paddle.

During our rounds, the relief nurse, dorm parents, Miz Wills, Arnold, Croucher, and Hairbrush favored me like a star pupil.

Croucher swooned at the sight of Mrs. Roosevelt. She requested her autograph on her autobiography, and on her newest book, *This Troubled World.* She showed off her slew of *Ladies' Home Journal* articles and yellowed "My Day" clippings.

"You must be so grateful Ruby's back, safe and sound," Mrs. Roosevelt said.

Croucher looked momentarily cattywampus, choking out, "Sure."

All the books signed, I was itchin for the First Lady to meet the girls I'd done my best to leave behind.

First came Clare, in her Coke-bottle-thick glasses. She curtseyed, one eye roving, and showed Mrs. Roosevelt the latest sheet of Easter seals she was selling.

"The president will be grateful."

Kitty, fragile but jitterbugging around, said brightly, "Pleased to meet you, Mrs. First Lady!" earning a laugh.

Mollie stuttered when she reached the *R* in the First Lady's name. I rescued her. "Call her ma'am, it's what she likes, and fetch Celesta."

"I'm pleased to meet you, ma'am," Mollie managed, and Mrs. Roosevelt replied she knew her name was a mouthful.

Before I let Dolores approach, I sniffed at her backside and didn't get a whiff of ammonia. The little panty-wetter was safe to introduce.

Thelma saw her chance and struck up a chat with Mrs. Roosevelt about opportunities with the Youth Administration, her 4-H ribbons, her yard demonstration project for the national 4-H award.

Celesta arrived last.

From the hallway came a percussion of limbs: a willful stomp, two clumps, the sound of something dragged, repeated slowly in 3/4 time, edging closer. Mysterious to none accustomed to the ravages of the crippler—especially the president's wife, watching expectantly.

Celesta appeared, her weight balanced on her wood-and-metal leather-braced boot, two crutches digging into her underarms.

"Mrs. Roosevelt," she breathed, her eyes shining.

The First Lady strode to Celesta, inquiring about her health. We were quiet as church mice, witnessing maybe the most miraculous thing any of us ever expected to see in a state home for neglected children.

Celesta shyly showed her the president's thank-you letter. "I keep it on my wall, as a reminder."

Mrs. Roosevelt's crystal-blue eyes glistened.

"Ma'am, can you get Celesta a spot at Warm Springs?" I asked.

She pulled a golden handkerchief from her pocket and dabbed at her eyes. The lace-edged tip with the embroidered letter *E* grazed her cheek and we were mesmerized at the notion of blowing snot into such a fancy, starched square of linen, awaiting the words that could save Celesta.

"We'll look into it, after we learn the details of your case. You're a brave girl, aren't you? Your disease requires effort which is so hard to make; step by step you must go forward, mentally, physically, to find happiness. You certainly are."

No one ever praised Celesta. She rose up, prideful.

"The warm springs have been beneficial to Mr. Roosevelt."

Celesta was too awestruck to say much except, "Thank you," but her eyes glistened.

"We must be on our way, Ruby. We're running late for my talk," the First Lady said, with a reluctance that looked real.

·   ·   ·

"I did so much enjoy these conversations with your friends, Ruby. I expect to speak with Dr. W. B. Carrell at Baylor tonight," she explained as we drove. "He helped organize the Texas Society for Crippled Children, and he's a professor of orthopedic surgery at the school of medicine. He's advocated a rehabilitative clinic for children in Gonzales, one that could rival my husband's polio retreat in Georgia."

"Yes, ma'am, I know all about Dr. Carrell; he says the twenty natural springs are the perfect temperature for hydrotherapy, 106 degrees, and everyone's in favor of it, the doctors, the Rotarians, the charitable ladies of Gonzales, even the education department. They held a big Easter seals campaign to raise money," I said.

I had the sensation of Clare shooting me a sinister look despite my distance. "We all helped," I added weakly. I'd have to pay Clare back pronto.

Mrs. Roosevelt regarded me like she'd come to expect my intelligent pronouncements.

"My husband is a supporter," she said. "His CCs are already there, developing Palmetto State Park with a fountain to create rock pools and waterfalls, and a bridge over the San Marcos River, all to enhance the surrounds of the facility for young infantile paralysis victims."

"Yes, ma'am. When will it be ready? We've been donating to the wishing well in town, for the March of Dimes . . ." I felt the presence of Clare, nodding vigorously.

"The NYA youth will start on the first hospital unit, a lovely Spanish stucco-style architecture, and—"

"Will it be soon? I mean, before anyone else has to have those terrible operations and that Bradford contraption to trap them in their hospital beds and wear those splints from Toronto?" My voice was insistent, rising to a shrill I didn't recognize.

"You sound very concerned about someone, dear. Your friend, Celesta?"

I was almost as surprised as she was.

•   •   •

That night, the First Lady had told her rapt audience we needed to set our own house in order and make democracy work because "democracy requires not the action of one man, but the conviction and courage of many" and make our most enduring contribution to the cause of peace She then genially acknowledged a standing ovation to boisterous applause.

She sent the superintendent back without me. We walked backstage to her dressing room.

"I have time before my train to Houston, Ruby, for a drive. You must take this candy back to your friends; they shower it on me at every whistle-stop. Will you accept a ride back home, so we can talk more?"

"Back home?" I couldn't believe my ears. "Home to my family?"

Mrs. Roosevelt patted the soft bench at the dressing table for me to sit beside her.

"The dust storm that brought us together on Saturday, three days ago?" She paused, struggling.

"Yes, ma'am," I urged, my hope fading.

"I've heard from Mr. Finnell, the president's top soil expert. He's gotten the latest report from an agronomist in Stillwater about that storm—"

A knock on the door interrupted her. It was the stage manager, saying they were ready to close. Mrs. Roosevelt said we'd be out in a moment.

"Take your time, ma'am. We are mighty big admirers of yours."

She nodded, then directed her eyes like headlamps on mine.

"The dust storms have become more serious in March, Mr. Finnell says, and in Amarillo, which I believe is pretty close to your farm, isn't it?"

I dipped my head, but didn't say nuthin. I knew what was coming.

"At Amarillo, the visibility on the day we met was zero, *zero*, for five hours, and the wind speed was recorded at sixty miles per hour. Think how fast that is, Ruby. Why, it would blow a small thing like you right off the face of the earth." She attempted a smile. "Even a big thing like me."

I'd heard enough. I knew what she was going to tell me. I opened the door, waiting for her to follow.

"Ruby, I need you to understand this. You can't breathe in air filled with dirt blowing like that. You're well enough now, but your lungs cannot take another assault by dust pneumonia."

She fixed her intelligent blue eyes on mine. I looked away.

"The reports from Mr. Finnell are the dust storm of March 11 put enough dirt in the air to cover five million acres, one foot deep. That dust storm took over one hundred thousand square miles of land."

When Pa sent me east for my health in 1935 with Will, he must have had a notion the loose flour bag of sackcloth holding our family of five was about to get ripped to shreds.

Like so many others across the High Plains, we were in trouble, and I'd have to find my own way home. And I wouldn't give up, not till we were family again.

I was down the stairs and ready to bolt but I heeded her voice, the familiar wavering absent.

"You've already found your home, Ruby, right here in Waco. Let's get you back there. Those State Home girls and boys who are loyal to you— you're lucky to have them for family."

CHAPTER FORTY-FIVE

The newspapers reported so many dusters in spring of 1939 they ran out of descriptions. Dusty conditions across Oklahoma, moderate- to gale-force winds carrying considerable dust in southwestern Kansas, frequent dust storms in Texas, local soils blowing in isolated parts of the Dust Bowl, widespread storms, a black gale here, a light dusting there, much erosion in farm fields, with gusting dust killing or damaging young seeds in all blowing areas. Dust made visibility low one day, cut it to one hundred yards the next, then reduced visibility decidedly. But never a drop of rain.

I read all the reports and heard only Pa's voice. *When it rains.*

•   •   •

Waco, as usual, was spared the bad blows. The air I breathed here, at least, was no enemy.

Mrs. Roosevelt mailed me a copy of *Collier's* from April with a note she'd penned over her byline. *For Ruby Lee, my companion in the air.* Her article, "Flying Is Fun," described how flight offered her a sense of freedom. She wrote it would become just as natural for boys and girls to want to fly as it was to drive an automobile. We'd need to learn, though, it is not courageous to be reckless.

Reckless would be risking my lungs to live in Hartless, I heard her pleasantly oscillating voice.

Chatter barnstormed the campus with news of a pen pal in the White House. I contrived nonchalance, but made dang sure Matron and Superintendent knew.

•   •   •

What really put Clay and the football gang back in good standing happened that fall.

The Hornets had such a winning football season in 1939 they went unbeaten and untied. Clay and some teammates made all-district, and heard talk of college scholarships. The Hornets shut out Hillsboro. They whipped Waxy, tamed Tyler, and outplayed Oak Cliff. The mighty and winningest team ever, the Waco High Tigers—who dubbed themselves "the pride of Waco"—were afraid to play the Hornets (so the rumors went). The good times on the field reverberated, not only on our campus, but all around town.

The coach was heaped with praise and took it all.

The football fever was for everyone except Red. Despite our hopes for harmony after that tapered leather ball united our home, things never got smoothed over for him. The coach held a grudge and a belief that for every slight, somebody would pay. His target was Red, and he had the backing of those who ruled, from the superintendent to Miz Arnold. Clay thought his little brother was naive enough to expect his innocence would prevail.

"Cannot be rehabilitated," the coach said of Red. "Inferior and no good."

The superintendent concurred. With no evidence beyond his streak of vengeance, the coach had prevailed. Red was sent to Gatesville for juvenile training. *Re-training*, we heard through horrified whispers, in a wicked teenage prison, where frequent clubbings were harsh. Where the unluckiest boys only got out by burial in the State Juvenile Training School Cemetery.

I wrote Mrs. Roosevelt for help.

•   •   •

The headlines about the new war in Europe that broke out when Hitler invaded Poland preoccupied the adults. France and Britain quickly declared war on Germany. In the president's September Fireside Chat, he'd reaffirmed America's commitment to neutrality, but implied the United States could be summoned to help what he called "a crippled humanity." The White House considered naval action after the British liner *Athenia* was torpedoed with Americans and Canadians aboard; Canada declared war on Germany September 10, 1939. In her "My Day" columns, Mrs. Roosevelt suggested the international situation was the only thing uppermost in every mind. But maybe the First Lady would find a moment for me.

•   •   •

We made Christmas lists of things we wanted costing a dollar. The only thing I wrote on my list was to go home. When the girl in front of me turned around to look at my paper, I covered it and kicked her desk. "Think up your own!" I breathed on her neck. It wasn't as if we didn't all want the same thing.

They set up a Christmas tree in the administration building, and a table with sparkly paper where we wrapped empty boxes for the tree. "So it's pretty for the state officials' visit," Matron said.

I had a letter from the White House, which caused excitement around the campus. The superintendent personally delivered it, waiting expectantly. I ran my fingers over the raised embossed ink of the return address with its engraving of the important house itself. I sensed the letter conferred some powerful magic to protect me. I tucked it in my pocket and thanked him, noting his disappointment. I'd open it later, when no one would see its contents.

•   •   •

The shorts they showed on movie nights heightened our loneliness. First off, Mickey and Minnie threw a Christmas party for a basket of orphaned kittens left on their doorstep in a blizzard. Next the elves were merrily at work fashioning toy soldiers and trains for Santa in his workshop. Then Professor Grampy transformed broken toys into sleds and wind-up turkeys and banjos for the children at the orphanage. The pitiable orphans were happy with their paltry lot.

The Lux Radio Theater presented a special program on Christmas, where Mr. Cecil B. DeMille introduced Walt Disney's *Pinocchio* and told us this enchanted night was for family reunions and stories by the fireplace.

An older kid tittered, "We only ever had a wood stove."

"When we had wood." Kids nodded. "Never enough to keep us warm."

I heard Clare's voice, more bitter. "Family? Which one? All of 'em broker than the Ten Commandments."

Mollie teared up. Putting Xs on her calendar since 1936, year after year, trusting her mother would come. Mollie and me, we shared hope; it was our creed. But trust, that's where Mollie took a wrong turn.

Everyone knew what happened to Red. And look where trust got him.

1940

CHAPTER FORTY-SIX

RUBY LEE

Spring and summer in 1940 passed with barnstormers doing aerial stunts at Rich Field on weekends, and 4-H preoccupying us after they left town. While we finished our projects, I envisioned my takeoff from the hayloft window, practicing jumps into hay bales below. Farmer caught me, bringing me back to earth with the threat of licks. He'd done worse, I knew, busting the jaw of a kid with his twisted-wood shillelagh. I hustled back to it, my flight path already determined.

In October we ate donated ice cream at the Brazos Valley Fair and posed for newspaper photographs. Monday was the day for colored children, Tuesday for white kids, and on Wednesday, the Methodist home and Waco State orphans got in free. We were among hundreds of kids there, divided by our lot in life, clamoring to shoot sitting ducks and win big fluffy bears.

A midway barker drew us to the Living Oddities of the World, shouting out their deformities—the man with a third leg, the lady with a heavy beard, two boys joined at their hips. I felt a kinship with those sideshow Oddities, treed like coonhound prey.

One teacher had Celesta, Mollie, and Kitty cornered, wagging her forefinger, "See what happens to retarded idiots? Not even good enough for their own families."

Kitty's lower lip trembled, and Mollie looked on the verge of tears.

I slipped beside them, linking arms, whispering. "Quit listening to her. She's got hateful words and that's all she's got. She can't hurt you."

To her, I shouted, "We ain't retards! And we ain't orphans, neither!"

We stood together like sisters. The Living Oddities regarded me with dumbfounded faces.

•   •   •

There was an unsettled mood at mealtimes as Thanksgiving approached. Most of the Hornets—Clay's teammates on the football team, who'd thrilled us with another winning season—had been talking to the US Army recruiters on campus. The boys were juniors, some older since they'd flunked a grade or two, and their youthful faces had grown mature as if by resolve. They pushed succotash around on their plates and downed dessert in one gulp. Crumbs from sugar cookies dotting their mouths, they bolted outside, Clay among them.

I left my overcooked meat loaf to follow them. Across the lawn, a US Army staff sergeant manned a sign that read, *Young Men, Enlist Now!* He called out names and the boys took the paperwork he doled out—applications to enlist in the regular army.

The Hubbards might enlist. My brothers, too.

"The Krauts are routing almost every country in Europe, and the Japs are running wild all over Asia. If you're twenty-one, you visit your draft board. But you're younger, right? If you're eighteen, Uncle Sam wants you to volunteer."

The boys were worked up. Some weren't eighteen yet, but they'd age out of the State Home when they were. The army offered a cot and three hots. "Nazis are bombing London, and war's on the horizon," the recruiter prodded.

The team's halfback, one of Clay's pals and the Hornets' most valuable player, was first in line. Seeing Dill step up, more boys decided on the spot, eagerly taking applications.

Clay stood back, hands in his pockets. As usual, his demeanor showed he was contemplating something. He was so like Will. I pictured my brother, nineteen now, with his smarts, crafty smile, and earnest brown eyes.

Clay's teammates looked up to him, like Will's would—probably captain of the debate club or Hartless high school president by now. On his way to the college he desperately wanted to attend. If the recruiters hadn't got to him yet.

I hoped he'd never see the kind of action where boys were blown up, and return like Red's shellshocked father, whose memories didn't survive. Or Pa, whose hands and arms bore scars from severe blisters when mustard gas blighted his battalion in the Great War. He never spoke of it.

"You're old enough," Clay's teammates badgered their captain. Dill called to him, "c'mon," but Clay refused. The boys complained about busting up the team.

"Disappointed you won't sign up," Dill said.

"Hey, Dillon, I already did." Clay spread his hands wide. "For the pilot training program. Going to ground school at Rich Field, getting my wings."

A boy who was Clay's favorite receiver had finished signing his application. He let out an *oof* we all recognized when he got tackled. But this was one of regret.

"Once I'm a pilot I'll be flying for Uncle Sam," Clay said.

The receiver with misgivings muttered *pilot school, damn it all to hell, went out too wide again, shit,* earning a sharp rebuke from the staff sergeant.

Dill shrugged off his chagrin and rejoined the ranks of football players-turned-soldiers, earning a thumbs-up.

Clay, flying? That lit me up. How'd he get into flying school?

"You take a test, Clay? Show your straight-A report card? How'd ya qualify?"

"What? No," he laughed. "I saved up for it. All it takes is money. Fifty bucks. And—you gotta be old enough," he said, reading the desire on my face.

I felt the blood rush to my cheeks. Fifty bucks. And Viola still owed me twenty.

Those boys were gone by Thanksgiving, and with it, everyone's exuberance.

• • •

At Christmastime the governor of Texas launched his 1940 Home for Christmas push—a gimmick to place us in some other family's home over the holidays, which reminded us we didn't have real homes. I wrote another letter home, pleading for somebody to come for me, having no real hope anyone was there. Pa, Will, even Earl might be in the army already.

The local papers were full of bad news, as Nazi forces bombed Liverpool, Southampton, and continued bombarding London. But it was deemed good news most State Home children would be Yule Adoptees. The governor himself would take a four-year-old who'd been rescued from dirt-poor subsistence. He resembled Pappy as a little boy, Mrs. O'Daniel thought. He'd spend Christmas at the governor's mansion in Austin.

The little ones were excited enough to wet their pants, staying with real families in real homes, departing for points west, east, north, and south.

The lady from the Texas Society of Crippled Children, who'd delivered all three Rudolph sisters four years ago, came for Celesta, who refused to leave her sister behind. The lady frowned, hemmed, and hawed, waiting out Celesta's entreaties and tears, before giving in. Holding hands, Clare and Celesta departed in glee.

Red had returned from Gatesville, taller, his muscles ropy. That crazy red hair was shorn short in military precision, accentuating new gaunt angles in his face. He was jumpy and his eyes were suspicious. From the taut set to his lips, his whistling days appeared over.

He'd helped build the manger's thatched roof before the pageant, keeping quiet, his features as sharp as the nails he slammed into the wood. He paid no mind to his surroundings, nor to me, intent on his carpentry.

But when a hammer thudded to the ground, he jerked his head up, alerting to the sound.

Nobody claimed Red for Christmas, either. But wasn't that how he wanted it?

The annual Christmas lights on the campus were turned on but the youngest missed the pageantry. The event attracted hundreds of nighttime sightseers—some for the lights, some to see us. We were Waco's own living oddities. The manger glowed beneath a giant star of Bethlehem.

Two days before Christmas Eve, despite the welcoming glow and rush of visitors, there were some seventy of us—all teenagers—who weren't cute enough to be claimed. Our consolation prize was a radio program of Christmas carols and donated venison for dinner.

In my dormitory's living room, a brand new Philco table radio—the state's gift—was tuned to the Governor's radio address. The new Patterson Hall was merrily lit with Christmas stars. At the baby cottage, Old Saint Nick's reindeer glowed, pulling a lighted sleigh. Across the lawn the infant new year fell from a sparkling sky by parachute, as Father Time scampered off.

By night we lived in a fantasy world.

"Home for Christmas," Governor O'Daniel enthused on air. "Pick out any little orphan boy or girl you want, and be their Christmas daddy or Christmas mother. They are nice, clean, wholesome boys and girls with all the life and fun and hope and aspirations of other little boys and girls who do have homes. Take them home for Christmas, Texas!"

I wasn't fooled. I'd seen Mollie get rejected by some smitten prospects from Mexia whose smiles froze when she stuttered over Santa's name.

I told that two-faced couple Mollie and I weren't available for Yuletide adoptions.

Not that anyone asked for me. Like Red, that was how I wanted it.

"We're already home, Mollie," I said, leading her to the truckload of gifts delivered from Texas State College for Women. "Let's pick something to replace your old calendar. Those babies must be six by now." For four years Mollie had marked her Xs, never noticing those Dionne quintuplets hadn't aged a day.

Mollie's eyes moistened, popping wide as a river ready to flood.

"Jes teasin, Mollie. I ain't gonna take away your dream."

One day you'll lose the feeling you have for your momma, I might have said. But I bit my words back.

CHAPTER FORTY-SEVEN

WILLA MAE

Madeleine's voice is hoarse, making it as painful for her to talk as it was for my art teacher in 1918. I remember Miss O'Keeffe's abrupt departure from the campus in Canyon on Valentine's Day like it was yesterday. I page through my logbook to continue my entry about my art classes at West Texas State Normal College.

Miss O'Keeffe's despondency since her college students enlisted to fight the Boche had given way to a respiratory ailment that gripped her after the fall term began, upon her return from her train tour of the Colorado Rockies, Denver, and Santa Fe. New Mexico's high mesa landscape had inspired her and she was painting a new series of watercolors, despite her worsening chest cold and severe cough.

In the new year, the virus had attacked viciously and she'd lost her speaking voice. In January, she taught in a whisper with a shadow of her vibrance. The injections her doctor administered did little to improve her condition. She risked succumbing to consumption, which felled her mother two years earlier, so it shouldn't have been a shock when she boarded the Santa Fe Chief for San Antonio. But—

Shelving books, the librarian casually dismisses me. I recognize Miss O'Keeffe's classroom books—Arthur Dow's Constructive Art-Teaching, *her book of Japanese woodblock prints, her well-thumbed philosophy and poetry books, the new pile of* Camera Works *journals her New York gallery donated.*

"You're white as a sheet," the librarian observes, adding, "Your art teacher's withdrawn and it's high time. Her doctor's sent her to San Antonio to get well. Got the TB, if you ask me."

Georgia had left her stash of prized books here.

Alarmed, I race to Georgia's rooming house, which is apparently being fumigated despite the chill, its windows open wide, curtains blowing in the brisk air. The landlady is sweeping out Georgia's bedroom. A crate of left-behind belongings set near the door are the only sign of the strong spirit who'd inhabited Canyon briefly and marked my soul indelibly. I bend to the crate and retrieve a bleached-out cow skull, one of many cattle bones she collected walking the plains on her long wanderings. The sheen of the skeleton is already beginning to dull.

When I get to the depot the sun is setting on her train, disappearing to the south, its plume resembling one of her watercolors. Train at Night in the Desert is my favorite and now she is aboard it.

For weeks, I was bereft and despondent. When my heart wasn't racing, my head throbbed, and I was plagued by unpredictable crying jags. The extraordinary weight of my graphite pencil kept me from sketching. The substitute the college hired was a feeble stand-in who taught the traditional art techniques Miss O'Keeffe eschewed and I couldn't bear to attend his class. I lost track of the days I hadn't risen from bed or dressed or eaten.

Madeleine, listening intently as I both narrate and write, scoots closer to place a warm hand upon my shoulder.

My mother telegrams. She'll see me for lunch in Amarillo before she changes trains en route to Denver to perform. We meet in the Santa Fe depot lunchroom. She takes in my melancholy, my haggard appearance, and fears I've contracted the Spanish influenza which is infecting young people in waves. She's brought me a wrapped gift from Marshall Field's. Her powdered face skews in alarm at my indifference. "You've forgotten your birthday," she murmurs, mistaken. I noted my seventeenth birthday but I am numb to the passing of time, my thoughts caught in quicksand and my purpose lost.

She gathers my limp hands in her determined grip and enjoins me to come home to Chicago where I can recover and study at the Art Institute. Her reasoning is sound. But I rebuff her.

Days before the term ends, facing a Fail on my final evaluation, I withdraw from the college.

1941

CHAPTER FORTY-EIGHT

RUBY LEE

The arithmetic teacher was reading Mrs. Roosevelt's January 22, 1941 column aloud in the faculty room, recounting the inaugural festivities as the president was sworn in for his third term. In her "My Day" account, the First Lady was thrilled by uniformed marchers parading from the NYA, CCC, and WPA, which we'd heard the broadcaster describe.

Mrs. Roosevelt's voice made me desperate for her wisdom. I'd never called the private number her secretary sent; I'd memorized it two years ago and stashed coins for the telephone in an invisible slit I'd cut in my mattress. The White House letter remained in its hiding place, a gap in the knotty-pine paneling at the dark end of the corridor.

The last line in Mrs. Roosevelt's letter prevailed and I heard her voice now, how she knew I had the courage to face my fears by myself.

•   •   •

A barn cat dropped another litter, and the whole squealing, squirming lot of them were in a flour sack a crew of boys carried to the river, for the ritual of drowning kittens. The barn would be overrun with cats without population control, Farmer Krewell insisted, and the new boys had to learn to do it.

Red hung back, leaning on a pitchfork outside the barn, watching with disdain. I hovered near the boys tromping down the ravine, creeping up to the one holding the sack. "Lemme have one peek," I pleaded in a whisper. "Please? I'll pay you a nickel."

"Two nickels." He glanced at Farmer leading the march, lecturing about cats in heat. One boy asked, "What's that, in heat?" Everyone snickered.

I shoved the coins in his pocket and he opened the sack. "Make it quick."

I stuck my hand in, yanking out the first ball of fur I grabbed. I ran up the ravine, into the woods, and examined the kitten, a soft gray thing whose eyes weren't open, mewling, pawing at me, suckling at air.

I couldn't hide the kitten for long in our dorm. Last year when somebody tried it, they quarantined his whole dorm on account of cats getting diphtheria from eating field mice. The kitten I held was so little she couldn't catch a mouse, much less eat it. Nobody was allowed puppies, kittens, bunnies—no pets—the dorm parents were strict. Farm animals were our only choice, but I'd never cuddle up to a cow after the government men with rifles had herded the starving ones into the pit.

I wanted to patch things up with Red. He'd been wary like a lone wolf, and Coach Beatty had guaranteed him a miserable existence. I found Red alone in the cow barn with my tiny gift warm and cupped in my hands.

"Still gonna be a Future Farmer, I see."

He startled, then yanked another teat. Milk hissed into the bucket. He moved to the next cow, his face unreadable. I blocked his path.

"Got something for ya. Here. Hold out your hands."

He extended his arms woodenly, palms flat and facing each other.

"You look like a toy soldier," I chided.

He didn't give up a hint of a smile.

"Cup your hands together, you know," I said, placing the furry bundle gently in his hands.

Red regarded me quizzically, his eyebrows dark with that lopsided slant I liked. I searched his eyes for something warm, some sign of his spirit beginning to surface. Maybe this would do it.

"Something to care about," I said, leaving quick before he could turn me down.

In June I started work in the nursery. A foundling was left in a wicker basket on the baby cottage's doorstep, like so many peaches.

The nurse was absorbed in the newspapers, reading about the hour-long flight the First Lady took in Alabama at Tuskegee Army Air Field with Chief Anderson, a self-taught flight instructor.

"A colored pilot, can you imagine that," she said, her newsprint-blackened fingerprints smudging her white uniform gray.

In the photograph, Mrs. Roosevelt beamed, all teeth, sitting in the trainer's cockpit with the pilot, wearing her flower-decked saucer hat. The airship, I noted, was a Piper J-3 Cub.

While the nurse read aloud, the foundling stirred and blinked her eyes at me, like baby Nell did.

I froze, my feet welded to the floor.

"Pick up the baby, Ruby, fer chrissakes, before she screams bloody murder." The nurse's eyes never left the newspaper. "It's time you learned to handle a baby."

I wanted to, I did. But what little I knew about mothering had expired with baby Nell.

Corinne jabbed me. The foundling emitted some squeaks, then a few insistent grunts, followed by a stream of anxious burbles, tossing her head side to side. Her wide-open eyes found me, rooted to the spot like a hickory tree.

The nurse shoved her chair back, and Corinne hurriedly pulled me to the baby. She explained how to swaddle her and shush her. From some long-ago memory my hands sought the baby blanket, and with no forethought or intention, I found myself rolling the baby into its folds, tucking it together papoose-style.

The girls watched me anxiously. The general impression was amazement I needed instruction on shushing a baby. Thelma approached with her hands outstretched and I shot her a look that turned her on her heels. Of course I could handle a foundling. With Momma prone to the trembles when she wasn't on tenterhooks, hadn't I been shushing Nell morning, noon, and night, right up until she passed?

The foundling fussed, squirmed, and warbled. Her cries grew fretful. I hugged her to me, shushing her, swaying in semi-circles, jiggling up and down, speaking softly to her, *calm down, little one, calm down.* She began a quavering wail. I tucked her blankets tighter, told her, *now now, there there,* yet her wail found a higher pitch. Corinne, Thelma, and the younger girls held their breath. The nurse's eyes drilled into me. The foundling's face was bright red, her tiny eyelids screwed tight. Tear droplets escaped and she caterwauled loud enough to compete with the tomcat in the barn.

I fell into a daze, swirling in a blackout, grabbing at breaths of air.

I needed silence. I enveloped the bundle I held more tightly to quell her pain—and mine, at feeling the life go out of Nell.

Ruby, let go, Ruby, you can let go now—

Corinne's voice broke through the baby's bawling and the soft keening coming from my lips, sounds I hadn't meant to be heard. I felt Corinne's hands collecting the foundling I'd nearly smothered before she could feel the emptiness of being abandoned.

•　•　•

That night I was last to wash up before lights out. No one would get near me, as if my handling of the foundling was a deadly disease they'd catch.

In the bathroom, someone left a straight razor. I knew it was meant for me.

The nurse had berated me in front of everyone after my shameful turn with the foundling. She'd threatened a whipping with the radiator brush used to quiet rowdy toddlers. Instead I was banished from the nursery. I'd be reported, she assured me, I was *not* cut out for children.

It had to be the nurse who placed the straight razor there, making sure I'd understood. I admired the delivery of her message. When I cut a shallow slice across my upper arm, a perfect red line arose slowly and beautifully.

•　•　•

Coach Beatty was still practicing his cruelty with relentless precision on the boys in his dorm when the war came and changed everything.

We were wakened early one Monday morning in December by the head matron. "The Japs attacked the navy's base in Hawaii yesterday, Sunday morning…It wasn't expected." Pearl Harbor Day, it would become known.

President Roosevelt called it, "December 7, 1941, a date that will live in infamy." The country was at war.

Later that week, we gathered around the Philco to hear the president tell us what we already knew: Our country had suffered a serious setback with the Pearl Harbor attack. Our forces were fighting bravely but taking a beating in the Philippines. He predicted a long and hard war with Japan.

As the news sank in, I realized there'd be plenty of airplanes now.

Two days later, we were at war with Germany and Italy, as well.

By Saturday, we learned Congress intended to draft men from eighteen to sixty-four for defense duties, which meant all the older boys were going to war. Will, too, if he hadn't already enlisted. And Earl? At seventeen, he wasn't old enough, but he might connive to pass as eighteen. Wouldn't they call up Pa, or did his mustard gas injuries disqualify him?

The new superintendent, who'd arrived in the fall, endorsed the coach's discipline methods. With patriotic fervor—and a keen need to escape the thrashings—the entire football team embraced the respite war offered. Everyone who was eighteen, or could fake it, scrammed to the war office.

They shipped out before Christmas.

•   •   •

On the eve of his departure Clay found me in the orchard, twilight waning. Wafting smoke from my cigarette entwined itself with the leafless branches.

He extended a slim envelope to me. "Our troop train's due out to Wichita Falls first thing."

Clay had earned his wings by spring, had a mechanic's job at Rich Field by summer, and enlisted in the Army Air Corps after Thanksgiving. He spent all his spare time working on airplane motors or flying, as driven as my brother Will had been by his studies. A week after the president declared war on Japan, Germany, and Italy, Clay was headed to the training center at Sheppard Field.

"You remind me of someone," I said, stubbing out my Potter's cigarette.

"Red?" He imitated his brother's quizzical eyebrows, waggling them up and down.

His eyes were tender, warm, I noticed for the first time, maybe because Red's had turned cold on me.

"What's in this." I flipped the envelope over. The flap was sealed.

"Open it tomorrow, after I'm gone."

Must be about Red. I shrugged, momentarily peeved.

"Take care of yourself, Ruby." His voice was sincere. "I know you do, but there's a new super here and he won't care about your guardian angel in the White House. Besides, she's got more on her mind."

"I'm seventeen," I said in a huff, inflating my age a few months and too riled to care. *I know how to take care of myself*, I began to assert, but stopped. Was it true? The memory of how I said nuthin to Will when he left Cousin Bess's, giving me his going-home money, flashed and filled me with shame.

I warmed to the heat of his body when Clay pulled me in for a hug. He laid his palm gentle on my hair, provoking a jolt of something I'd never felt before. I quick slipped out of his arms, calling good luck over my shoulder, feeling my ears burn red like Will's always did.

1942

CHAPTER FORTY-NINE

RUBY LEE

Everything happened so fast that year I turned seventeen.

Waco boomed once more, busy as a cotton supplier for the cots, mattresses, and tents the army needed. Waco Army Air Field opened for basic pilot training in May, and uniformed young men arrived by troop trains. I scanned the recruits' pinched faces, longing for a glimpse of my brothers, even Pa, imagining how tight I'd hold them. How could Momma bear it? She'd be all alone, missing her family. I pushed back tears, refusing to give her any sympathy.

Clay wrote from Biloxi, Mississippi, in basic training at Keesler Field, where the weather was balmy and sunny. The girls were nice but not as cute as the State Home girls. "They tried hard to make a man of me—quick!" he quipped in his onion-skin letter shared around the campus. He signed off, "We're in the army now! And how!!!" He made war sound fun.

•　　•　　•

High school social studies became rigidly topical, as battle locations taught us world geography. Everyone followed the exploits of the State Home boys who'd enlisted. Due to Japanese bombing raids on army air bases, I learned where Manila was (on the island of Luzon, in the Philippines), and thanks to Allied bombing successes, I could locate Penang (on Malaya's west coast) on the pull-down wall map. Months before Bataan fell to Japanese control, as US soldiers in foxholes succumbed to hunger, combat, and tropical diseases, and surrendered on Corregidor Island in May 1942, we dedicated ourselves to Far East study.

I pinpointed Biloxi with its base of balmy breezes on the Gulf Coast, calculating the distance from Waco.

Word came in June the Hornets' star halfback, Dill, who'd run, caught, and blocked his way to our winning year, was our first fatality overseas. As a prisoner of war during the Bataan Death March, he was one of thirty-six thousand feared lost in the Battle of the Philippines. A ripple of alarm crossed the campus. Corinne collapsed, wracked with sobs. She was waiting for Dillon, she wept, twirling her ring that coulda come from a Cracker Jack box. Watching Thelma comfort her, I understood. Will, even Earl, or Pa could end up dead, too.

I printed my address in large capitals after my signature and mailed another letter, hoping it would find Pa or my brothers. *Please come for me before you ship out. I'll take good care of the farm till you're home. Love, Ruby Lee*

•   •   •

Red's kitten slinked along my legs when I showed him another tinted postcard Clay sent, sunrise on the Gulf. He'd written, *Ruby, It's some life here. Hope you see this much water some day. Miss you and the gang*, and I'd rejoiced. Still alive.

More cat than kitten, she'd retained her gray fur around her eyes and ears, but had grown into white. She purred and I held her, stroking her head while Red studied the postcard so long I saw grass grow.

"What'd you name the cat?" I broke the silence.

"Nuthin."

A glint brightened his eyes for an instant. He might've been mocking me.

"Nuthin?" I retrieved my postcard.

"Little Bit a Nuthin, that's her name." The barest trace of a smirk.

When she squirmed from my grasp, Red fixated on my arm. "She just scratch you?" He touched the scars my razor had left. I yanked my arm away.

He was quiet, contemplating. We both were. We didn't dance so good together.

"A nanny goat had triplets and one kid's such a runt, might be a dwarf," he said. "Wanna see her?"

Red looked smitten with the newborn, long-necked and lean, her body compact and furry on wobbly little legs. Her coat was the color of cocoa, mixed with patches of salt-and-pepper fur. Between her ears was a splotch of white fur like a cap. Her blue eyes made her exotic.

"She's a dairy goat," Red said. "Her milk is high in butterfat, if she ever gets any. Farmer says she'll be a midget forever, no good for breeding." He swept her in his arms, his face softening. He murmured into her fur.

"You're in love," I teased. His face turned the color of his hair. When he set the goat down, she bleated with eyes so mournful he bent to hug her again. She nipped at the strap on his overalls. "No, Delilah, you cannot eat that. She'll eat about anything," he almost smiled.

"Her name's Delilah? Like in the Bible? You're kidding."

"That's what I call her." His face tightened.

Maybe he'd feel stronger, having that attachment. "It's a nice name, Red."

"Farmer Krewell thinks a runt like her's not worthy of a name. Said don't take a shine to her." He looked pained. "The little kids love to cuddle with her."

I couldn't remember ever getting cuddled.

"You worried about Clay?"

Red's face darkened. "Gotta get back to my chores." He turned defiantly.

"Thought you'd wanna know he's okay," I shouted at his back.

•   •   •

Though the days were getting hotter, I took to wearing long-sleeved shirts to cover the scars. Skin on bones, the boys said of me. Lanky, said the doctor at my yearly examination. Scrawny, the girls in my dorm said.

Like Mrs. Roosevelt said, they can only make me feel bad if I give them my permission.

I put myself on a shelf, up high, in a dusty corner, where nobody looked. Where nuthin could touch me.

•   •   •

The colonel who commanded the Waco Air Field visited the baby cottage with his wife. They adopted the foundling, who would never know the void left by being abandoned.

The Gonzales Warm Springs Rehabilitation Hospital for Crippled Children opened in tiny Ottine, 150 miles south, and Mrs. Roosevelt made good on her promise. She'd secured Celesta a bed in the president's pet polio project, the Spanish stucco-style hospital with two therapeutic pools bordered by dwarf palmettos, a river-fed fountain, and waterfalls. Palmetto State Park was newly transformed from bogs and swamp by the CCC for children struck by the crippler. With Clare's help and lots of Mollie's tears, Celesta packed up her Easter seals and crutches to board the Southern Pacific, hospital-bound.

Kitty's health faltered. She was confined in quarantine. When I visited, she was either coughing in small yips, or more ominously, completely silent. I read her favorite book, *Happy Days,* through the door.

Mollie's stutter came back, more so at the mention of Celesta. She kept on marking those Xs on her 1936 calendar, same as she'd done for six years, her hope a habit for her.

Some teen boys, Red's age, were placed out to local farmers looking for cheap hands, chopping cotton or working at the gins. Labor was scarce due to the draft, but cotton was flourishing. Strong, muscular teens were sought after for farm families they'd never met. Vocational education for young men, the superintendent called it, though they'd been plenty educated working our crops and animals for years.

The boys feared becoming indentured servants, doing heavy labor, living on a hay mattress in a barn. But they hadn't heard from their families in years and had nowhere to go after they aged out.

Red's muscles twitched—his entire body quivered—with disbelief at their acquiescence, having hardened since his stint at Gatesville. The barbed wire-ringed reformatory had three Kentucky dogs for tracking escapees; he'd tried. They'd tracked him. Later he was a farm squad inmate, leased out to farmers, a punishment doled out as easily as fifteen strokes. He'd never risk being placed out.

"Watch me disappear with no trace," he said, resolute, "I will cease to exist."

His steely eyes convinced me.

On my next visit to the dispensary, the door to Kitty's quarantine room was wide open, her bed empty. She got sent to the San Angelo sanatorium, the nurse said, for bed rest and the air.

"That's in West Texas, same air as the Panhandle."

The nurse shrugged. "Suppose so."

"Dusty as it is, could kill her quick."

"Kitty's lived her nine lives already. Once a lunger gets TB, a few years is all most get."

While Waco flushed with arrivals and activity, the State Home got lonelier.

•   •   •

What was happening to the boys in Beatty's dorm was an open secret, which the new superintendent had approved. Matrons who couldn't handle their smart-alecky teens hauled them over to Coach, who made sure they'd take their licks. But next door where a married couple were dorm parents, the discipline was handled within, until the day a girl asked why her sister was punished with her panties down. The conversation among her dorm mates at the long table in the dining hall stopped dead as she asked innocently, "Why does the dorm father take my sister to their bedroom?"

The girls whispered, their eyes widening. "That happened to you? You? You, too?" they asked one another.

Miz Wills dropped her fork to the linoleum with a clang and stood, her face ghostly. She ushered the girls out, and I followed.

She'd file a formal complaint on their behalf, she explained, and on behalf of the boys with visible scars from brutal whippings. There's plenty of evidence, she said, don't be afraid—Ruby wasn't when the barn burned. The teacher who never missed a trick cited me as a pillar of courage.

What about Viola, who owes me twenty bucks, I intended to say. But the words came out: "Whatever I think I cannot do, I must."

Miz Wills nodded emphatically.

She herded us into her classroom, sat before her shiny black Underwood Champion, and began typing furiously. One by one, each girl sat beside her desk and told her story, as Miz Wills's fingers flew across the typewriter keys and slammed the carriage back, keys clacking, carriage slammed, keys clacking, carriage slammed, sheaf of paper pulled out, another one fed into the roller, repeat. Next she'd write up the beatings some boys admitted to; she praised the girls for their bravery. They looked at one another uneasily. Miz Wills was determined to stop the abuse. She'd stop the superintendent from shipping Thelma and Viola and Corinne to the NYA for defense training before they graduated. She was irked about the State Home withholding their pay and cheating them of their diplomas.

I smiled. Viola and Corinne were so boy-crazy they couldn't wait to work near the cadets.

"Thelma's college-bound, with a scholarship! Your friend the First Lady would *not* approve of that," she fumed, continuing her frenzied typing, stacking papers, reading her words back to herself, nodding.

I collated the flimsy carbon copies. The girls were watchful, like a torpedo could detonate any moment.

Miz Wills stood triumphantly. "This is where it stops"—she flapped the stack of papers in the air—"for you brave girls. Don't worry."

The predictable stab of worry came, justified, I knew.

•   •   •

That evening I finalized my plan, wanting no part of any crusades for righteousness at a place that specialized in wrongness.

Before dark I looked for Red at the barn, intending to deliver Clay's envelope to him—my last chance to make things right.

I heard hollering and cuss words coming around the barn, where Red struggled to wrestle a sledgehammer from Farmer Krewell. Red prevailed. The two of them glared at each other, jaws clenched, huffing hard to get air, Krewell demanding the sledgehammer back. Red's dwarf goat was tied to a post between them. Red tensed, his eyes wild, and took a step forward, winding up to swing the sledgehammer at Krewell.

"Red!" I screamed. "Quit it!" He startled, shocked still in mid-swing. He threw the sledgehammer over the fence and freed his blue-eyed kid, lofting Delilah to his chest and shoving Krewell aside to run for the woods. She bleated over his shoulder as he disappeared.

Krewell turned on me, wagging a threatening finger. "He comes back with that goat, she's a goner, so's he. He comes back without that goat, he's still a goner. Either way. You tell him."

Red won't be back, I might have sneered. I wheeled around and didn't say nuthin.

I knew I'd lost Red, and fell back upon my childish habit, how I controlled what was out of control. Deep down I was ashamed I still behaved like a ten-year-old. I was seventeen.

When the nervous distress returned in spades that night, I shoved up my left sleeve and traced the scars I'd raised on my arm with the straight razor, a tendency I'd refined to dull the emptiness.

CHAPTER FIFTY

I woke up with a special feeling, my whole body tingling with it, like something out of the ordinary was going to happen.

It wasn't till late afternoon, though, when I was in the vegetable rows pulling weeds with my crew, that a tall youth pushed a wheelbarrow of mulch my way. His arms below his rolled-up sleeves were muscled and browned, and his big-brimmed straw hat was pulled down low over his face against the sun. I couldn't make out who he was. One of Farmer Krewell's new boys, I figured. The tall youth dumped a load of mulch at my row, tipped his hat, and walked off.

"Who's that," Clare said, hoeing some compost over the lettuce roots.

My limbs tingled once again. Of course they were, since I was set to cut and run tonight.

•   •   •

By suppertime, gossip was flying across the campus like double-struck lightning.

Miz Wills got fired.

There are some things of which we don't speak, I would have told her, if she hadn't said not to worry.

After supper, I followed Thelma and Corinne to a bench outside their dorm, where they sat murmuring in a huddle of girls, fearful about what would happen. I said Miz Wills could help them, but they'd have to track down our teacher, who had nothing to lose now by going to the newspapers. She'd helped me before, she'd help the girls, too, I said, hoping I was right.

I placed a collect call to the telephone number I'd memorized for the First Lady's private secretary. Miss Thompson answered at the White House, explaining Mrs. Roosevelt was aboard the *Ferdinand Magellan* Pullman with the president and couldn't be reached. "I have to talk to her," I insisted. Miss Thompson asked where she could reach me tomorrow. "She can't," I faltered—till she said to mail the First Lady at Hyde Park. I wrote Mrs. Roosevelt a hasty note about the plight of the girls being sent to the NYA without their diplomas and used the farm's return address.

I left word with one of Red's pals I'd wait for him at our tree in the fruit grove. Extracting my White House letter and Clay's envelope from their slots between the paneling, I pocketed them alongside my coins and straight razor. I loaded my belongings inside a potato sack and crept to the orchard to hide it in the brush.

There would be no moon tonight.

At lights out the girls in our dorm couldn't settle; they whispered ghost stories to scare one another. My skin crawled like screwworm infesting a herd. I shushed 'em all for the last time, itching for my escape.

I was shaking so hard from fright and excitement our bunk shimmied above me, and Mollie mumbled in her sleep, "Quit that, Ruby."

If they caught me sneaking out the punishment would be severe. We'd listened in terror to pitiful pleas after a girl was caught out after dark with a boy, and I'd seen the welts on her legs. If Beatty caught me—I practically blacked out, picturing it.

When everyone got quiet, I concentrated on their breathing, counting, matching theirs. Hours passed. The dorm was quiet as coffin air. I pulled my nightgown over my head, making a mound of it with my pillow under the blanket.

Once I left, there'd be no going back. It was home to the farm or banishment to reform school, and like Red, I vowed to vanish before I'd spend an hour at the State Training School for Girls in Gainesville.

I laid Kitty's favorite book, *Happy Days,* on the foot of Clare's bed and made for the door. My hand on the knob, I paused, saying a silent goodbye to the gently snoring sisters I was leaving behind.

That's when the fire bell's blare shattered the stillness.

•   •   •

"Dang!" I muttered, "If that don't scotch it! How can I sneak outta here now?"

Before I even budged an inch the door was flung open, squeezing me behind it, as Croucher flew in hollering to line up two by two and skedaddle, straining to pitch her voice over the shrieking fire alarm. I pulled Emma Sue in front of me as we lined up in pairs, praying Croucher wouldn't see my traveling clothes. She was so busy counting us, she never noticed.

Maybe I'd make a run for it while we were lining up in the yard. The children were sleepy and sloppy about their rows—they scuffled in confusion, somebody pushed somebody, somebody else shoved back, a good time to vanish. But Beatty blew his whistle for order and Matron chimed in with hers till the screeching shrill of whistles and the deafening fire alarm forced my hands over my ears.

I shrieked, which no one heard over the din, and here came four fire engines screaming onto the grounds, firemen jumping off trucks before they even braked, armed with axes, dragging hoses; and then the blasting horn of the hook and ladder signaled us to stand back as the firemen drove it beneath the dorm's upper floors. When they sent the ladder up, two hundred pairs of eyes followed the firemen to the second floor, third floor, while we waited to see flames shoot out the windows, holding our breath, nervous giggles escaping at the thrill of it.

Then the lights dimmed, first in our dorm and next, out all over the campus.

After a brief, edgy silence, the littlest ones began wailing with no moonlight to see by.

One child let out a bloodcurdling scream, which set everyone into a panic. "Fire! Fire!" they yelled and ran every which way.

A strong hand gripped my upper arm, but it was too dark to make out who. "Red?" I asked. "Red, is that you?" I was being hauled away from the scattering children towards the orchard edging the grounds, lashing out with my free hand for freedom.

In the grove of trees, the sturdy apple tree trunks blocked the darkened buildings. I couldn't see any signs of flames licking the windows or smell any acrid smoke rising. The voices of the children sounded weaker and I wriggled once more, quivering, my skin slick with sweat sliding loose, the familiar dark veil descending.

The tree trunks became thick ink-black strokes over the distant silhouettes of the dorms, where kids and caretakers milled around, ghostly shapes, no one recognizable. The tree leaves rustled, rasping a command. *You think you cannot do it, but you must.*

My eyes made no sense of anything in the blackness coming on, setting my skin to prickling, panic rising. I stumbled, and somehow landed on my hidden sack, holding my few earthly treasures. I pulled it tight to my chest

"Coach?" My voice cracked at being caught by him.

No answer. I turned in circles, peering wildly about, hoping I was advancing toward the gate.

It became easier to orient myself, my eyes adjusting to find the fence, and my breath settled.

I made a run for it.

But I was stopped dead. My heart near leapt out of my throat. There were two strong arms around me. Tightening their grip around me.

"Let go' a me!" I hollered into the coach's chest.

He whispered, "Shush, Ruby, easy, you're okay. It's me, Will . . . "

I was confused. Will? When had I given up on Will, how long ago? His size was arrested in my memory as a teenage boy. These arms belonged to someone muscular and so tall he was a man, not like the brother who left me six years ago, whose face I'd memorized and reminded myself by conjuring every night before sleep—until one forgettable night I'd quit dreaming of a far-fetched rescue.

"We're going back home," he said.

My heart was racing but I'd never let on he scared me outta my wits.

"You didn't even ask if I want to go," I railed, my voice rising.

He could tell with one look at me I did. I felt the heat of unabashed relief spread over my face. I musta glowed like a neon sign. But across the campus, all eyes were trained on the firemen, their hoses, their ladders.

I wrapped myself around him and let a few tears spill. I looked one last time for Red. Then we walked away from the shadows of the orchard out the back gate, unguarded in the pandemonium of the fire, and down the block, then down the next block and the next, until we were strolling along Main Street. Will whistled for the first yellow cab we saw.

"The train station, sir," I said, and he echoed my words, regarding me with esteem.

•   •   •

"What took you so long! Where've you been? Why didn't you come for me—" I pummeled his chest that felt hardened like a boulder.

"Where's Pa? Why didn't he fetch me? You didn't make him come for me, all these years gone by I lost track a how many. Why not?"

"Ruby—" His eyes somewheres in the distance, looking at something only he could see. "Pa's not right. Could be his heart giving out. He's a broken man . . . What a fine young gal you've got to be. Maybe you're what he needs, seeing what matters, maybe he'll come back to us."

"Come back? From where? Broken, what do you mean? What about his heart?" I fired off my questions.

But he just shook his head. "I wish I knew."

About Momma, we said nuthin.

CHAPTER FIFTY-ONE

"You hungry?"

Just like he'd asked me on our last, and first, train ride. We sat side by side, me at the window, like then. It was a lifetime ago, when Will first asked me if I was hungry on a train.

"Ain't that what you always say," I said. He allowed an unhurried smile, pulling two apples from his pack. We bit in to them together, sweeping me back to that frightening train ride we'd made to Waco against my will. Maybe against his, too.

The downtown lights winked in between trains streaking past on the Mary Avenue tracks, freight trains, troop trains, Pullman cars from the yards and warehouses at the Cotton Belt Bridge. Will leaned across to stare at a passing troop train, uttering, "I heard about it but never believed till—" He dragged his sleeve across his perspiring forehead.

"That's who we're fighting, Ruby. Those dirty Japs that bombed Pearl Harbor." I made out the faces of the enemy flashing by, hundreds on board, appearing young and scared.

After they'd passed, Will was trembling.

"How'd ya get here?" I asked to distract him.

A whole world of trouble crossed his pensive eyes before he answered. "We got lots of time to catch up."

He took a small black case with frayed edges from his pants pocket and put it in my lap. "Open it, Ruby."

The banged-up lid had faint white capitals, "THE CHROMATIC HARMONICA. The First and only Practical one. M. HOHNER." I could barely make out the faded words. I lifted the lid to find a slim harmonica nestled into satiny red folds. "Take it out. It won't bite ya, girl."

It was black and silver, smooth and cool to the touch, with gold trim and old-style letters engraved on top, and looked shiny as a new penny in its skanky case. I handed it to Will.

He put it to his lips, which I saw were chapped and edged with white like he'd spent time in the sun. His ruddy cheeks hollowed as he inhaled, and when he blew, the harmonica let its high notes sail over us and its lower notes waffle and warble around us. He played "Shenandoah," so soothing and sweet it made my heart ache for home, and the passengers in the train went quiet, listening to his doleful tune.

I watched his fingers drifting over the harmonica, surprised. Will hadn't been the musical type. Where'd he learn that?

Steam poured from the engine as the train found its rhythm along with Will and rattled along the track back to Hartless.

•   •   •

"How'd you find me, Will?" I squeezed his hand. "I was making a run for it when you showed up."

I'd given up on him, on all of them, but I wouldn't say so.

"I never quit thinking about you—about your situation—hope you know that, Ruby. Just thought you were better off with Bess, after Pa took up the drink." His eyes brimmed.

The drink? Pa? I was too shocked to press.

"Course I didn't know about Bess . . . and then I got sidetracked." Will's laugh was wry. "More 'n once."

Still spare with his words. I stared at Will, trying to equate the boy I looked up to with the man I sat beside. His eyes sunk deep but were the same serious dark brown that gave nuthin away. His profile—a straight nose, notched on its end, the angular jaw, wide cheekbones—had a prominence that brought Pa to mind. His light brown hair was straight, thick on top, but cut tight over his ears, like the army put clippers to it and it growed out in spite. He was a few inches over six feet, taller than Pa, with the strength of a laborer.

He was a man alright, but I saw the thoughtful boy always writing in his journal.

"Will. You still got your diary?"

His grin revealed his crooked front tooth, overlapping its lookalike, and he was the boy I'd kept hold of. "You remember that. Yeah, I've filled a few since then. A lot's happened."

I squirmed, impatient to hear it all. "Like what—" The train jolted to a stop and Will scanned the window. We'd progressed as far as Waco's rural outskirts with the train slowing frequently for street crossings.

"What is it?" I tugged on his shirtsleeve and saw how worn the faded blue cuff was.

"Gotta make sure of something," Will said, leaving wet palm prints on the window. His face had a queer look.

"You look like you seen a duster coming. What's the matter? Will?" The car felt close, suddenly, a sickly sweetness trapped inside with us.

He motioned for me to stand up, hastening down the aisle. He called my name softly. I stepped toward him with my sack of belongings but his eyes said no. His lips made the words, *leave it. Hurry.*

We slipped out the train door onto the platform between cars. He picked me up and put my feet on the ladder. "What?"

"Sssh, Ruby, climb up quick. I'm right behind you. You won't fall."

I wasn't worried about falling. I'd climbed plenty of rungs up and down my bunk every night. I was dang confused about why Will paid for our tickets when we were gonna ride on the roof.

•   •   •

"My bag? You gonna get it, Will?"

We were lying flat on our bellies on the top of the car, and Will shushed me again. He felt for his pocket and muttered something about his harmonica.

"Your harmonica? And your pack. They're still down there," I said, alarmed. How could he leave all that behind? Wasn't his money in the pack? "Your wallet?"

"Quiet, Ruby, I got my money clip in my stompers. Harmonica's right here" —he patted his hip pocket— "only the case is down there."

A finger to his lips, he pressed my head down gently next to his.

We laid there a while, hardly breathing. He threw his arm over me protectively. We'd busted out quick because the Home was on my trail. I shivered, whether from the thrill or the fear, I couldn't tell.

Below, footsteps crunched gravel, deep voices blended and grew louder as they approached the car we'd escaped. Heavy boots scraped the steel steps into the Pullman car we'd decked. Will's arm tightened around me.

The car shifted as they walked the aisle. Hadn't they noticed the bag and pack we left on our seats?

"We gotta run," I whispered, certain we'd be found.

Will clapped a hand hard over my mouth, eyes fierce.

We heard them clomp down the steps and breathed a sigh in unison. "Not yet. Stay put," Will cautioned, but he needn't have. I wasn't going anywhere without him.

Soon came the hiss of the locomotive releasing steam, and the powerful engine roared back to life. The train lurched, paused, jolted forward again, and I watched Will for a sign we'd climb down. But he lay there, head cocked my way, letting a lazy smile cross his face.

"Ever deck a train, Ruby Lee? You're about to."

I didn't say nuthin.

●　　●　　●

We decked her for a time, till he confessed he'd been pulling my leg. "Can't stay up here once she gets her speed up. I'll help you down." He swiveled me around on my belly so my feet were facing the ladder, and we scrambled down, me between him and the rungs, like a farm dog mounts a bitch in heat.

Will found us two seats in the rear of a half-full car where most folks were reading newspapers, intent on headlines of the war in Europe and now Asia. The Battle of Midway had ended with a US Navy victory over Japan, but German U-boats were sinking record numbers of Allied ships. The war had a way of preoccupying the adults.

"Be right back." Will slipped out to the platform between cars and disappeared into the next Pullman.

I watched that door, anxious, my breaths coming in bursts. Pins and needles crawled from my fingertips to my elbows and I focused on the window, where countryside whizzed by, putting miles between us and Waco. I wrung my hands. I could not halt the panic that descended like a veil.

When he returned with my sack, his pack, and a big grin, Will gave a thumbs up. I finally got a full tank of air in.

My voice juddered, asking, "my sack?" It contained Pa's unread telegram to Bess, my clothes and toiletries, the First Lady's letters and clippings, Clay's postcards. I felt my pocket, where my razor was tucked beside Clay's envelope.

He laid the sack on my lap, his palm steadying my arm, watchful as I settled.

"What was the Home like, Ruby?" Will asked.

"What'd you write about in your diary?" I said real sweet. He grinned and made to tickle me, and I kissed his rough cheek. Stubble. Another thing he didn't have last time I saw him.

•   •   •

"There wasn't no fire, was there, Will."

The train was nearing Wichita Falls when I came out of a bad dream close enough to smother me. I didn't so much ask as snatch a declarative sentence from the air. I'd hated English class, but I could diagram a sentence faster 'n a sneeze through a screen door.

He got that sly look in his eyes, the one I'd forgotten since his teasing jabs during the hard times. The corner of his mouth always twitched, a thick eyebrow always raised up.

"I'll admit to fearing a fire could break out."

"How'd ya find the box?"

"I've been in town a few days, working out my plan."

"It was you in the fields yesterday." I pictured his face, hidden under that big-brimmed straw hat, jaw clenched. How the muscles in his arms flexed.

He eased into a smile. "Hitched a ride to Waco from Kelly Field, went to Bess's house pronto. Found out it was sold."

That internal count started of its own accord. *One, two.* "After she passed."

He teared up. "I searched the obituaries at the *Weekly*'s office. Tracked down her sister-in-law, found out where you were."

"Six years ago." I bit back a flare of anger.

"Too much red tape in the front office at the State Home. I couldn't wait for them to sort out how I was your kin and release you. So I watched the Home yesterday, saw how things operated, fine-tuned my plan. Almost didn't recognize you in the garden, you got so tall. Smoking, too. Shouldn't ought do that."

"Those are asthma cigarettes. Nurse gave 'em to me for my breathing trouble."

"That so?" Will was quiet. "From the dust pneumonia."

I slowed my breathing and listened for wheezing. Seemed okay.

"Well you're a young lady now, Miss Ruby Lee." He tipped his cap with a wily grin that settled my nerves.

"Slick. That you are, Will. Always were the smart one. What about Pa? How's Earl?"

It was like a huge cloud passed over to darken a righteous sunny day. My heart started racing, so I changed the subject.

"You look like you lived outside for six years." His fair skin, always prone to sunburn, was bronzed like a copper kettle.

He had lived outside, he said, maybe too long but by choice, until he'd joined the CCs and then he'd worked outside, all across West Texas, from Balmorhea to the Davis Mountains to the Big Bend.

I had no idea where any of that was.

He sketched the life for me, the three hots and a cot guaranteed by the CCC along with an education, in exchange for building trails and lodges in state parks. Disciplined, he said, but with downtime and friendships. Secure.

Like having family.

"After I got home, I did go to school awhile—but I needed the work."

"And you never been back since?" I said. "You lived in tents, cut down trees, moved boulders, and built culverts over dry creeks? What about college, you get there?"

"Well," he mulled his thoughts, "not exactly how you'd picture it."

He still kept things close, shut off like always. He had a lot in common with Red.

I blew out my frustration in a torrent of questions.

"How's it you know so much about train hoppin? Why didn't Pa come for me? What's happened to the farm? Where's Momma—"

"Ruby," he said, eyes searching the ceiling of the compartment for answers he feared telling me. "A lot's happened. I'm awful glad you're coming home."

"What else ain't you tellin me?"

Reluctantly, he turned, his eyes keen on mine.

"Earl. He's gone. Last I heard to Boys Ranch in Tascosa."

"Like a camp?" I said. How could Pa afford a camp?

"No, a place for troubled boys who need a strong arm to get right. He ran wild with Pa gone so much chasing WPA work, helping the soil men—"

"They sent Earl to reform school? Like Gatesville. I know about that."

"Not like that, more like a ranch with chores, responsibilities, a boss . . . Earl could come home, I expect; it's his choice to stay."

"But that's not all, is it. There's more," I said, not trying to keep the accusation from my voice.

"Things back home are looking up, rain's coming back." He avoided my gaze. "Could jolt Pa out of his blue funk . . . Been a wet summer, I hear."

I grabbed his jaw, yanked it my way. "What else, Will."

"I enlisted. Due to ship out soon as I get you home—got assigned overseas in the Army Air Forces' weather unit."

Just as soon as he'd found me, I'd lose him again.

First Clay. Red, probably. Now Will. A contagion of enlistment was going around.

My face felt hot enough to scald a skunk.

I snapped at Will, "I don't need you, or Earl, or anyone."

I pulled my lumpy sack to my lap, locking my arms around it.

CHAPTER FIFTY-TWO

By the time the train delivered us to the Rock Island depot in Hartless, it was well past midnight. Will got Pa's old A-Model started up after two tries, and with the moon a mere sliver, we splashed through pools of muddy water that gouged ruts in the road, the Ford's headlamps too weak to light the fields. I fell into bumpy slumber despite the rough ride.

It was nearing first light when I bolted awake at the sound of a penetrating clap. I was in our farmhouse where Will must have settled me. Finally back where I'd longed to be for seven years, I was fearful of the air. I drew in shallow inhales. I breathed and listened, eyes closed, afraid I'd hear the rush of a black blizzard blowing in to smother me.

There was silence, one I didn't trust: no cackle of a rooster nor the squeaky clank of a windmill; no rustle from winds riffling the wheat; no muffled voices of Pa and my brothers hitching up mules, nor the clatter of the truck motor; no cows lowing. The stillness outside was as ominous as my dark fears, where my memories were of silt layered on the pine table, filling our tin cups, glazing Momma's hand-stitched quilts, coating the Bible's leather cover, blanketing Granny Alma's rosewood bureau, soiling the pearly white keys of her spinet from Chicago.

I listened for the sounds of the storms carrying black and brown and red dirt, never rain, and heard none.

Just that startling clap. In the nightmare it woke me from, the long-ago smells of Oklahoma and New Mexico and Texas soils mingled into an acrid assault on my throat and I'd coughed up dirt, panicking, my world as dark as Black Sunday.

What was that sharp crack—like a thunderbolt—that roused me from those dark times?

Still trembling from ghastly recollections, I opened my eyes to the familiarity of . . . 1935. All was as it had been in our house. I lifted the shade and the light was blinding, a rising summer sun with its glare aimed at me. I called out for Will, who walked from the backyard, wiping his palms on his dungarees. Beyond our fields, I saw crops in curved banks, and past those, big bluestem, buffalo grass, and black grama waving in a vivid landscape once drab and brown. Our fields were unplanted but tamed, with some mounds of sand in crazy windblown patterns evident here and there. The only growth was a stand of trees, more like greened-up saplings, maybe young elms, hackberries, bur oaks, and black walnuts. They were planted in neat rows on the west side of our farmhouse, which inside bore none of the improvements Pa had talked of making, seven years on.

It's so quiet. My eyelids heavy, I slept.

●   ●   ●

Much later, Will shook me awake. The afternoon sun made long shadows of us as we crossed the bare dirt yard. Drowsy still, I tried to make sense of his words which made no sense.

"There's some bad news, Ruby." His eyes reddened and brimmed wet. "It's Pa. He's gone."

Will didn't hush my mournful wails. He didn't stop my angry fists from beating on his chest. He didn't share how shocked he was and how he blamed himself; he didn't explain what caused Pa to die, or when, except to say, "It was his time." These were mysteries he left me to puzzle over, like the abrupt blast that interrupted my nightmare, answers I'd unearth another time.

He waited out my protests, my sobbing, my pleas, till I was rung dry as a twisted damp rag. Of Momma, he said her disappearance was a riddle he hadn't solved.

His silence held the power mine did—Momma's whereabouts being one of the unspoken things—things we don't even think of.

He had no words while we bumped over the two-rut road to town, skirting dunes left behind by the last big blow. I dosed off in denial of my yearnings and failings, falling into my dreams. We entered town and Will downshifted the Ford, catching me between worlds. Aware on some discomfiting level, yet soothed by hope. We'd pulled into the caliche drive of a comfortable house that mirrored the one in my fantasy, its lawn tended, its vegetable garden thriving. Graceful Chinese elms shaded the white-clapboard home in autumnal golds. The dormer windows were open, curtains lazily shifting within. Wicker chairs with floral cushions sat on the wide front porch, where a ceiling fan idly stirred the air. Healthy horses grazed in a pasture by the barn, pied cattle drank from a brimming tank in the fields. I rubbed my eyes and blinked. A boy pushed a mower across the greening grass of the front yard. I wished for my blade. Instead I pinched myself hard where my scars raised up, and peered closer.

It was as if the house and farm I'd conjured had sprung to life.

"We're at the doc's," Will said carefully. "You'll remember him from our visits to his clinic when you were sick." I recalled his soup kitchen where we ate, how he listened to my chest in the hospital.

Will reminded me he was due to ship out July 30. "Thursday. That's tomorrow. You're staying here in town with the doc while I'm overseas."

And like that, my dream was shattered—a proper home surrounded by my family—I'd nursed a fantasy that didn't exist.

When Will said Doc Lawler and his missus would be my family until we could all be together, I about spit at the irony of it. I'd come all this way, and my only family was back at the Waco State Home.

I didn't say nuthin, which he took as a good sign.

"Atta girl, Ruby, you're a tough one." His relief plain as day. "I'll help you settle before I head to the base."

Will's deep brown eyes held that distant look, wherever he went with his thoughts. He spoke real quiet, as if to himself. "It's powdery and slippery, the idea of family, sliding right through your fingers like flour through a sifter, dust through walls."

I waited for him to see I understood what he meant, nodding when he noticed me scrutinizing him.

What was the point in protesting? The US Army Air Forces he'd joined were attacking Nazi Germany. It was war and we were all caught in it. I'd find my own way to our farm. Until then, I figured I'd breathe easier in the Lawlers' sturdily constructed house, which I'd learn was nonsensical soon enough.

Uncertainty was the only constant in those hard times.

The adults were whispering in the parlor after they'd settled me in a bedroom, noting how groggy I was. Tired or not, I could hear the doc tell Will, "Your pa hasn't been in fine fettle for a few years now, with your ma . . . gone. It was the drink that got him," he added. "Lots of men turn to it when they can't earn a dime or support their families. The drink leads to worse, that's why your pa took his own—"

"It was his heart," Will snaps. "His heart went right out of him and you put that on the death certificate, Doc."

The truth, it stays unspoken.

Will's explanations of Pa, Momma, and Earl made no sense, but I was done questioning his bunk. Sometimes what you don't know is better than what you learn by digging deep. The signs were all there, the answers were all around me. But I didn't want the truth either. I might never want it.

That letter Momma wrote still languished in my lost cardboard suitcase somewheres back in Waco, unopened.

CHAPTER FIFTY-THREE

WILLA MAE

The country is at war again, and staff shortages mean we take extra shifts in the kitchens, at the laundry facilities, in the bakery, on the maintenance crews—in between our hydro treatments and hypos. *The inmates are running the asylum*, a popular joke goes around. In autumn of 1942 the recruiters are desperate enough for soldiers they set up outside the asylum grounds. Forcing myself not to imagine my sons enlisting, I scrub the sixth stock pot of my second shift and wonder what Miss O'Keeffe thinks about this war on the heels of the war to end all wars.

In November 1918 when the Great War ends, our men were arriving home by the trainloads. I was seventeen, adrift, and in need of a room and a job. In stepped Mr. Fred Harvey to solve my problems.

I'd noted the Harvey girls taking orders, lunching with my mother at the Amarillo Harvey House. They would smile in their ankle-length black dresses, hands tucked demurely in deep pockets of their white aprons—attire I could imagine the severe Miss O'Keeffe adopting. The Harvey Houses were a staple of the Santa Fe Railroad depots, offering newsstands, lunch counters, dining rooms, and at some, barbershops, soda fountains, bars, curio shops, even Photomatic photo booths since 1876. Mr. Harvey hired only wholesome-faced, decent young women who live in sheltered quarters he provided above the station, overseen by a matron to mind their ladylike manners. Although Mr. Fred Harvey had died nearly two decades earlier, his standards were still strictly adhered to. No girl in need of work batted an eye when told a condition of employment is she cannot marry until she puts in a full year of work. Decent pay, a room of my own, meals included, days that pass mindlessly as I followed orders—I signed on. My marriage prospects could wait. Until they couldn't.

In the asylum kitchen, I start in on the sink piled high with cups and saucers next, feeling my spirits descend as I revisit my dim fate in Canyon twenty-four years ago. How Miss O'Keeffe's illness and sudden departure upended my world . . . and how I knew my fortune had turned upon meeting Beck one afternoon at the Harvey newsstand counter . . . which led to a worse fate in the dust country.

My mind swirls like a sandstorm. *Will Beck ever come for me?* I wonder.

My face stings, the blowing dust swipes across it like sandpaper

From far off someone says, "Catch her, she's having a sinking spell . . ."

The once-bright day gets pitch black, darker than sin. "Where's the sun?" I cough . . . and fall back into the Black Sunday that took my mother and my baby.

Why did I accept my mother's help, I berate myself for the hundredth time. I can't forget her shock at finding me in childbirth under those conditions. Her insistence she'd stay to help, though her lungs couldn't withstand the dusters any more than my baby's. Innocent Nell, born into a destiny that ensnared us all.

How have I allowed this? My mother can't mask her horror and her face haunts me still.

I'm numb, rigid and rooted to the floor. I hear water rushing, a harsh voice shouting, "My feet are wet." It's the asylum's kitchen boss, cursing the lunatic. Me. Dishwater flows over the sink edge, my gown is drenched, my hands red and raw from the harsh soap, and I'm unable to move.

"I can't leave them, Beck," I plead, my lips moving but making no sound

"Restrain her," the boss commands an orderly. He shoves me aside, and stiff, I keel over.

"All alone," I say

1943

CHAPTER FIFTY-FOUR

RUBY LEE

"My pa always had the highest regard for the doc, Miz Lawler. Everyone did."

She clasped her hands, then stood, turning her wedding band round and round. Uselessly, a window fan blew hot air through her office. It was a crackling dry spring, 1943, six months since Doc's death.

On the September afternoon of his funeral, which had drawn a crowd bigger than any flying circus, I'd snuck away from the prayers and casseroles and tributes Pa never got when he'd died last July. My heart ached at losing Pa before I ever laid eyes on him again—I'd refused to feel the shock of the doc's death, too. I had to keep my mind from dwelling on the church service seven years ago that had turned an uncommon bright day into Black Sunday and upended my world.

I'd stolen away to our farm, as winter was teasing a late arrival with Indian summer weather. Our acreage appeared as abandoned as me, but the Aermotor blades still spun with their comforting clanking sound, urging me to climb thirty-seven feet to the platform. Far off to the southeast, beyond the Canadian River breaks, was the Boys Ranch in Tascosa where Earl labored. I was closer to the sky, closer than I'd ever get on the flat brown dying acreage Pa abandoned while he planted shelterbelts for FDR's Forestry Project. Closer to Will when he joined the Army Air Corps for flight school, closer to heaven if that's where Momma was.

From on high, dunes of dirt made brown patches in between light green pastures fresh with growth, forming giant squares across miles of even terrain that flattened into the horizon. Stands of young trees divided the acreage, and prairie grasses cloaked untilled sections. To the west was the hubbub of the new airfield, its barracks, hangars, and field hospital hastily constructed by Mexican braceros and locals for glider pilot war training. I watched an army-drab Aeronca Grasshopper with its white-on-blue star taxi down one of the grass runways, circle airborne, and return to make its landing, followed by a vivid yellow Piper Cub Cruiser circling wide and landing, the two planes repeating their coordinated dance. I daydreamed one of those pilots was Clay. The affection in his eyes and the throb I'd felt stayed with me since he'd hugged me goodbye, handing me the slim envelope.

"Open it tomorrow, after I'm gone," he'd said, and thinking he'd meant it for Red, I hadn't.

To my surprise, the enclosed fifty-dollar bill was meant for me. It came with a simple note. *Take flight—Clay*.

Watching the airplanes loop again and again above the patchwork of indifferent farm sections, I knew I'd learn to fly once I found means for the farm's revival.

Now Miz Lawler's voice, with its bitter edge, snapped me back to my purpose. "High regards never paid for seed, or hay, or the electric. The bank wouldn't accept any high regards to pay down his loan. Doc brought me out here to be a farm wife. His clinic was a kindness he did out of duty to the folks suffering here. It 'bout killed him."

Folks said it was the drouth that killed Doc Lawler. He was an asthmatic with the TB turned farmer who survived the Dirty Thirties. The Lawlers ran a soup kitchen, treated hoboes' maladies for pocket change, and doctored neighbors who paid with IOUs and blessings—like he'd done for our family. It was bad timing, taking up farming in a drouth.

"But running the clinic was a blessing to me," Miz Lawler was musing. "Operating the X-ray machine, developing films, managing the accounts, such that they were. Saved me from drudgery in his scorched fields, where he pictured golden grain and greening-up corn."

I was intent on getting my pilot's license, and impatient with home economics in high school, itching to learn business economics. The farming business couldn't differ much from the doctoring business when it came to running the numbers. I knew if I worked by her side, I'd learn how to keep books for the farm, too.

"You must be dog-tired after all these years, Miz Lawler."

"Right here's where I feel challenged. Useful." Her shoulders slumped. "And worn down."

I steered her to her husband's horsehair chair.

"Let me help with the accounts, ma'am. I've been working advanced calculations to earn my flight certificate," I said, embellishing, "I'll be the youngest to graduate flight school, eighteen, and the only girl." The instructor in my tables and instruments course said I had the aptitude for navigation but I'd need plenty of flight time.

Last summer and fall I had spent weekends trying to fit in some air time around the pilots training for war, when I wasn't overseeing the tenant farmer I'd hired using Will's monthly wages from the Army Air Forces. Griner was an old cowpunch who ran cattle for the XIT Ranch and learned farming after the vast ranch lands had gone under plow. He furrowed our fields for winter wheat, borrowing from the techniques brought in by the soil conservation men to slow the sand blow. Our deal included lodging in our half-sod house, which he'd fix up and roofed, along with the barn.

I kept that deal quiet, until I could make a success of growing grain.

Miz Lawler looked at me like she saw something in me. I stood taller. Nobody here knew I was still seventeen.

"Might could be good for you—this clinic was the university education my daddy wanted for me, when I was too headstrong to hear anything but my heart. Let that be a lesson, Ruby, don't hitch to some cowboy head over heels and let him steal your future."

Everyone was getting married in the war days, living like they never expected their men to return. It was a plague prompted by dispatches from the war's front lines, steady fodder in the newspapers. A constant supply of cadets arrived for glider training at the new base, along with infantry volunteers. Plenty of young men brought girlfriends to see them off. The justice of the peace was as busy as the owner of Gem Jewelers. Folks were sacrificing for the war, rationing their cooking oil, gasoline, sugar, but down the street the war brides in the boardinghouse were spending their husbands' service checks like it was the Roaring Twenties all over again.

Miz Lawler brought in a young Galveston doctor who'd graduated from the University of Texas Medical Branch, then hired a registered nurse. When the clinic got busy, this time with pregnant patients who could afford to pay their bills, she took me on. After two months of bookkeeping alongside her, she acknowledged my value with a raise. My next paycheck included a modest bonus. It all went straight to Co-op Supplies and Feed, where Griner was stocking up on my account. Soon our grain would be ready for harvesting.

•   •   •

Life among hasty brides whose new husbands had left them for the front lines was not so different from life among the children whose parents had left them at the State Home. The boardinghouse was busy with arrivals and departures, greetings and farewells. During evenings on the porch, listening to the chatter of new brides only a few years my senior, I learned about the intimacies of marriage, and how to get pregnant—a condition I resolved never to find myself trapped in. The brides and fiancées longed for V-Mail letters from their young men. They made do with their sugar and coffee rations, they shared a few pairs of silk stockings with mended runs, they planted greens and beans in their victory gardens. They laughed, gossiped, and communed like the family they'd fast become. When news came of a soldier feared missing, or buried at sea, they propped one another up against the grief. When the base chaplain arrived in the early morning hours to comfort the pregnant wife of the field officer killed in a glider crash, all the brides vowed to help her raise her fatherless baby.

They were a makeshift family and they fit me in like a kid sister, with some well-intended murmurs of sympathy for my father's untimely passing—which I spurned. Their inquiries about my brothers were polite if curious about Earl, and sensitive to the dangers Will faced on the front, what with their husbands and fiancés in similar straits. But I kept to myself. The brides allowed me the privacy of things unspoken—especially the whereabouts of my momma.

The doc's wife, on the other hand, wanted to mother me. I wasn't having it. She dispensed wisdom, broaching topics like feelings of shame or guilt, how secrets caused folks to suffer, but I shut her off like a spigot. I wouldn't let anyone try to tend my trauma.

A hurt dog snaps at anyone who goes near its wound.

The brides at the boardinghouse were too full of their fears for their GIs to pick at anyone else's scabs. I fell right in with them. They were generous and fun-loving, and after work and on weekends, I was their kid sister, at their suppers, going shopping, and socializing.

Holding my secrets close among them wasn't hard. Carrying them was the burden.

One evening a new bride, whose ghoulish habit involved scanning the columns of war dead in *The Panhandle Roundup* for names she'd recognize, began reciting the list aloud. She infected the entire boardinghouse with a case of the jitters.

Ida Rose, the doyenne of them all, stood to her full five-foot-eight-inch height (absent her perennial periwinkle pumps) and announced in her compelling, smoky voice that the only thing for it was to set up a canteen at the army airfield.

"Like the Stage Door Canteen," she said, shimmying theatrically, "the famous one in New York City, ladies. We'll take our phonograph and swing records, get some soda pop, and show the soldiers a good time."

Like a sudden shift of wind can blow a field of waving wheat stalks in reverse, the entire gaggle dabbed their eyes and began enthusiastic preparations for Saturday night at the base theatre.

CHAPTER FIFTY-FIVE

While they set about making the airfield canteen a magnet for all the single young women in Hartless and a hit with the fliers stationed there, I studied for my pilot's license. I stayed up nights poring over the farm's numbers and yields and government ag reports and wheat futures. I created a crash course of my own design by tuning in to KGNC, reading "Old Tack" in the Amarillo paper, and deciphering the *Farmer's Almanac*, teaching myself to predict the weather.

In town, I read the newspapers in the De Soto Hotel's lobby, scanning the increasingly lengthy lists of wounded and dead for two names: Becker and Hubbard.

On a Sunday afternoon in March 1943, I read a paragraph listing female names, reprinted from the *Waco Tribune-Herald*: "Eleven girls from the Waco State Home have joined the NYA and are learning various phases of defense work. Their progress is rapid and in a short time they will be assigned to defense plants."

Among the eleven names was Viola's; her studious roommate, Corinne; and dedicated Thelma, whose 4-H scholarship had meant everything to her.

From somewheres deep a shameful feeling stirred. I pushed it back in place, buried where it could not be exhumed. My skin prickled, hot all over.

I'd been a fool, putting my faith in any of them—even Miz Wills, and especially the First Lady, whom I'd never doubted. Till now. They'd failed those girls like they'd failed me. So had Bess, Will and Pa, my momma.

There was no one to trust but me.

Late that afternoon, the sky was rippling pinks and salmons, ambers and oranges, backlit in electric blues by the setting sun, and I climbed down from my thinking spot atop the windmill. I stared into the well awhile, willing myself to do what I feared.

When I pulled my straight razor from my pocket, a last ray of sun glinted off its sharp edge. I flung it into the dark void and listened for the satisfying clank at the bottom.

•   •   •

It was going on summer and the winds were blowing thirty, forty miles an hour across the plains.

"I'm not interested in being a farmer," I said.

My brother Earl squinted at me and gestured at the fields under terraced and contour-listed cultivation. The winter wheat had come back abundant that spring, surviving a cold snap and even a short-lived frost, and yields would be high come summer. Wheat prices were on a rise, I explained, what with all the war demand for industrial alcohol and for livestock feed, and reports were the country was on track to produce five hundred million bushels by the end of 1943.

"Sure making it look like you are, Ruby. Haven't seen a crop like this since—well, none I can remember." As Earl revolved to take it in, his mouth gaped open wide. "Can't even imagine what this'll be, now you've put your mind to it."

He was going on nineteen, but his face was as animated with awe as the eager eleven-year-old I'd left.

"I got my mind on our home—the house I'm building for us," I lectured. "The crops are just the means to pay for it. That wheat means nothing to me but cash. The tenant can plant bananas and raise monkeys for all I care, long as it brings a profit. He handles all this."

I walked with Earl to the shelterbelt trees, across the fresh-dug irrigation ditches bubbling with water I'd directed Griner to never spare. The trees nearly shaded the marker where Pa was laid to rest in the grave site Will dug. Earl lowered his head, lips moving in silent prayers, paying his respects.

I felt a rush of warmth for him, but when I stepped forward to put my arm around him, Earl's body tensed.

The wind gusted, carrying enough dirt to make me cough. He pulled me in and patted my back, and said, "There, there."

I cleared my throat. "I'll be making a home here for us."

"Gonna put all the pieces back together, are ya? Maybe you can," he said, his expression showing me how improbable he thought that was.

"It's all I've ever wanted," I said.

"Your head's in the sky, I hear from the flyboys at the base," Earl teased.

I hid a smile.

Earl had showed up all of a sudden, his body all growed and his mind done with the Boys Ranch, he said. It was room and board in exchange for ranch chores, with tough discipline, during the hard times. He didn't mention the legendary jams he'd got himself in around town which folks relayed in indulgent terms. "A young man finding his way" was the most charitable assessment of Earl's misdeeds. At school, teachers spoke of him as a no-account truant. Others called him lucky as a four-leaf clover. Amarillo tire salesman Cal Farley had offered Earl a shirttail to hang to, when he'd started up his ranch in Tascosa for boys nobody wanted. Miz Lawler said Earl had been among the first dozen delinquent boys he'd taken in, but she hadn't said why. And neither did Earl.

I'd heard the gossip. He'd helped himself to Bull Durham at the tobacco counter one too many times, borrowed a bicycle here and there, lifted someone's Christmas wreath right off their door, skipped school enough to get kicked out. He'd relieved the grocer of a fresh loaf of Julia Lee Wright's bread, though he delivered his illegal winnings from the pool hall every Friday to the bank that held Pa's mortgage. But the deed that got him put away, I figured, was getting caught window-peeping.

The windows were in the yellow house on the wrong side of the tracks, where Miss Walker's young ladies took discreet care of lawyers, bankers, business owners, and town councilmen. Which was another unspoken thing.

Earl looked lanky and sinewy that May morning he'd found me assessing the wheat crop. He was fresh-shaved, still freckled, but with his straggly pale-blond hair cut so short it looked white. Neat, quiet, and polite, with no semblance of his boyish fidgetiness nor his chronic gap-toothed grin. His eyes, once roving and curious, held a guarded look.

"I reckon I'll be drafted, now that I left the ranch." He said he'd come to make sure things were working out at the farm. "I want to learn radio."

I shoved down a lump forming in my throat.

"You'll stay though, won't you? A while?"

I counted, *one, two, one, two*, under my breath as my pulse quickened, and I foresaw my nervous distress ready to snatch me up. I stroked at the scars on my arms, calming down.

Earl's eyes skipped to the raised lines fading to dark pink from my daily exposure to the sun.

"I'm fixin to enlist, Ruby. In the Army Signal Corps."

I threw my arms around him as a hasty heart pang got me, jamming my head into his chest, and squeezed his tall, scrawny frame until his voice broke the spell.

"Let go now, little sister."

I clutched him tighter. "You get yourself back in one piece, Earl."

"You're more tenacious than our momma."

Momma.

That lump in my throat arose and prevented me from speaking. Earl took my hand.

"You remember the state she was in, don't you, before you got the dust pneumonia? She was in a terrified condition for weeks, till you got well enough to go east. That, she could not abide. She beat on Pa's chest and cried and yelled; she held him responsible for sending you away. She broke down, wouldn't eat, or sleep, or be consoled. She wanted no part'a Pa. She rubbed her hands raw, you remember that. Well, after that she started picking out her hair."

"No," I said, defiant. "No, Earl. I don't want to hear any more about her."

"She followed you, Ruby, you know that? She walked the tracks after your train pulled out, trudging on like a soldier till after dark. I chased after her, tried to stop her, begged her to turn around, but she never once took her eyes off where your train vanished. She fixated on walking clear to Waco. When a westbound freight bore down on us, I had to shove her off the track, she was so intent I'd swear she never even saw it. Once it passed by, she got right back at it, walking the track. Her compass was set on you."

His throat caught. "Me, Pa, our farm, none of it mattered to her as much as losing you. You musta known that. The next day, she collapsed on the tracks. Pa and me took her to Trinity Hospital. By then she was—broken— a nervous breakdown, the doctors called it. Said she'd gone mad. Pa said she was a danger to herself. They couldn't help her, she needed specialized treatment . . ."

Earl's voice cracked. Tears pooled and darkened his eyes.

"Driven mad by dust, the judge said. Pa took her to—"

I interrupted him. "The telegram."

"What telegram—"

I whirled round quick as a tumbleweed, at a run, my footfalls pounding out whatever he was saying. My breath was scarce as I tore into the house, racing for the bedroom where my valuables were. Pa's telegram—like all the dollar bills I ever earned since the banks failed—was stashed like precious cargo under the mattress. Dust rose up as I thrust my arm between the moldy mattress and box springs to extract the telegram that came for Cousin Bess as the Brazos flood was coming for us. The telegram I couldn't read then and was loath to read ever since.

Why I'd feared its contents, I'd never let myself consider. Now the urge to rip it open was as forceful as the flood waters that deluged Waco seven years ago. I read:

"Court ruled Willa unfit STOP Committed to North Texas State Hospital STOP Please keep Ruby safe - SIGNED Beck."

My mother, unfit? Insane? "That's not possible."

A rough yank on my shoulder and I faced Earl. Red-faced, with his eyebrows arched high, he signaled his incredulity.

"It's true, Ruby. I couldn't save her—Pa testified she went insane and the judge sent her to Wichita Falls—to the lunatic asylum, Ruby." His voice was coarse with regret. "Where they send people who go crazy."

But I was no longer listening, my hands clamped over my ears, shaking my head *no*, refusing to comprehend what Earl believed.

His voice rose to counter my denial, shouting, "Pa did it! Are you so dang blinkered you can't see what's right in front of your face, girl?"

He bent to retrieve the telegram flitting to the floor. His lips moved slowly, pronouncing each word in a whisper as he read it. His sad eyes rose to meet mine.

I said it, once. *No*. Firm.

He crumpled the lies into a wad he lobbed at my chest. When the screen door slammed, I let him go.

CHAPTER FIFTY-SIX

WILLA MAE

I stare out the window as a grave marker is placed at the tiniest, and newest, grave site, watching the gravedigger dig a second, adult-sized grave beside it. One of the pregnant patients, having been deemed morally defective and confined on the feebleminded ward, has died in childbirth. Before supper hour nears, I slip outside to the tiny grave where my most uncomfortable memories arise—of losing Nell. The sensation of my insufficient breasts haunts me, though eight years have passed. Undernourished as I was—as we all were—my milk was too scant to sustain my infant daughter. And her lungs were too small to filter out the dust.

I become aware the gravedigger is watching me, perhaps wanting to comfort me, feeling my loss as well. But I am too overcome to pay him any mind; I throw myself at the tiny marker engraved with nothing but a number, 504, and I weep uncontrollably for Nell for a long time.

The gravedigger's voice comes at me from inside a deep well. He speaks haltingly, his accent heavy, says, "I am sorry for your loss," and helps me up gently with a weathered hand. What could you know of my loss, I almost say, on the tip of my tongue, but I look around at all the grave sites he must have dug for the asylum over the years. Of course he knows loss.

"Thank you," I murmur. "You are?"

"Mr. Lorenzo," he replies, a foreign tinge to his pronunciation.

I speak softly. "My name is Willa Mae Eckhart."

"This is your child," he indicates the tiny grave. "No," I shake my head, "I don't know her. But I do know she didn't belong here."

I sit, my chest still heaving as I recover my breath and my composure. My cheeks are wet with tears. He removes a worn white handkerchief from his pocket and gives it to me.

I fold it carefully and place it beneath my hands in my lap, leaning back against a sturdy bur oak and closing my eyes. The lids feel so heavy.

When I open my eyes again, the light is golden and has bathed the grounds in warm late afternoon tones. The gravedigger is still there, seated beside me in the same spot but alert, as though he never budged. The silence between us is comfortable.

Later I say, "She reminds of someone."

The sun is going down and we have missed supper but I have no appetite for what they offer.

• • •

It becomes my habit to take my colored pencils and drawing papers outside to sit beneath the orderly rows of trees in the cemetery. The gravedigger always appears, sitting companionably with me as I work. His fingers are soiled under the nails, a working man's hands, like Beck's, and he speaks little. "Your daughter," he asks one day as I finish a portrait of Ruby. She's becoming a young woman. Her upright carriage is mine; her unflinching eyes are her father's; but her alluring face most resembles my mother's.

"Yes, she's seventeen, going on eighteen now," I explain. "Eleven when I lost her." He manages to understand me without any more dialogue. He raises his arms and rounds them, as if in an embrace, reading my eyes. He knows I ache to hold her in my arms.

We watch an airplane arcing overhead and into its white trail I send my love to Ruby.

1945

CHAPTER FIFTY-SEVEN

RUBY LEE

More than a year had flown by while I submerged myself in crop prices, accounting, and aeronautics. Kept my mind off my brothers, of whom I'd had no news. After hours of pilot training, studying flight manuals and instrumentation, passing my aeronautical engineering classes, all the drilling and the testing were behind me. I was finally ready to fly my first solo, in a fifty-horsepower Cub.

For good luck, I reread the book I'd borrowed permanently from Waco's Carnegie Library, *Women with Wings*, when traveling aerialists flew over en route to Rich Field for barnstorming shows. It had been five years ago; I could picture the old biplane buzzing the State Home one Saturday in 1940, and I caught out for the flying circus.

I wedged myself into a lineup of boys waiting for a ride. The Travel Air biplane soared, barrel-rolled, banked, looped, and turned for the landing strip. The pilot stepped onto the bright yellow wing of her blue biplane and lifted her flight goggles, her bright eyes flashing her excitement to the crowd. She tucked some errant curls back inside her leather flying helmet and motioned for her next rider. While two boys ahead of me tore into their pockets for change, I loped to the field and took her hand-up into the open cockpit. "I like to see an eager girl," she laughed, asking my name.

"I'm Genevieve. Been flying since I was born, but officially, for seven years." She thrust an oversize bomber jacket and goggles at me to don. "We'll squeeze in together, right up front. Gets cold up there, better button up.

This your first time? Don't worry, I haven't lost one yet! Strap in tight. You're in for it."

The propeller roared to life, drowning out any hope of chatter. Noise boomed in my ears, and we were off into a forever blue sky, wind gusting at our faces.

The thrill was instantaneous. I was hooked like a channel cat.

She banked the biplane for a view below, and the fields assembled themselves into neat quilt-patches, in burnt oranges, faded greens, and wan yellows, until we flew into clouds as gauzy as cotton batting. The grinding propeller and roar from the Wright engine became a low drone as I concentrated on the sensations, unaware I was mumbling, *one, two, one, two*, till we'd landed.

Genevieve glanced at me. "You counting the clouds up there, sweetie?"

I quit counting.

"Stay here in the cockpit, where I sit. Take the controls," she said. She held up a finger to the boys waiting their rides, and they groaned as I boosted myself over to her spot. She stood beside me on the yellow wing, leaning into the cockpit, close enough to smell the earthy leather of her flight jacket, the smoky Lucky Strikes on her breath, the spearmint gum she chewed.

She pointed out each window, lever, and switch in a dizzying array of instruments embedded in the black panel, explained each one's role, and finally placed my hand on the stick, cupping hers overtop mine.

"Close your eyes. Picture yourself guiding this ship down the runway, lifting, lifting, lifting, hi-i-i-i-i-iigh into the sky. On a path to wherever you want to go."

I did just that, replaying our takeoff and flight as if I was piloting my own plane, till I got myself dizzy.

She smiled vibrantly, her lips wide and coated in gleaming cherry-red lipstick, and gave me a thumbs up.

"I'll be back," I said.

For the rest of 1940 my head was in the clouds. On weekends during spring and summer, I hitched a ride to the flying circuses at Rich Field whenever I could. Waiting for a burger at the Dairy Queen, I dreamed of flying lessons. At the sporting goods store, I ogled the model airplane kits.

That fall, I swallowed my pride to attend free matinees for orphans, where the daring aviatrixes Trixie and Babe flew their air race in *Tail Spin*. I hid out in the balcony between showings, watching the picture again and again.

At the ending, the stunt pilot's name scrolled by in the credits. Genevieve Haugen—the aviatrix who'd given me my taste of freedom—had penned *Women with Wings*, which inspired *Tail Spin*. Her airplane ride, in turn, inspired me, setting me on my own flight path and ready to earn my wings.

• • •

The crusty instructor, who claimed he was a protégé of the Great War's flying ace Eddie Rickenbacker, had started me in the school's oldest Piper J-3, a two-seat monoplane painted a yellow as bold as French's mustard, stamped with a black flash reminiscent of a lightning bolt.

When we leaned into the cockpit, he said, "Okay now, you're gonna pre-flight her. Three things: Be sure our fuel's on; be sure we're trimmed; this here's the altimeter, very basic." He took me through the instruments, pointing to the fuel gauge—"Just a cork floating in the tank; the gasoline goes down, this vertical wire goes down"—eyes probing, ascertaining I followed him, showing me the sturdy lift struts, the cables that controlled the ailerons, the tightness of the flying wires.

"And it's a hand prop," he said, placing my hand on the propeller high atop the Cub's nose. I ran my palm over its smooth wood surface, following its curve. He waved another trainer over to swing the prop. "You're in the front seat today."

Almost there, I smiled to myself, the shiver of success overtaking me.

"The back seat, that's where you solo." He sized me up and took me down a peg. "Before you get ahead of yourself there, missy."

I climbed up quick, so's he wouldn't see my cheeks coloring.

Once I'd folded myself into my thimble-sized seat, my cramped legs astride the stick, a foot planted on each rudder pedal, he leaned forward, his voice alarmingly intimate up close. "This is a tail wheel. You're gonna learn to be ahead of it—anticipate things and be ready."

My toes prickled and the sensation shot up to my heart, which jumped a little. I could hardly wait to be airborne.

Straight and level, he drilled me, climb, glide, bank, turn and recover.

Soon after, I was taking the controls, addicted to the heady mix of gasoline, motor oil, and fresh-cut grass that blasted me as the little tail-dragger's engine fired. Poise, I whispered to myself, poise and patience, as I turned and pointed the high-wing trainer straight down the runway, jolting me with pleasure as its wheels bounced along the grass strip. I was eager for the Cub's tail to come up and signal she was ready to fly. It took only a matter of seconds that seemed like forever to me. Easing back on the stick, climbing, air rushing past my face, I was tipsy with joy.

Until the instructor lit into me, which he did every time I glanced at the altimeter—he'd holler to keep it straight and level by feel.

"You learn to fly by flying!" he'd lean forward to yell into my ear. "Straight and level! You're drifting! Allow for the wind—crab into it!"

"I am!" I'd scream from the open cockpit, words lost in the wind draft, as I frantically scanned the instruments—all four of them—for guidance on staying level. Until I'd flown enough to trust my own inner air speed indicator.

When we flew high enough above the plains for me to know I couldn't get into any real trouble, he'd holler at me.

"Lead your turns," he'd scream. "Anticipate!" I stepped on the rudder, got the nose moving, then the stick, and still he'd hammer at me. I never tired of practicing S-turns, steep climbs, lazy eights, hammerheads, loops, descents. In fact, I'd practice any maneuver in the ground school textbook or anything the crackerjack pilots did. When the door flapped up as I practiced stalls, the Cub falling like a leaf, I was ahead of it and recovered each time. But still he yelled.

"What's wrong with you? Can't you fly this thing?"

"Of course I can fly it!" I'd shoot back. "As well as anybody, in fact, better than any guy who hollers at me!"

"Straight and level!" he came back at me. "Now you're over-controlling it!"

By then I was too intent on flying by the feel of it, sensing how my body felt doing the maneuvers, learning to fly by flying. No longer hearing his barrage of commands. Ready to ace my first solo. Thirty-five solo hours later, I was ready for anything.

CHAPTER FIFTY-EIGHT

Sitting on the back steps one unseasonably warm evening that spring, I smoked my asthma cigarette and listened to the distant rumble of a train lumbering toward the depot, remembering the two young hoboes I met at Bess's back door.

It was a troop train throttling into the station, discharging restless men who pounded onto the platform and unloaded gear, filtered by night sounds. A Pullman train carrying their fiancées and brides couldn't be far behind. I heard the president's steady, affable voice ringing from the parlor radio, nearing the finish of another fireside chat. "I urge all Americans to buy War Bonds without stint!"

Shadows deepened in the backyard as the upstairs lights began going out. I took a deep breath, drew smoke into my lungs, held it there a few seconds. I was slowly exhaling the smoke when Ida Rose spoke from the kitchen, her voice like a breeze rustling through the screen door.

"Care for some company, doll?"

Without waiting for my answer, she sat beside me on the top step and reached for a drag from my cigarette, then promptly choked out the smoke.

"You're smoking loco weed?" She gagged theatrically. "You nutty? That stuff'll kill ya."

I took the cigarette from her fingers to finish it off. She watched my inhalation method with interest, examining the green box. "Dr. R. Schiffmann's Asthmador Cigarettes," she said. "'Relieves the distress of your bronchial asthmatic paroxysms.' That's swell. Let's see, you're a human adding machine for the clinic, you own your own prosperous farm, you can fly an airplane, you aren't tied down, and you positively excel at all that while you're an asthmatic."

She released her critique in a haughty way, unlike her, punctuated with a tart laugh. I replied like I hadn't caught on.

"They're therapeutic," I shrugged.

She was peeved, it was crystal clear, and likely hankering after something she lacked. But I steered clear of other folks' calamities. Ida Rose had plenty of pals who'd let her cry in their beers. Among all those GIs who lined up for a dance with her at the canteen, there were bound to be some whose ears were as big as their eyes.

I exhaled my last drag, long and smooth from my nose and mouth both, and stubbed out the cigarette. My breathing relaxed along with my bones, lifting my flesh and organs as if they were weightless. I was a feather, high on a cloud—the sensations I'd become accustomed to, since the very first draw of Potter's I'd taken outside the State Home infirmary. The sense of fullness in my lungs, of air expanding my chest, the unfettered access to as much oxygen as I could absorb, freed me in a way I almost never felt. Unless I was flying.

The breeze picked up and brought Ida Rose's dusky perfume beneath my nose, momentarily clogging my passages and intruding on my delirium.

She stood in the wan porch light in her bare feet, twirling slowly around in the darkened yard, her long arms outstretched and her head flung back.

"I do feel a bit . . . lighter. Let me try it again."

She took the last cigarette from my pack and lit it, taking in a slow, easy drag, and released it with a bit more finesse. "This is kind of—what, soothing, for a troubled soul . . ."

She had her eyes on the stars, as majestic and endless as always in the Panhandle night sky. Watching her whirl around, I grew a little dizzy. She gradually quit her twirling, then went limp like a noodle and flopped down beside me.

I let out a breath, in relief, at the stasis. She sure wasn't anyone to lean on.

"You got yourself the jitters," I said.

"I'm going to Amarillo for training at the Pantex plant. Hope I can get some of these smokes there." Ida Rose exhaled like I'd done. "I'll be inspecting artillery. A dream job, isn't it? In charge of quality control for killing. If I make the grade, I'll have to move there."

To anyone who didn't know of her supreme confidence and charm, she'd have sounded resentful.

"Women workers will win the war," I quoted the War Department posters we mocked, pasted on storefronts around town.

"I've been winning the war one soldier at a time." Again I heard it, more ominously then, the whiff of bitterness. "It's hard work: our crew's hauling canned food to hundreds of soldiers fresh off the trains every day and starving, then nights at the canteen, we're cheerfully showing the boys why they should come home with a win."

The Red Cross campaigned to prompt the brides and fiancées to write their soldiers more often—"You Write, He'll Fight!"—and to write better letters, instructing women to leave out the boring details of housekeeping, the challenges they faced with rationing, the troubles they encountered on the job and with the families they were raising. In *McCall's* and *TIME* and *The Saturday Evening Post*, all the big companies—the pen maker Sheaffer's, Martin Aircraft, Kodak, Dole Pineapple, Emerson Electric—all of 'em inundated women with advertisements to boost the soldiers' morale. Victory letters, properly written to "our loved ones and to others," would help win the war. "You're never too busy to write V-Mail . . . Tell him things are running smoothly . . . Make it short, keep it cheerful!"

"Soldier, can I buy you a drink—I'm so sick of asking them. Play you a round of ping-pong, fella? How 'bout we jitterbug, mister?" Ida Rose's voice had risen in a sing-song imitation of her canteen role. "I need a job that pays the bills since that no-good bombardier took off. He trained to hit his target, alright, he's been hitting every gal whose name ain't Tokyo Rose. Well, we're quits. Like all the boys at the canteen, they're hot to trot, but commitment? It makes their blood run cold."

She'd been real gung ho when her gang began the canteen. She was the epitome of the Victory Girl the propaganda posters exhorted to win the war on the home front, bolstering the troops' morale with her sparkling spirit and her stylish attire.

Rumor was she'd volunteered at the original Stage Door Canteen on Broadway, jitterbugging across the dance floor with any man in a uniform, and followed a flyboy who'd promised her a ring clear to Texas, lighting up every canteen she encountered along the tracks. Once her *Swing Time* quicksteps had been the envy of all the dancing fiancées. But now she looked more frazzled than fashionable, as defeated as the SS Panzer divisions in the Ardennes.

It wasn't surprising, how her flagging spirits underpinned the effortlessness she feigned. There'd been ugly talk around town about her outreach to not only our GIs at the canteen, but her efforts toward the German prisoners at the makeshift POW camp near the airfield, too. Miz Lawler said she hoped there'd be a German lady who'd offer the same kindnesses to her boy, if the Nazis captured him, the way Ida Rose did for the enemy. Every mother who's got a boy overseas would appreciate a reciprocal response, she told me. Miz Lawler's feelings didn't reflect those of most town folks, women who spoke darkly of the dirty Krauts enjoying fresh hots at the Fritz Ritz even as they had to cook their own rationed food, and fathers who warned of the dangerous Nazis whose presence threatened their daughters.

I'd been with Ida Rose when we'd heard them and had seen them throwing their jeers at her. She kept her upper lip stiff and her head held high, which at her height was considerably taller than most of them, adding to her natural ability to carry herself with a dignity they lacked. I had no notion she was bothered by any thing, or any of them.

But those Asthmador cigarettes had a way of easing more than airways.

I pocketed the empty tin.

"You sure put on a good show," I said.

"Got to keep the home fires burning," she snapped, followed by an apologetic smile.

Women had picked up where the men left off. When the president asked us to stick to the plow until we reached the end of the furrow, we did. We were the ones working for victory on the home front, female soldiers in overalls on the farm fields and in bib aprons at the factories. We were recruited to serve as WACs and WAVES, to volunteer for the American Red Cross and the USO, to serve as nurses near the front lines, to buy a war bond for a serviceman's baby, to write V-Mail letters till our hands cramped. We filled our War Stamp Albums with ten-cent stamps to "Stamp Out the Axis." We were Victory Volunteers, going door-to-door to raise money for every War Loan Drive, selling War Bond Rally auction tickets for Jack Benny's violin. We rationed our sugar and beef and gasoline, and canned quarts of vegetables we grew in our war gardens. The president called on us to sacrifice some of our comforts to the needs of the men in service, so we became riveters, welders, gear cutters, lathe operators, and mechanics.

Ida Rose had smoked my last cigarette. I'd have to hustle for a pack of Potter's or Schiffmann's on the black market before my early shift at the clinic tomorrow.

"Everything looks better in the morning, Miz Lawler always said," I told her. It was late, and as I stood I told her to sleep tight, ignoring the cross look she sent me, leaving her alone on the porch steps.

I longed for the feel of rain as I dozed off, dreaming of faces turned up to receive its gentle cleansing.

CHAPTER FIFTY-NINE

In April, President Roosevelt died from a cerebral stroke while he was at his Little White House near the Warm Springs hydrotherapy retreat for polios. Dazed and grief-stricken, many of us followed news of US Railcar No. 1, the wheelchair-equipped *Ferdinand Magellan* Pullman that carried Roosevelt's casket back home as he was honored by thousands of stunned mourners lining the Southern Railway tracks. When the grieving Mrs. Roosevelt wrote of her deep appreciation to the people who waited in the stations and along the railroads to pay their last respects, I longed to be among them. If she could walk by now, Celesta would have been there. The image of Celesta appeared vivid, how bright and hopeful she'd looked boarding the Southern Pacific bound for the rehabilitation hospital in Gonzales, bolstered by the president.

With the death of Mussolini two weeks later, then Hitler's death in May, there were near-daily surrenders of German forces occupying Europe. Okinawa finally fell to US forces on June 22, 1945, and everyone dared hope the war's end was in sight. I paid another visit to the army airfield, to bargain with the supply sergeant for a deal on what I speculated would soon be a surplus of Piper Cubs. They'd spewed by the thousands from Piper Aircraft factories, turning the skies golden with the little yellow tail-draggers favored by the War Training Service and the Army Air Forces for flight instruction. Before the start of the war, Mrs. Roosevelt had promoted the civilian pilot training program in a Cub flown by a Tuskegee Institute airman—I still had the yellowed newspaper clipping that showed her famous wide smile, the brim of her flower-trimmed hat skimming her sparkling eyes, comfortably seated behind the colored pilot who was Moton Aviation Field's chief flight instructor. Their half-hour flight over Alabama four years ago had made news across the country, the First Lady demonstrating her approval of the advanced training for colored pilots.

That's when I knew I'd be the one flying my own airplane one day.

I'd pored over the dog-eared pages of the book by stunt pilot Genevieve Haugen scores of times since leaving Waco. Its blue-sky cover was emblazoned in stirring gold lettering: *Women with Wings*: *A Novel of the Modern Day Aviatrix*. Reading it kept my passion for flight aloft.

At night I'd fall asleep practicing the insouciance of cross-country aerial derby flier Babe Dugan, in her ridiculous reply to a mechanic from the movie *Tail Spin*:

Bud: Say, don't you know better than to smoke around gasoline?
Babe Dugan: Oh, don't be so superstitious!

Of course I knew better than to smoke my asthma cigarettes anywheres but behind a tree and nowheres near an airplane. But I sure admired her spunk.

•   •   •

At the airfield, I walked among the yellow Piper J-3s that had trained many an aviator, looking for the Cub I'd soloed in. Fresh off the factory floor in 1939, the Cub sold for less than a new automobile. I peered in at the familiar bear in the logo on the altimeter, who wore a reassuring wink. With a tank in the spare seat, a spray boom under the wing, and a supply of Weedone, I'd have a fine crop duster. I approached the supply sergeant and we made a deal on the spot.

The plans I'd drawn for our house—with a dining room to handle a table for twelve, a sitting area, a massive living room beside a shelf-lined study, and six bedrooms along the east side with a long covered gallery facing west—were still just that. My drawings needed builders, but the war effort sucked every able-bodied male into the never-ending draft.

I needed a runway, too. It would be the layout I'd seen at Elliott Roosevelt's Dutch Branch Ranch, where Mrs. Roosevelt had taken me in her private Pullman car.

I'd need another banner harvest to pay for it all.

•   •   •

A dry spring was again threatening the crops. And the shortage of manpower was holding back the harvest.

Farmers had turned to hired help from Germany—the kind that needed a guard. All across Texas, from Marfa to Mexia, POW camps housed not just Germans, but Italians, even some Japanese.

At first they were a town curiosity, hearty-looking and suntanned, fed well enough, and plenty of them were learning to speak some English to the teen girls flirting on the other side of the fence. The shortage of field workers had grown acute. Where cotton needed chopping in the east, or fruit needed picking in the Rio Grande Valley, POWs became trusted substitutes for our drafted farmhands. Despite their earlier animosity, folks agreed the Germans especially had shown themselves to be good laborers.

At a small agricultural work camp nearby, German POWs were trucked in and farmed out from the air base, and housed in barracks fenced in by barbed wire. Some still didn't trust the POWs, but most farmers realized without their labor, we'd have lost the entire cotton crop in Texas last year. The German prisoners were resourceful with what little irrigation we could muster, and skilled at building. They were as disciplined at their work as the Texas sons and brothers who'd battled their kin overseas. It was ironic, but dodgy it was not. I figured the risk from the German prisoners was smaller than a gnat's whisker. Losing out on the harvest, on the other hand, would really put me on the spot.

And that yellow Piper J-3 was calling my name.

CHAPTER SIXTY

The team of German POWs I'd hired from the airfield work camp arrived near spring's end in 1945 with a carbuncle-faced young private guarding them. I showed them my drawings for our house, and where to lay out the field for my grass airstrip.

The German who was in charge of his work crew wore the faded green Wehrmacht tunic of the Nazi armed forces, minus several buttons and most of its emblems torn off, showing darker olive denim outlined by ragged stitch marks. On his back, like all the prisoners, were the stenciled letters *PW*. He looked to be some years older, and his bearing had an authority the others lacked; he was compact, and certain. They stood poised around him, waiting, respectful.

I took in his shoulder strap insignia, reminiscent of snakes entwined on a staff, a medical symbol I recognized from the clinic's stationery. The prisoners addressed him in their sharp, guttural language, *Jawohl, Herr Stabsarzt*, and he replied in heavily accented English. He kept his icy-blue eyes lowered around me, but wasn't shy about offering his opinions—on curving the runway for the Cub's S-turn taxi, altering the airstrip's location at an angle favorable to prevailing winds, grading its edges to encourage drainage during northers, even arguing in favor of widening it to allow for larger airplanes sure to come.

The German waited quietly as his recommendations were shot down by Griner, my tenant farmer, whose objections were all related to the potential impact on the crops.

"You'll work around that, use your irrigation ditches, what have you," I told Griner, irritated. "No crops have ever been hurt by a little airplane flying over."

I turned to Herr Stabsarzt. "Your men will lend a hand to the tenant when he needs you, since we look to be heading into a summer drouth." Noting the German's unflinching eyes travel to meet mine, I added, "And I accept your recommendations, Mr. *Stabsarzt*, is it? May I call you that?"

The prisoners suppressed smiles.

"I am Josef." He began laying out a plan to improve the irrigation as they dug out the airstrip, until the private, reddening and impatient, shut him up with a sneer and a shove, cursing under his breath and scowling at me.

Goddam Nazi lover. He said it under his breath, but I heard him and smacked him across his ruddy, carbuncle-pocked cheek.

"You damn well better not interfere here. These men are working for me on my farm."

He shouldered his rifle and leaned back on a fence post, pulling out a pack of Wrigley's cinnamon gum, and lazily shoved a stick in his smutty mouth. Griner trilled a whistle and swiped off his hat, a signal I took for disapproval. The prisoners hoisted their shovels and got back to it, and that's all I cared about.

•　　•　　•

There'd been no notices in the papers of the two names, now four. Earl had enlisted the day after our argument, and shipped out with the Army Signal Corps. Two Becks, two Hubbards. Brothers. No word from any one of 'em.

•　　•　　•

The six stonemasons among the prisoners had shown themselves to be quite skilled, and the house I'd envisioned was rising quicker than a dry creek in a gully washer, at an affordable ten cents an hour, wages I paid direct to the War Department.

The work crew leader, Josef, he'd called himself, was as dedicated to his job as I was to mine. We had spoken little during the months he supervised the prisoners, but I found myself wondering about him after an incident in the field. A prisoner took an accidental ax to the fleshy side of his hand, and Josef had quickly supplied a kit labeled *Deutsches Rotes Kreuz*, its bright red cross painted on white providing the translation. I watched, fascinated, while he expertly tended to the wound.

"*Stabsarzt*," I said. "Doctor?"

"Staff surgeon," he replied, without taking his eyes from the gut sutures he was pulling through flesh.

•　　•　　•

One weekend when she was back from her Pantex shift, Ida Rose had courted controversy by suggesting a canteen for the German POWs one night per month. It horrified the rooming house brides, and most roundly denounced her. She maintained it was Christian to treat them well, but few were willing to give her a hand.

A twinge of conscience seized me and I made a show of helping Ida Rose with the canteen for POWs, announcing my intent to keep my German laborers happy, and therefore more productive. Soon several fiancées, and some brides, came around.

If the sneering private who scorned the POWs reflected our soldiers' feelings, none were troubled enough to quit asking her for a drink or a dance. Ida Rose, vivacious and gracious, was ever the main attraction, appearing to know each GI on a first-name basis while avoiding a full-on fistfight over who'd get the last dance with her.

A war bride reported Ida Rose had written a *Dear John* letter to her bombardier boyfriend on the Pacific front lines, having learned he'd be shipping home to a wife up north. A wife! Ida had followed a married man west, they gossiped, in search of that elusive ring. Too hasty with her heart, what with all the fun she had at the canteen, someone said. Or maybe she'd known he was married all along, they snickered, Ida's reputation dashed as easy as that.

My mind was on the farm, the Beck brothers, and the Hubbard brothers.

While the canteen had been in full swing the last eighteen months, I'd been too preoccupied to patronize it. After 1943's good winter wheat crop came dry spells, cold snaps, then a freeze, which had turned into a plenty wet year overall, except for a few dry months in the early summer. The tenant farmer, Griner, had his crew leveling and ditching for irrigation with an Eversman land scraper he got at auction, which had improved our yield in 1944. This year's harvest had to make.

Even with the extra hands, managing the farm commanded my attention. I knew from boardinghouse gossip Ida Rose remained the darling of both canteens, and I stayed busy with the farm's books, Miz Lawler's accounts, plus any local businesses who could pay. I was raising barely enough extra cash to irrigate my winter wheat, to bankroll my airstrip, and to build my farmhouse, and I was counting on a good crop in 1945 to repay my seed loan. But the dry spring foretold a summer drouth.

I'd become a gambler, gazing at clouds, forcing a finger into parched earth. Betting on the come. Like Pa.

●　　　●　　　●

The Allies were regaining control in Italy, forcing more surrenders of German forces across Europe. Every day brought new hope the war would end. The back-to-back deaths in late April of Mussolini, then Hitler, followed with more victories, and we were joyfully stunned into the streets. That second week of May, the V-E Day celebrations made a glorious reprieve we desperately needed. We were giddy for a week as German troops in Europe laid down their arms. Banners, flags, and beer marked the joyful ceasefire celebrations around town.

Still there'd been no notices in the papers of the two names, now four. Earl's only letter, a short V-Mail for Will, arrived a few months after he'd shipped out with the Signal Corps. Picturing Earl, I could imagine him joking their paths might cross in the Pacific.

Two Beckers, two Hubbards. Brothers. No word from any of them.

CHAPTER SIXTY-ONE

The last day of July, Ida Rose was the first patient at the clinic.

"Back from Amarillo kind of early, aren't you?"

She cast her eyes onto pale cheeks. "I took sick leave from Pantex. They allowed me a day without pay and said don't come back looking green. I need that paycheck, but I'm half-deaf from all the gunfire. Let me in, will ya?"

I gave her the once-over.

"You do look a little peaked," I admitted. "We don't open till seven. Not even dawn yet—"

"I'm in the family way."

"Without a family." I covered my shock. "Well, Miz Lawler isn't here. And the new doc just left for Galveston."

"I'm not looking for him," she said miserably. "He wouldn't take my case."

"You can see the OB at Trinity Hospital—"

"You already know they won't help me," she interrupted. "They're afraid of getting prosecuted. The doctor's advice? 'Go see the baby's father, take a revolver. If he won't marry you, kill him on the spot.'"

"Gutless," I murmured. I'd overheard our young doctor tell a desperate patient to follow her minister's advice. But if Ida visited an illegal abortionist, she'd risk arrest. Why tell her what we all knew?

"Lookit, I've asked around. I had to chance it. No one can know, I'll be ruined—" She swallowed hard, her desperate eyes straying. "Don't judge me,

Ruby. You don't know . . . Everyone over there"—she jerked her head toward the rooming house— "they think I've got loose morals. What would they know about it, with those rings on their fingers? It's none of their business but they'll make it theirs."

Misery dulled her bright eyes.

"It's my problem, isn't it? Help me. Please."

She had no solution without risk. Every choice was deemed illegal, downright dangerous, or life-altering.

"Dot overheard me asking customers at the beauty parlor. She gave me this card." Ida averted her face as girls do when shamed. I recognized the name, an untrained abortionist who packed gauze into a pregnant uterus, inducing contractions, eventually expelling the fetus—a "miscarriage" of sorts. A patient we'd seen said it felt like her insides were being torn out.

"Our doctor treated a woman who hemorrhaged after a pack job, Ida . . . She died."

"I'm desperate, Ruby!" She stifled a sob. "I'll ask at Nettie's, her girls know what to do—"

"No. That's worse." What the paid girls did was dicey. I took her hands.

"Ida! Make some sense. How far along are you? This is just between us. Nobody else has to know anything. I'll call a midwife who's trustworthy."

"She'll charge a lot . . ." Ida seemed to shrink before my eyes. For the first time I saw how her airy nonchalance hid her vulnerability.

"C'mon, I've got enough coffee for two cups. Then I'll make that call for you." I measured a scant spoonful of rationed coffee into the percolator. Her predicament was a heavy presence.

"I can get the dough. In a few weeks."

Ida Rose had no time to waste, but I kept mum.

The percolator popped and perked.

Then Ida's smile surfaced, somewhat off-kilter. "I knew you'd be the soul of discretion, Ruby."

"I have some experience in that area," I replied.

A week later, Ida Rose turned up, a plea in her hollowed eyes. She needed to pay the midwife up front. Even after she cashed her paycheck and pawned the canteen phonograph, she was three hundred bucks short.

"What about the soldier?" I said.

She stared me down. "That's rich!"

"If you tell him, I'm sure he'd—" She cut me off.

"He says it's not his. He'd marry me if it was, but not without proof. As if I'd marry that rube and raise seven more like him."

"Who says you have to marry him?" I said, exasperated.

"Lift his wallet, then? That's what you expect me to do? And have the whole US Army gunning for me!"

Maybe she exaggerated, but a streak of fear crossed her face.

I weighed my options. I had a pile of cash set aside to cover my debts, which as farmers know, was a gamble on better times. I owed the bank on the leveler, a new combine, and seed; the co-op was floating me; the work crew's pay was due; and soon, Griner would claim his share of profits.

If we kept irrigating, we'd be harvesting soon, and a big payday would follow—with enough left to buy the Piper Cub I'd haggled for.

"I don't have that kind of dough . . ."

Ida Rose sized me up. She left without a word, and left my conscience teetering into recrimination.

•　　　•　　　•

Mid-August 1945 and I was jittery, pushing my peas around on my plate when a noisy distraction interrupted our supper. The clamor of honking car horns, screeching fire sirens, tolling church bells that swelled over screams and whistles and hollering could mean only one thing.

We ran outside, oblivious to the hot August wind pelting us, joined by women with joyous faces from the rooming house, turning onto the noisy Main Street amidst jubilant shouts rising above the caterwauling auto horns, whistles, sirens, and church bells. The entire town shuddered in elation: *It's over! The war is over! Victory! Victory over Japan!*

Only a week earlier, the war took a turn that made us dizzy with hope we'd soon see an end to rationing, shortages, war bonds, and above all, to the endless names of GI wounded and dead. The new atomic bomb made front-page headlines as "The most terrible destructive force in history, loosed upon Japan"—"Bombers Cremate Forewarned Cities."

We jammed into hog-wild throngs and grabbed the arms of airmen in sweat-stained khakis who whirled us around. We clasped hands with strangers and hugged neighbors in the surging crowd. We guzzled the beers pulled from pockets and shared in paper sacks, all of us cavorting with fresh-faced recruits, reveling in the news, overcome and shouting in the first full-throated belly laughter any of us had allowed ourselves for five long years. We danced and reveled long into the night, until tears dried salty on our cheeks, later washed off in an unexpected downpour that felt like a long-overdue double dose of good fortune.

When we linked arms to walk home, I conjured my brothers' surprise at the farm's transformation into the home Pa had promised. Wet and wide awake, I drove to the farm on fumes in the doc's old truck, its tank near empty on rationed gas.

The full moon bathed the last of the wheat tassels in light in contrast to the shadowed stalks and near-black earth. Our fields were full of golden hues and promise. Half the harvest was at the mill already. The sprawling farmhouse was dark, its tile roof illuminated by moonlight and awaiting its family to become a home.

I sat inside near the big picture window. I imagined myself in the Cub's cockpit, soloing and banking turns over our sections, and in my mind's eye I saw the patchwork of my hard work from the vantage of a lone nighthawk in flight.

•   •   •

The day after the V-J celebration, the rooming house was quiet but for rain pattering on the tin roof. It would be a day to sleep late and make plans for the newlyweds' lives to begin anew. I hadn't seen Ida Rose celebrating, in fact, not since she'd left the clinic, distressed, and me, guilt-ridden.

Her light glowed atop the stairs. I averted my eyes from the disarray of her room, stockings, tissues, panties, crumpled trousers, talcum powder, wet towels, and half-slips strewn about, with an opened closet door where dresses had hung, now in a fallen pile.

Maybe Ida Rose was in Amarillo, getting extra hours at Pantex, saving up to repay me.

The six fifty-dollar bills I'd left her two weeks ago, extracted from under my mattress, were gone, along with my hasty note.

For your procedure.
PS get the phonograph out of hock
—Ruby

I had little hope of being repaid unless Ida won the war bond lottery. Now I was reliant on the harvest to cover my debts and my airplane.

CHAPTER SIXTY-TWO

WILLA MAE

I've had a setback, the doctors tell me, after I threw myself against the tombstone inscribed with merely a number, 611, atop the fresh grave Mr. Lorenzo dug for the Duchess, screeching. "She's Madeleine! She has a name, she is Madeleine!"

Your hydro treatments must resume, the doctors say, continuing to debate the merits of a new procedure that's shown promise with the shell-shocked war veterans flooding asylums like ours.

Another doctor's voice, complaining, "It's clear we can't handle these numbers; we're too short-staffed. A quick surgical solution like Freeman and Watts are doing in Washington, DC could free up beds."

"The VA's had this lobotomy technique in use since 1943 to clear the mental wards," another opines. "A woman who's had numerous nervous breakdowns like this one"—he gestures at me—"also suffering from agitated depression, is an excellent candidate."

They nod, as though I'm merely a cadaver for their medical experiments, ignoring my panicky protestations. My questions go unanswered as the nurses roll me into treatment.

The longer I am here, the more likely I am to end up another number in the asylum cemetery.

In the shock of tonight's frigid hydrotherapy treatment my head explodes with an ungodly clamor of bells, sirens, crowds, cheers. It's a stifling August evening, our windows open to catch a nonexistent breeze, as I begin to lose consciousness. Are those shouts of *War Is Over!* Are they drifting across Holliday Creek from town, or inventions of my addled mind? Footsteps echo, staff roams the hallways, yell *Victory! Victory!* I'm numb, my thoughts jumbled, memories trapped as I succumb to the cold inertia of the bath . . .

I dream of the field where I lost myself, in 1931—the field familiar because it was the same field stretching to the endless flat horizon, set among similar fields, unrelenting, in all directions. It was the fertile field of Beck's belief that rain followed the plow, and it was the fallow field the bank threatened to repossess. But it might as well have been the field where a shadow catcher traveling in his photo wagon captured a Texline bachelor standing beside his farm who "wanted a kind and loving wife," boasting his homestead had "excellent prospects" on a nickel RPPC—a Real Photo Post Card—signed Wasson Photo. The hoe-man's picture and requirements for a wife ("must be a good housekeeper") were printed a decade before the card became a popular item at the Fred Harvey Newsstand in the Amarillo depot, where I sold dozens of real photo postcards, along with newspapers, magazines, and souvenirs, to the land seekers. After the 1919 cow-killer blizzard froze snow inside the cattle's nostrils—suffocating them—on the heels of 1918's deadly influenza season, the suitcase farmers had arrived by the trainload to snap up cheap rangelands.

The man who stood before me at the Harvey Newsstand counter in 1920 and bought that RPPC was a farmer of another kind, less shrewd investor and more true believer in the land. He later confessed he'd bought the card for the chance to make my acquaintance. When I lightly asked if he was the bachelor pictured, he replied with great seriousness that he, too, was in search of a wife. Henry Clyde Becker, the man I married, might have stepped from that scene right into the field I now painted intermittently, ten years later, in between chores and children—but for the plummeting wheat market since 1930 and the onset of sandstorms. After the decade-long plow-up of the Twenties, with abnormally steady rains yielding a wheat bonanza, Beck's belief in his land held steady even as the rain had ceased, and grain prices caved to unheard-of lows.

CHAPTER SIXTY-THREE

RUBY LEE

On my third cup of coffee at the café, I scanned the morning edition of the *Amarillo Daily News* a boy had been hawking at the courthouse. "Peace," the newsie called out over and over, "Japs surrender, read all about it," his high-pitched voice untiring. He was mobbed by customers. We couldn't get enough of it, two days after President Truman's radio broadcast Tuesday. "Peace! Read all about it," he said, shoving the newspapers into eager hands as quick as he could pocket their nickels. "War is over!"

Like every awed patron in the café, I absorbed each detail of Japan's unconditional surrender. It was Thursday, way past lunchtime, a hastily declared legal holiday. Even people with businesses to run and chores to finish stayed, sipping Dr Peppers and thrilling to the glorious news. We read greedily from a smorgasbord of newspapers diners passed around, sharing the reporting from Amarillo, Denver, Lubbock, Wichita Falls, Tulsa, San Angelo, Houston, New York.

The café cook was doling out warm slices of fresh-baked Dutch apple pie on the house when a newsie came in with the evening papers. I flipped him a nickel for the *Amarillo Globe*. Its headline made the diners erupt in cheers: "Gas Unrationed."

Despite the excited chatter, a tragic story, "Cruiser Indianapolis Lost to Enemy Action," had my heart racing. Twelve hundred sailors who should have been heading home to victory had faced untold horrors.

Folks were settling up their bills and rushing out to buy gasoline.

A familiar woman pushed her way inside, eyes casting about the patrons who'd remained, landing on mine. She clenched a crumpled telegram in her hand, her engagement ring flashing. Streaked tears slashed her face powder. Last night she'd swirled her skirts and danced wilder than anyone, jubilant her fiancé would be coming home.

Her voice flat, she read her telegram. "I deeply regret to inform you Ensign Finley Milton USNR is missing in action 30 July 1945 in the service of his country. You will be furnished with details when received. To prevent possible aid to our enemies do not divulge the ship's name or station unless general circumstances are made public in news stories."

She swooned and dipped dangerously near the floor. I hauled her into a chair, patting her cheeks till her eyes focused on mine.

"He was on the *Indianapolis*?" I shared the newspaper.

After a high-speed delivery of parts for the A-bomb, the famous flagship of the US Fifth Fleet was torpedoed on July 30 in the Philippine Sea, the navy reported. The cruiser plunged headfirst into shark-infested waters fifteen minutes later. Hundreds of men went down with her. Those not killed in the sinking—nearly eight hundred men—endured five days at sea with few lifeboats and scant sustenance before rescue arrived. By then, only three hundred-some sailors had survived the dehydration, exposure, noxious fuel oil slicks, saltwater poisoning, delirium, and shark attacks.

Her head bobbed up and down. "Not my Finley. He's coming home."

I dragged my forefinger down columns of names labeled *Deceased* occupying an entire page, recognizing none but her fiancé's. I felt my heart ease.

Gripping her hand tight, I scanned the telegram for her name. "Evelynne, I'm so sorry for your loss."

Evelynne heaved a sob, stood, then bawled unabated before running out.

I downed my coffee, noticing the USS *Indianapolis* list continued to the back page under the heading *Survived*.

My eyes raced down the names. I found none I knew, not Will nor Earl, Clay nor Red, until I reached the final column: *Status Questionable*.

And there he was.

"Oris Burton Hubbard. Believed to be among 316 survivors transported by USS Tranquillity *(AH-14) to Guam on 8 August 1945. Two survivors died en route; names withheld pending notification of kin."*

Red vanished without a trace, as promised. Or had he survived days adrift at sea, only to die after his rescue? It was too much to bear.

My stomach knotted. The café was so crazed nobody noticed my tears spilling as I muscled my way out. All the losses of the war, layered onto who the drouth claimed, the flood's victim, my State Home family, and the one I took real hard—Amelia Earhart's disappearance.

Losing Pa, who'd lost his lifelong dream. Pa and the farm so interchangeable I couldn't imagine one without the other. Yet Pa was dead and the farm was mine to lose.

What of the Hubbards—would I ever know? Would the Becker brothers make it back to see the farm?

I couldn't bear to contemplate Momma, the darkest blow of all, which I kept buried the deepest.

I caught my breath on a bench, glancing at another discarded newspaper. The headline hit like a bomb.

CLOSED

Pantex Ordnance Stops Production

Four thousand wartime jobs evaporated in an instant, like the cities the A-bombs annihilated. Ida Rose was out of a job.

I raced back to the office and pored over the books, reviewing bills, debts, and hoped-for profits, trying to squeeze blood out of turnips.

My projections buoyed me—if prices didn't fall and the crops paid. But I was two hundred short to buy my Piper Cub.

I deserved one win. Just one win.

I was so close. I rummaged through the indignities and setbacks of these last nine years in a frenzy, my breathing labored. I coughed and rasped till I quit breathing. I gasped for air, panicking, my skin prickling till perspiration prompted a sense of doom that pounded in my head, I forgot to count, I hacked my throat raw, I forgot how to breathe, I raced to the clinic to rifle through the medicines in the locked cabinets, my agitation mounting with each wheezing breath. I searched every shelf, finally found the One Night cough syrup, dusty and forbidden, the bottle boasting therapeutic results from its active ingredients: cannabis indica, F.E., chloroform, and morphia, sulph. Wild with the fear of no air at all, I fumbled the top off, gulping it right from the bottle. My vision darkened, I saw stars, blacked out, I pulled myself out of a tunnel that sucked the wind from my chest. I took another gulp, chased it with a swig from old Doc Lawler's fine aged Kentucky bourbon. I sank to the rug, chilled, wet, my heart beating faster than a propeller, my rib cage near bursting, my head exploding. Shivering, grasping myself, I held myself for dear life. I had no one else.

Late that night, while my mind drifted high into cotton ball clouds, panning out to reveal my plane's shadow crossing greening sections below, I soared over snowy mountains to an impossibly blue ocean, alone at my Cub's controls. Two rooming house brides brought a white-faced, failing housemate to the clinic, a blood-soaked bed sheet wrapped around her.

• • •

"No," Ida Rose protested, "no," her voice weak but her intent firm, she wouldn't go to the hospital; what she had done was illegal. It was six or seven days ago—she'd lost track—the doctor had injected a mail-order paste with a bulb syringe, packed her with a gauze tampon, and sent her away with two aspirin. Fearing police raids, he never took off his surgical mask. She couldn't know his name. It took only ten minutes on a cold metal table, in a sleazy rent room off an alley. There would be very little pain, he said, only mild cramping when she removed the gauze eighteen hours later. It would cause a natural miscarriage.

"Not a pack job, Ida, I warned you—"

"I couldn't afford the midwife. I've been bleeding nearly a week. It's so painful, I'm afraid I'll die . . ."

"Shush, we'll help you." Miz Lawler led her to the treatment ward, turning to me.

"Take the truck, fetch a doctor. She's lost lots of blood. She could have an air embolism, or blood poisoning."

"She wouldn't let us tell a soul," a stricken bride interjected. "After she collapsed in the bathroom we tried to help, but she wouldn't go to Trinity . . ."

Ida struggled to prop herself up.

"Ruby, no," she moaned. "Not there!"

Her face, no longer lovely, was shrouded by pain. She grimaced. "Help me . . ."

"Go now. Hurry," Miz Lawler implored me.

"Ida Rose, I'll help you." Her hand was clammy in mine. "I promise."

As determined as she was, I was more so. I gritted my words.

"I won't let you die."

I will not lose anyone else.

CHAPTER SIXTY-FOUR

The bugler was blowing "Reveille" as I pulled up to the gate. That pathetic carbuncle-pimpled private asked my business. Inside the barracks, lights came on. I made out prisoners rising, grumbling, and dressing in short order. I jammed on the horn. The men poured out and lined up to see what the commotion was about.

"I need the *Stabsarzt*, the staff surgeon," I shouted at the guard, searching the rows of prisoners. "Poco pronto! I've got an emergency." While the guard stood slack-jawed, I hollered, "Josef, I need you! It's me, Ruby Lee! Where are you, Josef? Come help!"

The war prisoners jabbered in German as a sergeant approached. Josef stepped from the line, his movements precise. "Grab your Red Cross bag, anything you need," I yelled before he ducked inside his barracks.

Touching the brim of his cap, the sergeant said, "Morning, ma'am, would you mind stepping out?"

I sprang out. "Sergeant, I need your *Stabsarzt* here; he's the only doctor in miles and I've got a life-or-death emergency. A lady's dying, she's desperate for medical attention."

Wearing a loaded pack, Josef neared the truck, his footsteps brisk and his kit in hand.

"Get in, I'll explain on the way."

The sergeant's hat shadowed his face, but he radiated a relaxed overconfidence. He looked about as sharp as scrambled eggs. With an appraising once-over, he tried to suppress a faint touch of surprise that crossed his face.

"That's enough, miss; hold your horses," he said. "You do know this is a German prisoner of war."

"You do know," I shot back, my voice rising, "the war is over, he's a doctor, and a woman is dying."

"You do know you're not in charge here," he kept at it, a smirk playing at his mouth. He pulled his hat brim lower, darkening his eyes.

"Josef, you all set?" I motioned him inside.

"I'll have to run this up the flagpole. I need a full report for the commander before I can okay that." The sergeant lifted his cap, scratched his head, and a whitened scar folded into his frown. As he lowered his hat, which landed askew, the edges of his lips ticked up. "Regrettably, ma'am."

He was nervy, given the stakes.

"Do you understand what emergency means?" I stood at his medal-bedecked chest, his lanky frame looming over me. "Like saving someone's life, or are you already used to people dying?"

His grin, which he may have thought was disarming, was familiar. Could have been grudging admiration. I slammed the truck door.

"Sir," Josef said, touching his medical insignia, "this is my calling. I must go."

A prisoner whistled, cheers rang out, and they all began clapping. The private hollered to cut it out and made menacing efforts, thrusting his bayoneted rifle at them.

I put the truck in gear, wheels grinding on the hardpan as I backed up. "I'm not waiting for your report or your flagpole, sergeant. Climb in back if you don't trust the doctor, and don't hold us up any longer."

The sergeant let a few seconds go by. When I was gunning it, he smacked the wheel cover and leapt nimbly into the rear bed.

"Get the prisoners to the canteen," he ordered the guard, standing tall in the truck bed and tugging the brim of his hat down tight. "Hand me your service revolver and cuffs."

"Hang on back there, it's a rough road," I yelled back, throttling off the base faster than a scalded cat, enjoying how he seesawed backwards in the rearview.

We pushed east into town, where the sun shoulda riz but was instead dark as a pocket. Tumbleweeds gusted along the fields. A farmer in the prayerful posture I attributed to my pa gazed at the sky, bruised in deep purples and grays.

Pa's voice in my head. "Weather comin on," I said, fearing for my crop in recognition of Pa's life of unease.

On the front porch, Miz Lawler grasped for the clinic sign which the wind swung wildly. The sergeant plucked the sign from the post, handing it to her with a small bow. Swirling dirt caused me a coughing spasm.

The sergeant attached a cuff to Josef's left hand and one to his own. Miz Lawler took in the POW stitching and the handcuffs with an alarmed look, but she led us to Ida Rose, who thrashed under the sheets in between bouts of mewling and sobs. Her skin had the frightening pallor I'd seen on Alma's and Nell's faces before we lost them one right after the other. I took hold of Ida's cold hand, her grip nonexistent.

"She's hemorrhaging; we've tried to contain it," Miz Lawler told the doctor. "She's in and out, and you can see—she's in a lot of pain."

Josef moved quickly to her, the attached sergeant not as quick. "I'm left-handed," Josef complained with a nod to his dominant hand, cuffed to the sergeant's.

Ida's eyes were closed, her breathing labored, and she flung her head from side to side.

I turned on the sergeant. "You're going to make the doctor revive her one-handed and backwards," I snapped, "instead of giving her a fighting chance?"

The sergeant was fixed on Ida, the color in his face disappearing faster than a runaway train. "Your patient's Rosie? From the canteen?"

"You gonna give her some privacy, aren't ya?" I jerked my head at the doorway, glaring. He sheepishly removed the handcuffs and stepped out.

"More light, please," the doctor asked, beckoning Miz Lawler to assist, examining Ida with practiced hands.

Inside the room of fumes and stifling air, my breath went raggedy on me, taking on the familiar whistling sound, and when I started up wheezing, Josef took note. He gave some quiet direction to Miz Lawler, who left for an instant, returning with cough syrup. She raised an eyebrow at the open label, but gave it to me, saying, "doctor's orders."

Hail pinged the tin roof while they worked. I was winded, so I squeezed past the sergeant at the porch door to get some fresh air. Cold dust flew through the air, needling my throat. I lit an Asthmador, fighting my dread, and while the quarter-sized balls of ice pounded the truck, the yard, and the barn, I willed my luck to change.

•　　•　　•

Inside the cab with prisoner and jailer crammed together for our return trip, the atmosphere was gloomy. It would be touch-and-go for Ida Rose, weakened and feverish, for a few days. She was struggling to fight off a localized infection that probably made her infertile and could still turn deadly poisonous. When she was released, she'd need bed rest, Josef said, aware my fieldstone ranch house had enough empty bedrooms for a recovering regiment.

The staff surgeon knew of the German physician who promoted the dangerous method of abortion used on Ida. He sold his Leunbach's Paste through the mail with promises of simplicity, safety, and ease. Much quicker than a surgical abortion, the German physician claimed, and no need for anesthesia. The danger was the likelihood a patient could die from an air embolism or poisoning. Before the war, German authorities had documented at least two dozen deaths from its use.

If Ida Rose made a full recovery from her infection, she'd be very lucky indeed. If she were to carry a child again, it would be a miracle.

Now he diagnosed my wheezing and coughing fits. Severe asthma, Josef said. Not likely to be controlled in a dust-prone environment. "Did you have lung problems as a child?" he wanted to know.

We were nearing the farm. The air had turned clear and crisp.

"Like dust pneumonia?" I asked, shunning the memory of those dark, delirious weeks in Trinity Hospital. I trained my eyes dead ahead as we rounded the bend to the farm.

The freak norther that hooked east flattened the prairie coneflowers and yellow bluestem in the fallow pastures, which shimmered with melting ice crystals. I followed the doctor's gaze along the glistening runway he and his men had labored over, where larger balls of hail glowed in the emerging sun. Mist rose from the last of my unharvested wheat, silvery threads meeting gray skies were backlit by bright streaks of sunshine piercing a cloudless blue. It would have been breathtaking except for the beaten-down shoots of wheat, endless acres of them, as crushed as my profits.

I slowed the truck, taking in the enormity of what I'd almost accomplished, the house complete but empty, the combine standing idle amidst the crop's remnants, the runway impotent without a plane. My eyes filled. I shuddered, refused to cry. These men would not see that weakness.

"I regret this loss," the doctor said, his voice kind.

"This place is yours?" The sergeant let out a low whistle. "The PW detail building the runway and farmhouse, planting your crops, they worked for you? That's how you knew Dr. Fritz here."

"Dr. Josef Richter," the staff surgeon corrected him as sternly as prisoner can captor. I turned to still my quivering chin.

"Where's the airplane?" the sergeant blundered on.

"*Der dummkopf.*" Josef placed his hand on my shoulder.

I blinked back tears. "Thick as cream gravy." I saw Josef tuck away a smile.

•   •   •

At the prisoner barracks, I thanked the staff surgeon, asking what would become of him with the war over.

Instead he told me the One Night cough syrup would cause more trouble than it fixed with its addictive ingredients, and to throw it away. He listened to my lungs. With his stethoscope positioned methodically up, over, down, and over my chest, Josef diagnosed my breathing irregularities more accurately than the local practitioners had ever managed.

Because I was exposed repeatedly to the fine silt particulates of the dusters with such high silica content, he explained, the small hair-like organs—the cilia—protecting the lungs from foreign particles couldn't function. The silt could enter deeper into the alveoli, which left my lungs irritated and inflamed, and resulted in dust pneumonia—the brown plague I survived as a child.

"Your lungs are likely permanently damaged," Josef said. Breathing grain dust from the harvest was the latest exacerbation. The windy norther with its sudden temperature drop had set off my wheezing and coughing. "The prognosis for continued exposure to dust is permanent lung scarring and restricted airways. Without treatment, the airway muscles in the lung enlarge, and won't relax, and won't allow as much air to pass through . . ." I quit listening, because he told me what I already knew and wouldn't face.

The very air I breathed was my enemy.

CHAPTER SIXTY-FIVE

WILLA MAE

I am flailing, battling the boredom along with the blowing dust, and still living in a one-room dugout Beck built when we married—now crowded with our three children. The promised wood-frame house with glass windowpanes and a clay tile roof fails to materialize after years of assurances. Denied time to pursue my art—and now denied money for tubes of paint and rolls of canvas (deemed frivolities while our unsold wheat stacks up beside more piles of unsold wheat at grain elevators across the Panhandle), my spirits are already low when a telegram comes from Chicago. It's my mother, sending word that Daniel Wilhelm Eckhart, my elusive father, died two weeks earlier, on April 28, 1931, in an oil explosion after bringing in a well in Gladewater, nine hundred miles from home.

Two weeks later on this rare day Beck doesn't need the mule, I lift Ruby Lee atop the docile creature with a picnic and my art kit and set off for the old XIT Ranch land that's not yet under plow. My six-year-old girl was born curious and tenacious, quite unlike her brothers—diligent, bookish Will and impulsive, rambunctious Earl. I've arrayed my spent remnants of pastels to paint the plains and heavens while Ruby's mesmerized by a butterfly, studying how it moves its wings. But after it flies away, Ruby rearranges my pastel stumps, losing the smaller bits to the crinkly grasses, frustrating my hard-to-summon inspiration. Poised over my paper, I try to conjure my father's face but instead see his leather satchel, bursting with geologic maps and surveys.

My prairie art session is suddenly less monotonous when a Model T Ford materializes in the wavy distance. The man who emerges wears a sombrero and sets up an easel, introducing himself as Zander. He visits family at a Texline ranch in summers on his way to paint in the Taos mountain air. Ruby inspects his supplies while he shuffles through my sketches, recognizing Palo Duro. He camped in the canyon he loves for three weeks, where he could survey soils and rock formations as a self-taught geology student. Zander talks of driving across the Staked Plains and feeling utterly small and helpless when the vast chasm suddenly opens up, referring to the canyon I walked with Miss O'Keeffe. We speak about the purples, lavenders, and grays that striate the brick-colored shale so typical of the Permian red beds, and I find my father's geology lessons at the tip of my tongue. Our conversations are so satisfying, a redemption since I've lost my art teacher and my father, we arrange to meet again to paint together.

Despite my intention on that May day to "explore the abstract," as Georgia O'Keeffe had often instructed, I find myself making her portrait, which Zander pauses to admire. She's wearing her black and white geometric stencil-print kimono, her expression austere as always, and I've captured her clean angles as she was in 1918. I've fallen into the very tendency she'd scolded me for: choosing what came easy rather than challenging my worldview.

I am pulled from the cold waters, wide awake, but the dream, so vivid, is a blur, a story I can't remember well enough to put down in my logbook. It's the dusters I remember, their arrival a harbinger of worse to come, as relentless as the dry, nonstop winds that brought choking storms and an end to my painting. I feel hollow with a loss I can't quite glimpse. I grasp at the details—they are as smeary as a palette of rich colors—until I finally re-create the remarkable ambidextrous painter Zander, whom I met on an undistinguished field in 1931, where he signed his art *A. H.*, and I never saw again.

1946

CHAPTER SIXTY-SIX

RUBY LEE

The regionally famed painter Alexandre Hogue of Dallas would be in town, Ida Rose had learned, visiting his relatives' ranch on his way to teaching at the Taos School of Art. While here, he would deliver a talk at the library, featuring his "banned" paintings of the Dust Bowl and talking about the "don't look up" mood that had gripped the farm boom promoters in the face of reality.

Still weak but desperate for any outing, Ida persuaded me to take her, despite my reluctance to revisit the conditions of my childhood. Maybe the artist will see signs of hope on the dusty horizon, she urged.

Hogue began with a brief history of the Panhandle's destruction, illustrated with lantern slides of his paintings. "The fence destroyed the grazing land here first. Then came the men with plows. Once the land was overplowed, drouth destroyed it. And the cycle continues to this day."

He paused at his slide of *Drouth Stricken Area*, an infamous painting, he said, which was banned for showing the truth. No different from Dorothea Lange's revealing photographs of abandoned farms and portraits, which he showed next—her famous image, *Woman of the High Plains*.

I gulped at the authenticity of Lange's photograph of a melancholy woman who could have been my momma; at the similarity of Hogue's painting to the farm I'd left as a child. "That could have been our farm," I whispered to Ida, pointing out layered dunes overtaking a wind-battered farm, a lone scrawny cow seeking water from a dirt-filled tank.

"I was here as the stage was set," Hogue said, "and I witnessed the fury of the dust storms. I saw the aftermath, how its beauty was terrifying, with my own eyes—smarting from dust." He passed around a well-thumbed *LIFE* magazine that featured his paintings of a lifeless country, vivid despite their despair, and black-and-white photographs of dusters and their devastation.

"My brother-in-law was literally plowed in on all sides by the suitcase farmers, like many of you." A few in the small audience were nodding, but many sat with lips set in grim lines. "Loose dirt, uncontrolled and pushed by the wind, gnawed away every sprig of grass that dared show above ground."

Hogue recalled the repeated warnings of ranchmen who'd predicted, "if you plow this country up, it will blow away," as he had painted his memories. He called the paintings his Erosion series. The series of artworks Hogue created in his Dallas studio were despised by local Hartless boosters who'd promoted the land sales. Where he'd viewed the Dust Bowl as a disaster brought on by men's careless overcultivation of the soil, using plows as the prime method of destruction, our local newspaper deemed him a traitor for his betrayal of the Panhandle.

By the time Hogue ended his talk with his predictions of another drouth—since historically, they'd arrived regular as clockwork every two decades—most of the audience had left. They'd gone politely, quietly, as people here do, shaking their heads with disgust written on their faces. Hogue finished by posing a question loud enough for them to hear him in the stairwell. "What will men do to prevent the devastation the next time?"

Ida Rose had sat spellbound throughout his presentation. As Hogue packed up, she turned excitedly to me. "I had no idea you survived that. How terrible for you and your family. Now look at your farm, Ruby, look how you've improved it! You must be so proud of your hard work. Let's go meet the painter. I'd love to buy you a painting, to always remind you of what you've accomplished."

I didn't want any paintings that showed the hard times we'd endured. I didn't need any reminder hanging on my wall that my dream of providing a home would fail with no family to share it. I grabbed at her arm as she rose, which she took to be willingness, and she swept us to the front of the room.

"Let me give you this gift, Ruby," she whispered, "for all you've done." Her eyes lit up, dancing for the first time in a while. How could I refuse her, I wondered. I could not disappoint this friend who'd become the only family I had.

From inside my chest arose a fit of coughing, probably the dusty air blowing in from the large open windows at the front of the room. I caught myself before the wheezing began, but not before my eyes moistened. By then Ida Rose was talking enthusiastically with the painter, who regarded my suppressed cough spasms in recognition.

"I know a place in New Mexico, maybe a day's drive from here, where the mountain air is dry and dust free," he was telling Ida as he eyed me. "Taos. I teach painting there most summers. You take your friend there, she'll find it easier to breathe."

Ida Rose finished her transaction with him. Praising my success, she exclaimed how eager she was to hang *Drouth Stricken Area* in my front room. All I could see were the ghosts of those I'd lost, who hadn't loved me enough—ghosts who haunted me still, and I feared Will would feel the same. But I couldn't refuse her gift.

I tracked that painter down before he left town and hired him to make a new painting of our farm. The same size as the one Ida gave me, all the same lines and angles and shapes, I directed Hogue. But he would paint the new one as our land was becoming—fertile and prosperous, its buildings trim, the cows well-fed, with abundant green fields and clear blue skies disappearing into the horizon. That would make a fine homecoming gift for Will.

"I find that *success* is what makes it easier to breathe," I told Alexandre Hogue.

CHAPTER SIXTY-SEVEN

Settled in the wing I'd built for my brothers, Ida Rose grasped my hand. Weeks past near-death and she still looked like chewed twine. But her grip was iron.

"I owe you so much, Ruby. You showed me a kindness few have. That aloof way you play people? I never knew you were my friend. You do care, don't you."

I lowered my eyes and said nuthin.

"I've embarrassed you, I didn't mean—what I mean is thank you. For your friendship."

I felt my cheeks flush and turned to open the curtains as my eyes moistened.

"I hoped there'd be a view of the wheat, waving as it does with a soft breeze," I said.

"You were counting on it, weren't you? I can't repay you yet, but I will. As soon as I get on my feet—"

I hushed her. "None of it matters till you're well."

I calculated how far my cash would go. Adding what I got from the damaged wheat to my savings, subtracting the loan payments, and settling my mercantile tab left nothing for living expenses, my Cub, or my crop-dusting business.

"You adding up some numbers in your head?" She smiled wanly. "Or else your lips are misbehaving."

"You trying to lighten my mood—" I quit before I got snarky.

When I counted, breathing in deep and out, she chimed along, "one-two, three-four."

"Bravo, we got to four." She looked more radiant.

"Lookit, stay as long as you need. Be nice to have you here. Like family."

Ida's eyes widened and just as quick shone luminous. She pushed herself up with effort and swung her feet to the floor. As she stood and wobbled, I lunged to steady her.

"Thank you." Her embrace was fierce. "Like family. We're both lonely that way, aren't we."

•   •   •

That night I pondered those years I'd grown to young adulthood at the State Home, where our dorm parents—married couples mostly—were anemic stand-ins for our own, at best; and at worst, brutal overseers for the unluckiest kids. They were ill-equipped to teach us plenty. But the one crucial thing they could have taught us, but didn't, was how babies were made.

"Don't ever hold a boy's hand," older girls gossiped to their little sisters, repeating what the house mothers told them. "If you do, you'll get pregnant."

They never tried to teach us how to grow up to be good parents, what was expected of a wife and mother, or what constituted a good father and husband. That good manners weren't the same as respect; that privileges and bribes didn't equal patient attention, and harsh punishments weren't good discipline. That some gifts came with strings attached. What genuine love felt like, and how to accept another person's caring. The way a child could thrive when she felt worthy.

Like the kitten I'd rescued for Red—"something to care about," I'd told him—Ida Rose was a new beginning for me. Some small atonement for Bess.

•   •   •

A large manila envelope came postmarked Waco. I tore it open.

I pulled out a black-and-white glossy photograph, stamped "Naval Base Hospital, Peleliu, 5 August 1945," showing a shirtless young man in white shorts on a cot. His navy haircut had grown out into curls, freckles crossed his cheeks like a teenager's, and dog tags swung over his hairless chest. Bandages wrapped his legs, one encasing his left hand. His nose and forehead were scabbed. His face would be boyish were it not so gaunt. His eyes were dead.

On the back of the photo, someone wrote: "HA1c Oris 'Red' Hubbard. USS *Indianapolis* Survivor."

I unfolded the enclosed letter from Miss Celesta Rudolph, a girl I hadn't given a gnat's thought to since the president died.

Dear Ruby,

Not much has changed around here since you left, except I'm walking with a little limp, without my braces. After Kenny treatment hot packs, therapists massaged and trained my leg muscles, and weeks later, put me in hydrotherapy in the warm springs. My legs got strong enough I could walk without my braces, and the doctors said I was ready to return to the State Home. Like that was a big prize.

I did miss Mollie while I was at Warm Springs (she stutters less often now), and, of course, Clare. She writes me every week—it's lonely here, since she left for clerical school.

Sometimes I wish I was still a cripple, floating in the springs, where the nurses were kind, looking out for our comfort and needs.

I have you to thank, for asking your good friend, Mrs. Roosevelt, to help me out. It was sure nice of you, Ruby. The NFIP, that's the National Foundation for Infantile Paralysis, is going to choose one child to be on next year's March of Dimes poster and the local chapter nominated me. Cross your fingers for me, Ruby—maybe I'll be selected! If I'm the poster child, I can get out of this dungeon two years early!

You can thank Mrs. Roosevelt for this letter to you at your pa's farm. She wrote you after you left, and put your forwarding address on the envelope, which

I copied down before I mailed it to you. I hope you are happy back home with your family, now that you're not an orphan anymore.

I reckoned you'd want to know about your friend from your times here, I guess maybe he was your best friend, Red. Since we got the news he'd been on the Indianapolis, *a reporter's been around asking about him. Well, Red is Waco's big hero now! "State Home Boy Makes Good," Coach keeps bragging, says discipline prepared his boys for war.*

Coach is still beating the boys in his dorm, and they're still running away. Red's a legend 'cause he succeeded.

The reporter gave me this picture he'd been showing around. I guess you recognized it's Red. His legs were burned bad in the oily water after the ship got torpedoed, plus he had shark bites on his hand and arm. He was a hero for saving some seamen when the ship first exploded. The reporter thinks Red will return to Waco once he's recovered. I told him, you're missing a few buttons off your shirt if you think Red would step foot here again. But if he does, I'll give him your pa's address so he can write you.

Well, wish me luck, Ruby. Maybe you'll see my smiling face on the March of Dimes posters soon! Write me back. I guess you know the address here.

Your State Home Family,

Celesta

Below Celesta's signature, a bounty of names appeared in scratchy scrawls, perfect penmanship, and variations in between. State Home kids, some teachers, and even dorm mothers signed her letter with x's and o's, good luck wishes, miss ya's. Mostly girls from the littles' dorm, Mollie, Emma Sue, Dolores, and Mrs. Croucher, Miz Wills, the nurses. The rest of the gang had aged out by now.

As if she knew I'd be wondering, Celesta had added a postscript.

PS Kitty never came back from the fresh air cure at the San Angelo TB Sanitarium. We knew she was frail and never figured she'd survive the wasting disease.

The superintendent sent twelve senior girls to work for a war factory after all, but Thelma cut loose. She said a measly $10.80 a month with room and board wouldn't keep her from commercial college.

Corinne and Viola were happy to get out, even if they didn't get their diplomas. Corinne sent us a V-Mail later from her London posting with Women's Army Corps. She was a teletype operator but couldn't say more since everything was hush-hush. Clare says she's a spy.

Viola married a gimpy infantryman, a T-Patcher on furlough from Camp Hood. They tied the knot quick before he went overseas. When his division attacked the Siegfried Line in Germany, he got trench foot and left a few toes there. Now he runs a Dr Pepper bottling plant, south of Waxahachie, not far. We visit on holidays. Viola says if it were up to her, we'd live there for good, but her husband's against it—says with another baby on the way, one gimp in the household is plenty. Clare never quits asking, though. She can't get used to being an orphan.

A stab of regret mixed with nostalgia froze my blood, followed by a hot longing for them all. For the first time in years, I contemplated what I'd left to follow my lost family and the fantasy home I'd conjured. Tears flowed, but I bit my tongue, hard, to stop the flood of emotions. A memory surfaced. Mrs. Roosevelt's keen blue eyes, observing in her wavery voice, *"You've already found your home, Ruby . . . Those State Home girls and boys who are loyal to you—you're lucky to have them for family."*

Ida appeared, her brow furrowed. "Ruby? What's wrong?"

"It's nuthin," I said, sliding the letter back in its manila envelope. The glossy photo fluttered from my grasp. Ida studied Red's face before handing it back.

"He means something to you, doesn't he."

From his picture, Red's spiritless eyes tugged at me, but I could decipher no message.

"Once. A long time ago." But did I ever mean anything to him? I set his photo on my desk to think about later.

She waited, the question in her eyes.

"Not anymore," I told her, with more finality than I felt.

I spent the day at Miz Lawler's office, balancing her accounts, trying not to think about how unbalanced mine were.

In town there were homecomings and celebrations, young men disembarking from troop trains into grateful waiting arms. Still no word from my brothers.

On the way home, I drove to the base to witness the dismantling of the once-bustling airfield.

Rules were relaxed at the guard post, and I was waved on through. I looped the area, lingering near the plane hangars. The Piper Cub I couldn't afford sat in a line of grounded airplanes, a bright yellow beacon of my hopes, dwarfed by big silver B-29 Superfortresses. I ran my hands along the airplane's fabric-covered steel frame, my fingers massaging each pock made by a hailstone as if I could mend her pitted body along with my broken heart.

Unlike mine, the damage to the Cub was purely cosmetic.

But her value to me was priceless. Which gave me an idea.

CHAPTER SIXTY-EIGHT

The sergeant turned up like a bad penny, emerging from the hangar, double-timing it with a lopsided gait.

He removed his cap and squinted. In the sunlight, his face was suntanned and his features were all angles. His rakish eyes drank in my newly curvy hips and full breasts. "Ruby. You're tough to catch up with."

"You never will."

"I reckon I won't. You don't remember me, do you."

"You have no idea how little I've tried." I strode to the hangar to find the man I'd bargained with for the Cub. The sergeant kept pace with me.

"Just as well you don't," he said. "Lemme buy you dinner."

"I've got no time for that." I pressed on ahead into the hangar, but my man wasn't around. Nobody was.

"Rumor is, orders are coming to sell off the military equipment," the sergeant gestured at the emptiness. "The Second Air Force training mission is done. The base'll be a storage depot for surplus till—"

"You're not telling me anything I didn't figure on." His persistence was irksome.

"And I'm assigned to manage that," he kept on, his smile self-satisfied.

I looked him over more carefully. With his close-cut hair and worn aviator jacket, he could have been any fast-talking flyboy—except for his flitting eyes, penetrating when they landed. Keen for the hunt.

"Now you're telling me something that matters to me," I said. "Still don't have a clue who you are."

I took some perverse pleasure in his crestfallen look.

"Well, like I said, that suits me fine. Let me introduce myself proper. I'm Wade Banks."

Cagey eyes, eager demeanor, I saw, my instincts on guard.

I shook his hand. "I'm Ruby Lee, and we have some business to talk over. Meet me tonight at Last Stop at six. Call ahead to get us a table."

●　　●　　●

I arrived early for a private spot in the bustling café, at a corner booth in the back. While I sipped sweet tea, the sergeant narrated a spiel about his dedicated service at the Army Air Field's training school, from cadets in gliders to actual pilots who flew a whole gamut of airplanes during target practice and flight drills. Drafted in Waco, Wade rocketed through the ranks here, and he facilitated it all. He rattled off a numerical blitz of training wings, bombardment groups, fighter missions, airplane models in a feat of sheer bombast that could have won the war if words were weapons. It made him thirsty. He held up a finger for a second beer.

"You're a flier, then," I said.

"Nope. Working my way up the chain of command. That's where the payola is."

"You don't even fly?"

His face flushed slightly. "Your family here?"

"Scattered," I said. "A hazard of life in the blow country."

"And war. I'd reckon."

"You got family," I asked while running through the menu. I considered grilled T-bone, but I hadn't eaten chicken-fried steak, the house specialty, in a month of Sundays. The entree list was mouthwatering enough, till my eyes lit upon desserts. Coconut cream pie, peach cobbler, and the special—until it ran out—chocolate meringue, a treat no longer rationed.

Wade Banks hadn't answered my half-hearted question. He didn't want to talk about his family any more than I did.

"Never met a fella didn't want to fly. But not you?"

"My ambition ain't to fly things. It's to run things."

I laughed. "Never met a fella didn't think he couldn't."

He studied the menu, revealing little. But I wasn't there to get to know him.

"You're quiet," I mused, mulling over meat loaf, the blue plate special.

He went to find the waitress for a beer.

"All that talking's made you thirsty," I observed as he downed the Jax he returned with.

He tipped back the longneck, eyes crinkling.

The waitress arrived, and Wade Banks pushed his empty at her, said to bring him another.

"Save me a slice of chocolate meringue pie." After I ordered, I looked up from the menu to find his bemused eyes fixed on mine.

He kept maddeningly silent. The sly smile widening across his cheeks was reminiscent of Earl in his least trustworthy moments.

"You said you had business to talk over," he prodded. "Go on, it's your nickel."

It had been ten years and Wade Banks had the powerful build and posture of a grown man, and the same wily gaze I'd known then. His eyes were still calculating.

"You owe me twenty dollars, plus interest," I said.

Wade didn't show a hint of surprise. From his billfold he counted out three twenties.

"That's not enough."

"Crazy broad," he smiled, added two more twenties to the pile. "That enough interest?"

"Not enough for the Piper Cub, is what I meant. But with the hail damage, I won't be paying the price I bargained for. That's where you come in."

My meat loaf arrived, smothered in cream gravy alongside a mound of mashed potatoes and a steaming pile of butter beans. I shoveled a few forkfuls into my mouth, savoring the biscuit I dragged through the gravy.

"Get me a Jax, will you," I told him.

He set two bottles on the table and watched me decimate my blue plate special. "Been a while since you ate, I'd say." He grinned in his winsome way, enjoying the show.

After I ate my fill, I said, "I'll pay half the price agreed on with your man at the hangar, in light of the hail dings and dents." I indicated his pile of twenties. "You can make this a down payment, mister officer in charge of surplus, can't you."

The waitress slid a piece of pie my way.

I stifled my pleasure at the first bite of chocolate meringue. With my mouth full, I continued, "The balance will come due six months from now. You won't have to wait ten years."

I dabbed at the meringue on the corners of my mouth, smirking behind the napkin.

Wade Banks appeared beguiled. His eyes danced. He had the con down. His hair was thick on top and a little wavy, and the way it fell onto his forehead lent him a rakish charm, which he'd cultivated since I'd seen him last—or more aptly, since he'd disappeared with my money and my suitcase.

"That all." He sounded tickled. "Well, I've got a promise for you." He signaled the waitress, said he'd have the chocolate meringue pie after all, and two Dr Peppers.

"I think I owe you that pop, too."

"What you owe me," I said, "is the truth about Viola, who's not your cousin, and never was. And you owe me an apology for stranding me without my suitcase and without a nickel to my name. Or is that too much to expect from a hustler like you?"

Wade Banks allowed his grin to go sheepish. "Like I said, it suited me fine you didn't remember me."

"Oh, I remembered you alright. And I always collect on my debts."

He leaned in, his entire body coiled to strike, and his voice surprised me with its intimacy. "You're a hustler, too, just like me."

He sat back, his body relaxed. His sharp eyes never left mine, nary a blink.

"I see you. I seen how you worked the angles on the Kraut doc. Hats off to you." He raised his pop in a toast. "You saved a life. Your hustle turned out good."

His eyes probed mine for a reaction, but my poker face was a well-honed talent.

"This time it did," he added, looking for a rise he didn't get.

Almost to himself, he said, "Admirable. Turned out better than most of mine did."

Then louder, "Damn decent of you, keeping Rosie's reputation clean."

He warmed to his pitch. "In point of fact, any down-and-out girl left at the Waco State Home who's restored her family's farm, built herself a home sweet home, laid out a runway to fly herself who knows where—well, she sure as shit employed a fair bit of hustle."

"What's hustle to a conniver like you, who stole money, and worse, hope, from an orphan, is pure grit," I threw back at him. "Don't ever forget it."

And then I said nuthin, having said more than I intended.

Unabashed admiration crossed his face.

"An orphan. I stole hope from an orphan." He rolled the syllables around on his tongue like marbles. "That's good. I plead ignorance and offer my deepest apologies."

He made a showy little bow, wobbling a bit.

We'd all hated being called orphans. I said nuthin.

He remained standing—weaving, more like. "Waiting," he claimed, for forgiveness.

"Forgiveness is earned."

"Then I'll earn it."

I rolled my eyes. He slid beside me in the booth. "Let me see you again— I've got something for you."

I raised an eyebrow.

"Something that'll please you," he insisted. "To make up for stealing from an orphan."

I allowed a corner of my mouth into a slight smile, and he moved in for the kill.

"Now about that promise," he said, provoking me to mouth a steely *no*. Who needs a promise from a con man?

Our Dr Peppers arrived.

"Alright. My promise'll be there when you're ready. Meanwhile, here's to hustle"—he raised his fountain glass to tap mine—"and to Viola, not my cousin at all, as you rightly perceived, but a good kisser nonetheless."

He was shameless.

CHAPTER SIXTY-NINE

WILLA MAE

After the war the asylum overflows with shell-shocked soldiers, bedded down in hallways, porches, common areas. I grieve for Madeleine. I search the blank eyes of the young men, looking for my sons, fearing I might find them. I absorb the guilt of the deaths I've caused, my mother's, my baby's. I write letters to Ruby. I expect nothing from Beck.

I meet a curious veteran who believes he's the painter Vincent van Gogh. He calls himself *fou roux*—the mad redhead. He wears a bandage on his ear, like his idol, but absent the wound. With wild, wide eyes, he paints *The Yellow House* madly and fiercely, over and over again, outside on the asylum cemetery grounds. He mutters to himself, the same words, a little chant:

Oh Mother, dear Mother, it's sad to relate,
Your poor boy has met a most horrible fate.
We flew through the flak, oh so brave and so bold,
We flew through the flak but he died of the cold.

He laments as he paints. "It was June in '44 when an Allied bombing raid to destroy the bridges over the Rhône destroyed van Gogh's yellow house," he relates as I watch his lusty, bold brushstrokes emulate his idol's technique. "Right before my infantry group landed on the beaches of Southern France, to break the Siegfried Line—in August, only two months later." He was a T-Patcher, who'd served in the Thirty-Sixth Infantry

Division, the Texas Division, and claimed his psychosomatic symptoms resulted not from his battle scars during raging combat, but from his deep despair over the loss of van Gogh's *Maison Jaune* at 2 Place Lamartine in Arles, bombed by the Allies.

For a while he's missing, suffering one of his depressive episodes, I assume. After a few months, and several shock treatments, the Mad Redhead returns one day but has tired of painting his yellow house. He shows me a sketch he'd like me to model for. "Girl in White," he says, referencing my white standard-issue gown, I suppose, my interest in his flamboyant brushstrokes piqued. When time allows, I pose in my hospital gown, wearing a fanciful scarlet hat which belonged to the Duchess. For our next session he wants to paint me outdoors, to capture the north light on my three-quarter profile. He begins to lay paint on his canvas, transforming me. I wear a flowing white dress, cinched tight across bodice and waist; on my head, a broad-brimmed yellow hat topped with a knot of sky-blue ribbons. "One of my last paintings, *Jeune fille en blanc,*" he sighs, signing it, *fou roux.*

I notice Mr. Lorenzo keeping watch. He takes an occasional break from his caretaking duties in the cemetery to observe with his usual silent protectiveness, and unwittingly becomes another subject for a work the painter is beginning. He calls it *Garden of the Asylum.*

He's more talkative today and his words come rapidly. "I use red ochre, green saddened with gray, black outlines to give rise to the feelings of anxiety we wretches suffer from," the Mad Redhead explains of the lightning-struck tree and autumnal flowers which bore no relation to our asylum garden, if it could even be called such. He works in a small dark figure prowling between the trunks, shovel over his shoulder, which I realize is the gravedigger.

"They've proposed the transorbital lobotomy to control my frenetic outbursts of energy, my sleeplessness, and what they call my delusions, but say it may ruin my creative capacity." He whistles as his flat brush makes short, vibrant strokes. "They say even if my creative artistry is sacrificed, my agitation and depression can be managed—then I can go home. *Home.*"

I am shaking my head, no, and he takes a piece of charcoal to his paper to sketch what looks like a steel chisel, shaped like an ice pick, beside a slim silver hammer. "It's quick, ten minutes or less, practically painless—I'll need only a bit of novocaine. They will hammer this orbitoclast about seven centimeters into my upper eye sockets. A quick thrust up and around destroys my offending brain tissue and I won't feel a thing. My eyes will be blackened . . . but it won't be the first time. Ha!" His eyes flare as he emits one shrill laugh. "Then I'll be released, they've assured me, like all the veterans they've operated on . . ."

With widening eyes I regard him in horror. "But your talent, you can't let them take that from you—"

"Lobotomy gets them home, " he sings, his brushstrokes coming in rapid bursts.

Autumn gives way to a cold North Texas winter and the Mad Redhead makes his studio in the asylum attic. I follow him up there, curious, eager for solitude to write and sketch. That's where I find the suitcases. Stacked on rows of shelves, they number in the hundreds. All the suitcases, even trunks and crates, that belong to patients whose lives are mere numbers in the cemetery; and the belongings of patients who've never left—like mine. I race through the aisles until my fingers land on the leather suitcase I took to college in Canyon three decades ago, when my independence seemed assured. It's stuffed with my writings, logbooks, drawings, every portrait I've ever made of Ruby, every letter I've written, in sealed, addressed envelopes— never mailed.

CHAPTER SEVENTY

RUBY LEE

Wade was right. He had something that pleased me, alright, as he'd insisted. Scared me, too. But it didn't make up for stealing from an orphan, which I wasn't.

He arrived at my house with a fragrant bouquet of fresh-cut roses, unseen since before the war, the back of his service truck laid out like a picnic table, covered in a red-and-white checkered oilcloth, boasting a basket of formerly rationed cheeses, cold cuts, canned fish, butter biscuits, jarred jams, and confections with the sugar and chocolate we'd craved during the war years. We drove south of town to Rita Blanca Lake, where WPA workers had dammed up Rita Blanca and Carisso Creeks for flood control back in 1939, Wade explained, an event I'd missed.

The waterfowl on the lake were putting on a sunset show, whooping cranes and geese covering the water's glinting surface by the thousands, flushing in a flurry of white that burst up as we neared. When they settled again, Wade pointed out flocks of cormorant, heron, egret, duck, teal. "They're all just passing through, not like you," he remarked. "A woman who knows her place."

"You're hollerin down a well if you expect me to laugh at your double meaning, Wade."

"No harm meant, my lady," he replied as serious as I'd seen him, lending a hand up to the back bed.

"I came all this way from Waco, Ruby, to deliver something to you I been safeguarding all these years," he said, extracting my cardboard suitcase from beneath the checkered oilcloth. "My deepest regret is that it's taken me so long to find you."

"There you go with the double meanings again," I mumbled to choke back tears springing up.

He touched my cheek, tilted my chin up, and looked me right in my brimming eyes. "That means only one thing, girl. Now that I've found you, I know what I been looking for." The scar in his brow disappeared into a crease as he lowered his lids and his lips met mine with an electric jolt that lingered. Startled, I found myself kissing him back.

Later I reflected on Viola's claim her cousin stole my suitcase and decided maybe so, but back then, we were kids. Now Wade was hell-bent on earning my forgiveness and I enjoyed letting him. That evening we first kissed, we feasted on Wade's picnic in between more snatched kisses, until we laid back to watch the stars emerge, one by one, to clot the vast Panhandle sky in twinkling light.

•   •   •

After Wade had seen me home in the wee hours, I set my shabby cardboard suitcase beside me on my bed and contemplated my momma's letter. Its envelope was coated in a layer of dust. Though I'd long since given up hope of seeing it again, I'd never forgotten it. Her letter had remained there, unopened, along with her fine tortoiseshell hairbrush and comb, her once too-large kid leather gloves, and her oversized cloche hat, since the day Pa put me on the train.

Earl had torn my certainty from me when he'd insisted it was Pa who'd sent me to Waco because of the dust pneumonia. My momma's compass was set on me, he'd said; she hadn't abandoned me, far from it. She'd tried to follow me. Since then, even as I held my shame and guilt close to protect my heart, that shield was slowly disintegrating. I needed to know Momma's true thoughts. Her intentions were in that letter, maybe. I hoped there'd even be some love for me.

I lifted the yellow-haired rag doll from the suitcase and placed her in my lap. Her blue eyes looked up at mine. I turned the letter over and over, nervous, grappling with what I'd long believed and daring to wonder if I'd been wrong, my hands damp, a lump lodging in my throat, before I finally tore it open and devoured its few words.

CHAPTER SEVENTY-ONE

The dark sedan barreled toward me, sucking up the runway.

I was pummeling hail pocks from the Cub—far easier than healing the pits in my heart. My stomach did a barrel roll and I climbed down the stepladder to meet the olive drab Plymouth staff car that stopped short with a screech.

A stranger in uniform emerged as the passenger door swung wide and Wade walked to me. The soldier handed me a telegram.

My head spun with my worst fears. Will, killed in combat on Okinawa. Earl, died in captivity on Kyushu. Clay, killed by mortar fire. Red, succumbed to sepsis. Who would it be, which one, I shook with dread; the telegram fluttered to the earth. Woozy, I bent for it, crumpling.

Wade's arms were around me, propping me up.

The soldier handed it back to me. They watched me read the unbearable words.

"This is about my brother." I felt the blood drain from my face and longed to be piloting the Cub, the engine's full-throated roar eliminating any thought.

Wade tightened his grip, speaking insistently, voice low, his breath warm on my neck.

"I knew you'd need a strong shoulder to lean on. Remember meeting at the café? I wanted to make it up to you, what I did, right then. The promise you didn't want to hear . . . " He pulled me into the curve of his body. "I'll never let you down again. I'll be the man you can count on, no matter what."

My knees buckled, and he caught me. "I got you, Ruby, now and always. I promise."

"Those are fine words." I separated myself to stand on my own two feet. I read the telegram again, hoping for a different conclusion.

The Secretary of War desires me to express his deep regret that Pvt. Earl Everett Becker, Radar Repairman, Airborne Equipment, is reported missing in action after a surprise attack on the 1094 Th. Signal C. O. Service group in Burauen, Leyte, Philippine Islands, on December 6, 1944. Presumed dead. Remains not recovered. To prevent possible aid to our enemies this notice has not been timely delivered. Letter follows. —The Adjutant General

"MacArthur declared the liberation of the Philippine Islands in 1945, in July—" I protested, recalling the much-ballyhooed news.

Wade conferred with the soldier, who described a battle over an airstrip, where fanatical Japs infiltrated the American lines. After the Allies' victory over Japan was celebrated, reports reached high command of belated guerrilla action, minor and isolated . . .

"Minor." I wobbled. Again, Wade steadied me.

I read the telegram—*has not been timely delivered*—a third time. Missing and presumed dead since 1944.

Not Earl! Not after I shirked him.

•   •   •

Ida Rose stayed close in the dark months that followed—when I refused to believe we'd lost my brother, and the crops, and feared I'd built a house for an empty dream and a dented plane. She allowed me privacy for the crying jags I couldn't predict, whenever shame and secrets bubbled up. She filled my house with laughter and love, perversely, hosting baby showers for war brides she'd roomed with, their bellies now expectant with life. She took in new mothers whose husbands were still overseas, allowing them modest rents which covered our cash shortfall. In return Ida relieved them from the many sleepless hours they spent with their newborns. She rose to the most mind-numbing repetitive tasks that came with new motherhood, while she atoned for losing her own. The scents of baby powder and pablum and Ivory suffused the house.

I was allowed to wallow in my guilt for only so long as she deemed cathartic. She walked the fence line with me, the one that divided my nervous distress and panicky regret from full-out emotional collapse.

"We've already faced the worst of it," Ida reminded me again and again. "We've got some cash on hand, we'll replant, we'll pay off the loans. We'll be in the black again." She'd hold me as the prickling began and shivers took me.

"Will's safe, still on active duty, stationed at Nagoya Air Base; he'll be back," she said. "He's fine." But she couldn't shake my certainty about Earl, who I'd shunned for shining light on the unspoken, who'd simply tried to pry loose my shame.

"The telegram said, '*Presumed dead. Remains not recovered.*' Earl's coming home," I insisted.

•　　•　　•

Later, Ida said, while I clung to false hopes, cultivating a breakdown, she'd kept me from cutting and my nervous distress at bay. The one thing she couldn't keep me from was Wade.

Wade Banks made good on his promise, always there if I needed a hand with the crops, double-checking my accounts payable, collecting my receivables. He cheered me with stories of his sales prowess at the new Chrysler dealer where New Yorkers and Town & Country Woodies were jumping off the lot. He brought his never-ending party of recently discharged GIs over for drinks, arriving with card games, magic tricks, a bottle of Johnnie Walker Black, a new record to whip up his gang.

When his parties kicked into gear, the former canteen girl who'd yearned for an acting career (but had settled for the dance floor at New York's real Stage Door) nested herself in her bedroom with a good book. She snubbed the swinging swaying sounds of Sammy Kaye that cascaded from the Bakelite radio-phonograph.

The bebop rhythm of those eighth-note triplets was irresistible, and I'd haul a protesting Ida from her room to show me the swing steps. No sooner had I mastered a swing hammerlock, or a swing barrel roll, she'd slip back to her book.

On my darker days Wade arrived with a slim little volume he'd consult, *The Stork Club Bar Book*, to separate an egg white into a highball and mix me a restorative Morning Glory Fizz. At lunch, he poured a foamy White Daisy into an etched claret glass. Evenings, he'd whirl a Snow White in the new Waring mixer he acquired, or serve a concoction he called the Ruby Julep, which involved much muddling of mint, shaving of ice, a generous jigger of bourbon, and a floater of cognac. Later, he propped me up, walking me to my bedroom.

In my bed he nuzzled my neck and kissed me breathless as he undressed me, patient with my refusal to remove my long-sleeved blouse—until the night he whispered we need not fear one another, my secrets were his, there was no truth he would not accept. I peeled off my blouse without hesitating. I offered my scarred arms with defiance, and he cradled my wrists and traced the cuts with his lips, tenderly, showing me a grace I'd denied myself.

The nightmares returned. I'd lowered my guard and nearly allowed an examination of the unspoken things. Sleeping, Momma's screams terrified me; I heard them clear as the night I lost Nell, Alma, then her. I pressed my hands over my ears but couldn't block out her keening wail.

"You're howling, Ruby, shush, it's okay." Wade pulled me into his chest, muffling my screams. "Tell me what's the matter, baby, we'll fix it."

There are things, I wanted to tell him, *unspoken things that can never be fixed.*

But I said nuthin.

•   •   •

Before his honorable discharge—he'd made more payola in auto sales than in the air force—Wade had secured the Piper Cub, per our deal, and had it delivered to my runway, complete with two bottles of fine champagne. One he broke across the nose to christen my mustard-yellow tail-dragger, the other he poured into two Waterford coupes which fizzed up and bubbled over onto the runway amidst my tears, our laughter, and his toasts.

I wasn't the only pilot who wanted to fly for a living—those returning air force boys had the same idea, and surplus two-wing two-seaters were going for a song. While everyone welcomed the fliers home with victory parades and joyous celebrations, I got a head start on my crop-dusting business. I installed a tank, fixed a spray boom beneath the wing, added a small pressure pump. With my Cub rigged and loaded with insecticide, I practiced my drops, flying low on a field with wheels skimming the crops, pulling up sharp at field's end. I trained my eyes for obstacles that loomed up sudden and could take me down—fenceposts, standpipes, windmills. Wade stood his ground below as my flagman, keeping me on course, flagging me to the next section I'd spray. Once my wheels grazed him close enough for a buzz cut, and he dove like a duck. Circling back after my abrupt pull-up, I saw his head thrown back in laughter, his body shaking, the thrill of the close call as intoxicating to him as me.

That was how flying became my drug of choice, as my crops flourished, my dusting business took off, and for a few good seasons, nobody talked about next year when it rains.

1948

CHAPTER SEVENTY-TWO

RUBY LEE

Snow threatened under low skies sketched gray on the day Miz Lawler asked me to bring Wade for coffee at her clinic. It was still winter, 1948, and when we arrived, Ida Rose was settled in the living room, a knitted shawl around her shoulders—doing her best not to look around at the dispensary that held those memories of horror for her, I guessed. I pulled my chair closer and took Ida's hand, which was as cold as her eyes were icy.

As Miz Lawler poured coffee, she fretted the wheat prospects looked poor after the dry spells we'd endured since summer; thank goodness, she said, she'd quit the gambling habit. The one that lured her late husband to the blow country during its only steady years of rainfall and fertility on record since the century began.

"Gambling?" Wade raised an eyebrow.

"Wheat," I whispered. "A few good crops amidst the losses and it gets addictive."

"Water over the dam now, isn't it," she smiled to herself. "Though I'll allow you're making a good run at it, Ruby."

"Diversified, she is," Wade interjected, puffing up proud with his arm around my shoulder. "Ruby's hedged her bets with her crop-dusting business."

"Like you hedged yours, Wade?" Ida's voice, edgy and sharp.

During the brief uncomfortable silence, Ida's dig bored into Wade.

"Ironic, isn't it," Ida Rose continued, her eyes darting my way, "how a Dust Bowler takes up dusting. With help." She settled her steely gaze on Wade.

My face was suddenly hot. She didn't need to tell me all that dust I breathed was risky, and I was relying more on Wade. I tamped down a cough.

Since Ida had begun working evenings at the clinic, she'd slyly tried to persuade me Wade wasn't the marrying kind.

Now she put me in mind of Miz Lawler, lecturing me not to hitch to a cowboy head over heels, letting him steal my future.

"What brings us here to visit?" I changed the subject, uneasy. Had they joined forces to uncover Wade's shady side? Had they discovered my childhood hustling?

Miz Lawler settled back into the divan. "I'm ready to retire. I aim to go to San Antonio where I've got family, but folks here need doctoring, and like we all know, a doctor's days as a horse-and-buggy man with his medical bag are long gone."

I let myself breathe again.

"Everybody's got a car and an itch to get somewhere. They're coming here, soldiers settling here, babies coming, plenty enough patients to maintain this clinic, even expand it, and Lord willing, one day operate it in the black." She added another spoon of sugar to her coffee.

I nodded, wondering who on earth would take on the not-inconsiderable debts I'd tracked over the years.

"You all know that young Galveston doctor I hired straight out of the Medical Branch didn't last. He got a better offer in Houston. But I don't want to see the clinic close," Miz Lawler said. "I've found someone who's ready to step in, but first, I need to exact a promise from each of you."

I kicked Wade's ankle before he could ask what she had in mind while exchanging a glance with Ida. His name was on the tip of her tongue, too, I could tell.

It surprised none of us that Miz Lawler named Ida's surgeon, the former prisoner of war, Dr. Josef Richter.

He was one of a handful of former German soldiers who'd applied for visas to remain here after they were released from the prison camps. Most were from work camps in Dumas, Amarillo, or Lubbock, and had found employment during harvests or in city machine shops. They were tolerated, if not welcomed, as hard workers, fastidious, even dedicated. Increasingly, they'd been regarded as honest. A few had married, which was scandalous at first. But spare hands are never turned down on a farm. There'd been grudging acceptance, especially among residents with German heritage.

My pa's grandparents were farmers from Bavaria. He had loved his grandmother's apple kuchen, a rare treat. I knew the German lullaby Momma taught me by heart, "*Guten Abend, gute Nacht, lullaby, and good night, thy mother's delight . . .*" passed down by Pa's mother.

Miz Lawler said, "We both agreed it's very important Doctor—"

Wade was on his feet before she could say Richter.

"Richter!? *That Nazi?* Don't you know we fought a war against that country—"

"Wade," I stopped him with a look. "Josef wasn't a fighter, or a killer. He saved lives."

"He was the enemy," he muttered, "my prisoner, that dirty Jerry . . ." building up to another outburst.

Ida Rose cleared her throat.

"We should hear Mrs. Lawler out." The color of Ida's skin had faded to match the bone china cup trembling slightly in her hand.

"My dears, Josef is a fine surgeon"—Miz Lawler ignored Wade's protests— "and a fine man who only wants to be reunited with his family and practice medicine. He was educated in the top medical schools in Berlin. He's trying to secure passage for his wife and their young children to escape the horrors of war. Dr. Richter was trained to care for people. He was never a Nazi."

When Wade fumed, she put up her hand. "He isn't your enemy, though most of them were. The Nazis forced Josef into service for his medical skills. Because of that, he never suffered the fate of killing—having to kill GIs. All he ever did was save lives . . ."

Ida Rose mumbled something none of us could make out.

"Speak up," I prodded her.

"He saved me. I would have died," she said, her voice small, her eyes steady on Wade.

Miz Lawler nodded approvingly. "That's where the promise comes in, all three of you. We know the prejudice Josef will face. You are evidence of it, Wade, and I understand why. But he won't succeed here if he's not trusted, and if he's forced out, there won't be a doctor and there won't be a clinic."

She let that sink in, watching Wade.

"Dr. Richter's very determined to serve this town well, and he'll treat first, request payment later. He'll accept what his patients can afford to pay. He comes from a farming family, and back in Germany, he saw the challenges we face."

We all raised our coffee cups, sipping tentatively. Buying time.

I spoke first. "He'll be an excellent addition to this town, but only if he has everyone's trust."

Miz Lawler finished the last of her coffee. "Indeed. And I do trust him. But if he becomes known as an abortionist, unfairly of course, but if there's even one whiff he aided in the debacle that befell Ida, he'll be tainted. He'll be ostracized, even worse than he was as a . . . *dirty Kraut*."

It was shocking to hear Miz Lawler spit out the vile term everyone used for the hated Germans. I'd said it, too, until I'd gotten to know them.

"He'll be ruined, and this town will be without a decent man who's a gifted doctor," Miz Lawler hammered on. I'd never seen her as adamant.

"You three must promise you will never, ever speak of how he saved Ida's life. Once you leave my parlor, that topic is *verboten*."

"Forbidden," I echoed, nodding. Miz Lawler's face was unflinching, set stern while she spoke, but her eyes danced the tiniest bit as she repeated the German word.

I nodded, my mind made up. I owed Ida that much anyways.

Ida Rose gulped gratefully. "By all means, yes."

"I agree to that." I underscored it, as did Ida Rose, more forcefully. I clasped her hand. There was no upside for her if that story got out.

Then three pairs of eyes were on Wade.

He looked cornered, or to put it the way he might've, hustled. What could he say? He didn't have to like it, but he'd have to learn to get along with the German he'd never even fought.

Wade hadn't seen any real action, not like the men who'd returned battle-scarred or worse. He'd served his time right here, oblivious to threats or danger. He'd never been missing in action, like Earl, or survived an exploding ship and sharks like Red. Wade had a lotta nerve, which I telegraphed to him with a wicked stare.

He found a speck of lint to flick from his creased trousers.

"You might need a doctor someday yourself, Wade," I said.

"Or Ruby might," Ida finished.

And trapped like a treed fox, he pledged his secrecy, too.

CHAPTER SEVENTY-THREE

We'd settled into a rhythm in the last few years of the decade, with rain plentiful enough to spur demand for my crop-dusting business, and by late 1948, Griner was getting us decent yields with hybrid crops that were less thirsty.

"With wheat over two bucks a bushel, we're running with the big dogs." Griner allowed a smile of satisfaction, a rarity for him.

Wade was managing the entire dealership by now, top salesman every year on his sheer magnetism alone, and was about to open a new location on the other side of town, too. He'd been nosing around the latest drilling boom to hit the Panhandle—not oil, but water. Deep wells were going in to tap what Wade called the underground rain, straight up from the Ogallala aquifer beneath us. Newer drills that dug farther and faster had been spurred by war technology, and Wade was keen to invest in their manufacturing. He believed the farm profits could fund his pipe dream, but so far, I wasn't having any of it. I did my best to hide my skepticism from Wade, but like a good flimflam man, he never confronted me outright. With attentiveness and small kindnesses, he worked me good.

I saw through that, too, but still let myself be drawn to his allure. He began talking about settling down. I usually indulged his musings awhile, then changed the subject.

Ida Rose was immersed in her part-time jobs, juggling hours at the new soil conservation district with the expanding electric co-op. Most evenings, after a hasty supper, she lent her organizational skills to the clinic, where Dr. Josef's medical expertise was in demand despite the accident of his birth. Convictions died hard and heartless here, and anti-German sentiment was no exception—unless your wife was fixin to deliver your baby breach, or your child was struck with the sudden paresthesia and paralysis of polio. Then the nationality of the only doctor in two counties didn't matter too much. Gradually Josef had been overcoming his patients' reluctance to be treated by a German, even seeing patients for nonemergency care, too.

Ida Rose kept her room here but we saw little of her, except on weekends. Most weeknights she stayed in town in the boardinghouse where I'd met her, or (I suspected) in the rooms Josef occupied in the clinic. She was smitten with him, and perhaps he was with her, but Josef held to a foolhardy hope his German wife, the mother of his two sons, would travel to America to reunite their family. Josef's moral code was honorable, even admirable, if unrealistic. It was four years post-V-E Day and he'd heard little from Germany. I thought he deserved a woman like Ida—and she him.

It was Thursday in late November, and time for my supply run into town. The spring and summer crops had been abundant, with enough rainfall until fall to make my dusting business go gangbusters. But by fall, the dwindling rainfall had soured the ag men in Washington on a bumper winter wheat crop next year.

I was more optimistic. My almanac said otherwise, and I could see plenty more well water irrigating the fields with my own eyes, every day I flew. I'd been eyeing a second plane, to expand my territory and take on another pilot. In Lubbock, the legendary airplane designer Fred Weick had joined the Aircraft Research Center at Texas A&M College to build an airplane specifically for agricultural use, to spread insecticides, broadcast seeds, and fertilize fields. I was saving for the new AG-1, touted as structurally safer and more efficient—or if not that plane, something newer with a closed cockpit.

While I was settling my mercantile account, perusing the latest products at the register, a new item caught my eye. As I reached for it, the clerk spoke up.

"Just got these newfangled rain gauges in. Don't know why you'd need a thing to tell you what you can see with your eyes. Look at the earth and you can tell it's dry."

I laughed, said add it to my order.

"Yes ma'am, don't mind taking your hard-earned money," he winked.

I was optimistic, sure, but I'd always believed preparation was the best form of prevention.

My next stop was the post office, where the customers scrutinized me the instant I stepped inside. The mail clerk, counting stamps out for a customer, stopped mid-sentence to call out, "Miss Ruby Lee Becker, there's a package for you."

"I'm expecting some parts for my Cub." I raised a finger in acknowledgment. "Plane's wearing down after spraying thousands of acres, need some extras on hand."

The murmuring customers had gone silent when the mail clerk whisked into the back room. He returned with a large box wrapped in brown shipping paper and tied up with twine, plunking it on the counter before me.

Puzzled, I lifted the box. Too light to be the parts I'd ordered. We both stared at the capitals stamped in red under his stubby finger, POSTAGE DUE, and beside it, the return address. Wichita Falls State Hospital.

"Don't think this here's parts." He shifted. "Unless the half-wits are manufacturing airplanes at the bughouse these days."

My face reddened at the communal titter and right quick I felt hot as a hornet. One glance at the busybodies told me they'd been speculating about my package all morning.

A woman I recognized from the employment office laid a gentle palm on my arm. Her eyes radiated sympathy. She whispered. "I've thought often of your mother, since your older brother Will came in to join the CCs. That was before your father passed. I hope you have some good news from her."

My mother, alive?

I gripped the counter to steady myself, made myself note the familiar prickling in my arms. *Was that even possible?* I began counting, silently, the postal patrons just as silent, their eyes avoiding mine.

Evidently so, and a long-time patient at the asylum for the mentally insane in Wichita Falls. A shameful truth I would finally face up to, even as it went unspoken. A droning buzz pounded in my head; my vision blurred. I forced myself to focus.

Convictions died hard alright.

The employment office lady gripped my arm more tightly. Her hand felt warm but maybe it was me, perspiration moistening my face. I turned to her; she met my eyes knowingly.

With what poise I could muster, I carried my package out. Apparently it had been an open secret all these years about my mother's whereabouts and only I was in the dark, and perhaps Earl and Will, though I doubted it. Wasn't that what Earl was trying to tell me, when I shirked him? And Will, always reticent, or protective, hadn't he known? Or suspected as much? In any event, their deception was still secure overseas. And Miz Lawler, whom I'd trusted—she must have known. If she'd still been in town I'd be grilling her about her years of silence, but she lived with her San Antonio relatives now.

Late that night, two fingers of Scotch down, and after I'd reread the letter from Momma that was tucked into my cardboard suitcase—the one I'd resisted believing—I unsealed the box. It was bursting at the seams with drawings, notes, sketchpads, letters, journals, haphazard writings, some crumpled, some carefully folded, many in envelopes addressed to our farm, none stamped. Obviously none were ever mailed. I pulled out a random letter. It was dated September 27, 1936—the same time as Waco's worst flood of history, when the telegram arrived I couldn't read, and had long forgotten.

CHAPTER SEVENTY-FOUR

WILLA MAE

September 27, 1936
Wichita Falls State Hospital

My dear Ruby,

I know I am not insane—I am not going mad. Even though they say I am driven mad by dust, I am driven only by my love for you, dear Ruby Lee.

I never wanted to lose you, darling girl, please believe me. Your pa sent you to Waco against my wishes, for how could a child so tender as you be separated from her mother?

It was for your own good, Beck insisted, so you wouldn't suffer from the dust pneumonia.

You were strong enough to overcome it, I knew. I could nurse you back to health, I was certain. And I feared you could not overcome a life without your momma.

But I couldn't stop your pa once he got his mind fixed.

I couldn't bear for you to go without my goodbye!

I followed your train on foot, long after the smoke plume vanished into the next duster sweeping east, where you were headed with Will. Poor Earl, I ignored his pleas to return home as he trailed me, begging me, long after dark until I collapsed on the tracks, your loss too much to bear.

The judge said I'd lost the ability to care for my family and sent me here to the state hospital to recover, but he understood nothing about mothering.

For what choice is that to give a mother, that to save her adored daughter she must give her up? Without even one last kiss upon her brow, one last tuck of a loose lock of her hair behind her ear, one last whisper of love and confidence? Your pa didn't trust me to do the right thing for you—and kept me from looking in your eyes to make you understand how much you are loved, how fiercely I want to protect you!

I will do the only thing I can—accept their treatments for this dust madness they say I have, to regain my sanity they say I've lost.

I pray for your return every moment until this vengeful swirling dirt leaves our skies and grants us the safety to breathe again, to live again.

I am including more drawings I made of your dear face, and a poem I wrote for you. I'll write you every week, sweet girl.

With all my love,
Your momma Willa Mae

1949

CHAPTER SEVENTY-FIVE

RUBY LEE

The newspapers in March 1949 hit me like a double whammy. Nearly every major paper in the state speculated it was twenty years since the last drouth and time for another, and ran an eight-part exposé about the grim conditions in Texas mental hospitals. Called "The Shame of Texas," the series detailed the gruesome treatment, overcrowding, and neglect patients faced, housed in what the reporter termed "the nation's worst hospitals."

It had taken months of letters, phone calls, and pressure, but I'd been able to confirm my mother was indeed a patient at Wichita Falls State Hospital, as she had been by court order in a jury trial since 1935—her commitment indefinite. She'd been judged insane, with my pa's consent, but I knew from her many writings she'd been driven to the edge by her preempted dreams, followed by the loss of her mother and baby, and not driven mad by dust.

At the Hartless depot fourteen years ago, about to board the train for Waco with Will, my father had pinned my name on my coat and I'd watched in vain for a mother who'd never appeared, certain I'd made myself so unlovable she no longer wanted me.

It had been easier, thinking she was gone forever. If she never comes back.

Twelve jurors, a judge, the court stenographer, the sheriff and deputies—so many knew where Momma was, yet no one thought her own child deserved to know. The worst betrayal, of course, was my father's. He took a secret to his grave he had no right to withhold, and sentenced my mother to a wretched life in a cesspool of insanity.

I'd read enough of the shocking report. I was still reeling as I put my truck in gear, my vision blurred by tears, driving the route to town I knew blind. When I reached the clinic, Josef was seeing patients. I settled myself in the parlor to await Ida Rose and enlist their help in bringing my mother back home.

•   •   •

The patient information Josef had requested from the Wichita Falls asylum came by mail a few weeks later. He'd wanted to understand my mother's condition and treatment history before we collected her. "She had some type of psychotic break, evidently, after her writings and sketches were shipped to you. They want to attempt a new intervention."

He read aloud to Ida Rose and me from a sheaf of papers that consisted of my mother's chart: "All forms of medical and psychiatric treatment up to this time have not been of more than temporary benefit. Unless a more drastic therapy is carried out, there will be little hope of any improvement… The treatment suggested is a delicate brain operation, which involves cutting certain nerve pathways controlling the basic emotions. This is known technically as psycho-surgery or prefrontal leukotomy."

"Brain surgery? Is that a good idea? It sounds so . . . drastic." I paused, willing the pooling tears not to overflow. "I can't believe she's in such dire straits. You have to examine her first."

Josef looked stricken. "I'm not trained as a psychiatrist, but I am a surgeon. I would never sanction surgery to alter one's emotions. It would be extraordinarily risky to operate on the brain, with no certainty of success. I've asked my colleagues about this Dr. Walter Freeman, the man who is promoting his treatment they call an ice-pick lobotomy. He's been using this procedure quite frequently in overcrowded hospitals that treat shell-shocked war veterans, with the VA's approval. The intent is to sever the connections of the frontal cortex, and especially to interrupt the projections which connect the frontal regions with the thalamus and hypothalamus. It's intended to inhibit certain psychic manifestations. But my colleagues caution it can cause seizures, incontinence, emotional outbursts, a flat affect, memory loss, even death. And there's little research to back up the results he claims," Josef concluded somberly.

"How awful," Ida Rose whispered, pulling me into a hug.

I flipped through the chart myself, noting the many treatments my mother had undergone with horror. Josef explained them to me, the ice packs, the hydrotherapy, the insulin shock injections, the Metrazol procedures—and still my mother had the presence of mind to write those many diary entries, letters, logbooks, and poems; she'd made countless predictive portraits of me as I'd aged that were perfect likenesses. Surely a mind that had endured throughout those "treatments" was not insane.

I turned to the chart's final page. "She cannot have surgery. In fact, they can't do any more to her. We have to bring her back and I need your help."

Now my tears were overflowing. I couldn't pull myself together to read the last entry aloud. Ida Rose took over.

"Dr. Walter Freeman, who developed the ice-pick lobotomy, will be at the asylum on July second and already has three patients scheduled for transorbital lobotomies," she read. "The last is Patient W. M. E., who 'shows her years, and at the rate she is going she will probably wear herself out before long. She is gradually deteriorating physically and something should be done about it now. Lobotomy is recommended in this case, primarily as a means of terminating the disturbed behavior, hoping it may affect favorably the long-term course of the illness before she becomes critically ill.'"

I stammered, "Patient W. M. E. That's Willa Mae Eckhart. My mother."

•　　•　　•

I made the cockpit comfortable for two while I tamped down my sense of unworthiness. My dread of being abandoned no longer suited me, I was realizing, and I thought again about the belief I'd clung to—my mother blamed me for Nell, so she'd rejected me. I hoped I was wrong. It was time to find out.

Ida Rose was already eastbound by train, waiting for us in Wichita Falls. Josef and I made ready to fly to the old Sheppard Field, where we'd hire a car for the half-hour drive to the state hospital. The insane asylum.

It was the last day of June and I recognized crops thirsty for rain in the sections we passed as we drove to the asylum, which was six miles from anywhere. The FW&DC tracks and Lake Wichita—neither of which the patients could access—lay to the east of the entrance. We'd taken two rooms in town the night before, after we'd been denied after-hours entry. "The patients are asleep," we were scolded. We'd walked the grounds in the twilight, observing some thirty-odd red-brick buildings and another sixty frame structures. The campus wasn't unlike the State Home but in worse shape; its cluster of red-brick buildings trimmed with limestone had splintered white trim, broken windows, and sagging roofs long overdue for repairs. When we looped the grounds, a mysterious man emerged from the cemetery, watching us. It was anyone's guess where my mother could be . . . but the solemn, dark-eyed man in heavy rubber boots who pocketed a harmonica introduced himself as Mr. Lorenzo. He would be our best bet.

The next morning I spotted Mr. Lorenzo, shovel in hand. He'd been digging a fresh grave, I realized, shivering. He tugged at his thick salt-and-pepper mustache, motioning to a row of trees.

"Ruby Lee," he said, surprising me with my name, "your mother has been waiting for you." He pointed to a spot beneath a tree. "She always sits here. I would know you anywhere, from your mother's portraits."

The box they'd shipped me contained dozens of drawings and paintings of me as I'd aged, most of them uncanny in their accuracy. "Where is she, my mother?"

The gravedigger pointed to the main building where the windows were blacked out. "She always has a bad day after the electroshock. Come back tomorrow." The man's features were forced together, like they'd been repositioned. With a slight bow, he walked away.

• • •

I ran to the entrance where Josef waited with Ida. "He's not allowed to see Willa officially as her doctor," Ida said, despite Josef's efforts. "But he can discuss her response to the lobotomy with the surgeon. It's scheduled for tomorrow." She touched my arm, kindly.

My skin was prickling but I wasn't counting. I stormed inside to the reception desk, demanding to see my mother. The harassed desk clerk spoke shortly. "Not today. In recovery from treatment."

I felt the rage building as I raised my voice, insisting on my mother's immediate release. None of the staff responded, moving on about their business as if I were another pleading patient.

A loud bell began ringing, its sound reverberating down halls that stretched in all directions. The echoing took me right back to the State Home on the night of my escape, which prompted an idea. I pounded on the desk to no avail. Deciding the coast was clear, I took a tour around. I averted my eyes from the steel-braided glass in the locked doors, afraid of what I'd see.

When I found what I was looking for, a passing aide directed me to the lobby. "Nobody can be released without a court order. And you're not allowed back here. The asylum is liable."

•   •   •

Josef, Ida, and I huddled outside, finalizing our plan. After a restless night in our hotel, we were back at dawn. I watched Josef don his white surgical coat, the mask tied loosely around his neck, looking every inch the competent doctor I knew him to be. He strode inside with Ida, who wore nurse's attire. I kept an eye on them from the entrance. He introduced himself in his commanding manner and told the receptionist to show them to the surgical suite to prepare for procedures Dr. Freeman would be performing. During the maddening wait, I lit up a hoarded Kellogg's cigarette. An hour passed. Finally they were directed to the stairwell. As soon as they entered it, I stubbed out the asthma cigarette while the second hand on my wristwatch made five long revolutions. I snuck in, sounded the fire alarm I'd located yesterday, and dashed out.

Beside the auto I watched the chaos build, first with eagerness, then dismay. Orderlies and nurses urged the patients out—a number nearly naked, some in jackets with sleeves tied behind their backs, many barefoot, unbathed, or with unbandaged wounds, babbling gibberish; most were dressed shabbily, protesting, or looking resigned, a few cowering fearfully.

Ida Rose emerged with a washed-out woman much older than my mother, whose eyes were vacant. Strips of white streaked her dark, oily hair. In her threadbare gown, she was rail-thin. With her expression subdued and her eyes blank, my mother looked dazed. I ached for her.

Josef followed closely, herding a trio of patients. His pace was impatient with the last man who shuffled slowly. Oblivious to the sirens, bells, screeching, wailing, and crazed pandemonium, his eyes were downcast to follow his footsteps. My mother caught sight of the doleful man Josef was steering out. When they reached the bottom of the steps the doleful man lifted his eyes—both black and blue like a beaten boxer's—which landed on my mother. She drifted toward him, hands outstretched. They both wore the same dirty hospital attire except for his addition, a cockeyed beret. The man spoke carefully, as though speech was an effort.

"Au revoir, ma cherie, n'arrête jamais de peindre."

My mother replied to him, also in French, her voice so faint I didn't catch it.

Josef conferred with the three patients he'd escorted, all of whom had black eyes, and after a final once-over he joined Ida. Together they coaxed my mother to our waiting auto. Close on the wheels of a speeding pumper came a hook-and-ladder, clattering between us and the building. That's when the odd gravedigger turned up, calmly assessing the commotion. His observant black eyes darted from me to my mother and I saw something in him ease. Taking note of him, she called out. "Look after them."

Momma, I think I said, but she didn't acknowledge me; the gravedigger recognized me. "She found you, Willa Mae Eckhart," Mr. Lorenzo's voice was awed. "Your daughter, there—" he pointed to me. But my mother's gaze was on Mr. Lorenzo, who looked lost as Ida helped her into the auto. Again my mother spoke, mysteriously, "Take care of them, Mr. Lorenzo. I don't want them to be alone."

I held my mother's face in my hands, my eyes only on hers. Waiting for her to know me again. Not seeing recognition in her eyes, I pulled her into me. "I won't let you be alone, Momma," I whispered.

Mr. Lorenzo, his face torn, watched her. "That's my job here. Who else would do it?"

•   •   •

Later in the auto Josef explained he'd quickly made his way to surgery, where he had words with the balding, Van Dyke-bearded Dr. Freeman, clad in neither surgical gloves nor mask. The lobotomist had folded his spectacles and inserted them in his shirt pocket, then hastily packed his orbitoclast and hammer into its black leather case, unplugged his portable electroshock machine, and departed that instant under cover of the havoc unleashed by the alarm. His patients still laid inert upon the tables. Josef had made certain Freeman knew those patients on whom he'd already performed his ice-pick lobotomy—the three whose eyes were blackened—would be his last in Wichita Falls.

After witnessing the lobotomy's aftermath on those patients, I deliberated whether Momma knew she'd come close to a total disintegration of her personality.

We spent another night in the hotel to allow my mother to adjust. I worried her mind had been dismantled by years of harsh treatments in confinement. I was troubled she didn't know me. Josef reassured me it would take time.

After a sleepless night, I was content to let Ida and Josef accompany the mother who didn't know me to their clinic. But I wouldn't let her go without a goodbye. From the train platform, I waved her off—as if that could dismiss our past.

Flying back solo gave me time to reflect on her years of entrapment. Why didn't she walk away? Something she'd written in her diaries tugged at me—how she had absorbed the guilt for the deaths she'd caused, her mother's and her baby's. Maybe she'd got herself stuck, doing her penance, thinking it's what she deserved. How it would absolve her. That was something I could understand.

CHAPTER SEVENTY-SIX

Sometime in late 1949 the skies began to go dry, but we didn't notice it at first. Drouth in the Panhandle wasn't entirely absent a rainfall; it crept on stealthily, a little rain here, a sprinkling there, never enough to soak in. The soil showed cracks, the moisture so sparse the wheat couldn't head out, and we started to X out the dry days on the John Deere wall calendar.

The old-timers who'd survived the drouth of the dirty thirties became the bellwether for clouds that carried rain or were just empties. Their café counter debates weren't winnable but they heralded an undeniable fact: the ground was drying out and crops were withering. I saw it with my own eyes, flying over my customers' browning fields with my crop duster tanks empty. Farmers had quit spraying—no need to fertilize wheat that won't head out. The 1950s' worst drouth of record, far more tenacious than the destructive weather in the 1930s dust bowl years, was still on the horizon, and we still had cause to hope for rain. *When it rains*, I thought, the phrase farmers like my pa spoke in 1935, ever optimistic despite the fearsome black dusters that upended my childhood.

It was two shades hotter 'n hell when I began my climb up the Aermotor, missing the familiar clank-clap of shiny new blades silenced on a windless day. The unaccustomed heaviness in my belly slowed my pace. That was my secret to tell, when I was ready. No doctor or husband would pressure me to slow down and take it easy, not while this farm was still mine to lose. Some thirty-seven feet up and panting, I heaved myself on to the windmill platform and took in the views past the sole tombstone in our family cemetery. The New Mexico mountains, a purplish constant in the hazy west. To the north, where the James family had run cattle till the dried-out, overgrazed ranch land blew dirt across Oklahoma and Kansas in the thirties, native grasslands now held the soil.

Our sections were still green, with ancient aquifer water flowing from our once-dry well, newly deep and now one of four. I hadn't been up to my thinking perch since the drouth of the 1930s ended and I finally got back home, a few months after Pearl Harbor. Those depression years, aggravated by the drouth, had bankrupted Texas farmers and scattered thousands of Panhandle families like ours and millions of unemployed in every direction the dust blew. They had little choice, with a hundred million acres overtaken by dusters in 1935 alone. In those hard times, homeless children turned into tramps on trains, jobless men rode the rails, and hunger was the norm. Boys like my two brothers were looking for a lump at the back door, a day's work for food, a hand up. I was looking for a place where the very air I breathed wasn't my enemy.

•   •   •

Fall brought a norther. It swept in, howling out of a blue-black sky that turned dirty brown. I ran for the house and hauled the storm windows down, slamming the double-hungs shut against the dust. Scared as a sinner in a cyclone, I held my breath as if that small act of defiance would keep the sandy particles out. With my lungs near bursting, I let go and breathed— and found the air was silt-free. Breathable. Racing from room to room, I traced my finger along the darkening windowsills, picking up nary a whit of dust. I poured two jiggers of Scotch over one cube of ice and topped it with soda. Then I sank into the deep cushions of my armchair, sipping my Scotch, my breathing even inside my sealed house as the brown blizzard scoured the earth bare.

I hoped my mother's quarters in Josef's sanitarium were as airtight, so she wouldn't flash back to the terror of the dirty thirties. Josef had her there under observation, doing mental exercises he deemed appropriate. With

Ida's tenderhearted care and a nutritious diet, her hygiene improved, she slept amply, and gained weight. Josef was cautiously optimistic she'd heal from the traumas she'd endured.

"Her health needs must be met first. She's very fragile still," Ida said. "Trying to uncover herself, who she is, Josef says, will come next—and then, learning to trust again."

Unconsciously I fingered the scars beneath my sleeve. That's what I was doing, too.

During my daily visits, I read aloud from her writings and letters, having put them in a semblance of chronological order, and showed her the drawings that corresponded, gently nudging her to remember this or that. But my mother's faraway look was maddening in its willfulness. Months passed, with Joseph assuring me she needed time to acknowledge her memories. To remember them, after all, was why she wrote so much.

"Your mother wanted to keep her memory, understand. Reading to her helps," he chided me. "Read everything over and over again if that's what it takes. Until the day she smiles upon you because she knows you as the daughter she has so much love for."

I wiped a tear from my eye and nodded, pressing my hand to his with a whisper, *thank you,* my resolve returned. Tomorrow I would take her some charcoal sticks, pastels, and a new sketchpad, so her love of making art might revive her.

•   •   •

The air smelled almost clean the next day. Except for bedraggled crops, it could have been a gullywasher come through. But in the Cub, each spraying flight was a test of my breathing stamina—with no way to keep out dust and cold air. It pricked away at my throat until I couldn't contain the coughing and I had to land.

All that was forgotten a week later. The first sleet storm of winter slammed us, bringing fresh breathable air and melting hail. The temperatures dropped, leaving a soupy frozen crust on the fields.

Our fears of another drouth were overlooked when the flimsy red-white-and-blue V-Mail letter arrived—Will's, writing from Japan. He'd grown tired of pushing paper and supervising requisitions from his air forces desk in a repurposed Quonset hut and was itching to get home.

After dusting the last fields for the day, I drove to the clinic, taking the stairs two at a time to my momma's room, eager to share the news of Will coming home. She stared at me blankly, as she always did, the daughter she was loath to lose and now knew not at all.

•   •   •

We were filling out the marriage license application at the courthouse. "Your father was Wade Banks Sr. and your mother was Beulah K. Banks," I read aloud. "She got a maiden name?"

"Krausen, I think," Wade said. "Everyone called her Curly."

"For her hair?" I mused.

"No. That's what her maiden name meant. Her hair was straight as a board."

"German?"

"From Mississippi. Probably Czech." The uneven white scar on Wade's forehead disappeared into a crease, which it was prone to do when he was on the spot.

"They still around?"

He shrugged. We had that in common.

His full name was Wade Mason Banks Jr., born 1920 in Waco, McClellan County, which he'd already told me. The license proved he wasn't embellishing for some hustle.

"That's right, Miss Ruby Lee, about to marry one Wade Banks and drive off into the sunset in my brand new 1949 Club Coupe with a four-speed Presto-Matic." Wade relished his role as top salesman at both Chrysler dealerships, where GIs were still snapping up the new V8-powered automobiles.

A buying spree was going on. We acquired GE clock-radios, Maytag automatic dryers, slant-needle Singers, and Kelvinator ranges. There were even deals on acreage—land adjacent to ours was offered at seven dollars an acre, but valued lower by the Federal Land Bank. Two sections were a bargain that doubled our property.

Wade haggled with the John Deere salesman on a Model M with cultivator attached, raised and lowered by a Touch-O-Matic hydraulic control, and equipped with a padded seat—a first among tractors.

"It's what pretty little derrières deserve," he claimed. "Like yours."

Never mind I spent my days on a hard leather seat behind the flight controls, laying down insecticides and fertilizers on farms all over the Panhandle. Wade never let facts get in his way.

"Actually, we're about to *fly* off into the sunset in my Cub," I corrected him, smiling. We didn't have our travel plans settled yet. We'd be honeymooning in Houston's new eighteen-story Hotel Shamrock, built by oil tycoon Glenn McCarthy, infamous King of the Wildcatters. His resort hotel had opened on St. Patrick's Day with fireworks, Hollywood stars, and a million-dollar celebration. Wade wanted to drive to Fort Worth and catch the Santa Fe Chief down.

I knew I'd prevail.

Wade looped an arm around my waist as I filled out the marriage license. "Just making sure you're of age," he kidded, watching me enter 1925.

He exaggerated a sigh of relief. "Miss Ruby Lee, twenty-four and legal."

I printed my name below my signature. He bent down for closer scrutiny.

"Ruby Lee . . . Becker? You're not Ruby Lee. You're—" His ruddy coloring drained.

"Ruby Lee Becker I am," I said. "You thought Lee was my last name all this time? Never figured you for a sucker—"

"How could you be—Becker? Dang. You're Ruby Becker . . ." he trailed off.

"Wade," I drew out his name into two syllables. "I don't see why it matters."

When that man was thinking hard, I'd swear I could hear all the gears grinding away in there.

"Wade, is there a problem?"

And like he'd flipped a switch, he smiled wide, his usual devil-may-care mask back on. Down on one knee he went.

"Ruby Lee … Becker"—his voice caught for a split second— "may I have your hand in marriage?" Then the wink, and his aside, "Wanted to be sure I proposed to the right gal."

• • •

I'd clung to my hopes for Earl. Still officially missing in action and because they hadn't identified his remains, presumed dead—I refused to allow him to be. Wade and Ida were skeptical of my belief, so I tucked it away where they couldn't take it from me. Their contrary evidence fell on my deaf ears.

Before I'd stand with Wade at the JP, I insisted on waiting for Will to get home from Nagoya Air Base, any day now. *Home.* It would be a good surprise for Will, having a proper home to come back to.

Ida Rose protested when I showed her our marriage license. "It was the flying that saved you, Ruby. Not Wade."

"Ida, you're not jealous, are you?" I teased. "You'll still live here, of course, there's plenty of room, even after Will gets back, and Momma's well enough to come home …"

Her loan long since repaid, she'd helped with expenses while I got on my feet and launched my crop-dusting business. She put her part-time clerking and office work earnings towards whatever project we had going on. She never asked what she should contribute; she kept her eyes open, and if she saw a need, took care of it. That was how we got our electric hook-up when the REA came in, followed by a double-wall Speed Queen washer, an Emerson Electric fan for every room, new lamps for the end tables and desks. She kicked in the balance due on the chicken coop I had built, and took on the cultivating of our vegetable garden. After the REA brought in telephones and power, Ida found full-time employment at the new Rita Blanca Electric Co-op front office. Right quick, got herself promoted to manager. The dreamy, dancing, good-time girl lay buried beneath the mature, competent guise she'd assumed.

I relied on her sensibility, her unwavering support. Her caring friendship, her honesty—her loyalty—meant everything to me.

"You'll stay here, won't you?" My question, repeated, came out in a fearful gulp. "We're like family now, Ida, you said it yourself. My only sister . . ." I quit my prattling, lest my terror of being abandoned get obvious.

She pulled me close for a hug. "You're my only sister, too. It's not that, Ruby, it's—what you've done, everything you've been through, what you've made here . . . You didn't need anyone to help you. It was all you. You don't have to marry the first guy you ever fell for."

She leveled her intense eyes at me. "Is Wade the one? Or just the first to ask?"

CHAPTER SEVENTY-SEVEN

We both knew Ida Rose meant Red, whose glossy photo showed him to be a survivor like me. Red was someone I ached for when I let myself remember him. But he'd never responded to the letter I sent him, in care of Celesta, nor to another I'd written to him later in care of the navy. The last I'd heard about him was almost four years ago, right before Christmas in 1945.

One of the boarders Ida Rose had taken was Evelynne, the bewildered fiancée whose ensign had gone down with the USS *Indianapolis*. And Evelynne planned to attend the very public court-martial of the ship's captain that December.

It became Ida's habit to pore over the morning and afternoon papers. One evening she shared some startling news. Many crew members testified on behalf of Captain Charles B. McVay III, whose conviction for "negligence in executing evasive maneuvers to avoid the Japanese torpedoes" would end his twenty-six-year career. One of those giving supporting testimony was among the 316 survivors, Hospital Apprentice First Class Oris Hubbard. Red.

With Evelynne as courier, I had one last chance to reach Red with a letter.

A character witness, Red testified Captain McVay took charge of a scattered group of men struggling in spreading fuel oil, many injured, burned, thirsty, and starving. "He was as fine a commander as we could have had for those five desperate days," Hospital Apprentice First Class Oris Hubbard testified, "when the navy lost track of its flagship."

I could imagine the contemptible disgust on Red's face, maintaining his poise for the court while mocking the navy's failure to realize its own ship was missing.

Nonetheless, the verdict was guilty, destroying his captain's ambitions. But I hoped Red had grasped a revived purpose. And that Ensign Milton's melancholy fiancée, Evelynne, who we never saw again, had delivered the letter I'd sent with her.

•   •   •

Ida Rose's gentle voice brought me back. "Ruby, why don't you give him some time? A man who's been to hell and never figured on making it back might need to get on his feet before he feels deserving of you."

"How much more time?" I couldn't say what I really thought. *I'm not deserving of him.*

"If Red's the one you long for, Wade will be a poor substitute," she said.

But Wade was the one I deserved.

Post-war wedding ceremonies were still as contagious as cholera and I'd been four years abstinent. Wade was right that night at the Last Stop diner, calling us hustlers. He'd echoed that with a sympathy I never expected from him the night he'd unbuttoned my shirt, tugged my long sleeves down, and let his eyes widen an instant, before tracing his finger reverently along my cutting scars.

"Each one of these has cost you," he said, touching his lips to scar after scar. "These are the stories of how you got your grit."

With that he'd earned my forgiveness, as prescribed.

"Your badges of honor," Wade said, helping me to accept myself.

During the nights we spent together, I found someone I trusted enough to let myself feel the sensual stirrings to end my abstinence. What I'd once seen as conniving in him had become something more. Our coupling was a thrill I craved—rocky, but underlaid by a stability that let me feel free if I needed to.

I showed Ida the marriage license. I pointed to the line where I hoped she'd sign as a witness, beside Will's signature.

Despite her misgivings, Ida Rose, who'd spent those months recovering in my house, then caring for me and other women's babies, agreed to be our witness.

I'd seen what her ordeal had cost her. "I never gave two cents about kids or being a mother, until I knew I couldn't," she said. Now it was a sorrow she carried like a cloak on her shoulders.

Ida Rose hadn't visited the midwife she could trust when she got in trouble. Once she'd recovered from the butchering, we saw her together. Ida wanted the midwife to examine her, tell her she'd healed, be able to have children. The midwife could no more offer her that assurance than the staff surgeon who'd saved her would.

When Ida's face crumpled, I shoved a hanky her way. She refused it, held her composure with those glowing amber eyes glistening. She insisted she'd return the money I'd loaned her. Told me to put it aside for my Cub, or my firstborn, her voice cracking.

The midwife had explained the measures which prevented unwanted pregnancies, and I listened carefully, my dread of being trapped by pregnancy acute. Her advice was less than reassuring. "None of these methods are fail-safe, so if you want to be sure, abstinence is your only option." And abstinent I was, until Wade persuaded me we'd be lovers who married.

Ida Rose always said the name of the man who got her pregnant would go to her grave with her—and it went unspoken. By then, I trusted her like the sister I'd never had.

But sometimes I wondered if he'd been Wade.

CHAPTER SEVENTY-EIGHT

When Will showed up, dressed in Air Force blues, he came unannounced.

He found me gazing at the tombstone erected for Pa under the shelterbelt trees he'd planted for the SCS with the soil men. Opposite Pa's grave marker, I sat on the granite bench which waited for Earl—a place for me to rest and watch for his return.

Will approached as cautious as a barn cat, his eyes ricocheting from tombstone to bench to mine and back, darting around, taking in the stone-and-timber house, the red barn, the cranking windmill, the full tank, the runway where my Piper Cub rested, the fields sprouting wheat to the horizon.

His boyish face had matured beyond his years, more serious and even more cautious, but didn't conceal the curiosity in his eyes.

"Welcome home, Will," I said, embracing him. "To our family home."

He held me, reticent at first, then fully and wholly, as if to never let go.

He restrained a sob and I rubbed his back before I gently separated myself from him. I kept hold of his hand, my own tears ready to spill over. I breathed in deeply, finding the spring air fresh and clean.

Of the farm, I said, "I took care of things while you were gone. This is all ours now, yours and mine. Your bedroom and study are in the wing on the left."

His lips parted and his shock gave way to pleasurable surprise. When I spoke again, it was my turn to be surprised—at the faltering in my voice.

Of Earl, I said, "He's gone, they say. With honors. But I'm not giving up on him."

Of Pa, I said, "You shoulda told me the truth, Will."

Of Momma, I said nuthin. Yet.

•   •   •

First we surveyed the farm, Will and I, in the cockpit of my Cub. From the air, brown patches creeping in here and there weren't evident. Will's admiration for my stewardship of our sections was genuine.

"What you've done here, Ruby, how you've brought us back from the brink—it's remarkable," Will said after we touched down from our short hop over our greening fields.

If he bore me any ill will from my takeover, he gave no hint.

"You're a fine pilot, too." He'd flown with enough to know, he added.

Will was animated by ideas he'd spent time thinking about since we'd been in Waco. "There's new ways to tap the underground water, Ruby," he said, his enthusiasm unstifled. "The aquifer's like a sponge with trillions of gallons of water. Pumps and drills are powerful now, fuel's cheap—we can bring up thousands of gallons, plenty enough to irrigate the entire farm."

It crossed my mind, later, did Will realize the 1950s drouth of record was already on our doorstep?

"We won't suffer in the next drouth," he said on the back porch. We entered the kitchen, plucked pop-up ice cubes from our new Coolerator icebox, and poured two glasses of sweet tea. Will whistled at the sight of our modern kitchen appliances.

"Rita Blanca Electric Co-op finally got around to us," I said. "XIT Rural Co-op's bringing in the telephone next."

"Look what you've done." Will's voice was thick. "You got spunk, Ruby. That stubborn streak of yours served you well while I've been overseas."

I put my hand on his arm. I didn't have words for how glad I was to have him home. I tamped down tears lest they overflow.

The two paintings in our front hall commanded his attention. I'd hung the 1934 painting Ida Rose bought from the artist's Dust Bowl series next to the painting I'd commissioned of our flourishing farm.

"That's Hogue's art, from the Texas Centennial . . ." Will said with a start, a weariness furrowing his brow. He ran a finger gently over the brushstrokes. "Half-expecting to feel some Kansas soil blown into this paint. *Drouth Stricken Area*. It's our farm, ghosts and all—" His body quavered. He was shaking off our whole blown-apart world. I showed him the newer painting that depicted greening fields, a full tank for well-fed cows, the house I'd built, wheat bales, prosperity.

"Our farm." I squeezed his arm before gloomy memories could sweep over him.

He wandered into the parlor, drawn to our grandmother's spinet from Chicago, running his fingertips over its carved legs. The walnut piano gleamed like it had since a drifter had come through in search of fieldwork and set to it during the night he spent in the barn. That morning I had been awakened by a melody I hadn't heard since Granny Alma played it, the piano's tone the warm mellow sound I remembered. I listened hard for her lilting voice. "*The Very Thought of You*." I stumbled out to the barn.

"Couldn't sleep at all, ma'am, once I saw the cobwebs and dirt smothering this sweet spinet," the drifter had said, finishing the tune.

"Signed by Starke, a real beauty. Had to restore her. Tricky to tune though." He'd been a piano tuner by trade, a bit rusty, owing to little work in the hard times. Wouldn't take a penny for it, just grateful to sleep under a roof.

"Found something tucked inside, ma'am," the tuner had said, "in the hammer rail."

Will sat on the bench with his hands raised over the ivories, poised to play. "Tuned, is it?" he asked.

I lifted the piano lid and extracted three railroad tickets, still tucked in the hammers where the tuner had found them.

"Tickets," Will said. "To Chicago?"

I nodded. "A mystery."

"I remember Granny Alma gave me cash to gas up Pa's Ford." Will studied the tickets like they were cuneiform scripts withholding ancient secrets. I jabbed at him playfully.

He raised unsmiling eyes to mine. "She was fixin to carry you, the baby, and Momma to Chicago. But she got the dust pneumonia. Accused Pa of being too stubborn or too soused to think straight —"

I lost hold of the piano fallboard I held up; Will withdrew his hands quick as it banged down hard, shooting me a side glance.

"Pa told Alma, my Willa Mae's gone 'round the bend."

That prickly sensation crawled up my arms. I needed air. "It's stifling hot in here, Will. Let's step outside."

We toured the house outside and in, discussing the floor plan and improvements I'd made—the electric power, airtight windows, indoor plumbing—narrating my thinking while pins needled at my skin.

The screen door slammed. Will about jumped out of his loafers, whirling around, tensed.

Wade strode in like he owned the joint—though he wouldn't, not even when we tied the knot. I'd hired an attorney to draw up the papers.

Wade cinched his arm around my waist and kissed my cheek, his eyes never leaving Will's.

"Stripes," he said to Will, his voice measured. "You sure get around."

"Slide," Will nodded, his lips tight, eyes wary. A chill in that one word.

"Sonny *the Slide*," Will added, spitting his disdain.

"Sonny?" I turned to Wade, the one-carat diamond ring on my left hand flashing in the lamp light. "Wade Banks, groom, meet Will Becker, brother. And best man."

The silence grew uncomfortable. My face felt flushed. I cleared my throat.

"This is your fiancé?" Will exploded. His disbelieving expression telegraphed what I'd already accepted: Wade's not the marrying kind.

A scalding-hot stinging erupted all over. Before the panic took hold, I breathed in deeply, my release slow as molasses.

"Do I detect some history here, Sonny—and Stripes, is it? Well, you'll have a lifetime to tell me all about how you two got your nicknames. Wade, let's toast our upcoming nuptials, since the best man's home from the war and we can finally be family."

Will's body was rigid, his hands clenched. Wade's grip around my waist tightened. With a defiant glance at Wade, I forced my other arm inside Will's and led them to the bar.

Whatever was between them felt heavy and we spoke of everything but, downing our stirred martinis, toasting endings and beginnings.

Tomorrow we'd make time to visit the clinic. Will could get reacquainted with our momma, and we'd abandon those things unspoken.

CHAPTER SEVENTY-NINE

At bedtime, as I had ever since Wade returned my cardboard suitcase, I took it from beneath the bed, laying out Momma's fine leather gloves, her best cloche hat, her hairbrush and comb set, the doll with my eyes. I would take them along when Will and I visited Momma, to brush out her silver-laced hair and comb the fine tendrils, to nestle her cloche hat on her head, and put her kid gloves on her hands. The doll she'd made me—with the yellow hair I desired and the blue eyes that matched mine—would help her remember me. Then we could bring her home with us and be family again.

Last, I unfolded the letter she meant for me when Pa sent me to Waco with Will in 1935.

Before sleep would come, I'd need to read it again.

CHAPTER EIGHTY

WILLA MAE

June 1935

My darling Ruby,

These gloves are stitched with my love for your father, and when you fit your hands inside them, your hands rest inside his, and mine. Let our hands hold you and guide you.

When you use my comb and hairbrush, it will be your momma styling your hair with love.

Nestle my best hat atop your head and feel my warmth, always with you, no matter where.

Tuck your blue-eyed doll beneath the covers with you each night and sing her a lullaby as I sang to you.

Before you close your eyes, know your heart is held inside mine, and my love song to you is forever.

Your loving momma,
Willa Mae

AUTHOR'S NOTE

Women have always persevered. That much is known but little noted in books written by and for men, heroes all, with minor roles delegated to women—if indeed they are featured at all. UNSPOKEN is my contribution to this new surge of historical literature which uncovers the pioneering and resilient heroics women have long demonstrated.

* * *

UNSPOKEN is Book One of the *DUST* series, set in the mythical town of Hartless, Texas, where real historical events provide fertile ground for invented adventurers. For a glimpse of the sequel on the horizon, follow their dusty trail at <u>JannAlexander.com</u>.

ACKNOWLEDGMENTS

In 2016, while pondering my mother-in-law's somewhat fractious upbringing, I wondered how Lorene, who'd never been satisfactorily mothered, could become a good mother herself. Lorene Beck was Texas-born, with a rich heritage of family names: her own momma's, Willie Mae Farmer (the child-bride of Lorene's beloved daddy, William "Willie" Beck); and those of her aunts and stepmothers: Ruby, Jewel, Pearl, Lucile, Ida.

I'd been diving deep into Texas Panhandle history, researching the "Dirty Thirties." It was the era of the Dust Bowl and the Great Depression, with environmental and economic ramifications as devastating as the impacts on families. In the epicenter of the Dust Bowl, the elderly and the young were dying from the very air they breathed—they called it dust pneumonia. Parents who were starving, with no work available and no means of support, left their children in State Homes—just until they could get back on their feet. Such state-run homes had been established countrywide under various names to house children deemed "Throw Away Kids."

Further east in Texas, far from the Panhandle's black blizzards, Waco had such a State Home, with a well-documented reputation, largely due to present-day accounts by former residents. In a time when children were dying from dust pneumonia, it might well have been a logical choice for a girl who couldn't breathe—who would grow up without her mother's guidance, forever seeking family.

That's when Ruby Lee Becker's voice inhabited my head. I could hear her speak:

"I had never seen anyone dead before."

She told her story insistently, and Lorene's ancestors found new life as the invented characters who lived in Ruby's world. Their fictional stories were propelled by substantial quantities of research about actual historic occurrences that sparked my imagination. I'm extremely grateful for every source I found—nonfiction, oral histories, maps, photographs, paintings, blogs, historical sites, and online repositories.

My gratitude extends to many, first among them Reagan Rothe and the publishing team at Black Rose Writing, for taking on my debut novel.

I relied on several notable memoirs and first-person accounts. John C. Dawson, Sr.'s *High Plains Yesterdays*, 1985, and Sherry Matthews' *We Were Not Orphans*, 2011, were riveting and detailed nonfiction accounts of their childhoods, and provided invaluable inspiration for Ruby Lee Becker's fictional youth. Along with Eleanor Roosevelt's daily "My Day" columns (particularly those she wrote from 1937-1945), and her two memoirs, *This Is My Story*, 1938, and *You Learn By Living*, 1960, all were important primary sources in establishing the historical basis for Unspoken. To read more from the sources I consulted (too many to list here), a Selected Bibliography follows.

My novel took shape and was honed with Laurie Chittenden's brilliant editorial eye, editor Rebecca Allen's sharp blue pencil, having begun under the deft guidance of Caroline Leavitt in her Story Structure program, and with continuing encouragement from dear friends here and on each coast. I learned how to talk Texan thanks to Texas natives Paula and Tom Coopwood. And no one has been more steadfast than my own personal Texan—Lorene's son and my eternally proud husband. Thank you, Karl, for your willingness to talk storylines, learn the publishing business, and especially for your unwavering support and love.

SELECTED BIBLIOGRAPHY

Among numerous historical sources I drew from, these stand out:

The Portal to Texas History digital archives, University of North Texas

Farm Security Administration Collection digital archives, Library of Congress

Taming the Land: The Lost Postcard Photographs of the Texas High Plains, John Miller Morris, 2009

Land of the Underground Rain: Irrigation on the Texas High Plains, 1910-1970, Donald E. Green, 1973

Dust Bowl: The Southern Plains in the 1930s, Donald Worster, 1979, 2004

High Plains Yesterdays, John C. Dawson, Sr., 1985

Letters from the Dust Bowl, Caroline Henderson, 2003

The Worst Hard Time, Timothy Egan, 2005

The Dust Bowl: An Illustrated History, Dayton Duncan and Ken Burns, 2012

Alexandre Hogue: An American Visionary, Susie Kalil, 2011

The Dust Bowl Children: Memories of Growing Up in Dalhart, R. Edward Waite, Barbara Reynolds Alkofer, and Zelda Law Lang, 2011

Riding the Rails: Teenagers on the Move During the Great Depression, Errol Lincoln Uys, 2014

Tramps of America, Thomas Minehan, 1934

East to the Dawn: The Life of Amelia Earhart, Susan Butler, 1997

Weeping in the Playtime of Others: America's Incarcerated Children, Kenneth Wooden, 1976

We Were Not Orphans, Sherry Matthews, 2011

Closing Corsicana: Lessons From a Shuttered Youth Detention Center, TEXAS TRIBUNE, Maurice Chammah, 2004

While the Locust Slept, Peter Razor, 2001

The Orphanage, Richard Bergeron, 2012

The Home: A Memoir of Growing Up in An Orphanage, Richard McKenzie, 2019

The Polio Years in Texas, Heather Green Wooten, 2009

Harvey Houses of Texas: Historic Hospitality from the Gulf Coast to the Panhandle, Rosa Walston Latimer, 2014

Georgia O'Keeffe's Wartime Texas Letters, Amy Von Lintel, 2020

Covered Wagon Geologist, Charles Newton Gould, 1959

Women of the Asylum: Voices From Behind The Walls, 1840-1945, Jeffrey L. Geller and Maxine Harris

Life at the Texas State Lunatic Asylum, 1857-1997, Sarah C. Sitton, 1943

The Lives They Left Behind: Suitcases from a State Hospital Attic, Darby Penney and Peter Stastny, 2008

Fair Park Deco: Art and Architecture of the Texas Centennial Exposition, Jim Parsons and David Bush, 2012

Bound for Beaumont: Eleanor Roosevelt's 1939 Train Trip through East Texas and Beyond, EAST TEXAS HISTORICAL JOURNAL, Mary L. Scheer, 2016

"My Day" syndicated newspaper columns, Eleanor Roosevelt, 1937-1945

This Is My Story, Eleanor Roosevelt, 1938

You Learn By Living, Eleanor Roosevelt, 1960

Franklin and Eleanor: An Extraordinary Marriage, Hazel Rowley, 2011

The WPA Guide to Texas, Workers of the Writers' Program of the Works Progress Administration, 1940

The WPA Dallas Guide and History: 1936-1942, Workers of the Writers' Program of the Works Progress Administration, 1992

A Mouthful of Rivets: Women at Work in World War II, Nancy Baker Wise, 1994

ABOUT THE AUTHOR

Jann Alexander is a 20-year resident of central Texas and creator of the Vanishing Austin photography series. Her lifelong storytelling habit and her more recent passion for Texas history merged to become the historical novel *Unspoken*, her first book in the Dust Series. She holds a B.S. from the University of Maryland. When Jann is not reading, writing, or creating, she bikes, hikes, skis, and kayaks. Jann always brakes for historical markers.

NOTE FROM JANN ALEXANDER

Word-of-mouth is crucial for any author to succeed. If you enjoyed *Unspoken*, please leave a review online—anywhere you are able. Even if it's just a sentence or two. It would make all the difference and would be very much appreciated.

Thanks!
Jann Alexander

We hope you enjoyed reading this title from:

www.blackrosewriting.com

Subscribe to our mailing list – *The Rosevine* – and receive **FREE** books, daily deals, and stay current with news about upcoming releases and our hottest authors.
Scan the QR code below to sign up.

Already a subscriber? Please accept a sincere thank you for being a fan of Black Rose Writing authors.

View other Black Rose Writing titles at www.blackrosewriting.com/books and use promo code **PRINT** to receive a **20% discount** when purchasing.